°38'
64°36'
Lake
Snug Harbour
Skull Rock
anchor
SKULL ISLAND
1763
Wherein lies the booty from the X
°38'
64°36'
64°34'

THE BOOK OF PIRATES

Essay, chapter introductions, and biographies by
Robert E. and Jill P. May

Illustrations by
Michael Custode

TASCHEN

THE TALES

INTRODUCTION

by Robert E. and Jill P. May

Truth or Vision? Piracy of the Past

Robert E. and Jill P. May

Throughout history there has been a tendency to romanticize characters on the wrong side of the law, something that does not exclude criminals who once terrorized the high seas. In recent years especially this has manifested itself in faddish, outlandish, and largely roguish cultural forms, leading us to ask why people continue to celebrate these lawless looters in this way, and even indulge in dressing up and engaging in similar behavior themselves (since 1995, people in English-speaking countries have light-heartedly observed "The International How to Talk Like a Pirate Day"). Current stereotypes of pirates derive to no small degree from earlier literary and artistic representations of them, and these constitute the main subject of this book. Some of the most significant and memorable depictions of pirates in literature and art over the centuries are included here, allowing us to trace how our understanding of pirates has changed over time.

Pieces of Eight

Piracy has afflicted civilization throughout recorded history. As long ago as the 14th century B.C., cuneiform texts on clay tablets attest to sea raiders mounting attacks on the island of Cyprus. In Classical times, pirates appeared in the works of ancient Greece's most illustrious historian, Thucydides, and in the epic poems of Homer, and they continued to plague Mediterranean trade in the time of the Roman Republic. Indeed, Julius Caesar himself was taken captive by pirates and later sought revenge. Cilician pirates operating from their hideaways on the southeastern coast of what is now Turkey were a frequent blight on Rome's trade with the eastern Mediterranean, at least until the Roman military leader Pompey the Great led a huge force against them in 67 B.C., destroying some 120 pirate bases and killing thousands of the marauders. All the centuries since have witnessed piracy. In recent decades, swift-boat attacks have been made by pirates on oil supertankers, pleasure cruisers, private yachts, and other vessels at maritime choke points such as the Gulf of Aden off the horn of east Africa and the Malacca Strait between Indonesia and Malaysia. These assaults have shocked the world's powers and have sometimes resulted in hefty ransoms for the modern pirates.

Despite piracy's persistence through the centuries, the larger-than-life marauders who inspired the literary and illustrative contents of this book mostly did their pillaging during a compressed 200-year span from about 1520 to the mid-1720s, a period that included the so-called "Golden Age" of piracy beginning in the late 1600s. Captain (William) Kidd, Henry Avery, Henry Morgan, Stede Bonnet, Bartholomew Roberts ("Black Bart"), Samuel ("Black Sam") Bellamy, Edward

Page 6
Howard Pyle
The Buccaneer Was a Picturesque Fellow, oil on canvas, 1905

Page 8
George Roux
"The Squire raised his gun, the rowing ceased"; engraving from the first illustrated edition of Treasure Island, 1885

Benjamin Cole
"Blackbeard the Pirate", from Captain Charles Johnson's A General History of the Pyrates, 1724

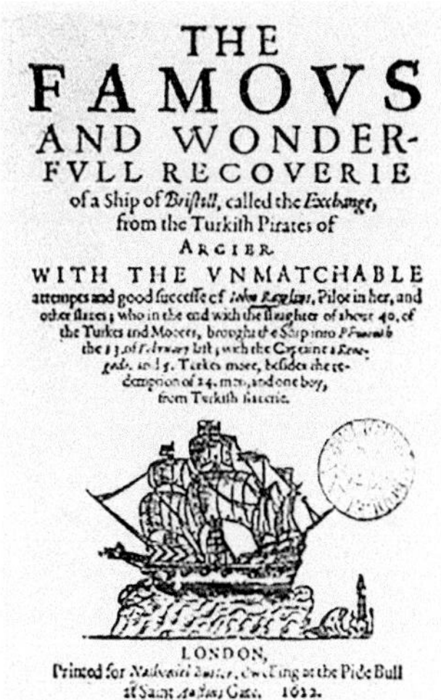

THE FAMOVS AND WONDERFVLL RECOVERIE of a Ship of Bristll, called the Exchange, from the Turkish Pirates of Argier.
WITH THE VNMATCHABLE attempts and good successe of John Rawlins, Pilot in her, and other slaves; who in the end with the slaughter of about 40. of the Turkes and Moores, brought the Ship into Plimouth the 13. of February last; with the Captaine a Renegado, and 5. Turkes more, besides the redemption of 24. men, and one boy, from Turkish slaverie.
LONDON,
Printed for Nathaniel Butter, dwelling at the Pide Bull at Saint Austins Gate. 1622.

John Rawlins
Title-page of The Famous and Wonderfull Recoverie of a Ship of Bristoll, 1622

(or Ned) Low, and Edward Thatch (sometimes Teach or Thache) or "Blackbeard" all sailed the seas during piracy's heyday. In total, some 2,000 pirates of Anglo-American origin alone prowled the high seas during this period, and were given all sorts of different names in the process, such as corsair, privateer, freebooter, buccaneer, and filibuster. Sometimes these words meant the same thing as pirate; sometimes they did not.

Piracy, an international crime, was punishable at this time by death, and some 600 English and Anglo-American pirates were hanged just in the decade between 1716 and 1726. Stede Bonnet was hanged before a crowd of onlookers in Charles Town (today Charleston) in England's South Carolina colony, on December 10, 1718 (ill. p. 19 r.), after being taken into custody by the local colonial authorities following a fight at nearby Sullivan's Island the month before; in the same month, in the capital of the Bahama Islands at Providence, Britain's governor and other observers watched as eight convicted pirates were hanged at the same time. Meanwhile, many Golden Age pirates wound up hanged at Execution Dock in London. Privateers, in contrast to pirates, held legal status under international law, which included presumed immunity from execution if they were taken into custody: their vessels had contractual authority from a government at war – usually in the form of official letters of marque and reprisal – to attack and rob ships belonging to an enemy power (often but not always under stipulation that the authorizing governments receive a share of the proceeds from captured vessels and their cargoes). It was under this aegis of a government or sovereign's approval that Sir Francis Drake (*c.* 1540–1596) was emboldened to raid territories on the Spanish main on behalf of Elizabeth I (1533–1603), most notably during his circumnavigation of the globe (1577–80) on board the *Golden Hind* (ill. p. 15). Many of the most famous pirates of the Golden Age claimed legitimacy from such privateering commissions at one time or another, even if sometimes these claims were based on false pretenses.

The majority of pirate attacks during the Golden Age occurred in the Indian Ocean, the western Mediterranean, along the Atlantic coastline of England's colonies in North America, or against the "Spanish Main" – a term indicating the mainland coast of Spanish-controlled northern South America but often applied to the whole Caribbean basin. From the 1500s to the 1700s, Spain ruled today's U.S. Gulf Coast, Mexico, Central America, and South America (with the exception of Portuguese Brazil), and some of the Caribbean islands, including Cuba; consequently, marauders of the Golden Age bent on appropriating the vast gold, silver, and other wealth of Spain's New World empire had what might today be called "targets of opportunity"

Herman Padtbrugge
Map of Panama, from Alexandre Exquemelin's De Americaensche Zee-Roovers (The Buccaneers of America), 1678

Herman Padtbrugge
Henry Morgan attacking the forts at Chagre, Panama, from The Buccaneers of America, 1678

throughout the Main. The French corsair Jean Fleury (or Florin), for example, attacked Spanish vessels as they were returning to European waters laden with New World wealth in 1523, just two years after the Spanish *conquistadores* had captured the native Aztecs' capital of Tenochtitlán (today's Mexico City), at the dawning of Spain's New World empire. Pirate fiction alludes to Spanish coinage as "pieces of eight" and "doubloons" for good reason.

"Dead Man's Chest"

Given the significance of piracy in early modern history, especially in the Spanish Main, it is no coincidence that many notable works about pirates in western literature, including a number of accounts of people who were held captive by pirates, date from the late 1500s through the early 1700s and feature tropical locations. The first fanciful pirates, products entirely of the imagination, were descendants of the historical figures described in diaries, newspapers, court records, or oral remembrances by men who had survived captivity. Their narratives were tailored for readers who rarely knew anything about piracy from their own personal experience, and as a result, such retold episodes relied on their readers' capacity to suppress their disbelief and accept at face value the survival narratives of men whose vessels had been overtaken by pirates, who had been bound into servitude or were held for ransom, but who would eventually regain their freedom. As historical pirates morphed into literary representations, authors and illustrators began to create images that roughly fit with the information known about sea rovers and their escapades.

One early narrative, *The Famous and Wonderfull Recoverie of a Ship of Bristoll, called the* Exchange, *from the Turkish Pirates of Argier* (1622, ill. p. 11), represents the genre very well in all its aspects. As an "official retelling" by John Rawlins of his experiences with Turkish Muslim pirates who had earlier captured two English ships and were now using them to pillage, *Wonderfull Recoverie* includes elements common to pirate lore, such as the marooning and enslavement of captives, and their eventual escape: Rawlins and his crew (and their two ships) were overtaken by pirates and, after a long and strenuous battle, defeated. The pirate captains believed they had acquired too many English captives and so marooned 12 of them before proceeding on their way. Of the remaining prisoners, some became pirates' servants, while others were sold into slavery. In the end, a group of the captives, some of whom converted to Islam to save their lives, managed to free themselves and return to England.

Such accounts fascinated contemporary readers, partly because piracy was a genuine threat to travelers

H. P. de Bruÿge inv. et f.

Herman Padtbrugge
Portraits of Henry Morgan, styled as "Johan Morgan" (far left), and Bartholomew the Portuguese (near left), both with a backdrop of a naval battle, from The Buccaneers of America, 1678

and residents of seaports at the time, and partly because of their narrative embellishments. Detailed descriptions of places where pirate attacks occurred and masterfully drawn maps (for their time) compelled book consumers to accept these stories as accurate and true.

No early modern author did more to integrate piracy into Western literature than the prolific English writer Daniel Defoe (1660–1731). Pirates appeared so frequently in his fiction that some experts attribute to him the highly influential and illustrated "non-fiction" book from 1724 entitled *A General History of the Pyrates* (supposedly the work of "Captain Charles Johnson", a historically invisible figure), which profoundly influenced virtually all later accounts of Golden Age piracy (ills. pp. 10, 16/17, 36/37). By then, Defoe had perfected his own narrative devices for representing fictional pirates, especially the distinctive variants of captivity tales. He routinely indicated that his own tales had first been related to him by men who had themselves been captured by pirate rogues. Later fiction writers and illustrators often patterned their tales of imagined seamen and literary pirates in Defoe's mold, drawing on each other to a degree that verged on plagiarism. Robert Louis Stevenson (1850–1894), the author of *Treasure Island*, arguably the most influential piece of pirate fiction of all, mused that he had taken inspiration for his book and the phrase "Dead Man's Chest" from the English clergyman Charles Kingsley's (1819–1875) *At Last: A Christmas in the West Indies*. The character of Billy Bones, furthermore, and much of *Treasure Island*'s first chapters were derived from the writings of the U.S. author Washington Irving (1783–1859), the skeleton on Treasure Island itself was taken from the work of Edgar Allan Poe (1809–1849), while Long John Silver's parrot (ill. p. 18) was inspired by Defoe's *Robinson Crusoe* (ill. p. 22).

Nothing Defoe published touching piracy had more influence on his own and later generations than *Robinson Crusoe*, a wildly popular English novel that came out in 1719 and was regularly republished, having never been out of print since (ills. pp. 20–23). Although not a piracy book *per se*, *Crusoe* replicates themes and authorial stratagems that may be found in earlier published accounts of pirates. Narrating his own story, Crusoe, a well-trained sailor, falls into pirate captivity after his vessel is captured by Turkish pirates in the course of a fierce sea battle. But it is Crusoe's later experiences on an uninhabited island off the South American coast for 28 years that have fascinated readers. Defoe's expansive narrative centers on Crusoe's self-reliance in his isolation. He forages, finds animal companions, and becomes master of his island landscape. His solitary life envelops his storytelling, and

Royal Letters Patent issued from Elizabeth I to Sir Francis Drake regarding the Capture of Cádiz, 1587

John Gilbert
Francis Drake knighted by Elizabeth I aboard the Golden Hind, 1851

Benjamin Cole
"Captain Bartholomew Roberts", from Captain Charles Johnson's A General History of the Pyrates, 1724

what his readers remember is the island scenery and occurrences during his stay there, such as the spoils he recovers from his wrecked ship (ills. pp. 21, 82), rather than any details of Crusoe's previous servitude under North African corsairs. Defoe's clever deployment of literary devices, such as his narrator's expressed self-reproach, also help to keep readers attentive, as, for instance, when Crusoe tells them that he should never have gone to sea in the first place. He confesses that he is the son of an honorable man and that he determined to be a sailor against his parents' wishes, leaving home without even telling them. Instead of studying law or choosing to follow some other sensible occupation, he made the fateful decision to enlist with an honest captain and learn the sea-voyaging trade. At one reflective point in the story, Crusoe admits that being on shore never worked well for him.

Jules Verne's (1828–1905) adventure novel *L'Île mystérieuse* (*The Mysterious Island*, 1875), also featured in the selection of tales presented here, unambiguously draws inspiration from the plotlines and devices of *Robinson Crusoe*. Like Defoe's novel, it set pirates at the periphery of the narrative action, not at its center, but exhibited similar (or in some cases identical) flourishes of piracy: whether it be a wrecked vessel at the mercy of the elements, the discovery of an exotic island, a message in a bottle or treasure chests washed ashore (ills. pp. 28–29).

Pag. 202.

Frank Schoonover
Treasure Island, oil on canvas, 1920
Long John Silver is here shown in traditional pirate attire, with his parrot Captain Flint on his left shoulder.

Captain Charles Johnson
Stede Bonnet, portrayed alongside the first known depiction of the Jolly Roger flag, from The History and Lives of All The Most Notorious Pirates, 1725

The hanging of Stede Bonnet, from Historie de Zee-Rovers, *a Dutch edition of Johnson's* General History of the Pyrates, 1725

Defoe's writing about pirates, including *Robinson Crusoe*, was enabled by the sizable cache of contemporary source material that he had at his disposal, including but not limited to a number of captivity narratives. Book authors, newspapers editors and writers, balladeers, and playwrights on both sides of the Atlantic understandably paid close attention to these legendary rogues during piracy's Golden Age in the 1600s and 1700s, as pirates were both overtaking ships at sea and pillaging citizens along the coastlines of the countries they traversed. Long-range travel became hazardous, and international commerce was threatened, both in harbors and on the high seas. The hanging of Captain Kidd on the afternoon of May 23, 1701 at Execution Dock inspired an immediate outpouring of broadsides and sermons, together with *Captain Kid's Farewell to the Seas* (also known as *The Dying Words of Capt. Robert Kidd* or *The Ballad of Captain Kidd*). This 22-verse narrative, in its original extent, covering Kidd's career on the high seas and his subsequent imprisonment and execution, became the longest-lasting folk ballad in music (in its American version) about pirate life.

The publication in Dutch in 1678 of Alexandre O. Exquemelin's (*c.* 1645–1707) *De Americaensche Zee-Roovers* (*Buccanneers of America*, ills. pp. 12–14), soon afterwards translated into English, French, and Spanish, marked another of the milestones in early pirate literature and history, for its claimed authenticity. Presented as the "autobiographical account" of a one-time indentured servant of the French West India Company who wound up in the pirate nest of Tortuga Island (off the coast of today's Haiti), and then joined Henry Morgan's buccaneers in raiding the Caribbean in the early 1670s after buying his own freedom, this book profoundly affected later literary treatments of piracy and anticipated Defoe's *Robinson Crusoe*. After Exquemelin determined to "enter into the wicked order of the Pirates or Robbers at Sea"[1] he related many aspects of pirate culture and behavior, including the articles of agreement they bonded themselves to keep and their preference to set prisoners on land after capturing a ship, while keeping back only a few captives as servants. In contrast to the savagery pirates sometimes display, they could also be liberal comrades in the crunch. Were a pirate to lose his goods or money, others would bail him out. While on shore, sea rovers made certain to pay their tavern bills so as to avoid being sold into servitude themselves.

Democracy on the Seas

So, what should we believe of early pirate literature, and how do these stories square with what is known from history? To begin with, it is important to note that historical research bears out what Exquemelin high-

Frank Godwin
Cover illustration from Robinson Crusoe, *depicting the protagonist alongside his servant Friday*, 1925

Newell Convers Wyeth
Title-page illustration from Robinson Crusoe, 1920

Frank Godwin
Crusoe amongst the spoils recovered from his wrecked ship, 1925

lighted concerning the contractual nature of pirating in the Golden Age. These articles of agreement, negotiated before their vessels weighed anchor, specified for the individual men when and where the ships would sail and whether an attack on another vessel would be decided by majority vote of the crew. Pirates accorded far less power to their ship captains than was common on merchant and naval ships, as they typically came from lower-class backgrounds and had often served as crewmen on naval and merchant ships before becoming freebooters. They intentionally consented to minimal authority and would assert the right for a replacement of the captain by a vote of the crew at any time. The articles, most importantly, specified how their takings should be shared, anticipating that disputes or fights concerning the profits might evolve. Furthermore, these contracts specified how injuries incurred during battles might be compensated. Finally, because these men abhorred hierarchical divisions, they adopted relatively flat pay scales, with everyone receiving roughly the same pay.

Although pirate democracy might seem appealing, historical sources also document the fact that the buccaneers committed heinous atrocities. Such behavior hardly deserves romanticizing, while any attempt to make fun of it does a disservice to the actual crimes, although it should also be acknowledged that some pirates did exercise restraint during their attacks and escapades. Surprisingly, historians have been unable to find that Blackbeard ever killed anyone prior to the battle in which he lost his own life. Nevertheless, many pirates were without doubt killers, and executed naval as well as commercial seamen, not to

FRANK

FRANK
GODWIN

Frank Godwin
Crusoe's parrot Poll, which provided the inspiration for Captain Flint in Treasure Island, 1925

Right and below
John Clark, John Pine
Title image and world map delineating the voyage of Robinson Crusoe, published in the book's first edition, 1719

mention passengers on captured ships and the inhabitants of ports. They were also known to torture their captives, especially captured merchant captains who had reportedly treated their men poorly or refused to disclose where the valuables aboard their ships were stored. Many of the pirates had earlier served autocratic captains and had been abused. They were not above using the methods they had earlier observed. For instance, Henry Morgan's men, while sacking Panama City in 1671, raped the inhabitants and tortured people to find out where the treasure was. Some unverifiable accounts of atrocities are stomach-turning.

Readers who turned to stories of pirates and their adventures in the 19th and early 20th centuries,

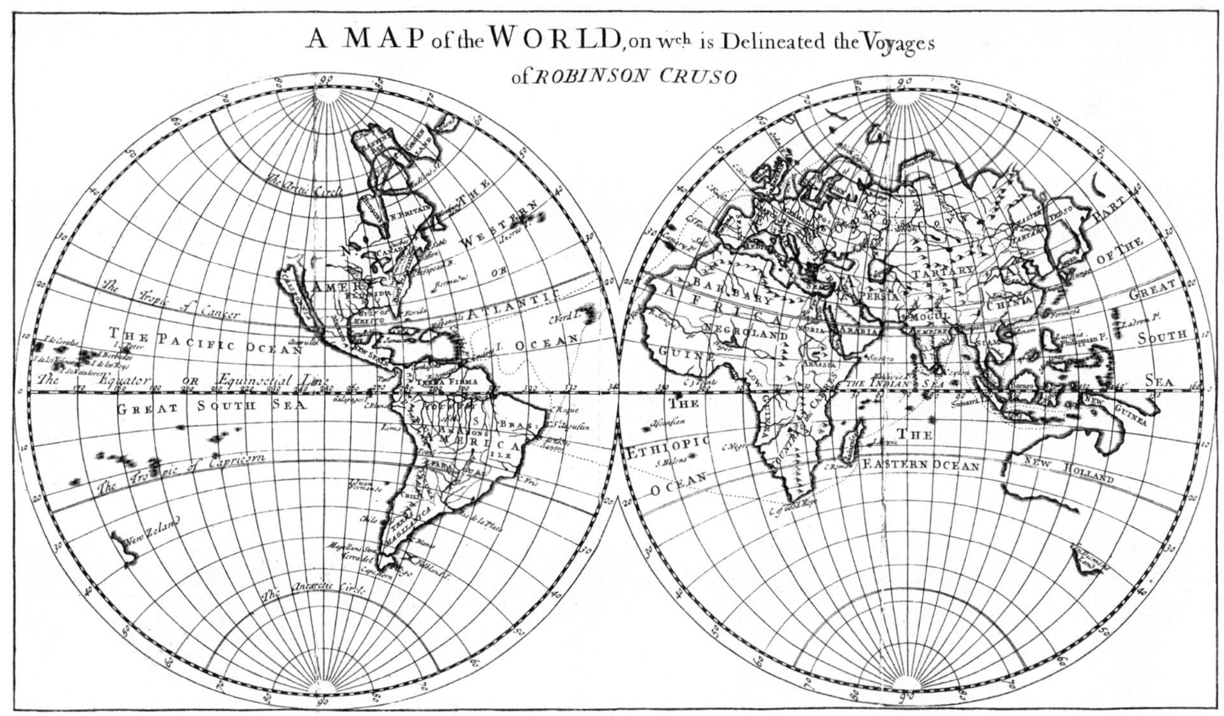

Newell Convers Wyeth
Cover Illustration for Treasure Island,
oil on canvas, 1911

Newell Convers Wyeth
"Oh, Morgan's men are out for you; and Blackbeard–buccaneer!",
oil on canvas, 1917
Wyeth's seascape depicts the infamous Blackbeard alongside his crew.

however, found stories that downplayed the cruelty of piracy, perhaps because there were few threats to travel, commerce, and vessels from encounters on

the high seas. Indeed, chronicles of these episodes wax and wane in maritime history, and major military powers often have committed ample resources to protecting vessels and shorelines from seafaring exploitation. During late feudal times, for instance, when power in northern Europe was localized and sovereign rulers were weak, piracy thrived in the surrounding waters. In the 1390s, German pirates known as the *Vitalienbrüder* (Victual Brothers), operating from the island of Helgoland in the North Sea, almost succeeded in closing down Baltic Sea shipping with the extent of their marauding, until eventually they were defeated by the Hanseatic League fleet in a sea battle in the summer of 1401. The pirates' leader Klaus Störtebeker (1360–*c.* 1401) and some 70 of his men were executed after being put on trial in Hamburg, and their heads were then impaled on spikes so that the full measure of their punishment would be there for all to see. In myth, the historically elusive Störtebeker evolved into a legendary antihero who has regularly been the subject of tales and also songs (ills. pp. 44 r., 45, 52–54), especially in Germany where he is sometimes compared to the English folk hero Robin Hood. After 1715, and especially during the so-called "Pax Britannica" between the end of the Napoleonic Wars and the beginning of World War I (1815–1914), Britain's navy helped eradicate or reduce piracy in many parts of the world.

Howard Pyle
Vignettes for the title-page and dedication of Pyle's Book of Pirates, 1921

Howard Pyle
Pirate Captain Keitt, the protagonist of Pyle's short story The Ruby of Kishmoor, *on deck – as illustrated on the cover of his* Book of Pirates, 1921

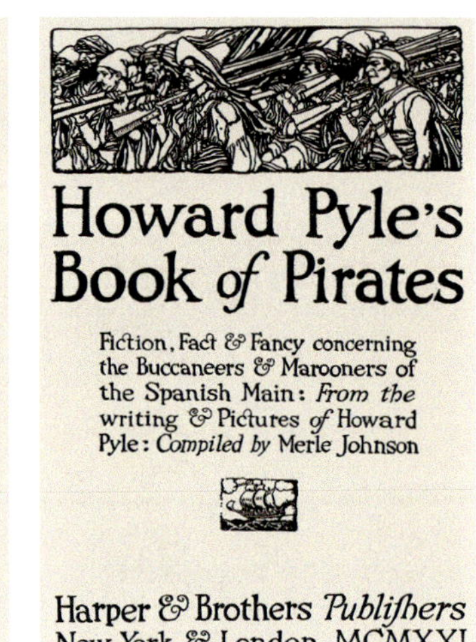

Undoubtedly the tone of W.S. Gilbert (1836–1911) and Arthur Sullivan's (1842–1900) hilarious operetta *The Pirates of Penzance; or, The Slave of Duty*, which premiered in New York City on December 31, 1879, a spoof about warmhearted, bumbling marauders rather than an exposé of actual buccaneer life, owed something to the diminishing menace of piracy in previous decades (ills. pp. 30–31).

"It's like enough you've heard of me before"

As the threat from pirates lost momentum, authors could more readily create romantic figures with an appealing nature, even if they were rarely portrayed entirely without fault. Stevenson's pirates in *Treasure Island*, for instance, were drunkards almost to a man. As a general rule, however, pirates in literature were ruthless to outsiders whilst maintaining democratic standards within their own circles: they ruled their ships according to fixed laws, and selected their leaders by vote. They were also forbidden to steal from each other, or to take up arms and accost a fellow pirate. In addition, they could be moralistic, as when protecting the honor of a "prudent" woman or dividing their booty amongst one another, in largely equal shares.

The renowned U.S. author and illustrator Howard Pyle (1853–1911), whose art and writing often dealt with pirate subject matter, was acquainted with much earlier printed material about their escapades. Among his writings was a parallel of sorts to Exquemelin's classic account, which he wrote and illustrated for the August and December 1887 issues of *Harper's New Monthly*

Zdeněk Burian
Cover illustration for a Czech edition of L'Île Mystérieuse (Tajuplný ostrov), 1939

Newell Convers Wyeth
Cover illustration for The Mysterious Island, 1919

Magazine and entitled "Buccaneers and Marooners of the Spanish Main", a tale that was later included in his posthumous publication, *Howard Pyle's Book of Pirates*, in 1921. The story contained a masterful image of a shipwrecked seaman, entitled "Marooned", one of the iconic pirate illustrations in literature (ill. pp. 344/45). Pyle then edited Exquemelin's work on piracy, and included it in his own *Buccaneers and Marooners of America* (1891). As an adult, Pyle recalled in an autobiographical sketch how his mother had read *Robinson Crusoe* to him as a child. In addition to these childhood memories, he may well have had pirate articles of clothing amongst the various costumes he collected to guide his artwork.

Pyle's stories, which concentrated on the pirates of the Golden Age who sailed between U.S. ports and their Caribbean bases, succeeded in humanizing these characters to a degree that many of their victims would have disputed vigorously, although there was a known basis for his depictions. During the late 1600s, many of England's Atlantic Coast colonies were financially impeded by English mercantile restrictions on trade between the colonists and other foreign countries, driving up prices for imported goods. In this context, pirates sometimes made positive contributions to the economies of seaside communities by supplying cheaper products, so much so that their robberies

were encouraged and their presence welcomed locally, while they were also often regarded as respectable seamen. At times, they were pardoned for their crimes and became legendary figures. Growing up on the

Jules Férat
Cover illustration to the original, Hetzel edition of L'Île Mystérieuse, 1875

Jules Férat
"'The black flag!', cried Ayrton": the castaways espy a pirate ship adorned with the Jolly Roger from afar, in an illustration from L'Île Mystérieuse, 1875

Delaware coastline, Pyle worked to recreate an accurate depiction of these men within his writings. Yet, in the end, he is remembered more for his illustrations of buccaneers than his narratives about them.

Although several of the American illustrators who studied with him would remember Pyle reading his stories to them as they worked together in their shared studio, many of them never followed him into the world of fiction writing. Instead, they remembered Pyle's fascination with legendary tales of piracy and created their own illustrations that included dramatic scenes and detailed representations in various adaptations of the stories contained in this volume. Two students who studied closely with Pyle, Newell Convers Wyeth (1882–1945) and Frank Schoonover (1877–1972), remained in the Delaware area where piracy's hold had helped inspire their mentor's work. Perhaps the surroundings also sparked their creative output in the field of pirate illustration.

Much like Defoe's *Crusoe*, Pyle's pirate tales depended upon predictable elements found in early writings. In *Jack Ballister's Fortunes*, first published in 1895, while the plot is partly based on earlier accounts of Blackbeard, Pyle's conventional framing allows his reader to predict the story's ending, and he resorts to the common literary device of the orphan's tale to frame Jack's adventures. As an English youngster who

CH BARBANT

PIRATES OF PENZANCE,

CHARLES D'ALBERT.

LONDON: CHAPPELL & Co 50, NEW BOND St W.

ENT. STA. HALL.

PRICE SOLO . . . 4/-
" DUET 4/-

Alfred Concanen
Color lithograph covers to Charles d'Albert's galop (left), quadrille (below left) and polka (below right) arrangements to The Pirates of Penzance, 1880

is 16 when the story starts, Jack is alone in the world after his mother died when he was four and his father when he was 14. After his father's death, Jack's uncle has him impressed into indentured servitude in Virginia.

Once in Virginia, Jack soon becomes immersed in the traditional hero's journey: he meets a young woman whose family owns a plantation, is sent to live with her rakish uncle who is indebted to Blackbeard, rescues the

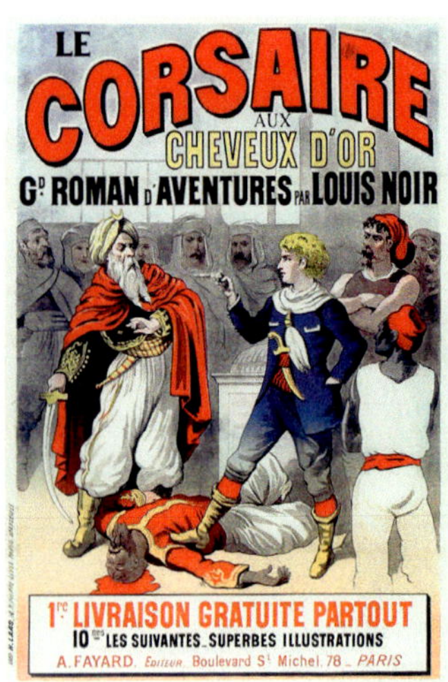

Auguste Berlin
Cover illustration for Louis Noir's adventure novel Le corsaire aux cheveux d'or, 1880

Howard Pyle
"The Song of Captain Kidd", one of Pyle's earliest pirate illustrations, published in Harper's New Monthly Magazine, 1879

"Mr. Campbell as Blackbeard the Pirate", from a set of theatre posters, c. 1831/32

young woman from Blackbeard when she is captured for ransom, and is finally revealed as the heir to a sizable inheritance who must return to his native England and attend college there. Later, he returns to America and marries the plantation owner's daughter. This plot, of the poor wandering orphan who is saved and saves others, was already standard in pirate lore by Pyle's day.

In *Jack Ballister's Fortunes,* Pyle illuminated the very real ties that existed between some New World pirates and England's North American colonies. At one point, Blackbeard overhears someone asking who he is, and replies that he is "Teach... Captain Teach, and I hail from North Carolina. It's like enough you've heard of me before,"[2] allowing Pyle to acknowledge the fact that his readers at the time would likely already have been familiar with tales of Blackbeard. Furthermore, as a writer whose audience included both youngsters and adults, Pyle fused two popular literary styles of the day, the adventure story and the romance novel, and in doing so he also bridged the age gap. *Jack Ballister's Fortunes* is collaborative literature, literature that depends upon the audience's knowledge of pirate lore and their literary understanding of the avarice and transformative experiences often depicted in novels of romance.

Pyle would surely have read Stevenson's *Treasure Island* when he was writing his own works about

The Song of CAPTAIN KIDD

Oh, my name was Robert Kidd, as I sail'd, as I sail'd;
Oh, my name was Robert Kidd, as I sail'd.
My sinful footsteps slid; God's laws they did forbid;
But still wickedly I did, as I sail'd.

I'd a Bible in my hand when I sail'd, when I sail'd;
I'd a Bible in my hand when I sail'd.
I'd a Bible in my hand, by my father's great command,
And I sunk it in the sand, when I sail'd.

I spied three ships of France, as I sail'd, as I sail'd;
I spied three ships of France, as I sail'd.
I spied three ships of France; to them I did advance,
And took them all by chance, as I sail'd.

I spied three ships of Spain, as I sail'd, as I sail'd;
I spied three ships of Spain, as I sail'd.
I spied three ships of Spain; I fired on them amain,
Till most of them were slain, as I sail'd.

I murdered William Moore, as I sail'd, as I sail'd;
I murdered William Moore, as I sail'd.
I murdered William Moore, and I left him in his gore,
Not many leagues from shore, as I sail'd.

I'd ninety bars of gold, as I sail'd, as I sail'd;
I'd ninety bars of gold, as I sail'd.
I'd dollars manifold, and riches uncontrolled,
And by these I lost my soul, as I sail'd.

Mr. CAMBELL as BLACK BEARD the PIRATE.

A Debelle del
Huart sc

Christian Pitois
The female pirate Mary Read reveals herself before a vanquished enemy, from Histoire des pirates et corsaires, 1846

Illustration of Mary Read in combat, from Historie de Zee-Rovers, 1725

pirates, and indeed the books of both authors initially appeared in serialized formats, sometimes within the same magazines. *Jack Ballister's Fortunes* was serialized in the children's periodical *St. Nicholas Magazine* between May 1894 and September 1895. Pyle's use of brief episodes allowed him to leave his readers dangling with cliffhanging plot turns at the end of each installment, and he also embellished the tales with his own illustrations. *The Century Illustrated Monthly Magazine* compared Pyle's *Ballister* to Stevenson's *Kidnapped* (1886), which also first appeared in a serialized version, predicting that his adventure saga would be as graphic and interesting to readers as Stevenson's had been. Both Pyle and Stevenson depended on this kind of magazine publication for extra income and also relied on it to spur the public's interest in their writings. Stevenson wrote *Treasure Island* after he had created a map and then been encouraged by his 12-year-old stepson to write a real pirate's story. Because he was ill, he wrote the book a chapter at a time, reading each one aloud to his family. Looking back, Stevenson's wife wrote, "Had it not been a serial, I doubt if it would ever have been finished."[3]

Contemporary reviews of Pyle's book instantly connected *Jack Ballister's Fortunes* to earlier pirate literature. When the story was released in book form, *The Literary World* declared Pyle's new pirate narrative to be as good as the earlier publications of Defoe and Stevenson, noting in particular its enhancement by the full-page woodcuts that accompanied the text and

Pag. 117.
B. Cole sculp.

Pages 36/37
Benjamin Cole
"Anne Bonny and Mary Read", from Captain Charles Johnson's A General History of the Pyrates, 1724

George Varian
Jim Hawkins peers into cabin of the Hispaniola, *where Israel Hands and his companion are locked in combat, in an illustration for* Treasure Island, 1918

Frank Schoonover
Pirate with Flintlock, oil on board, 1921
Dust jacket illustration for the Harper & Brothers edition of Treasure Island.

which they deemed to contain the "verisimilitude of history".[4]

As fanciful as *The Pirates of Penzance* in its way, *Treasure Island* had realistic elements, especially in the sense that it portrayed pirate violence both explicitly and indirectly. For example, the buccaneer Billy Bones, who in the novel's opening scene visits the Admiral Benbow Inn, bears a sabre cut across his cheek, while much later in the book, after Jim has fled to a thicket to escape Long John Silver's mutinous cohort on Treasure Island, he witnesses Silver fell a disaffected conspirator by throwing a tree branch at his back, and then, without giving the fellow a moment to recover and make a fair fight of it, finish him off. Silver "buried his knife up to the hilt," Stevenson relates, "in that defenceless body."[5]

Also embedded into the plot of *Treasure Island*, more than any other work of piracy, are the distorted fancies that modern popular culture most associates with pirates, such as walking the plank (ill. p. 50 b.), "black spot" curses, maps showing the location of buried treasure, and colorful, invented lingo, including "shiver my timbers" and "Yo-ho-ho, and a bottle of rum!" In reality, pirates, who tended to spend their monies on booze and prostitutes at portside taverns, simply did not hoard their loot on beaches for future use; and they did not condemn each other with black spots or compel prisoners to walk the plank to a

Frank Schoonover
Pirate with Skull and Crossbones,
charcoal and crayon on board, 1922
Schoonover's illustration of a pirate gesturing towards the Jolly Roger flag was featured in the first, 1922 edition of Ralph D. Paine's novel Blackbeard, Buccaneer.

Clyde Osmer Deland
The Blades Rang Together,
oil on canvas, 1924
Deland's painting of a pirate duel was used as an illustration in Rafael Sabatini's Captain Blood, *also published in 1924.*

watery grave. Historians have found very few incidents of people having to walk the plank, and all of them occurring long after piracy's Golden Age. While a few creative retellings have asserted that Blackbeard made French sailors walk the plank after two of their ships had been captured – the *Toison d'Or* and *Rose Emelye* – in 1718, the truth would actually appear to be that Blackbeard let the French escape on the former vessel, declaringthat they would have been hurled into the sea had there not been a ship available for their return to France. Similarly, although there is no hard evidence for the legend that Captain Kidd buried gold dust, silver, diamonds, and other loot on Gardiner's Island, off the coast of Long Island in England's New York colony in 1699, legends persisted that he did and that the treasure remains there, thus providing a source of compelling subject matter for mythmakers. "Kidd at Gardiner's Island", a magazine illustration by Howard Pyle which accompanied a story about him, depicts Kidd in full pirate regalia standing beside a treasure chest, supervising two plainly dressed seamen wearing bandanas as they dig a hole in the sand to bury the treasure.[6]

"Weapons Grim and Gory"

Stories of piracy were labeled as "boys' literature" and considered family reading, although the tales did gradually evolve in terms of narrative style. Early writing on the subject was penned by adults who supposedly found themselves in actual encounters with groups of men who welcomed and went in search of adventure, who deliberately broke social norms, and lived communally. However, tales of the Victorian era made adolescent youths, not pirates, their heroes. These first-person narratives recounted to readers how, following their adventurous experiences, the

Howard Pyle
Who Shall Be Captain?, oil on canvas, 1908
Pyle's depiction of a pirate duel, watched by onlookers, was subsequently printed in his Book of Pirates.

Frank Schoonover
Pirates Hide and Watch, charcoal and crayon on board, 1922
The pirates Trimble Rogers and Bill Saxby, in an illustration subsequently used for Paine's Blackbeard, Buccaneer.

post-buccaneering adult returns to his proper place in polite society. The archetypal young, often orphaned, heroes, of which Jack Ballister was a classic example, also typically described how they were transformed by their adventures, embarking on a *Bildungsroman* journey of psychological, social, and moral change.

As for pirate stories on stage, and whether they were increasingly resembling children's literature too, one cannot deny that early staged plays featuring pirates or shipwrecks were written for adults: Shakespeare's *Hamlet* and *The Tempest* were hardly children's fare. Later stage productions with pirate themes retained some aspects from the earlier plays but they also engaged with the societal norms of their own day. Pirates on the stage, given their gripping adventures, outwardly held commonalities with their predecessors in books and magazines, though their actions were also guided by responses to current geopolitics. Furthermore, the adventures of these pirates often ironically commented on "polite society" and their dialogue was designed to entertain audiences that might include both men and women (and youngsters too), being directed as it was at the ruling classes.

Gilbert and Sullivan's *Pirates of Penzance* depicted pirates as English gentlemen. There is little actual piracy in this production, in the sense of the characters being seafaring robbers. Rather, the appeal of *The Pirates of Penzance* depended upon finding a reaction in an audience already schooled in earlier literature about pirates, and particularly the orphan trope it employed. Gilbert and Sullivan's pirates are orphans, and they are all single. As full-grown men, they still bear the literary trappings of the English orphan, and, because they come from good families, they know the stock conventions of their own characterization and the typical pirate plot. Indentured to pirates as a youth, Frederic is an honorable and naïve young man who has completed his apprenticeship and falls in love with the daughter of a local gentleman: the Major General, a man with good upbringing and education. After his daughters are captured by the pirates, he pretends to be an orphan himself, and in this way, he usurps the well-known literary trope of the orphan in an attempt to mine it for his own profit: specifically, that the pirates show him sympathy and release his daughters. Once the Major General and his daughters learn that the pirates are actually English gentlemen, however, he declares they are acceptable: "Peers will be peers, and youth will have its fling. Resume your ranks and legislative duties, And take my daughters, all of whom are beauties."

Gilbert and Sullivan were hardly depicting authentic pirates from the Atlantic. For all their allusions to the "brave black flag" and "weapons grim and gory",[7] they were using the motif of the pirate as a means to

Howard Pyle
"Burning the Ship", published in
Howard Pyle's Book of Pirates, 1921

Right and opposite
Alfred Roloff
Cover illustrations for the issues
A Fight in Wadden Sea *(right)*
and The Sea Battle of Helgoland
(opposite) of the serialized dime novel
Klaus Störtebecker, der gefürchtete Herrscher der Meere, 1932/33

stage an ironic parody on the gentlemanly habit of literary stealing. On the one hand, this is a story about pirates invading a place on land and pillaging, but on the other it is a narrative about the pillaging of something quite different.

The Pirates of Penzance illustrates how geopolitical shifts allow the literary and visual devices found in pirate stories to be understood in divergent ways. Such devices encourage audiences to engage with the text in multiple ways. Is the pirate the hero of the story, or does he become a symbolic characterization of the abuses of power? The readers of early pirate stories would have been able to nod in recognition at the familiar elements from earlier plots and characterization within conventional pirate literature. This understanding would also have affected the audience at later staged works such as *The Pirates of Penzance*. Embedded within the public embrace of these staged pirates was an unconscious acknowledgment that the dramatist had pilfered someone else's literary tradition, perhaps even their sociopolitical heritage. Stage audiences (and equally readers of the literary tales) recognized additionally the degree to which the depictions of pirates were to be interpreted as political satire.

By the time James Barrie (1860–1937) turned to writing a play that spoke to urbane British audiences who were already familiar with literary and stage

Alice Bolingbroke Woodward
Watercolor illustrations depicting Peter Pan in close combat with Captain James Hook, 1907

Francis Donkin Bedford
Cover illustration for the first edition of Peter and Wendy, *published by Charles Scribner's Sons, New York*, 1911

pirates, the idea of playing with plots and characterizations in traditional literature was an established form. When *Peter Pan* opened in London in 1904 it was considered a *tour de force* consonant with popular adventure literature and the Victorian ideals of British colonialism. It seemed to be a representation of early colonial exploitation by British men who wanted to rule, whether in the new world or at home.

Barrie's play also crossed the geopolitical boundaries between British colonialism and American historicism, re-imagining pirate lore once again in the process. Howard Pyle had rewritten the history of piracy in highly dramatic stories that appeared episodically so that he could first publish them in magazines and later gain a second income from the story when it was published in book format. His tales featured pirates who were regional legendary figures in the Americas, but these new pirates as presented by Gilbert and Sullivan pillaged the literary works of other authors. Barrie, with his own agenda, tapped into obsessions with maleness in Anglo-American culture.

When Barrie first introduced Peter Pan in *The Little White Bird* (1902), Peter was betwixt and between man and bird. Having flown out of his nursery, he lived in the park of Kensington Gardens. In the play, Peter emerged as a child who loved to play games, who enjoyed folklore, and longed to have a mother but refused to become a man. When the theatrical Peter is admired and sought after by two civilizations – "Indians" and orphan English boys who have been forgotten by

George Varian
"From the ship, we could see nothing of the house or stockade"; illustration for Treasure Island, 1918

George Varian
Jim Hawkins watches from afar, as the pirates disembark from canoes, with the Hispaniola *in the background; illustration for* Treasure Island, 1918

their mothers or nannies – we notice shades of colonial exploitation within the plot. The play's children and Indians remain under Peter's rule while they are in Neverland, and this dependence is rooted in racialist depictions of stereotypically dependent savage cultures in conquered lands of Britain's historical worldwide empire. Peter Pan is more than capable of handling the "others", pirates and "Indians" alike, that he comes up against, including, of course, Captain Hook. In a telling early version of the play, Barrie wrote a scene implying that the Indian princess Tiger Lily fantasized about Peter attacking her: "If [Peter] Paleface chase Tiger Lily – she no run fast – she tumble into a heap, what then?"[8] Tiger Lily's faltering English, as it is thus styled, only diminishes her stature further in regard to Peter Pan and the culture he represents.

At the same time, *Peter Pan*'s straightforward plot and stock characters filled a theatrical void for children that enthralled audiences in England and America alike. It imposed pirates upon a magical land where boys crow and strut about as they engage with fairies, mermaids, Indians, and pirates in battles for physical and verbal supremacy. Despite the fact that there are now serious works about women pirates and that women's history is taken far more seriously today than in Barrie's time, it is worth considering that most pirate talk and swagger in modern popular culture originates in literature and stage productions that were primarily designed for males. Such works leave the sense that girls should identify with Wendy's domestic characteristics and her storytelling for lost boys, or accept the fate of a young woman who finds herself saved by a Jack Ballister or a Frederic who stepped into the fray to champion her cause. Viewed in this light, pirate literature is conventional, reinforcing the *status quo*. At times, reading a traditional pirate story can feel exhilarating because it holds the kernel of the orphan story, and in the end the orphan is the hero. Still, just like Peter Pan, we may be in danger of losing all semblance of truth if we look too fondly on these unruly ways of living.

One of the ways *Peter Pan* has changed understandings of pirates in popular culture is through its upending of gender imagery. When the play was turned into a book for young readers, the illustrator selected was Alice Bolingbroke Woodward (1862–1951), the daughter of a revered scientist who had largely been home-schooled, just as the Darling children had been in Barrie's story. Her emphasis throughout her illustrations is on the children and their adventures, although attention is also paid to Peter's duels with Captain Hook (ills. pp. 46–47). Peter Pan is definitely a boy in the story, not a young woman as he is portrayed on the stage, and his dependence on Wendy as a mother figure is aptly shown. Yet they are never depicted as adults.

Guy Arnoux
"Les Pirates", illustration from Dessinateurs et humoristes, 1900–1916

Howard Pyle
Walking the Plank, oil on canvas, 1887
A pirate, blindfolded and with his arms bound, is sent to his demise, in a painting later repoduced in Harper's Magazine.

Louis Rhead
Israel Hands is shot by Jim Hawkins after a prolonged conflict in Rhead's illustration for Treasure Island, 1915

Woodward's illustrations, first published in 1907, have given her viewers a child's fantasy that could easily be considered a fairyland. In 1980, some three generations later, the American illustrator Trina Schart Hyman (1939–2004) illustrated *Peter Pan* for a new audience, one who might have seen Peter played on the stage by a woman. Hyman's watercolor pictures hold a suggestion of Barrie's possible intention: is Peter male, female, or androgynous?

"Portraiture of Death"

In the excerpts that follow from some of the classic literary works on pirates, their hybrid blend of realism and imagination, perhaps more so than is found in most literary genres, should be both apparent and something to bear in mind. Although a lot is known about pirate military operations and their depredations, far less is understood about pirates than popular culture suggests. For instance, a lot is known about pirate ships. Though pirates tended to man modest-sized sloops built primarily for speed, to overtake their victims and escape with booty, they sometimes sailed in fearsome war vessels comparable to the best naval ships of the day. This they accomplished by capturing large merchant ships and government warships and converting them for pirate service. After Blackbeard's squadron overtook the French slaving

Alfred Roloff
Cover illustrations for issues of Klaus Störtebecker, der gefürchtete Herrscher der Meere*:* The Riddle of the Crypt *(left);* Waldemar Zappy *(below);* The Raid on Strelasund *(right)*, 1932/33

vessel *La Concorde* (a ship with portals for 40 cannon) near the Windward Islands in November 1717, he made it his flagship, the *Queen Anne's Revenge*. In contrast, understanding is limited, at best, of pirate attire. The likelihood is that pirates clothed themselves much like common seamen of the time, since they often had prior experience either as "Jack Tars" on merchant vessels or as sailors on military vessels. Sailors on trading vessels generally wore linen shirts, baggy breeches, jackets, stockings, and caps, and many had tattoos on their forearms. But since few contemporary descriptions of pirate clothing have survived, past and present writers, artists, and illustrators, not to mention today's cinema costume designers, have taken considerable amounts of leeway when imagining them.

Likewise, pirate flags are another area of uncertainty, since no authentic pirate standards from the Golden Age have made their way into modern museum collections. It is assumed that pirate flags were black and distinctively designed, especially in the early 1700s when commentators did allude to the "Jolly Roger" or "Old Roger". A newspaper report on the execution of some of Edward Low's pirate crewmen in Newport, Rhode Island in July 1723 mentioned that their gallows were sited under their "Black Flag, with the Pourtrature of Death having an Hour-Glass in one Hand and a Dart in the other," which suggests that pirate colors emphasized death to intimidate targeted ships into quickly surrendering as pirate vessels closed with them.[9] It is probable that some Golden Age pirate flags featured the skull and crossbones insignia, since a pirate flag seized by the Royal Navy in 1780 had that exact design, but that flag capture occurred a half century after the Golden Age.[10]

Alfred Roloff
Cover illustration for the issue Vitalientreue *from* Klaus Störtebecker, der gefürchtete Herrscher der Meere, 1932/33

Newell Convers Wyeth
Cover illustration for The Ladies' Home Journal, *volume 39*, March 1922

Pages 56/57
Newell Convers Wyeth
The Duel on the Beach, oil on canvas, 1926

The jury remains out too regarding attitudes to race and gender among pirates. While there *were* female pirates in the Age of Sail (around 1571–1862), such as Anne Bonny and Mary Read (ills. pp. 34–37), the world of high-seas piracy was almost exclusively homosocial. Similarly, it is difficult to generalize about pirates' racial attitudes. Because they sailed at a time when the international slave trade was legal and flourishing, pirates seized many captives from vessels that were engaged in slave trading. On the one hand, pirates sometimes fully integrated captured Black slaves into their crews, even allowing them a rough equality with the existing crew and allocating them a share of the spoils. Nearly a third of pirate crews during this era were of African derivation. But other historians emphasize that European and Euro-American pirates routinely relegated Black people to drudgework aboard ship and that they often sold captured slaves along with their other takings when they reached port. Furthermore, some pirates had sufficient social pretensions to retain them as servants to wait on them aboard ship.

These debates make pirate literature all the more interesting. The following adventure-packed selections nevertheless stand on their own merits as well, and offer elements of realism, myth, stereotypes, and romance, all waiting to be sorted out in light of what is known and what remains mysterious about pirate life and culture.

© N.C.WYETH

THE TALES

ROBINSON CRUSOE

Daniel Defoe, 1719
Illustrations by Edward Henry Wehnert, Walter Paget, and Newell Convers Wyeth

Awash with battles, brutalities, shipwrecks, marooned victims, exotic tropical locales, parrots, and with a cast of all-male characters, Daniel Defoe's *Robinson Crusoe* has many of the common trappings of a pirate tale. It recounts, in the first person, the life story of an adventure-seeking son of an English merchant, who, obsessed with the idea of going to sea, ships out as a captain's "companion" on a voyage to the west coast of Africa, and when that episode ends, determines to make money in the Guinea trade. The bulk of Crusoe's account describes how he eventually went to Brazil (then a Portuguese colony) to plant tobacco and sugar cane; his experiences after being shipwrecked for 28 years on a Caribbean island off the Spanish-controlled coast and waters of northern South America (in the vicinity of the mouth of the Orinoco River in Venezuela and Trinidad island); his later brief return there, and his experiences in the China trade and traveling back to Europe via Russia. The only pirates *per se* peopling these pages appear early on, when a trading vessel Crusoe is on is seized by the "Moorish pirates of Sallee" – an allusion to the North African Barbary corsairs who were known as Sallee Rovers and their port base of Salé on the Atlantic coast of Morocco. Crusoe has a relatively comfortable time as a servant to the Rovers' "pirate-chief", but plots to escape from the start of his captivity and pulls it off a couple of years later. It is little wonder that *Crusoe* became an instant success, given its action-packed chapters filled with dangerous cannibals and the like. The tale shows how easy it is to accept certain distasteful ideas uncritically when they are delivered in first-person narratives that tend to be self-justifying. Early in Crusoe's stay on the island, he fantasizes about capturing native "savages" who live there and making them into his slaves, and he eventually follows through with this idea, in part, with a "savage" whose life he saves and who he names Friday. True, Crusoe cares for Friday, clothes and feeds him, teaches him English and weans him off eating human flesh. But he also makes Friday into his personal servant and instructs him to call him "Master". In passages omitted from the excerpts that follow, Defoe indicated that Crusoe was engaged in a voyage to Guinea to acquire slaves for his plantation in Brazil when he was shipwrecked on his island; and that later in life he was involved in selling opium in China. Robinson Crusoe is thus no paragon of virtue by modern standards, and yet it should of course be remembered that during the years that the fictional Crusoe lived imperialism was thoroughly engrained into English culture and slavery was still legal in English, Spanish, and Portuguese colonies.

START IN LIFE

I was born in the year 1632, in the city of York, of a good family, though not of that country, my father being a foreigner of Bremen, who settled first at Hull. He got a good estate by merchandise, and leaving off his trade, lived afterwards at York, from whence he had married my mother, whose relations were named Robinson, a very good family in that country, and from whom I was called Robinson Kreutznaer; but, by the usual corruption of words in England, we are now called – nay we call ourselves and write our name – Crusoe; and so my companions always called me.

START IN LIFE

I had two elder brothers, one of whom was lieutenant-colonel to an English regiment of foot in Flanders, formerly commanded by the famous Colonel Lockhart, and was killed at the battle near Dunkirk against the Spaniards. What became of my second brother I never knew, any more than my father or mother knew what became of me. Being the third son of the family and not bred to any trade, my head began to be filled very early with rambling thoughts. My father, who was very ancient, had given me a competent share of learning, as far as house-education and a country free school generally go, and designed me for the law; but I would be satisfied with nothing but going to sea; and my inclination to this led me so strongly against the will, nay, the commands of my father, and against all the entreaties and persuasions of my mother and other friends, that there seemed to be something fatal in that propensity of nature, tending directly to the life of misery which was to befall me.

My father, a wise and grave man, gave me serious and excellent counsel against what he foresaw was my design. He called me one morning into his chamber, where he was confined by the gout, and expostulated very warmly with me upon this subject. He asked me what reasons, more than a mere wandering inclination, I had for leaving father's house and my native country, where I might be well introduced, and had a prospect of raising my fortune by application and industry, with a life of ease and pleasure. He told me it was men of desperate fortunes on one hand, or of aspiring, superior fortunes on the other, who went abroad upon adventures, to rise by enterprise, and make themselves famous in undertakings of a nature out of the common road; that these things were all either too far above me or too far below me; that mine was the middle state, or what might be called the upper station of low life, which he had found, by long experience, was the best state in the world, the most suited to human happiness, not exposed to the miseries and hardships, the labour and sufferings of the mechanic part of mankind, and not embarrassed with the pride, luxury, ambition, and envy of the upper part of mankind. He told me I might judge of the happiness of this state by this one thing – viz. that this was the state of life which all other people envied; that kings have frequently lamented the miserable consequence of being born to great things, and wished they had been placed in the middle of the two extremes, between the mean and the great; that the wise man gave his testimony to this, as the standard of felicity, when he prayed to have neither poverty nor riches.

He bade me observe it, and I should always find that the calamities of life were shared among the upper and lower part of mankind, but that the middle station had the fewest disasters, and was not exposed to so many vicissitudes as the higher or lower part of mankind; nay, they were not subjected to so many distempers and uneasinesses, either of body or mind, as those were who, by vicious living, luxury, and extravagances on the one hand, or by hard labour, want of necessaries, and mean or insufficient diet on the other hand, bring distemper upon themselves by the natural consequences of their way of living; that the middle station of life was calculated for all kind of virtue and all kind of enjoyments; that peace and plenty were the handmaids of a middle fortune; that temperance, moderation, quietness, health, society, all agreeable diversions, and all desirable pleasures, were the blessings attending the middle station of life; that this way men went silently and smoothly through the world, and comfortably out of it, not embarrassed with the labours of the hands or of the head, not sold to a life of slavery for daily bread,

My father, a wise and grave man, gave me serious and excellent counsel.

nor harassed with perplexed circumstances, which rob the soul of peace and the body of rest, nor enraged with the passion of envy, or the secret burning lust of ambition for great things; but, in easy circumstances, sliding gently through the world, and sensibly tasting the sweets of living, without the bitter; feeling that they are happy, and learning by every day's experience to know it more sensibly.

After this he pressed me earnestly, and in the most affectionate manner, not to play the young man, nor to precipitate myself into miseries which nature, and the station of life I was born in, seemed to have provided against; that I was under no necessity of seeking my bread; that he would do well for me, and endeavour to enter me fairly into the station of life which he had just been recommending to me; and that if I was not very easy and happy in the world, it must be my mere fate or fault that must hinder it; and that he should have nothing to answer for, having thus discharged his duty in warning me against measures which he knew would be to my hurt; in a word, that as he would do very kind things for me if I would stay and settle at home as he directed, so he would not have so much hand in my misfortunes as to give me any encouragement to go away; and to close all, he told me I had my elder brother for an example, to whom he had used the same earnest persuasions to keep him from going into the Low Country wars, but could not prevail, his young desires prompting him to run into the army, where he was killed; and though he said he would not cease to pray for me, yet he would venture to say to me, that if I did take this foolish step, God would not bless me, and I should have leisure hereafter to reflect upon having neglected his counsel when there might be none to assist in my recovery.

I observed in this last part of his discourse, which was truly prophetic, though I suppose my father did not know it to be so himself – I say, I observed the tears run down his face very plentifully, especially when he spoke of my brother who was killed: and that when he spoke of my having leisure to repent, and none to assist me, he was so moved that he broke off the discourse, and told me his heart was so full he could say no more to me.

I was sincerely affected with this discourse, and, indeed, who could be otherwise? and I resolved not to think of going abroad any more, but to settle at home according to my father's desire. But alas! a few days wore it all off; and, in short, to prevent any of my father's further importunities, in a few weeks after I resolved to run quite away from him. However, I did not act quite so hastily as the first heat of my resolution prompted; but I took my mother at a time when I thought her a little more pleasant than ordinary, and told her that my thoughts were so entirely bent upon seeing the world that I should never settle to anything with resolution enough to go through with it, and my father had better give me his consent than force me to go without it; that I was now eighteen years old, which was too late to go apprentice to a trade or clerk to an attorney; that I was sure if I did I should never serve out my time, but I should certainly run away from my master before my time was out, and go to sea; and if she would speak to my father to let me go one voyage abroad, if I came home again, and did not like it, I would go no more; and I would promise, by a double diligence, to recover the time that I had lost.

It was not till almost a year after this that I broke loose, though, in the meantime, I continued obstinately deaf to all proposals of settling to business, and frequently expostulated with my father and mother about their being so positively determined against what they knew my inclinations prompted me to. But being one day at Hull, where I went casually, and without any purpose of making an elopement at that time; but, I say, being there, and one of my companions being about to sail to London in his father's ship, and prompting me to go with them with the common allurement of seafaring men, that it should cost me nothing for my passage, I consulted neither father nor mother any more, nor so much as sent them word of it; but leaving them to hear of it as they might, without asking God's blessing or my father's, without any consideration of circumstances or consequences, and in an ill hour, God knows, on the 1st of September 1651, I went on board a ship bound for London.

Never any young adventurer's misfortunes, I believe, began sooner, or continued longer than mine. The ship was no sooner out of the Humber than the wind began to blow and the sea to rise in a most frightful manner; and, as I had never been at sea before, I was most inexpressibly sick in body and terrified in mind. I began now seriously to reflect upon what I had done, and how justly I was overtaken by the judgment of Heaven for my wicked leaving my father's house, and abandoning my duty. All the good counsels of my parents, my father's tears and my mother's entreaties, came now fresh into my mind; and my conscience, which was not yet come to the pitch of hardness to which it has since, reproached me with the contempt of advice, and the breach of my duty to God and my father.

All this while the storm increased, and the sea went very high, though nothing like what I have seen many times since; no, nor what I saw a few days after; but it was enough to affect me then, who was but a young sailor, and had never known anything of the matter. I expected every wave would have swallowed us up, and that every time the ship fell down, as I thought it did, in the trough or hollow of the sea, we should never rise more; in this agony of mind, I made many vows and resolutions that if it would please God to spare my life in this one voyage, if ever I got once my foot upon dry land again, I would go directly home to my father, and never set it into a ship again while I lived; that I would take his advice, and never run myself into such miseries as these any more. Now I saw plainly the goodness of his observations about the middle station of life, how easy, how comfortably he had lived all his days, and never had been exposed to tempests at sea or troubles on shore; and I resolved that I would, like a true repenting prodigal, go home to my father.

NEVER ANY YOUNG ADVENTURER'S MISFORTUNES BEGAN SOONER, OR CONTINUED LONGER THAN MINE.

These wise and sober thoughts continued all the while the storm lasted, and indeed some time after; but the next day the wind was abated, and the sea calmer, and I began to be a little inured to it; however, I was very grave for all that day, being also a little sea-sick still; but towards night the weather cleared up, the wind was quite over, and a charming fine evening followed; the sun went down perfectly clear, and rose

I went on board a ship bound for London.

so the next morning; and having little or no wind, and a smooth sea, the sun shining upon it, the sight was, as I thought, the most delightful that ever I saw.

We had not, however, rid here so long but we should have tided it up the river, but that the wind blew too fresh, and after we had lain four or five days, blew very hard. However, the Roads being reckoned as good as a harbour, the anchorage good, and our ground-tackle very strong, our men were unconcerned, and not in the least apprehensive of danger, but spent the time in rest and mirth, after the manner of the sea; but the eighth day, in the morning, the wind increased, and we had all hands at work to strike our topmasts, and make everything snug and close, that the ship might ride as easy as possible. By noon the sea went very high indeed, and our ship rode forecastle in, shipped several seas, and we thought once or twice our anchor had come home; upon which our master ordered out the sheet-anchor, so that we rode with two anchors ahead, and the cables veered out to the bitter end.

By this time it blew a terrible storm indeed; and now I began to see terror and amazement in the faces even of the seamen themselves. The master, though vigilant in the business of preserving the ship, yet as he went in and out of his cabin by me, I could hear him softly to himself say, several times, "Lord be merciful to us! we shall be all lost! we shall be all undone!" and the like. During these first hurries I was stupid, lying still in my cabin, which was in the steerage, and cannot describe my temper: I could ill resume the first penitence which I had so apparently trampled upon and hardened myself against: I thought the bitterness of death had been past, and that this would be nothing like the first; but when the master himself came by me, as I said just now, and said we should be all lost, I was dreadfully frighted. I got up out of my cabin and looked out; but such a dismal sight I never saw: the sea ran mountains high, and broke upon us every three or four minutes; when I could look about, I could see nothing but distress round us; two ships that rode near us, we found, had cut their masts by the board, being deep laden; and our men cried out that a ship which rode about a mile ahead of us was foundered. Two more ships, being driven from their anchors, were run out of the Roads to sea, at all adventures, and that with not a mast standing.

We had a good ship, but she was deep laden, and wallowed in the sea, so that the seamen every now and then cried out she would founder. It was my advantage in one respect, that I did not know what they meant by *founder* till I inquired. However, the storm was so

I was so surprised that I fell down in a swoon.

violent that I saw, what is not often seen, the master, the boatswain, and some others more sensible than the rest, at their prayers, and expecting every moment when the ship would go to the bottom. In the middle of the night, and under all the rest of our distresses, one of the men that had been down to see cried out we had sprung a leak; another said there was four feet water in the hold. Then all hands were called to the pump. At that word, my heart, as I thought, died within me: and I fell backwards upon the side of my bed where I sat, into the cabin. However, the men roused me, and told me that I, that was able to do nothing before, was as well able to pump as another; at which I stirred up and went to the pump, and worked very heartily. While this was doing the master, seeing some light colliers, who, not able to ride out the storm were obliged to slip and run away to sea, and would come near us, ordered to fire a gun as a signal of distress. I, who knew nothing what they meant, thought the ship had broken, or some dreadful thing happened. In a word, I was so surprised that I fell down in a swoon. As this was a time when everybody had his own life to think of, nobody minded me, or what was become of me; but another man stepped up to the pump, and thrusting me aside with his foot, let me lie, thinking I had been dead; and it was a great while before I came to myself.

We worked on; but the water increasing in the hold, it was apparent that the ship would founder; and though the storm began to abate a little, yet it was not possible she could swim till we might run into any port; so the master continued firing guns for help; and a light ship, who had rid it out just ahead of us, ventured a boat out to help us. It was with the utmost hazard the boat came near us; but it was impossible for us to get on board, or for the boat to lie near the ship's side, till at last the men rowing very heartily, and venturing their lives to save ours, our men cast them a rope over the stern with a buoy to it, and then veered it out a great length, which they, after much labour and hazard, took hold of, and we hauled them close under our stern, and got all into their boat. It was to no purpose for them or us, after we were in the boat, to think of reaching their own ship; so all agreed to let her drive, and only to pull her in towards shore as much as we could; and our master promised them, that if the boat was staved upon shore, he would make it good to their master: so partly rowing and partly driving, our boat went away to the northward, sloping towards the shore almost as far as Winterton Ness.

We were not much more than a quarter of an hour out of our ship till we saw her sink, and then I understood for the first time what was meant by a ship foundering in the sea. I must acknowledge I had hardly eyes to look up when the seamen told me she was sinking; for from the moment that they rather put me into the boat than that I might be said to go in, my heart was, as it were, dead within me, partly with fright, partly with horror of mind, and the thoughts of what was yet before me.

SLAVERY AND ESCAPE

An irresistible reluctance continued to going home; and as I stayed away a while, the remembrance of the distress I had been in wore off, and as that abated, the little motion I had in my desires to return wore off with it, till at last I quite laid aside the thoughts of it, and looked out for a voyage.

It was my lot first of all to fall into pretty good company in London, which does not always happen to such loose and misguided young fellows as I then was; the devil generally not omitting to lay some snare for them very early; but it was not so with me. I first got acquainted with the master of a ship who had been on the coast of Guinea; and who, having had very good success there, was resolved to go again. This captain taking a fancy to my conversation, which was not at all disagreeable at that time, hearing me say I had a mind to see the world, told me if I would go the voyage with him I should be at no expense; I should be his messmate and his companion; and if I could carry anything with me, I should have all the advantage of it that the trade would admit; and perhaps I might meet with some encouragement.

I embraced the offer; and entering into a strict friendship with this captain, I went the voyage with him, and carried a small adventure with me, which, by the disinterested honesty of my friend the captain, I increased very considerably; for I carried about £40 in such toys and trifles as the captain directed me to buy. These £40 I had mustered together by the assistance of some of my relations whom I corresponded with; and who, I believe, got my father, or at least my mother, to contribute so much as that to my first adventure.

This was the only voyage which I may say was successful in all my adventures, which I owe to the integrity and honesty of my friend the captain; under whom also I got a competent knowledge of the mathematics and the rules of navigation, learned how to keep an account of the ship's course, take an observation, and, in short, to understand some things that were needful to be understood by a sailor; for, as he took delight to instruct me, I took delight to learn; and, in a word, this voyage made me both a sailor and a merchant; for I brought home five pounds nine ounces of gold-dust for my adventure, which yielded me in London, at my return, almost £300; and this filled me with those aspiring thoughts which have since so completed my ruin.

WE BROUGHT EIGHT OF OUR GUNS TO BEAR ON THAT SIDE, AND POURED IN A BROADSIDE UPON HIM.

I was now set up for a Guinea trader; and my friend, to my great misfortune, dying soon after his arrival, I resolved to go the same voyage again, and I embarked in the same vessel with one who was his mate in the former voyage, and had now got the command of the ship. This was the unhappiest voyage that ever man made; for though I did not carry quite £100 of my new-gained wealth, so that I had £200 left, which I had lodged with my friend's widow, yet I fell into terrible misfortunes.

The first was this: our ship making her course towards the Canary Islands, or rather between those islands and the African shore, was surprised by a Turkish rover of Sallee, who gave chase to us with all the sail she could make. We crowded also as much canvas as our yards would spread, or our masts carry, to get clear; but finding the pirate gained upon us, and would certainly come up with us in a few hours, we prepared to fight; our ship having twelve guns, and the rogue eighteen. About three in the afternoon he came up with us, and bringing to, by mistake, just athwart our quarter, instead of athwart our stern, as he intended,

For when I had fish on my hook I would not pull them up, that he might not see them.

we brought eight of our guns to bear on that side, and poured in a broadside upon him, which made him sheer off again, after returning our fire, and pouring in also his small shot from near two hundred men which he had on board. However, we had not a man touched, all our men keeping close. He prepared to attack us again, and we to defend ourselves. But laying us on board the next time upon our other quarter, he entered sixty men upon our decks, who immediately fell to cutting and hacking the sails and rigging. We plied them with small shot, half-pikes, powder-chests, and such like, and cleared our deck of them twice. However, to cut short this melancholy part of our story, our ship being disabled, and three of our men killed, and eight wounded, we were obliged to yield, and were carried all prisoners into Sallee, a port belonging to the Moors.

The usage I had there was not so dreadful as at first I apprehended; nor was I carried up the country to the emperor's court, as the rest of our men were, but was kept by the captain of the rover as his proper prize, and made his slave, being young and nimble, and fit for his business. At this surprising change of my circumstances, from a merchant to a miserable slave, I was perfectly overwhelmed; and now I looked back upon my father's prophetic discourse to me, that I should be miserable and have none to relieve me, which I thought was now so effectually brought to pass that I could not be worse; for now the hand of Heaven had overtaken me, and I was undone without redemption; but, alas! this was but a taste of the misery I was to go through, as will appear in the sequel of this story.

As my new patron, or master, had taken me home to his house, so I was in hopes that he would take me with him when he went to sea again, believing that it would some time or other be his fate to be taken by a Spanish or Portugal man-of-war; and that then I should be set at liberty. But this hope of mine was soon taken away; for when he went to sea, he left me on shore to look after his little garden, and do the common drudgery of slaves about his house; and when he came home again from his cruise, he ordered me to lie in the cabin to look after the ship.

Here I meditated nothing but my escape, and what method I might take to effect it, but found no way that had the least probability in it; nothing presented to make the supposition of it rational; for I had nobody to communicate it to that would embark with me – no fellow-slave, no Englishman, Irishman, or Scotchman there but myself; so that for two years, though I often pleased myself with the imagination, yet I never had the least encouraging prospect of putting it in practice.

After about two years, an odd circumstance presented itself, which put the old thought of making some attempt for my liberty again in my head. My patron lying at home longer than usual without fitting out his ship, which, as I heard, was for want of money, he used constantly, once or twice a week, sometimes oftener if the weather was fair, to take the ship's pinnace and go out into the road a-fishing; and as he always took me and young Maresco with him to row the boat, we made him very merry, and I proved very dexterous in catching fish; insomuch that sometimes he would send me with a Moor, one of his kinsmen, and the youth – the Maresco, as they called him – to catch a dish of fish for him.

ALAS! THIS WAS BUT A TASTE OF THE MISERY I WAS TO GO THROUGH.

It happened that he had appointed to go out in this boat, either for pleasure or for fish, with two or three Moors of some distinction in that place, and for whom he had provided extraordinarily, and had, therefore, sent on board the boat overnight a larger store of provisions than ordinary; and had ordered me to get ready three fusees with powder and shot, which were on board his ship, for that they designed some sport of fowling as well as fishing.

I got all things ready as he had directed, and waited the next morning with the boat washed clean, her ancient and pendants out, and everything to accommodate his guests; when by-and-by my patron came on board alone, and told me his guests had put off going from some business that fell out, and ordered me, with the man and boy, as usual, to go out with the boat and catch them some fish, for that his friends were to sup at his house, and commanded that as soon as I got some fish I should bring it home to his house; all which I prepared to do.

After we had fished some time and caught nothing – for when I had fish on my hook I would not pull them up, that he might not see them – I said to the Moor, "This will not do; our master will not be thus served; we must stand farther off." He, thinking no harm, agreed, and being in the head of the boat, set the sails; and, as I had the helm, I ran the boat out near a league farther, and then brought her to, as if I would fish; when, giving the boy the helm, I stepped forward to where the Moor was, and making as if I stooped for something behind him, I took him by surprise with my arm under his waist, and tossed him clear overboard into the sea. He rose immediately, for he swam like a cork, and called to me, begged to be taken in, told me he would go all over the world with me. He swam so strong after the boat that he would have reached me very quickly, there being but little wind; upon which I stepped into the cabin, and fetching one of the fowling-pieces, I presented it at him, and told him I had done him no hurt, and if he would be quiet I would do him none. "But," said I, "you swim well enough to reach to the shore, and the sea is calm; make the best of your way to shore, and I will do you no harm; but if you come near the boat I'll shoot you through the head, for I am resolved to have my liberty;" so he turned himself about, and swam for the shore, and I make no doubt but he reached it with ease, for he was an excellent swimmer.

I could have been content to have taken this Moor with me, and have drowned the boy, but there was no venturing to trust him. When he was gone, I turned to the boy, whom they called Xury, and said to him, "Xury, if you will be faithful to me, I'll make you a great man;

I took him by surprise with my arm under his waist, and tossed him clear overboard into the sea.

but if you will not stroke your face to be true to me" – that is, swear by Mahomet and his father's beard – "I must throw you into the sea too." The boy smiled in my face, and spoke so innocently that I could not distrust him, and swore to be faithful to me, and go all over the world with me.

While I was in view of the Moor that was swimming, I stood out directly to sea with the boat, rather stretching to windward, that they might think me gone towards the Straits' mouth (as indeed any one that had been in their wits must have been supposed to do): for who would have supposed we were sailed on to the southward, to the truly Barbarian coast, where whole nations of negroes were sure to surround us with their canoes and destroy us; where we could not go on shore but we should be devoured by savage beasts, or more merciless savages of human kind.

But as soon as it grew dusk in the evening, I changed my course, and steered directly south and by east, bending my course a little towards the east, that I might keep in with the shore; and having a fair, fresh gale of wind, and a smooth, quiet sea, I made such sail that I believe by the next day, at three o'clock in the afternoon, when I first made the land, I could not be less than one hundred and fifty miles south of Sallee; quite beyond the Emperor of Morocco's dominions, or indeed of any other king thereabouts, for we saw no people.

Yet such was the fright I had taken of the Moors, and the dreadful apprehensions I had of falling into their hands, that I would not stop, or go on shore, or come to an anchor; the wind continuing fair till I had sailed in that manner five days; and then the wind shifting to the southward, I concluded also that if any of our vessels were in chase of me, they also would now give over; so I ventured to make to the coast, and came to an anchor in the mouth of a little river, I knew not what, nor where, neither what latitude, what country, what nation, or what river. I neither saw, nor desired to see any people; the principal thing I wanted was fresh water. We came into this creek in the evening, resolving to swim on shore as soon as it was dark, and discover the country; but as soon as it was quite dark, we heard such dreadful noises of the barking, roaring, and howling of wild creatures, of we knew not what kinds, that the poor boy was ready to die with fear, and begged of me not to go on shore till day.

We made on to the southward continually for ten or twelve days, living very sparingly on our provisions, which began to abate very much, and going no oftener to the shore than we were obliged to for fresh water. My design in this was to make the river Gambia or Senegal, that is to say anywhere about the Cape de Verde, where I was in hopes to meet with some European ship. At length, doubling the point, at about two leagues from the land, I saw plainly land on the other side, to seaward; then I concluded, as it was most certain indeed, that this was the Cape de Verde, and those the islands called, from thence, Cape de Verde Islands. However, they were at a great distance, and I could not well tell what I had best to do; for if I should be taken with a fresh of wind, I might neither reach one or other.

In this dilemma, as I was very pensive, I stepped into the cabin and sat down, Xury having the helm; when, on a sudden, the boy cried out, "Master, master, a ship with a sail!" and the foolish boy was frighted out of his wits, thinking it must needs be some of his master's ships sent to pursue us, but I knew we were far enough out of their reach. I jumped out of the cabin, and immediately saw, not only the ship, but that it was a Portuguese ship; and, as I thought, was bound to the coast of Guinea, for

negroes. But, when I observed the course she steered, I was soon convinced they were bound some other way, and did not design to come any nearer to the shore; upon which I stretched out to sea as much as I could, resolving to speak with them if possible.

With all the sail I could make, I found I should not be able to come in their way, but that they would be gone by before I could make any signal to them: but after I had crowded to the utmost, and began to despair, they, it seems, saw by the help of their glasses that it was some European boat, which they supposed must belong to some ship that was lost; so they shortened sail to let me come up. I was encouraged with this, and as I had my patron's ancient on board, I made a waft of it to them, for a signal of distress, and fired a gun, both which they saw; for they told me they saw the smoke, though they did not hear the gun. Upon these signals they very kindly brought to, and lay by for me; and in about three hours' time I came up with them.

They asked me what I was, in Portuguese, and in Spanish, and in French, but I understood none of them; but at last a Scotch sailor, who was on board, called to me: and I answered him, and told him I was an Englishman, that I had made my escape out of slavery from the Moors, at Sallee; they then bade me come on board, and very kindly took me in, and all my goods.

It was an inexpressible joy to me, which any one will believe, that I was thus delivered, as I esteemed it, from such a miserable and almost hopeless condition as I was in; and I immediately offered all I had to the captain of the ship, as a return for my deliverance; but he generously told me he would take nothing from me, but that all I had should be delivered safe to me when I came to the Brazils. "For," says he, "I have saved your life on no other terms than I would be glad to be saved myself: and it may, one time or other, be my lot to be taken up in the same condition. Besides," said he, "when I carry you to the Brazils, so great a way from your own country, if I should take from you what you have, you will be starved there, and then I only take away that life I have given. No, no," says he: "Seignior Inglese" (Mr. Englishman), "I will carry you thither in charity, and those things will help to buy your subsistence there, and your passage home again."

The generous treatment the captain gave me I can never enough remember: he would take nothing of me for my passage, gave me twenty ducats for the leopard's skin, and forty for the lion's skin, which I had in my boat, and caused everything I had in the ship to be punctually delivered to me; and what I was willing to sell he bought of me, such as the case of bottles, two of my guns, and a piece of the lump of beeswax – for I had made candles of the rest: in a word, I made about two hundred and twenty pieces of eight of all my cargo; and with this stock I went on shore in the Brazils.

WRECKED ON AN ISLAND

I had not been long here before I was recommended to the house of a good honest man like himself, who had an ingenio, as they call it (that is, a plantation and a sugar-house). I lived with him some time, and acquainted myself by that means with the manner of planting and making of sugar; and seeing how well the planters lived, and how they got rich suddenly, I resolved, if I could get a licence to settle there, I would turn planter among them: resolving in the meantime to find out some way to get my money, which I had left in London, remitted to me.

I got to the mainland, where, to my great comfort, I clambered up the cliffs of the shore.

In short, I took all possible caution to preserve my effects and to keep up my plantation. Had I used half as much prudence to have looked into my own interest, and have made a judgment of what I ought to have done and not to have done, I had certainly never gone away from so prosperous an undertaking, leaving all the probable views of a thriving circumstance, and gone upon a voyage to sea, attended with all its common hazards, to say nothing of the reasons I had to expect particular misfortunes to myself.

But I was hurried on, and obeyed blindly the dictates of my fancy rather than my reason; and, accordingly, the ship being fitted out, and the cargo furnished, and all things done, as by agreement, by my partners in the voyage, I went on board in an evil hour, the 1st September 1659, being the same day eight years that I went from my father and mother at Hull, in order to act the rebel to their authority, and the fool to my own interests.

The same day I went on board we set sail, standing away to the northward upon our own coast, with design to stretch over for the African coast when we came about ten or twelve degrees of northern latitude, which, it seems, was the manner of course in those days. We had very good weather, only excessively hot, all the way upon our own coast, till we came to the height of Cape St. Augustino; from whence, keeping further off at sea, we lost sight of land, and steered as if we were bound for the isle Fernando de Noronha, holding our course N.E. by N., and leaving those isles on the east. In this course we passed the line in about twelve days' time, and were, by our last observation, in seven degrees twenty-two minutes northern latitude, when a violent tornado, or hurricane, took us quite out of our knowledge. It began from the south-east, came about to the north-west, and then settled in the north-east; from whence it blew in such a terrible manner, that for twelve days together we could do nothing but drive, and, scudding away before it, let it carry us whither fate and the fury of the winds directed; and, during these twelve days, I need not say that I expected every day to be swallowed up; nor, indeed, did any in the ship expect to save their lives.

In this distress, the wind still blowing very hard, one of our men early in the morning cried out, "Land!" and we had no sooner run out of the cabin to look out, in hopes of seeing whereabouts in the world we were, than the ship struck upon a sand, and in a moment her motion being so stopped, the sea broke over her in such a manner that we expected we should all have perished immediately; and we were immediately driven into our close quarters, to shelter us from the very foam and spray of the sea.

It is not easy for any one who has not been in the like condition to describe or conceive the consternation of men in such circumstances. We knew nothing where we were, or upon what land it was we were driven – whether an island or the main, whether inhabited or not inhabited. As the rage of the wind was still great, though rather less than at first, we could not so much as hope to have the ship hold many minutes without breaking into pieces, unless the winds, by a kind of miracle, should turn immediately about. In a word, we sat looking upon one another, and expecting death every moment, and every man, accordingly, preparing for another world; for there was little or nothing more for us to do in this. That which was our present comfort, and all the comfort we had, was that, contrary to our expectation, the ship did not break yet, and that the master said the wind began to abate.

Now, though we thought that the wind did a little abate, yet the ship having thus struck upon the sand, and sticking too fast for us to expect her getting off, we were in a dreadful condition indeed, and had nothing to do but to think of saving our lives as well as we could. We had a boat at our stern just before the storm, but she was first staved by dashing against the ship's rudder, and in the next place she broke away, and either sunk or was driven off to sea; so there was no hope from her. We had another boat on board, but how to get her off into the sea was a doubtful thing. However, there was no time to debate, for we fancied that the ship would break in pieces every minute, and some told us she was actually broken already.

In this distress the mate of our vessel laid hold of the boat, and with the help of the rest of the men got her slung over the ship's side; and getting all into her, let go, and committed ourselves, being eleven in number, to God's mercy and the wild sea; for though the storm was abated considerably, yet the sea ran dreadfully high upon the shore, and might be well called *den wild zee*, as the Dutch call the sea in a storm.

And now our case was very dismal indeed; for we all saw plainly that the sea went so high that the boat could not live, and that we should be inevitably drowned. As to making sail, we had none, nor if we had could we have done anything with it; so we worked at the oar towards the land, though with heavy hearts, like men going to execution; for we all knew that when the boat came near the shore she would be dashed in a thousand pieces by the breach of the sea. However, we committed our souls to God in the most earnest manner; and the wind driving us towards the shore, we hastened our destruction with our own hands, pulling as well as we could towards land.

AS WE MADE NEARER AND NEARER THE SHORE, THE LAND LOOKED MORE FRIGHTFUL THAN THE SEA.

What the shore was, whether rock or sand, whether steep or shoal, we knew not. The only hope that could rationally give us the least shadow of expectation was, if we might find some bay or gulf, or the mouth of some river, where by great chance we might have run our boat in, or got under the lee of the land, and perhaps made smooth water. But there was nothing like this appeared; but as we made nearer and nearer the shore, the land looked more frightful than the sea.

After we had rowed, or rather driven about a league and a half, as we reckoned it, a raging wave, mountain-like, came rolling astern of us, and plainly bade us expect the *coup de grâce*. It took us with such a fury, that it overset the boat at once; and separating us as well from the boat as from one another, gave us no time to say, "O God!" for we were all swallowed up in a moment.

Nothing can describe the confusion of thought which I felt when I sank into the water; for though I swam very well, yet I could not deliver myself from the waves so as to draw breath, till that wave having driven me, or rather carried me, a vast way on towards the shore, and having spent itself, went back, and left me upon the land almost dry, but half dead with the water I took in. I had so much presence of mind, as well as breath left, that seeing myself nearer the mainland than I expected, I got upon my feet, and endeavoured to make on towards the land as fast as I could before another wave should return and take me up again; but I soon found it was impossible to avoid it; for I saw the sea come after me as high as a great hill, and as furious as an enemy, which I had no means or strength to contend with: my business was to hold my breath, and raise myself upon the water if I could; and so, by swimming, to preserve my breathing, and pilot myself towards the shore, if possible, my greatest concern now being that the sea, as it would carry me a great way towards the shore when it came on, might not carry me back again with it when it gave back towards the sea.

The wave that came upon me again buried me at once twenty or thirty feet deep in its own body, and I could feel myself carried with a mighty force and swiftness towards the shore – a very great way; but I held my breath, and assisted myself to swim still forward with all my might. I was ready to burst with holding my breath, when, as I felt myself rising up, so, to my immediate relief, I found my head and hands shoot out above the surface of the water; and though it was not two seconds of time that I could keep myself so, yet it relieved me greatly, gave me breath, and new courage. I was covered again with water a good while, but not so long but I held it out; and finding the water had spent itself, and began to return, I struck forward against the return of the waves, and felt ground again with my feet. I stood still a few moments to recover breath, and till the waters went from me, and then took to my heels and ran with what strength I had further towards the shore. But neither would this deliver me from the fury of the sea, which came pouring in after me again; and twice more I was lifted up by the waves and carried forward as before, the shore being very flat.

The last time of these two had well-nigh been fatal to me, for the sea having hurried me along as before, landed me, or rather dashed me, against a piece of rock, and that with such force, that it left me senseless, and indeed helpless, as to my own deliverance; for the blow taking my side and breast, beat the breath as it were quite out of my body; and had it returned again immediately, I must have been strangled in the water; but I recovered a little before the return of the waves, and seeing I should be covered again with the water, I resolved to hold fast by a piece of the rock, and so to hold my breath, if possible, till the wave went back. Now, as the waves were not so high as at first, being nearer land, I held my hold till the wave abated, and then fetched another run, which brought me so near the shore that the next wave, though it went over me, yet did not so swallow me up as to carry me away; and the next run I took, I got to the mainland, where, to my great comfort, I clambered up the cliffs of the shore and sat me down upon the grass, free from danger and quite out of the reach of the water.

I was now landed and safe on shore, and began to look up and thank God that my life was saved.

All the remedy that offered to my thoughts at that time was to get up into a thick bushy tree like a fir, but thorny, which grew near me.

I was now landed and safe on shore, and began to look up and thank God that my life was saved, in a case wherein there was some minutes before scarce any room to hope. I believe it is impossible to express, to the life, what the ecstasies and transports of the soul are, when it is so saved, as I may say, out of the very grave: and I do not wonder now at the custom, when a malefactor, who has the halter about his neck, is tied up, and just going to be turned off, and has a reprieve brought to him – I say, I do not wonder that they bring a surgeon with it, to let him blood that very moment they tell him of it, that the surprise may not drive the animal spirits from the heart and overwhelm him.

I cast my eye to the stranded vessel, when, the breach and froth of the sea being so big, I could hardly see it, it lay so far off; and considered, Lord! how was it possible I could get on shore?

After I had solaced my mind with the comfortable part of my condition, I began to look round me, to see what kind of place I was in, and what was next to be done; and I soon found my comforts abate, and that, in a word, I had a dreadful deliverance; for I was wet, had no clothes to shift me, nor anything either to eat or drink to comfort me; neither did I see any prospect before me but that of perishing with hunger or being devoured by wild beasts; and that which was particularly afflicting to me was, that I had no weapon, either to hunt and kill any creature for my sustenance, or to defend myself against any other creature that might desire to kill me for theirs. In a word, I had nothing about me but a knife, a tobacco-pipe, and a little tobacco in a box. This was all my provisions; and this threw me into such terrible agonies of mind, that for a while I ran about like a madman. Night coming upon me, I began with a heavy heart to consider what would be my lot if there were any ravenous beasts in that country, as at night they always come abroad for their prey.

All the remedy that offered to my thoughts at that time was to get up into a thick bushy tree like a fir, but thorny, which grew near me, and where I resolved to sit all night, and consider the next day what death I should die, for as yet I saw no prospect of life.

CLAIMING PROVISIONS

A little after noon I found the sea very calm, and the tide ebbed so far out that I could come within a quarter of a mile of the ship. And here I found a fresh renewing of my grief; for I saw evidently that if we had kept on board we had been all safe – that is to say, we had all got safe on shore, and I had not been so miserable as to be left entirely destitute of all comfort and company as I now was. This forced tears to my eyes again; but as there was little relief in that, I resolved, if possible, to get to the ship; so I pulled off my clothes – for the weather was hot to extremity – and took the water.

I swam round her twice, and the second time I spied a small piece of rope.

But when I came to the ship my difficulty was still greater to know how to get on board; for, as she lay aground, and high out of the water, there was nothing within my reach to lay hold of. I swam round her twice, and the second time I spied a small piece of rope, which I wondered I did not see at first, hung down by the fore-chains so low, as that with great difficulty I got hold of it, and by the help of that rope I got up into the forecastle of the ship. Here I found that the ship was bulged, and had a great deal of water in her hold, but that she lay so on the side of a bank of hard sand, or, rather earth, that her stern lay lifted up upon the bank, and her head low, almost to the water. By this means all her quarter was free, and all that was in that part was dry; for you may be sure my first work was to search, and to see what was spoiled and what was free. And, first, I found that all the ship's provisions were dry and untouched by the water, and being very well disposed to eat, I went to the bread room and filled my pockets with biscuit, and ate it as I went about other things, for I had no time to lose. I also found some rum in the great cabin, of which I took a large dram, and which I had, indeed, need enough of to spirit me for what was before me. Now I wanted nothing but a boat to furnish myself with many things which I foresaw would be very necessary to me.

It was in vain to sit still and wish for what was not to be had; and this extremity roused my application. We had several spare yards, and two or three large spars of wood, and a spare topmast or two in the ship; I resolved to fall to work with these, and I flung as many of them overboard as I could manage for their weight, tying every one with a rope, that they might not drive away. When this was done I went down the ship's side, and pulling them to me, I tied four of them together at both ends as well as I could, in the form of a raft, and laying two or three short pieces of plank upon them crossways, I found I could walk upon it very well, but that it was not able to bear any great weight, the pieces being too light. So I went to work, and with a carpenter's saw I cut a spare topmast into three lengths, and added them to my raft, with a great deal of labour and pains. But the hope of furnishing myself with necessaries encouraged me to go beyond what I should have been able to have done upon another occasion.

My raft was now strong enough to bear any reasonable weight. My next care was what to load it with, and how to preserve what I laid upon it from the surf of the sea; but I was not long considering this. I first laid all the planks or boards upon it that I could get, and having considered well what I most wanted, I got three of the seamen's chests, which I had broken open, and emptied, and lowered them down upon my raft; the first of these I filled with provisions – viz. bread, rice, three Dutch cheeses, five pieces of dried goat's flesh, and a little remainder of European corn, which had been laid by for some fowls which we brought to sea with us, but the fowls were killed. There had been some barley and wheat together; but, to my great disappointment, I found afterwards that the rats had eaten or spoiled it all. As for liquors, I found several, cases of bottles belonging to our skipper, in which were some cordial waters; and, in all, about five or six gallons of rack. These I stowed by themselves, there being no need to put them into the chest, nor any room for them. While I was doing this, I found the tide begin to flow, though very calm; and I had the mortification to see my coat, shirt, and waistcoat, which I had left on the shore, upon the sand, swim away. As for my breeches, which were only linen, and open-kneed, I swam on board in them and my stockings. However, this set me on rummaging for clothes, of which I found enough, but took no more than I wanted for present use, for I had other things which my eye was more upon as, first, tools to work with on shore. And it was after long searching that I found out the carpenter's chest, which was, indeed, a very useful prize to me, and much more valuable than a shipload of gold would have been at that time. I got it down to my raft, whole as it was, without losing time to look into it, for I knew in general what it contained.

My next care was for some ammunition and arms. There were two very good fowling-pieces in the great cabin, and two pistols. These I secured first, with some powder-horns and a small bag of shot, and two old rusty swords.

I looked on both sides for a proper place to get to shore, for I was not willing to be driven too high up the river: hoping in time to see some ships at sea, and therefore resolved to place myself as near the coast as I could.

I RESOLVED TO GET TO THE SHIP; SO I PULLED OFF MY CLOTHES AND TOOK THE WATER.

At length I spied a little cove on the right shore of the creek, to which with great pain and difficulty I guided my raft, and at last got so near that, reaching ground with my oar, I could thrust her directly in. But here I had like to have dipped all my cargo into the sea again; for that shore lying pretty steep – that is to say sloping – there was no place to land, but where one end of my float, if it ran on shore, would lie so high, and the other sink lower, as before, that it would endanger my cargo again. All that I could do was to wait till the tide was at the highest, keeping the raft with my oar like an anchor, to hold the side of it fast to the shore, near a flat piece of ground, which I expected the water would flow over; and so it did. As soon as I found water enough I thrust her upon that flat piece of ground, and there fastened or moored her, by sticking my two broken oars into the ground, one on one side near one end, and one on the other side near the other end; and thus I lay till the water ebbed away, and left my raft and all my cargo safe on shore.

I went to work to make me a little tent with the sail and some poles which I cut for that purpose: and into

My raft was now strong enough to bear any reasonable weight.

this tent I brought everything that I knew would spoil either with rain or sun; and I piled all the empty chests and casks up in a circle round the tent, to fortify it from any sudden attempt, either from man or beast.

When I had done this, I began to work my way into the rock, and bringing all the earth and stones that I dug down out through my tent, I laid them up within my fence, in the nature of a terrace, so that it raised the ground within about a foot and a half; and thus I made me a cave, just behind my tent, which served me like a cellar to my house.

In the interval of time while this was doing, I went out once at least every day with my gun, as well to divert myself as to see if I could kill anything fit for food; and, as near as I could, to acquaint myself with what the island produced. The first time I went out, I presently discovered that there were goats in the island, which was a great satisfaction to me; but then it was attended with this misfortune to me – viz. that they were so shy, so subtle, and so swift of foot, that it was the most difficult thing in the world to come at them; but I was not discouraged at this, not doubting but I might now and then shoot one, as it soon happened; for after I had found their haunts a little, I laid wait in this manner for them: I observed if they saw me in the valleys, though they were upon the rocks, they would run away, as in a terrible fright; but if they were feeding in the valleys, and I was upon the rocks, they took no notice of me; from whence I concluded that, by the position of their optics, their sight was so directed downward that they did not readily see objects that were above them; so afterwards I took this method – I always climbed the rocks first, to get above them, and then had frequently a fair mark.

The first shot I made among these creatures, I killed a she-goat, which had a little kid by her, which she gave suck to, which grieved me heartily; for when the old one fell, the kid stood stock still by her, till I came and took her up; and not only so, but when I carried the old one with me, upon my shoulders, the kid followed me quite to my enclosure; upon which I laid down the dam, and took the kid in my arms, and carried it over my pale, in hopes to have bred it up tame; but it would not eat; so I was forced to kill it and eat it myself. These two supplied me with flesh a great while, for I ate sparingly, and saved my provisions, my bread especially, as much as possibly I could.

"DID NOT YOU COME, ELEVEN OF YOU IN THE BOAT? WHY WERE THEY NOT SAVED, AND YOU LOST? WHY WERE YOU SINGLED OUT?"

I had a dismal prospect of my condition; for as I was not cast away upon that island without being driven, as is said, by a violent storm, quite out of the course of our intended voyage, and a great way, viz. some hundreds of leagues, out of the ordinary course of the trade of mankind, I had great reason to consider it as a determination of Heaven, that in this desolate place, and in this desolate manner, I should end my life. The tears would run plentifully down my face when I made these reflections; and sometimes I would expostulate with myself why Providence should thus completely

I killed a she-goat, which had a little kid by her.

ruin His creatures, and render them so absolutely miserable; so without help, abandoned, so entirely depressed, that it could hardly be rational to be thankful for such a life.

But something always returned swift upon me to check these thoughts, and to reprove me; and particularly one day, walking with my gun in my hand by the seaside, I was very pensive upon the subject of my present condition, when reason, as it were, expostulated with me the other way, thus: "Well, you are in a desolate condition, it is true; but, pray remember, where are the rest of you? Did not you come, eleven of you in the boat? Where are the ten? Why were they not saved, and you lost? Why were you singled out? Is it better to be here or there?" And then I pointed to the sea. All evils are to be considered with the good that is in them, and with what worse attends them.

Then it occurred to me again, how well I was furnished for my subsistence, and what would have been my case if it had not happened (which was a hundred thousand to one) that the ship floated from the place where she first struck, and was driven so near to the shore that I had time to get all these things out of her; what would have been my case, if I had been forced to have lived in the condition in which I at first came on shore, without necessaries of life, or necessaries to supply and procure them?

After I had been there about ten or twelve days, it came into my thoughts that I should lose my reckoning of time for want of books, and pen and ink, and should even forget the Sabbath days; but to prevent this, I cut with my knife upon a large post, in capital letters – and making it into a great cross, I set it up on the shore where I first landed – "I came on shore here on the 30th September 1659." Upon the sides of this square post I cut every day a notch with my knife, and every seventh notch was as long again as the rest, and every first day of the month as long again as that long one; and thus I kept my calendar, or weekly, monthly, and yearly reckoning of time.

I COULD NOT FORBEAR LOOKING OUT TO SEA, IN HOPES OF SEEING A SHIP.

And now it was that I began to keep a journal of every day's employment; for, indeed, at first I was in too much hurry, and not only hurry as to labour, but in too much discomposure of mind. Some days after this, and after I had been on board the ship, and got all that I could out of her, yet I could not forbear getting up to the top of a little mountain and looking out to sea, in hopes of seeing a ship; then fancy at a vast distance I spied a sail, please myself with the hopes of it, and then after looking steadily, till I was almost blind, lose it quite, and sit down and weep like a child, and thus increase my misery by my folly.

But having gotten over these things in some measure, and having settled my household staff and habitation, made me a table and a chair, and all as handsome about me as I could, I began to keep my journal; of which I shall here give you the copy (though in it will be told all these particulars over again).

"THE ISLAND OF DESPAIR"

September 30, 1659. – I, poor miserable Robinson Crusoe, being shipwrecked during a dreadful storm in the offing, came on shore on this dismal, unfortunate island, which I called "The Island of Despair"; all the rest of the ship's company being drowned, and myself almost dead.

"THE ISLAND OF DESPAIR"

I saw about ten or twelve ears come out, which were perfect green barley, of the same kind as our European – nay, as our English barley.

All the rest of the day I spent in afflicting myself at the dismal circumstances I was brought to – viz. I had neither food, house, clothes, weapon, nor place to fly to; and in despair of any relief, saw nothing but death before me – either that I should be devoured by wild beasts, murdered by savages, or starved to death for want of food. At the approach of night I slept in a tree, for fear of wild creatures; but slept soundly, though it rained all night.

In the managing my household affairs, I found myself wanting in many things, which I thought at first it was impossible for me to make. In the middle of all my labours it happened that, rummaging my things, I found a little bag which had been filled with corn for the feeding of poultry – not for this voyage, but before, as I suppose, when the ship came from Lisbon. The little remainder of corn that had been in the bag was all devoured by the rats, and I saw nothing in the bag but husks and dust; and being willing to have the bag for some other use (I think it was to put powder in, when I divided it for fear of the lightning, or some such use), I shook the husks of corn out of it on one side of my fortification, under the rock.

It was a little before the great rains that I threw this stuff away, taking no notice, and not so much as remembering that I had thrown anything there, when, about a month after, or thereabouts, I saw some few stalks of something green shooting out of the ground, which I fancied might be some plant I had not seen; but I was surprised, and perfectly astonished, when, after a little longer time, I saw about ten or twelve ears come out, which were perfect green barley, of the same kind as our European – nay, as our English barley.

It is impossible to express the astonishment and confusion of my thoughts on this occasion. I had hitherto acted upon no religious foundation at all; indeed, I had very few notions of religion in my head, nor had entertained any sense of anything that had befallen me otherwise than as chance, or, as we lightly say, what pleases God, without so much as inquiring into the end of Providence in these things, or His order in governing events for the world. But after I saw barley grow there, in a climate which I knew was not proper for corn, and especially that I knew not how it came there, it startled me strangely, and I began to suggest that God had miraculously caused His grain to grow without any help of seed sown, and that it was so directed purely for my sustenance on that wild, miserable place. This touched my heart a little, and brought tears out of my eyes, and

All this while I sat upon the ground very much terrified and dejected.

I began to bless myself that such a prodigy of nature should happen upon my account; and this was the more strange to me, because I saw near it still, all along by the side of the rock, some other straggling stalks, which proved to be stalks of rice, and which I knew, because I had seen it grow in Africa when I was ashore there.

I BEGAN TO SUGGEST THAT GOD HAD MIRACULOUSLY CAUSED HIS GRAIN TO GROW WITHOUT ANY HELP OF SEED SOWN.

I not only thought these the pure productions of Providence for my support, but not doubting that there was more in the place, I went all over that part of the island, where I had been before, peering in every corner, and under every rock, to see for more of it, but I could not find any. At last it occurred to my thoughts that I shook a bag of chickens' meat out in that place; and then the wonder began to cease; and I must confess my religious thankfulness to God's providence began to abate, too, upon the discovering that all this was nothing but what was common; though I ought to have been as thankful for so strange and unforeseen a providence as if it had been miraculous; for it was really the work of Providence to me, that should order or appoint that ten or twelve grains of corn should remain unspoiled, when the rats had destroyed all the rest, as if it had been dropped from heaven; as also, that I should throw it out in that particular place, where, it being in the shade of a high rock, it sprang up immediately; whereas, if I had thrown it anywhere else at that time, it had been burnt up and destroyed.

The very next day I had almost had all my labour overthrown at once, and myself killed. As I was busy in the inside, behind my tent, just at the entrance into my cave, I was terribly frighted with a most dreadful, surprising thing indeed; for all on a sudden I found the earth come crumbling down from the roof of my cave, and from the edge of the hill over my head, and two of the posts I had set up in the cave cracked in a frightful manner. I was so much amazed with the thing itself, having never felt the like, nor discoursed with any one that had, that I was like one dead or stupefied.

While I sat thus, I found the air overcast and grow cloudy, as if it would rain. Soon after that the wind arose by little and little, so that in less than half-an-hour it blew a most dreadful hurricane; the sea was all on a sudden covered over with foam and froth; the shore was covered with the breach of the water, the trees were torn up by the roots, and a terrible storm it was. This held about three hours, and then began to abate; and in two hours more it was quite calm, and began to rain very hard. All this while I sat upon the ground very much terrified and dejected; when on a sudden it came into my thoughts, that these winds and rain being the consequences of the earthquake, the earthquake itself was spent and over, and I might venture into my cave again. With this thought my spirits began to revive; and the rain also helping to persuade me, I went in and sat down in my tent. But the rain was so violent that my tent was ready to be beaten down with it; and I was forced to go into my cave, though very much afraid and uneasy, for fear it should fall on my head. This violent rain forced me to a new work – viz. to cut a hole through my new fortification, like a sink, to let the water go out, which would else have flooded

I began to be very easy, applied myself to the works proper for my preservation.

my cave. After I had been in my cave for some time, and found still no more shocks of the earthquake follow, I began to be more composed. And now, to support my spirits, which indeed wanted it very much, I went to my little store, and took a small sup of rum; which, however, I did then and always very sparingly, knowing I could have no more when that was gone. It continued raining all that night and great part of the next day, so that I could not stir abroad; but my mind being more composed, I began to think of what I had best do; concluding that if the island was subject to these earthquakes, there would be no living for me in a cave, but I must consider of building a little hut in an open place which I might surround with a wall, as I had done here, and so make myself secure from wild beasts or men; for I concluded, if I stayed where I was, I should certainly one time or other be buried alive.

June 20. – No rest all night; violent pains in my head, and feverish. June 27. – The ague again so violent that I lay a-bed all day, and neither ate nor drank. I was ready to perish for thirst; but so weak, I had not strength to stand up, or to get myself any water to drink. Prayed to God again, but was light-headed; and when I was not, I was so ignorant that I knew not what to say; only I lay and cried, "Lord, look upon me! Lord, pity me! Lord, have mercy upon me!"

I suppose I did nothing else for two or three hours; till, the fit wearing off, I fell asleep, and did not wake till far in the night. When I awoke, I found myself much refreshed, but weak, and exceeding thirsty. However, as I had no water in my habitation, I was forced to lie till morning, and went to sleep again. In this second sleep I had this terrible dream: I thought that I was sitting on the ground, on the outside of my wall, where I sat when the storm blew after the earthquake, and that I saw a man descend from a great black cloud, in a bright flame of fire, and light upon the ground. He was all over as bright as a flame, so that I could but just bear to look towards him; his countenance was most inexpressibly dreadful, impossible for words to describe. When he stepped upon the ground with his feet, I thought the earth trembled, just as it had done before in the earthquake, and all the air looked, to my apprehension, as if it had been filled with flashes of fire. He was no sooner landed upon the earth, but he moved forward towards me, with a long spear or weapon in his hand, to kill me; and when he came to a rising ground, at some distance, he spoke to me – or I heard a voice so terrible that it is impossible to express the terror of it. All that I can say I understood was this: "Seeing all these things have not brought thee to repentance, now thou shalt die;" at which words, I thought he lifted up the spear that was in his hand to kill me.

"THE ISLAND OF DESPAIR"

I saw but a prospect of living and that I should not starve and perish for hunger.

No one that shall ever read this account will expect that I should be able to describe the horrors of my soul at this terrible vision. I mean, that even while it was a dream, I even dreamed of those horrors. Nor is it any more possible to describe the impression that remained upon my mind when I awaked, and found it was but a dream.

I had, alas! no divine knowledge. What I had received by the good instruction of my father was then worn out by an uninterrupted series, for eight years, of seafaring wickedness, and a constant conversation with none but such as were, like myself, wicked and profane to the last degree. I do not remember that I had, in all that time, one thought that so much as tended either to looking upwards towards God, or inwards towards a reflection upon my own ways; but a certain stupidity of soul, without desire of good, or conscience of evil, had entirely overwhelmed me; and I was all that the most hardened, unthinking, wicked creature among our common sailors can be supposed to be; not having the least sense, either of the fear of God in danger, or of thankfulness to God in deliverance.

In the relating what is already past of my story, this will be the more easily believed when I shall add, that through all the variety of miseries that had to this day befallen me, I never had so much as one thought of it being the hand of God, or that it was a just punishment for my sin – my rebellious behaviour against my father – or my present sins, which were great – or so much as a punishment for the general course of my wicked life.

When I was on the desperate expedition on the desert shores of Africa, I never had so much as one thought of what would become of me, or one wish to God to direct me whither I should go, or to keep me from the danger which apparently surrounded me, as well from voracious creatures as cruel savages. But I was merely thoughtless of a God or a Providence, acted like a mere brute, from the principles of nature, and by the dictates of common sense only, and, indeed, hardly that. When I was delivered and taken up at sea by the Portugal captain, well used, and dealt justly and honourably with, as well as charitably, I had not the least thankfulness in my thoughts. When, again, I was shipwrecked, ruined, and in danger of drowning on this island, I was as far from remorse, or looking on it as a judgment. I only said to myself often, that I was an unfortunate dog, and born to be always miserable.

It is true, when I got on shore first here, and found all my ship's crew drowned and myself spared, I was surprised with a kind of ecstasy, and some transports of soul, which, had the grace of God assisted, might have

In the morning I took the Bible; and beginning at the New Testament, I began seriously to read it.

come up to true thankfulness; but it ended where it began, in a mere common flight of joy, or, as I may say, being glad I was alive, without the least reflection upon the distinguished goodness of the hand which had preserved me, and had singled me out to be preserved when all the rest were destroyed, or an inquiry why

THIS WAS THE FIRST TIME I COULD SAY, IN THE TRUE SENSE OF THE WORDS, THAT I PRAYED IN ALL MY LIFE.

Providence had been thus merciful unto me. Even just the same common sort of joy which seamen generally have, after they are got safe ashore from a shipwreck, which they drown all in the next bowl of punch, and forget almost as soon as it is over; and all the rest of my life was like it. Even when I was afterwards, on due consideration, made sensible of my condition, how I was cast on this dreadful place, out of the reach of human kind, out of all hope of relief, or prospect of redemption, as soon as I saw but a prospect of living and that I should not starve and perish for hunger, all the sense of my affliction wore off; and I began to be very easy, applied myself to the works proper for my preservation and supply, and was far enough from being afflicted at my condition, as a judgment from heaven, or as the hand of God against me: these were thoughts which very seldom entered my head.

July 4. – In the morning I took the Bible; and beginning at the New Testament, I began seriously to read it, and imposed upon myself to read a while every morning and every night; not tying myself to the number of chapters, but long as my thoughts should engage me. It was not long after I set seriously to this work till I found my heart more deeply and sincerely affected with the wickedness of my past life. The impression of my dream revived; and the words, "All these things have not brought thee to repentance," ran seriously through my thoughts. I was earnestly begging of God to give me repentance, when it happened providentially, the very day, that, reading the Scripture, I came to these words: "He is exalted a Prince and a Saviour, to give repentance and to give remission." I threw down the book; and with my heart as well as my hands lifted up to heaven, in a kind of ecstasy of joy, I cried out aloud, "Jesus, thou son of David! Jesus, thou exalted Prince and Saviour! give me repentance!" This was the first time I could say, in the true sense of the words, that I prayed in all my life; for now I prayed with a sense of my condition, and a true Scripture view of hope, founded on the encouragement of the Word of God; and from this time, I may say, I began to hope that God would hear me.

THE FOOTPRINT

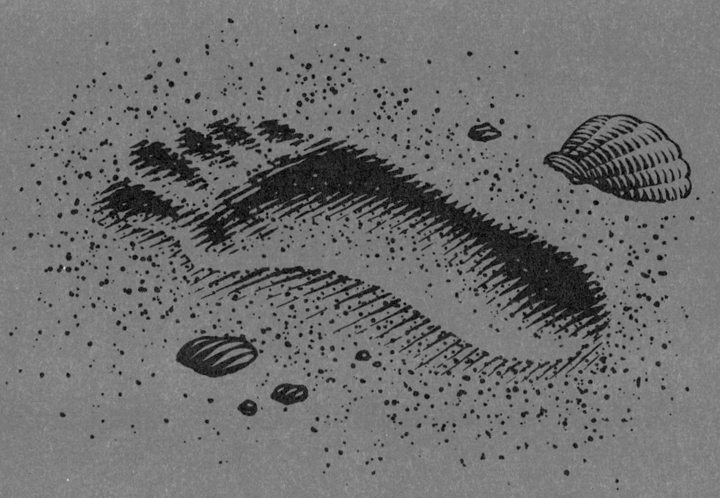

I could not tell what part of the world this might be, otherwise than that I knew it must be part of America, and, as I concluded by all my observations, must be near the Spanish dominions, and perhaps was all inhabited by savages, where, if I had landed, I had been in a worse condition than I was now; and therefore I acquiesced in the dispositions of Providence, which I began now to own and to believe ordered everything for the best; I say I quieted my mind with this, and left off afflicting myself with fruitless wishes of being there.

Besides, after some thought upon this affair, I considered that if this land was the Spanish coast, I should certainly, one time or other, see some vessel pass or repass one way or other; but if not, then it was the savage coast between the Spanish country and Brazils, where are found the worst of savages; for they are cannibals or men-eaters, and fail not to murder and devour all the human bodies that fall into their hands.

With these considerations, I walked very leisurely forward. I found that side of the island where I now was much pleasanter than mine – the open or savannah fields sweet, adorned with flowers and grass, and full of very fine woods. I saw abundance of parrots, and fain I would have caught one, if possible, to have kept it to be tame, and taught it to speak to me. I did, after some painstaking, catch a young parrot, for I knocked it down with a stick, and having recovered it, I brought it home; but it was some years before I could make him speak; however, at last I taught him to call me by name very familiarly.

But being now in the eleventh year of my residence, and, as I have said, my ammunition growing low, I set myself to study some art to trap and snare the goats, to see whether I could not catch some of them alive; and particularly I wanted a she-goat great with young. At length I set three traps in one night, and going the next morning I found them, all standing, and yet the bait eaten and gone; this was very discouraging. However, I altered my traps; and not to trouble you with particulars, going one morning to see my traps, I found in one of them a large old he-goat; and in one of the others three kids, a male and two females.

But now I come to a new scene of my life. It happened one day, about noon, going towards my boat, I was exceedingly surprised with the print of a man's naked foot on the shore, which was very plain to be seen on the sand. I stood like one thunderstruck, or as if I had seen an apparition. I listened, I looked round me, but I could hear nothing, nor see anything; I went up to a rising ground to look farther; I went up the shore and down the shore, but it was all one; I could see no other impression but that one. I went to it again to see if there were any more, and to observe if it might not be my fancy; but there was no room for that, for there was exactly the print of a foot – toes, heel, and every part of a foot. How it came thither I knew not, nor could I in the least imagine; but after innumerable fluttering thoughts, like a man perfectly confused and out of myself, I came home to my fortification, not feeling, as we say, the ground I went on, but terrified to the last degree, looking behind me at every two or three steps, mistaking every bush and tree, and fancying every stump at a distance to be a man. Nor is it possible to describe how many various shapes my affrighted imagination represented things to me in, how many wild ideas were found every moment in my fancy, and what strange, unaccountable whimsies came into my thoughts by the way. When I came to my castle (for so

I STOOD LIKE ONE THUNDERSTRUCK, OR AS IF I HAD SEEN AN APPARITION.

I think I called it ever after this), I fled into it like one pursued.

I slept none that night; the farther I was from the occasion of my fright, the greater my apprehensions were, which is something contrary to the nature of such things, and especially to the usual practice of all creatures in fear; but I was so embarrassed with my own frightful ideas of the thing, that I formed nothing but dismal imaginations to myself, even though I was now a great way off. Sometimes I fancied it must be the devil, and reason joined in with me in this supposition, for how should any other thing in human shape come into the place? Where was the vessel that brought them? What marks were there of any other footstep? And how was it possible a man should come there? But then, to think that Satan should take human shape upon him in such a place, where there could be no manner of occasion for it, but to leave the print of his foot behind him, and that even for no purpose too, for he could not be sure I should see it – this was an amusement the other way. I considered that the devil might have found out abundance of other ways to have terrified me than this of the single print of a foot; that as I lived quite on the other side of the island, he would never have been so simple as to leave a mark in a place where it was ten thousand to one whether I should ever see it or not, and in the sand too, which the first surge of the sea, upon a high wind, would have defaced entirely. All this seemed inconsistent with the thing itself and with all the notions we usually entertain of the subtlety of the devil.

Thus my fear banished all my religious hope, all that former confidence in God, which was founded upon such wonderful experience as I had had of His goodness. I reproached myself with my laziness, that would not sow any more corn one year than would just serve me till the next season, as if no accident could intervene to prevent my enjoying the crop that was upon the ground.

How strange a chequer-work of Providence is the life of man! and by what secret different springs are the affections hurried about, as different circumstances present! To-day we love what to-morrow we hate; to-day we seek what to-morrow we shun; to-day we desire what to-morrow we fear, nay, even tremble at the apprehensions of. This was exemplified in me, at this time, in the most lively manner imaginable; for I, whose only affliction was that I seemed banished from human society, that I was alone, circumscribed by the boundless ocean, cut off from mankind, and condemned to what I call silent life; that I was as one whom Heaven thought not worthy to be numbered among the living, or to appear among the rest of His creatures; that to have seen one of my own species would have seemed to me a raising me from death to life, and the greatest blessing that Heaven itself, next to the supreme blessing of salvation, could bestow; I say, that I should now tremble at the very apprehensions of seeing a man.

In the middle of these cogitations, apprehensions, and reflections, it came into my thoughts one day that all this might be a mere chimera of my own, and that this foot might be the print of my own foot, when I came on shore from my boat: this cheered me up a little, too, and I began to persuade myself it was all a delusion; that it was nothing else but my own foot; and why might I not come that way from the boat, as well as I was going that way to the boat? Again, I considered also that I could by no means tell for certain where I had trod, and where I had not.

Now I began to take courage, and to peep abroad again, for I had not stirred out of my castle for three days and nights, so that I began to starve for provisions; for I had little or nothing within doors but some

It was some years before I could make him speak; however, at last I taught him to call me by name very familiarly.

barley-cakes and water; then I knew that my goats wanted to be milked too, which usually was my evening diversion: and the poor creatures were in great pain and inconvenience for want of it; and, indeed, it almost spoiled some of them, and almost dried up their milk. Encouraging myself, therefore, with the belief that this was nothing but the print of one of my own feet, and that I might be truly said to start at my own shadow,

For there was exactly the print of a foot – toes, heel, and every part of a foot.

I began to go abroad again, and went to my country house to milk my flock: but to see with what fear I went forward, how often I looked behind me, how I was ready every now and then to lay down my basket and run for my life, it would have made any one have thought I was haunted with an evil conscience, or that I had been lately most terribly frightened; and so, indeed, I had. However, I went down thus two or three days, and having seen nothing, I began to be a little bolder, and to think there was really nothing in it but my own imagination; but I could not persuade myself fully of this till I should go down to the shore again, and see this print of a foot, and measure it by my own, and see if there was any similitude or fitness, that I might be assured it was my own foot: but when I came to the place, first, it appeared evidently to me, that when I laid up my boat I could not possibly be on shore anywhere thereabouts; secondly, when I came to measure the mark with my own foot, I found my foot not so large by a great deal. Both these things filled my head with new imaginations, and gave me the vapours again to the highest degree, so that I shook with cold like one in an ague; and I went home again, filled with the belief that some man or men had been on shore there; or, in short, that the island was inhabited, and I might be surprised before I was aware; and what course to take for my security I knew not.

While this was doing, I was not altogether careless of my other affairs; for I had a great concern upon me for my little herd of goats: they were not only a ready supply to me on every occasion, and began to be sufficient for me, without the expense of powder and shot, but also without the fatigue of hunting after the wild ones; and I was loath to lose the advantage of them, and to have them all to nurse up over again. For this purpose, after long consideration, I could think of but two ways to preserve them: one was, to find another convenient place to dig a cave underground, and to drive them into it every night; and the other was to enclose two or three little bits of land, remote from one another, and as much concealed as I could, where I might keep about half-a-dozen young goats in each place; so that if any disaster happened to the flock in general, I might be able to raise them again with little trouble and time: and this though it would require a good deal of time and labour, I thought was the most rational design.

Accordingly, I spent some time to find out the most retired parts of the island; and I pitched upon one, which was as private, indeed, as my heart could wish: it was a little damp piece of ground in the middle of the hollow and thick woods. Here I found a clear piece of land, almost an enclosure by nature; at least, it did not want near so much labour to make it so as the other piece of ground I had worked so hard at.

I immediately went to work with this piece of ground; and in less than a month's time I had so fenced it round that my flock, or herd, call it which you please, which were not so wild now as at first they might be supposed to be, were well enough secured in it: so, without any further delay, I removed ten young she-goats and two he-goats to this piece, and when they were there I continued to perfect the fence till I had made it as secure as the other; which, however, I did at more leisure, and it took me up more time by a great deal. All this labour I was at the expense of, purely from my apprehensions on account of the print of a man's foot; for as yet I had never seen any human creature come near the island; and I had now lived two years under this uneasiness, which, indeed, made my life much less comfortable than it was before, as may be well imagined by

Accordingly, I spent some time to find out the most retired parts of the island.

any who know what it is to live in the constant snare of the fear of man. And this I must observe, with grief, too, that the discomposure of my mind had great impression also upon the religious part of my thoughts; for the dread and terror of falling into the hands of savages and cannibals lay so upon my spirits, that I seldom found myself in a due temper for application to my Maker; at least, not with the sedate calmness and resignation of soul which I was wont to do: I rather prayed to God as under great affliction and pressure of mind, surrounded with danger, and in expectation every night of being murdered and devoured before morning; and I must testify, from my experience, that a temper of peace, thankfulness, love, and affection, is much the more proper frame for prayer than that of terror and discomposure: and that under the dread of mischief impending, a man is no more fit for a comforting performance of the duty of praying to God than he is for a repentance on a sick-bed; for these discomposures affect the mind, as the others do the body; and the discomposure of the mind must necessarily be as great a disability as that of the body, and much greater; praying to God being properly an act of the mind, not of the body.

But to go on. After I had thus secured one part of my little living stock, I went about the whole island, searching for another private place to make such another deposit; when, wandering more to the west point of the island than I had ever done yet, and looking out to sea, I thought I saw a boat upon the sea, at a great distance. I had found a perspective glass or two in one of the seamen's chests, which I saved out of our ship, but I had it not about me; and this was so remote that I could not tell what to make of it, though I looked at it till my eyes were not able to hold to look any longer; whether it was a boat or not I do not know, but as I descended from the hill I could see no more of it, so I gave it over; only I resolved to go no more out without a perspective glass in my pocket. When I was come down the hill to the end of the island, where, indeed, I had never been before, I was presently convinced that the seeing the print of a man's foot was not such a strange thing in the island as I imagined: and but that it was a special providence that I was cast upon the side of the island where the savages never came, I should easily have known that nothing was more frequent than for the canoes from the main, when they happened to be a little too far out at sea, to shoot over to that side of the island for harbour: likewise, as they often met and fought in their canoes, the victors, having taken any prisoners, would bring them over to this shore, where, according to their dreadful customs, being all cannibals, they would kill and eat them; of which hereafter.

When I was come down the hill to the shore, as I said above, being the SW. point of the island, I was perfectly confounded and amazed; nor is it possible for me to express the horror of my mind at seeing the shore spread with skulls, hands, feet, and other bones of human bodies; and particularly I observed a place where there had been a fire made, and a circle dug in the earth, like a cockpit, where I supposed the savage wretches had sat down to their human feastings upon the bodies of their fellow-creatures. I turned away my face from the horrid spectacle; my stomach grew sick, and I was just at the point of fainting, when nature discharged the disorder from my stomach; and having vomited with uncommon violence, I was a little relieved, but could not bear to stay in the place a moment; so I got up the hill again with all the speed I could, and walked on towards my own habitation.

The mouth of this hollow was at the bottom of a great rock, where, by mere accident (I would say, if I did not see abundant reason to ascribe all such things now

to Providence), I was cutting down some thick branches of trees to make charcoal; and before I go on I must observe the reason of my making this charcoal, which was this – I was afraid of making a smoke about my habitation, as I said before; and yet I could not live there without baking my bread, cooking my meat, &c.; so I contrived to burn some wood here, as I had seen done in England, under turf, till it became chark or dry coal: and then putting the fire out, I preserved the coal to carry home, and perform the other services for which fire was wanting, without danger of smoke. But this is by-the-bye. While I was cutting down some wood here, I perceived that, behind a very thick branch of low brushwood or underwood, there was a kind of hollow place: I was curious to look in it; and getting with difficulty into the mouth of it, I found it was pretty large, that is to say, sufficient for me to stand upright in it, and perhaps another with me: but I must confess to you that I made more haste out than I did in, when looking farther into the place, and which was perfectly dark, I saw two broad shining eyes of some creature, whether devil or man I knew not, which twinkled like two stars; the dim light from the cave's mouth shining directly in, and making the reflection. However, after some pause I recovered myself, and began to call myself a thousand fools, and to think that he that was afraid to see the devil was not fit to live twenty years in an island all alone; and that I might well think there was nothing in this cave that was more frightful than myself. Upon this, plucking up my courage, I took up a firebrand, and in I rushed again, with the stick flaming in my hand: I had not gone three steps in before I was almost as frightened as before; for I heard a very loud sigh, like that of a man in some pain, and it was followed by a broken noise, as of words half expressed, and then a deep sigh again. I stepped back, and was indeed struck with such a surprise that it put me into a cold sweat, and if I had had a hat on my head, I will not answer for it that my hair might not have lifted it off. But still plucking up my spirits as well as I could, and encouraging myself a little with considering that the power and presence of God was everywhere, and was able to protect me, I stepped forward again, and by the light of the firebrand, holding it up a little over my head, I saw lying on the ground a monstrous, frightful old he-goat, just making his will, as we say, and gasping for life, and, dying, indeed, of mere old age. I stirred him a little to see if I could get him out, and he essayed to get up, but was not able to raise himself; and I thought with myself he might even lie there – for if he had frightened me, so he would certainly fright any of the savages, if any of them should be so hardy as to come in there while he had any life in him.

I was now recovered from my surprise, and began to look round me, when I found the cave was but very small – that is to say, it might be about twelve feet over, but in no manner of shape, neither round nor square, no hands having ever been employed in making it but those of mere Nature. I observed also that there was a place at the farther side of it that went in further, but was so low that it required me to creep upon my hands and knees to go into it, and whither it went I knew not; so, having no candle, I gave it over for that time, but resolved to go again the next day provided with candles and a tinder-box, which I had made of the lock of one of the muskets, with some wildfire in the pan.

THE SPANISH SHIPWRECK

I was now in the twenty-third year of my residence in this island, and was so naturalised to the place and the manner of living, that, could I but have enjoyed the certainty that no savages would come to the place to disturb me, I could have been content to have capitulated for spending the rest of my time there, even to the last moment, till I had laid me down and died, like the old goat in the cave.

There were no less than nine naked savages sitting round a small fire they had made.

It was now the month of December, as I said above, in my twenty-third year; and this, being the southern solstice (for winter I cannot call it), was the particular time of my harvest, and required me to be pretty much abroad in the fields, when, going out early in the morning, even before it was thorough daylight, I was surprised with seeing a light of some fire upon the shore, at a distance from me of about two miles, toward that part of the island where I had observed some savages had been, as before, and not on the other side; but, to my great affliction, it was on my side of the island.

I was indeed terribly surprised at the sight, and stopped short within my grove, not daring to go out, lest I might be surprised; and yet I had no more peace within, from the apprehensions I had that if these savages, in rambling over the island, should find my corn standing or cut, or any of my works or improvements, they would immediately conclude that there were people in the place, and would then never rest till they had found me out. In this extremity I went back directly to my castle, pulled up the ladder after me, and made all things without look as wild and natural as I could.

Then I prepared myself within, putting myself in a posture of defence. I loaded all my canon, as I called them – that is to say, my muskets, which were mounted upon my new fortification – and all my pistols, and resolved to defend myself to the last gasp – not forgetting seriously to commend myself to the Divine protection, and earnestly to pray to God to deliver me out of the hands of the barbarians. I continued in this posture about two hours, and began to be impatient for intelligence abroad, for I had no spies to send out. After sitting a while longer, and musing what I should do in this case, I was not able to bear sitting in ignorance longer; so setting up my ladder to the side of the hill, where there was a flat place, as I observed before, and then pulling the ladder after me, I set it up again and mounted the top of the hill, and pulling out my perspective glass, which I had taken on purpose, I laid me down flat on my belly on the ground, and began to look for the place. I presently found there were no less than nine naked savages sitting round a small fire they had made, not to warm them, for they had no need of that, the weather being extremely hot, but, as I supposed, to dress some of their barbarous diet of human flesh which they had brought with them, whether alive or dead I could not tell.

As soon as I saw them shipped and gone, I took two guns upon my shoulders, and two pistols in my girdle, and my great sword by my side without a scabbard, and with all the speed I was able to make went away to the hill where I had discovered the first appearance of all;

and as soon as I got thither, which was not in less than two hours (for I could not go quickly, being so loaded with arms as I was), I perceived there had been three canoes more of the savages at that place; and looking out farther, I saw they were all at sea together, making over for the main. This was a dreadful sight to me, especially as, going down to the shore, I could see the marks of horror which the dismal work they had been about had left behind it – viz. the blood, the bones, and part of the flesh of human bodies eaten and devoured by those wretches with merriment and sport. I was so filled with indignation at the sight, that I now began to premeditate the destruction of the next that I saw there, let them be whom or how many soever. It seemed evident to me that the visits which they made thus to this island were not very frequent, for it was above fifteen months before any more of them came on shore there again – that is to say, I neither saw them nor any footsteps or signals of them in all that time; for as to the rainy seasons, then they are sure not to come abroad, at least not so far. Yet all this while I lived uncomfortably, by reason of the constant apprehensions of their coming upon me by surprise: from whence I observe, that the expectation of evil is more bitter than the suffering, especially if there is no room to shake off that expectation or those apprehensions.

During all this time I was in a murdering humour, and spent most of my hours, which should have been better employed, in contriving how to circumvent and fall upon them the very next time I should see them – especially if they should be divided, as they were the last time, into two parties; nor did I consider at all that if I killed one party – suppose ten or a dozen – I was still the next day, or week, or month, to kill another, and so another, even *ad infinitum*, till I should be, at length, no less a murderer than they were in being man-eaters – and perhaps much more so. I spent my days now in great perplexity and anxiety of mind, expecting that I should one day or other fall into the hands of these merciless creatures; and if I did at any time venture abroad, it was not without looking around me with the greatest care and caution imaginable. And now I found, to my great comfort, how happy it was that I had provided a tame flock or herd of goats, for I durst not upon any account fire my gun, especially near that side of the island where they usually came, lest I should alarm the savages; and if they had fled from me now, I was sure to have them come again with perhaps two or three hundred canoes with them in a few days, and then I knew what to expect. However, I wore out a year and three months more before I ever saw any more of the savages, and then I found them again. It is true they might have been there once or twice; but either they made no stay, or at least I did not see them; but in the month of May, as near as I could calculate, and in my four-and-twentieth year, I had a very strange encounter with them.

I LOADED ALL MY CANON, AND ALL MY PISTOLS, AND RESOLVED TO DEFEND MYSELF TO THE LAST GASP.

It blew a very great storm of wind all day, with a great deal of lightning and thunder, and a very foul night it was after it. I knew not what was the particular occasion of it, but as I was reading in the Bible, and taken up with very serious thoughts about my present

I laid me down flat on my belly on the ground, and began to look for the place.

condition, I was surprised with the noise of a gun, as I thought, fired at sea. This was, to be sure, a surprise quite of a different nature from any I had met with before; for the notions this put into my thoughts were quite of another kind.

I started up in the greatest haste imaginable; and, in a trice, clapped my ladder to the middle place of the rock, and pulled it after me; and mounting it the second time, got to the top of the hill the very moment that a flash of fire bid me listen for a second gun, which, accordingly, in about half a minute I heard; and by the sound, knew that it was from that part of the sea where I was driven down the current in my boat. I immediately considered that this must be some ship in distress, and that they had some comrade, or some other ship in company, and fired these for signals of distress, and to obtain help. I had the presence of mind at that minute to think, that though I could not help them, it might be that they might help me; so I brought together all the dry wood I could get at hand, and making a good handsome pile, I set it on fire upon the hill. The wood was dry, and blazed freely; and, though the wind blew very hard, yet it burned fairly out; so that I was certain, if there was any such thing as a ship, they must needs see it. And no doubt they did; for as soon as ever my fire blazed up, I heard another gun, and after that several others, all from the same quarter. I plied my fire all night long, till daybreak: and when it was broad day, and the air cleared up, I saw something at a great distance at sea, full east of the island, whether a sail or a hull I could not distinguish – no, not with my glass: the distance was so great, and the weather still something hazy also; at least, it was so out at sea.

I looked frequently at it all that day, and soon perceived that it did not move; so I presently concluded that it was a ship at anchor; and being eager, you may be sure, to be satisfied, I took my gun in my hand, and ran towards the south side of the island to the rocks where I had formerly been carried away by the current; and getting up there, the weather by this time being perfectly clear, I could plainly see, to my great sorrow, the wreck of a ship, cast away in the night upon those concealed rocks which I found when I was out in my boat; and which rocks, as they checked the violence of the stream, and made a kind of counter-stream, or eddy, were the occasion of my recovering from the most desperate, hopeless condition that ever I had been in in all my life. Encouraged by this observation, I resolved the next morning to set out with the first of the tide; and reposing myself for the night in my canoe, under the watch-coat I mentioned, I launched out. It was a dismal sight to look at; the ship, which by its building was Spanish, stuck fast, jammed in between two rocks. When I came close to her, a dog appeared upon her, who, seeing me coming, yelped and cried; and as soon as I called him, jumped into the sea to come to me. I took him into the boat, but found him almost dead with hunger and thirst. Besides the dog, there was nothing left in the ship that had life; nor any goods, that I could see, but what were spoiled by the water. There were some casks of liquor, whether wine or brandy I knew not, which lay lower in the hold, and which, the water being ebbed out, I could see; but they were too big to meddle with. I saw several chests, which I believe belonged to some of the seamen; and I got two of them into the boat.

FRIDAY'S RESCUE

I lived in this condition near two years more; but my unlucky head, that was always to let me know it was born to make my body miserable, was all these two years filled with projects and designs how, if it were possible, I might get away from this island.

FRIDAY'S RESCUE

I was then obliged to shoot at him first, which I did, and killed him at the first shot.

I made this conclusion: that my only way to go about to attempt an escape was, to endeavour to get a savage into my possession: and, if possible, it should be one of their prisoners, whom they had condemned to be eaten, and should bring hither to kill. But these thoughts still were attended with this difficulty: that it was impossible to effect this without attacking a whole caravan of them, and killing them all; and this was not only a very desperate attempt, and might miscarry, but, on the other hand, I had greatly scrupled the lawfulness of it to myself; and my heart trembled at the thoughts of shedding so much blood, though it was for my deliverance. I need not repeat the arguments which occurred to me against this, they being the same mentioned before; but though I had other reasons to offer now – viz. that those men were enemies to my life, and would devour me if they could; that it was self-preservation, in the highest degree, to deliver myself from this death of a life, and was acting in my own defence as much as if they were actually assaulting me, and the like; I say though these things argued for it, yet the thoughts of shedding human blood for my deliverance were very terrible to me, and such as I could by no means reconcile myself to for a great while. However, at last, after many secret disputes with myself, and after great perplexities about it (for all these arguments, one way and another, struggled in my head a long time), the eager prevailing desire of deliverance at length mastered all the rest; and I resolved, if possible, to get one of these savages into my hands, cost what it would. My next thing was to contrive how to do it, and this, indeed, was very difficult to resolve on; but as I could pitch upon no probable means for it, so I resolved to put myself upon the watch, to see them when they came on shore, and leave the rest to the event; taking such measures as the opportunity should present, let what would be.

With these resolutions in my thoughts, I set myself upon the scout as often as possible, and indeed so often that I was heartily tired of it; for it was above a year and a half that I waited; and for great part of that time went out to the west end, and to the south-west corner of the island almost every day, to look for canoes, but none appeared. This was very discouraging, and began to trouble me much, though I cannot say that it did in this case (as it had done some time before) wear off the edge of my desire to the thing; but the longer it seemed to be delayed, the more eager I was for it: in a word, I was not at first so careful to shun the sight of these savages, and avoid being seen by them, as I was now eager to be upon them. Besides, I fancied myself able to manage one, nay, two or three savages, if I had them, so as to make them entirely slaves to me, to do whatever I should direct them, and to prevent their being able at any time to do me any hurt. It was a great while that I pleased myself with this affair; but nothing still presented itself; all my fancies and schemes came to nothing, for no savages came near me for a great while.

MY HEART TREMBLED AT THE THOUGHTS OF SHEDDING SO MUCH BLOOD.

About a year and a half after I entertained these notions (and by long musing had, as it were, resolved them all into nothing, for want of an occasion to put them into execution), I was surprised one morning by seeing no less than five canoes all on shore together on my side the island, and the people who belonged to them all landed and out of my sight. The number of them broke all my measures; for seeing so many, and knowing that they always came four or six, or sometimes more in a boat, I could not tell what to think of it, or how to take my measures to attack twenty or thirty men single-handed; so lay still in my castle, perplexed and discomforted. However, I put myself into the same position for an attack that I had formerly provided, and was just ready for action, if anything had presented. Having waited a good while, listening to hear if they made any noise, at length, being very impatient, I set my guns at the foot of my ladder, and clambered up to the top of the hill, by my two stages, as usual; standing so, however, that my head did not appear above the hill, so that they could not perceive me by any means. Here I observed, by the help of my perspective glass, that they were no less than thirty in number; that they had a fire kindled, and that they had meat dressed. They were all dancing, in I know not how many barbarous gestures and figures, their own way, round the fire.

While I was thus looking on them, I perceived, by my perspective, two miserable wretches dragged from the boats, where, it seems, they were laid by, and were now brought out for the slaughter. I perceived one of them immediately fall; being knocked down, I suppose, with a club or wooden sword, for that was their way; and two or three others were at work immediately, cutting him open for their cookery, while the other victim was left standing by himself, till they should be ready for him. In that very moment this poor wretch, seeing himself a little at liberty and unbound, Nature inspired him with hopes of life, and he started away from them, and ran with incredible swiftness along the sands, directly towards me; I mean towards that part of the coast where my habitation was. I was dreadfully frightened, I must acknowledge, when I perceived him run my way; and especially when, as I thought, I saw him pursued by the whole body: and now I expected that part of my dream was coming to pass, and that he would certainly take shelter in my grove; but I could not depend, by any means, upon my dream, that the other savages would not pursue him thither and find him there. However, I kept my station, and my spirits began to recover when I found that there was not above three men that followed him; and still more was I encouraged, when I found that he outstripped them exceedingly in running, and gained ground on them; so that, if he could but hold out for half-an-hour, I saw easily he would fairly get away from them all.

There was between them and my castle the creek, which I mentioned often in the first part of my story, where I landed my cargoes out of the ship; and this I

FRIDAY'S RESCUE

I smiled at him, and looked pleasantly, and beckoned to him to come still nearer.

saw plainly he must necessarily swim over, or the poor wretch would be taken there; but when the savage escaping came thither, he made nothing of it, though the tide was then up; but plunging in, swam through, landed, and ran with strength and swiftness. When the three persons came to the creek, I found that two of them could swim, but the third could not, and that, standing on the other side, he looked at the others, but went no farther, and soon after went softly back again. I immediately ran down the ladders with all possible expedition, fetched my two guns, for they were both at the foot of the ladders, as I observed before, and getting up again with the same haste to the top of the hill, I crossed towards the sea; and having a very short cut, and all down hill, placed myself in the way between the pursuers and the pursued, hallowing aloud to him that fled, who, looking back, was at first perhaps as much frightened at me as at them; but I beckoned with my hand to him to come back; and, in the meantime, I slowly advanced towards the two that followed; then rushing at once upon the foremost, I knocked him down with the stock of my piece. I was loath to fire, because I would not have the rest hear. Having knocked this fellow down, the other who pursued him stopped, as if he had been frightened, and I advanced towards him: but as I came nearer, I perceived presently he had a bow and arrow, and was fitting it to shoot at me: so I was then obliged to shoot at him first, which I did, and killed him at the first shot. The poor savage who fled, but had stopped, though he saw both his enemies fallen and killed, as he thought, yet was so frightened with the fire and noise of my piece that he stood stock still, and neither came forward nor went backward, though he seemed rather inclined still to fly than to come on. I hallooed again to him, and made signs to come forward, which he easily understood, and came a little way; then stopped again, and then a little farther, and stopped again; and I could then perceive that he stood trembling, as if he had been taken prisoner, and had just been to be killed, as his two enemies were. I beckoned to him again to come to me, and gave him all the signs of encouragement that I could think of; and he came nearer and nearer, kneeling down every ten or twelve steps, in token of acknowledgment for saving his life. I smiled at him, and looked pleasantly, and beckoned to him to come still nearer; at length he came close to me; and then he kneeled down again, kissed the ground, and laid his head upon the ground, and taking me by the foot, set my foot upon his head; this, it seems, was in token of swearing to be my slave for ever. I took him up and made much of him, and encouraged him all I could. But there was more work to do yet; for I perceived the savage whom I had knocked

And then he kneeled down again, kissed the ground, and laid his head upon the ground, and taking me by the foot, set my foot upon his head.

down was not killed, but stunned with the blow, and began to come to himself: so I pointed to him, and showed him the savage, that he was not dead; upon this he spoke some words to me, and though I could not understand them, yet I thought they were pleasant to hear; for they were the first sound of a man's voice that I had heard, my own excepted, for above twenty-five years. But there was no time for such reflections now; the savage who was knocked down recovered himself so far as to sit up upon the ground, and I perceived that my savage began to be afraid; but when I saw that, I presented my other piece at the man, as if I would shoot him: upon this my savage, for so I call him now, made a motion to me to lend him my sword, which hung naked in a belt by my side, which I did. He no sooner had it, but he runs to his enemy, and at one blow cut off his head so cleverly. But that which astonished him most was to know how I killed the other Indian so far off; so, pointing to him, he made signs to me to let him go to him; and I bade him go, as well as I could. When he came to him, he stood like one amazed, looking at him, turning him first on one side, then on the other; looked at the wound the bullet had made, which it seems was just in his breast, where it had made a hole, and no great quantity of blood had followed; but he had bled inwardly, for he was quite dead. He took up his bow and arrows, and came back; so I turned to go away, and beckoned him to follow me, making signs to him that more might come after them. Upon this he made signs to me that he should bury them with sand, that they might not be seen by the rest, if they followed; and so I made signs to him again to do so. He fell to work; and in an instant he had scraped a hole in the sand with his hands big enough to bury the first in, and then dragged him into it, and covered him; and did so by the other also; I believe he had him buried them both in a quarter of an hour. Then, calling away, I carried him, not to my castle, but quite away to my cave, on the farther part of the island: so I did not let my dream come to pass in that part, that he came into my grove for shelter. Here I gave him bread and a bunch of raisins to eat, and a draught of water, which I found he was indeed in great distress for, from his running: and having refreshed him, I made signs for him to go and lie down to sleep, showing him a place where I had laid some rice-straw, and a blanket upon it, which I used to sleep upon myself sometimes; so the poor creature lay down, and went to sleep.

THEY WERE THE FIRST SOUND OF A MAN'S VOICE THAT I HAD HEARD, MY OWN EXCEPTED, FOR ABOVE TWENTY-FIVE YEARS.

After he had slumbered, rather than slept, about half-an-hour, he awoke again, and came out of the cave to me, for I had been milking my goats which I had in the enclosure just by: when he espied me he came running to me, laying himself down again upon the ground, with all the possible signs of an humble, thankful disposition, making a great many antic gestures to show it. At last he lays his head flat upon the ground, close to my foot, and sets my other foot upon his head, as he had done before; and after this made all the signs to me of subjection, servitude, and submission imaginable, to let me know how he would serve me so long as he lived.

FRIDAY'S RESCUE

I was greatly delighted with him, and made it my business to teach him everything that was proper.

It is true he went awkwardly in these clothes at first.

In a little time I began to speak to him; and teach him to speak to me; and first, I let him know his name should be Friday, which was the day I saved his life; I called him so for the memory of the time. We came back to our castle; and there I fell to work for my man Friday; and first of all, I gave him a pair of linen drawers, which I had out of the poor gunner's chest I mentioned, which I found in the wreck, and which, with a little alteration, fitted him very well; and then I made him a jerkin of goat's skin, as well as my skill would allow (for I was now grown a tolerably good tailor); and I gave him a cap which I made of hare's skin, very convenient, and fashionable enough; and thus he was clothed, for the present, tolerably well, and was mighty well pleased to see himself almost as well clothed as his master. It is true he went awkwardly in these clothes at first: wearing the drawers was very awkward to him, and the sleeves of the waist-coat galled his shoulders and the inside of his arms; but a little easing them where he complained they hurt him, and using himself to them, he took to them at length very well.

I was greatly delighted with him, and made it my business to teach him everything that was proper to make him useful, handy, and helpful; but especially to make him speak, and understand me when I spoke; and he was the aptest scholar that ever was; and particularly was so merry, so constantly diligent, and so pleased when he could but understand me, or make me understand him, that it was very pleasant for me to talk to him. Now my life began to be so easy that I began to say to myself that could I but have been safe from more savages, I cared not if I was never to remove from the place where I lived.

THE PRISONERS RETRIEVED

When the settled season began to come in, as the thought of my design returned with the fair weather, I was preparing daily for the voyage. And the first thing I did was to lay by a certain quantity of provisions, being the stores for our voyage; and intended in a week or a fortnight's time to open the dock, and launch out our boat. I was busy one morning upon something of this kind, when I called to Friday, and bid him to go to the sea-shore and see if he could find a turtle or a tortoise, a thing which we generally got once a week, for the sake of the eggs as well as the flesh.

Friday had not been long gone when he came running back, and flew over my outer wall or fence, like one that felt not the ground or the steps he set his foot on; and before I had time to speak to him he cries out to me, "O master! O master! O sorrow! O bad!" – "What's the matter, Friday?" says I. "O yonder there," says he, "one, two, three canoes; one, two, three!" By this way of speaking I concluded there were six; but on inquiry I found there were but three. "Well, Friday," says I, "do not be frightened." So I heartened him up as well as I could. However, I saw the poor fellow was most terribly scared, for nothing ran in his head but that they were come to look for him, and would cut him in pieces and eat him; and the poor fellow trembled so that I scarcely knew what to do with him. I comforted him as well as I could, and told him I was in as much danger as he, and that they would eat me as well as him. Then I took four muskets, and loaded them with two slugs and five small bullets each; and my two pistols I loaded with a brace of bullets each. I hung my great sword, as usual, naked by my side, and gave Friday his hatchet. When I had thus prepared myself, I took my perspective glass, and went up to the side of the hill, to see what I could discover; and I found quickly by my glass that there were one-and-twenty savages, three prisoners, and three canoes; and that their whole business seemed to be the triumphant banquet upon these three human bodies: a barbarous feast, indeed! but nothing more than, as I had observed, was usual with them. I observed also that they had landed, not where they had done when Friday made his escape, but nearer to my creek, where the shore was low, and where a thick wood came almost close down to the sea. This, with the abhorrence of the inhuman errand these wretches came about, filled me with such indignation that I came down again to Friday, and told him I was resolved to go down to them and kill them all; and asked him if he would stand by me. He had now got over his fright, and his spirits being a little raised with the dram I had given him, he was very cheerful, and told me, as before, he would die when I bid die.

In this fit of fury I divided the arms which I had charged, as before, between us; I gave Friday one pistol to stick in his girdle, and three guns upon his shoulder, and I took one pistol and the other three guns myself; and in this posture we marched out. I took a small bottle of rum in my pocket, and gave Friday a large bag with more powder and bullets; and as to orders, I charged him to keep close behind me, and not to stir, or shoot, or do anything till I bid him, and in the meantime not to speak a word. In this posture I fetched a compass to my right hand of near a mile, as well to get over the creek as to get into the wood, so that I could come within shot of them before I should be discovered, which I had seen by my glass it was easy to do.

I TOOK ONE PISTOL AND THE OTHER THREE GUNS MYSELF; AND IN THIS POSTURE WE MARCHED OUT.

I had now not a moment to lose, for nineteen of the dreadful wretches sat upon the ground, all close huddled together, and had just sent the other two to butcher the poor Christian, and bring him perhaps limb by limb to their fire, and they were stooping down to untie the bands at his feet. I turned to Friday. "Now, Friday," said I, "do as I bid thee." Friday said he would. "Then, Friday,"

They were, you may be sure, in a dreadful consternation.

And with that I fired again.

says I, "do exactly as you see me do; fail in nothing." So I set down one of the muskets and the fowling-piece upon the ground, and Friday did the like by his, and with the other musket I took my aim at the savages, bidding him to do the like; then asking him if he was ready, he said, "Yes." "Then fire at them," said I; and at the same moment I fired also.

Friday took his aim so much better than I, that on the side that he shot he killed two of them, and wounded three more; and on my side I killed one, and wounded two. They were, you may be sure, in a dreadful consternation: and all of them that were not hurt jumped upon their feet, but did not immediately know which way to run, or which way to look, for they knew not from whence their destruction came. Friday kept his eyes close upon me, that, as I had bid him, he might observe what I did; so, as soon as the first shot was made, I threw down the piece, and took up the fowling-piece, and Friday did the like; he saw me cock and present; he did the same again. "Are you ready, Friday?" said I. "Yes," says he. "Let fly, then," says I, "in the name of God!" and with that I fired again among the amazed wretches, and so did Friday; and as our pieces were now loaded with what I call swan-shot, or small pistol-bullets, we found only two drop; but so many were wounded that they ran about yelling and screaming like mad creatures, all bloody, and most of them miserably wounded; whereof three more fell quickly after, though not quite dead.

"Now, Friday," says I, laying down the discharged pieces, and taking up the musket which was yet loaded, "follow me," which he did with a great deal of courage; upon which I rushed out of the wood and showed myself, and Friday close at my foot. As soon as I perceived they saw me, I shouted as loud as I could, and bade Friday do so too, and running as fast as I could, which, by the way, was not very fast, being loaded with arms as I was, I made directly towards the poor victim, who was, as I said, lying upon the beach or shore, between the place where they sat and the sea. The two butchers who were just going to work with him had left him at the surprise of our first fire, and fled in a terrible fright to the seaside, and had jumped into a canoe, and three more of the rest made the same way. I turned to Friday, and bade him step forwards and fire at them; he understood me immediately, and running about forty yards, to be nearer them, he shot at them; and I thought he had killed them all, for I saw them all fall of a heap into the boat, though I saw two of them up again quickly; however, he killed two of them, and wounded the third, so that he lay down in the bottom of the boat as if he had been dead.

He killed two of them, and wounded the third, so that he lay down in the bottom of the boat as if he had been dead.

While my man Friday fired at them, I pulled out my knife and cut the flags that bound the poor victim; and loosing his hands and feet, I lifted him up, and asked him in the Portuguese tongue what he was. He answered in Latin, Christianus; but was so weak and faint that he could scarce stand or speak. I took my bottle out of my pocket and gave it him, making signs that he should drink, which he did; and I gave him a piece of bread, which he ate. Then I asked him what countryman he was: and he said, Espagniole; and being a little recovered, let me know, by all the signs he could possibly make, how much he was in my debt for his deliverance. "Seignior," said I, with as much Spanish as I could make up, "we will talk afterwards, but we must fight now: if you have any strength left, take this pistol and sword, and lay about you." He took them very thankfully; and no sooner had he the arms in his hands, but, as if they had put new vigour into him, he flew upon his murderers like a fury, and had cut two of them in pieces in an instant; for the truth is, as the whole was a surprise to them, so the poor creatures were so much frightened with the noise of our pieces that they fell down for mere amazement and fear, and had no more power to attempt their own escape than their flesh had to resist our shot; and that was the case of those five that Friday shot at in the boat; for as three of them fell with the hurt they received, so the other two fell with the fright.

I kept my piece in my hand still without firing, being willing to keep my charge ready, because I had given the Spaniard my pistol and sword: so I called to Friday, and bade him run up to the tree from whence we first fired, and fetch the arms which lay there that had been discharged, which he did with great swiftness; and then giving him my musket, I sat down myself to load all the rest again, and bade them come to me when they wanted. While I was loading these pieces, there happened a fierce engagement between the Spaniard and one of the savages, who made at him with one of their great wooden swords, the weapon that was to have killed him before, if I had not prevented it. The Spaniard, who was as bold and brave as could be imagined, though weak, had fought the Indian a good while, and had cut two great wounds on his head; but the savage being a stout, lusty fellow, closing in with him, had thrown him down, being faint, and was wringing my sword out of his hand; when the Spaniard, though undermost, wisely quitting the sword, drew the pistol from his girdle, shot the savage through the body, and killed him upon the spot, before I, who was running to help him, could come near him. Friday, being now left to his liberty, pursued the flying wretches, with no weapon in his hand but his hatchet: and with that he despatched those three who as I said before, were wounded at first, and fallen, and all the rest he could come up with: and the Spaniard coming to me for a gun, I gave him one of the fowling-pieces, with which he pursued two of the savages, and wounded them both; but as he was not able to run, they both got from him into the wood, where Friday pursued them, and killed one of them, but the other was too nimble for him; and though he was wounded, yet had plunged himself into the sea, and swam with all his might off to those two who were left in the canoe; which three in the canoe, with one wounded, that we knew not whether he died or no, were all that escaped our hands of one-and-twenty: three killed at our first shot from the tree; two killed at the next shot; two killed by Friday in the boat; two killed by Friday of those at first wounded; one killed by Friday in the wood; three killed by the Spaniard; four killed, being found dropped here and there, of the wounds, or killed by Friday in his chase of them; four escaped in the boat, whereof one wounded, if not dead: twenty-one in all.

Those that were in the canoe worked hard to get out of gun-shot, and though Friday made two or three shots at them, I did not find that he hit any of them. Friday would fain have had me take one of their canoes, and pursue them; and indeed I was very anxious about their escape, lest, carrying the news home to their people, they should come back perhaps with two or three hundred of the canoes and devour us by mere multitude; so I consented to pursue them by sea, and running to one of their canoes, I jumped in and bade Friday follow me: but when I was in the canoe I was surprised to find another poor creature lie there, bound hand and foot, as the Spaniard was, for the slaughter, and almost dead with fear, not knowing what was the matter; for he had not been able to look up over the side of the boat, he was tied so hard neck and heels, and had been tied so long that he had really but little life in him.

When Friday came to him I bade him speak to him, and tell him of his deliverance; and pulling out my bottle, made him give the poor wretch a dram, which, with the news of his being delivered, revived him, and he sat up in the boat. But when Friday came to hear him speak, and look in his face, it would have moved any one to tears to have seen how Friday kissed him, embraced him, hugged him, cried, laughed, hallooed, jumped about, danced, sang; then cried again, wrung his hands, beat his own face and head; and then sang and jumped about again like a distracted creature. It was a good while before I could make him speak to me or tell me what was the matter; but when he came a little to himself he told me that it was his father. It is not easy for me to express how it moved me to see what ecstasy and filial affection had worked in this poor savage at the sight of his father, and of his being delivered from death; nor indeed can I describe half the extravagances of his affection after this: for he went into the boat and out of the boat a great many times: when he went in to him he would sit down by him, open his breast, and hold his father's head close to his bosom for many minutes together,to nourish it; then he took his arms and ankles, which were numbed and stiff with the binding, and chafed and rubbed them with his hands; and I, perceiving what the case was, gave him some rum out of my bottle to rub them with, which did them a great deal of good. This affair put an end to our pursuit of the canoe with the other savages, who were now almost out of sight; and it was happy for us that we did not, for it blew so hard within two hours after, and before they could be got a quarter of their way, and continued blowing so hard all night, and that from the north-west, which was against them, that I could not suppose their boat could live, or that they ever reached their own coast.

ROBINSON CRUSOE

MUTINEERS

In a little time, however, no more canoes appearing, the fear of their coming wore off; and I began to take my former thoughts of a voyage to the main into consideration; being likewise assured by Friday's father that I might depend upon good usage from their nation, on his account, if I would go. But my thoughts were a little suspended when I had a serious discourse with the Spaniard, and when I understood that there were sixteen more of his countrymen and Portuguese, who having been cast away and made their escape to that side, lived there at peace, indeed, with the savages, but were very sore put to it for necessaries, and, indeed, for life.

I asked him all the particulars of their voyage, and found they were a Spanish ship, bound from the Rio de la Plata to the Havanna, being directed to leave their loading there, which was chiefly hides and silver, and to bring back what European goods they could meet with there; that they had five Portuguese seamen on board, whom they took out of another wreck; that five of their own men were drowned when first the ship was lost, and that these escaped through infinite dangers and hazards, and arrived, almost starved, on the cannibal coast, where they expected to have been devoured every moment. He told me they had some arms with them, but they were perfectly useless, for that they had neither powder nor ball, the washing of the sea having spoiled all their powder but a little, which they used at their first landing to provide themselves with some food.

I asked him what he thought would become of them there, and if they had formed any design of making their escape. He said they had many consultations about it; but that having neither vessel nor tools to build one, nor provisions of any kind, their councils always ended in tears and despair. I asked him how he thought they would receive a proposal from me, which might tend towards an escape; and whether, if they were all here, it might not be done. I told him with freedom, I feared mostly their treachery and ill-usage of me, if I put my life in their hands; for that gratitude was no inherent virtue in the nature of man, nor did men always square their dealings by the obligations they had received so much as they did by the advantages they expected. I told him it would be very hard that I should be made the instrument of their deliverance, and that they should afterwards make me their prisoner in New Spain, where an Englishman was certain to be made a sacrifice, what necessity or what accident soever brought him thither; and that I had rather be delivered up to the savages, and be devoured alive, than fall into the merciless claws of the priests, and be carried into the Inquisition. I added that, otherwise, I was persuaded, if they were all here, we might, with so many hands, build a barque large enough to carry us all away, either to the Brazils southward, or to the islands or Spanish coast northward; but that if, in requital, they should, when I had put weapons into their hands, carry me by force among their own people, I might be ill-used for my kindness to them, and make my case worse than it was before.

He answered, with a great deal of candour and ingenuousness, that their condition was so miserable, and that they were so sensible of it, that he believed they would abhor the thought of using any man unkindly that should contribute to their deliverance; and that, if I pleased, he would go to them with the old man, and discourse with them about it, and return again and bring me their answer; that he would make conditions with them upon their solemn oath, that they should be absolutely under my direction as their commander and captain; and they should swear upon the holy sacraments and gospel to be true to me, and go to such Christian country as I should agree to, and no other; and to be directed wholly and absolutely by my orders till they were landed safely in such country as I intended, and that he would bring a contract from them, under their hands, for that purpose. Then he told me he would first swear to me himself that he would never stir from me as long as he lived till I gave him orders; and that he would take my side to the last drop of his blood, if there should happen the least breach of faith among his countrymen. He told me they were all of them very civil, honest men, and they were under the greatest distress imaginable, having neither weapons

It was now harvest, and our crop in good order: it was not the most plentiful increase I had seen in the island, but, however, it was enough to answer our end.

nor clothes, nor any food, but at the mercy and discretion of the savages; out of all hopes of ever returning to their own country; and that he was sure, if I would undertake their relief, they would live and die by me.

Upon these assurances, I resolved to venture to relieve them, if possible, and to send the old savage and this Spaniard over to them to treat. But when we had got all things in readiness to go, the Spaniard himself started an objection, which had so much prudence in it on one hand, and so much sincerity on the other hand, that I could not but be very well satisfied in it; and, by his advice, put off the deliverance of his comrades for at least half a year. The case was thus: he had been with us now about a month, during which time I had let him see in what manner I had provided, with the assistance of Providence, for my support; and he saw evidently what stock of corn and rice I had laid up; which, though it was more than sufficient for myself, yet it was not sufficient, without good husbandry, for my family, now it was increased to four; but much less would it be sufficient if his countrymen, who were, as he said, sixteen, still alive, should come over; and least of all would it be sufficient to victual our vessel, if we should build one, for a voyage to any of the Christian colonies of America; so he told me he thought it would be more advisable to let him and the other two dig and cultivate some more land, as much as I could spare seed to sow, and that we should wait another harvest, that we might have a supply of corn for his countrymen, when they should come; for want might be a temptation to them to disagree, or not to think themselves delivered, otherwise than out of one difficulty into another. "You know," says he, "the children of Israel, though they rejoiced at first for their being delivered out of Egypt, yet rebelled even against God Himself, that delivered them, when they came to want bread in the wilderness."

It was now harvest, and our crop in good order: it was not the most plentiful increase I had seen in the island, but, however, it was enough to answer our end. Having a full supply of food for all the guests I expected, I gave the Spaniard leave to go over to the main, to see what he could do with those he had left behind him there. I gave him a strict charge not to bring any man who would not first swear in the presence of himself and the old savage that he would in no way injure, fight with, or attack the person he should find in the island, who was so kind as to send for them in order to their deliverance; but that they would stand by him and defend him against all such attempts, and wherever they went would be entirely under and subjected to his command; and that this should be put in writing, and signed in their hands. How they were to have done this, when I knew they had neither pen nor ink, was a question which we never asked. Under these instructions, the Spaniard and the old savage, the father of Friday, went away in one of the canoes which they might be said to have come in, or rather were brought in, when they came as prisoners to be devoured by the savages. I gave each of them a musket, with a firelock on it, and about eight charges of powder and ball, charging them to be very good husbands of both, and not to use either of them but upon urgent occasions.

This was a cheerful work, being the first measures used by me in view of my deliverance for now twenty-seven years and some days. I gave them provisions of bread and of dried grapes, sufficient for themselves for many days, and sufficient for all the Spaniards – for about eight days' time; and wishing them a good voyage, I saw them go.

And wishing them a good voyage,
I saw them go.

It was no less than eight days I had waited for them, when a strange and unforeseen accident intervened, of which the like has not, perhaps, been heard of in history. I was fast asleep in my hutch one morning, when my man Friday came running in to me, and called aloud, "Master, master, they are come, they are come!" I jumped up, and regardless of danger I went, as soon as I could get my clothes on, through my little grove, which, by the way, was by this time grown to be a very thick wood; I say, regardless of danger I went without my arms, which was not my custom to do; but I was surprised when, turning my eyes to the sea, I presently saw a boat at about a league and a half distance, standing in for the shore, with a shoulder-of-mutton sail, as they call it, and the wind blowing pretty fair to bring them in: also I observed, presently, that they did not come from that side which the shore lay on, but from the southernmost end of the island. Upon this I called Friday in, and bade him lie close, for these were not the people we looked for, and that we might not know yet whether they were friends or enemies. In the next place I went in to fetch my perspective glass to see what I could make of them; and having taken the ladder out, I climbed up to the top of the hill, as I used to do when I was apprehensive of anything, and to take my view the plainer without being discovered. I had scarce set my foot upon the hill when my eye plainly discovered a ship lying at anchor, at about two leagues and a half distance from me, SSE., but not above a league and a half from the shore. By my observation it appeared plainly to be an English ship, and the boat appeared to be an English long-boat.

I cannot express the confusion I was in, though the joy of seeing a ship, and one that I had reason to believe was manned by my own countrymen, and consequently friends, was such as I cannot describe; but yet I had some secret doubts hung about me – I cannot tell from whence they came – bidding me keep upon my guard. In the first place, it occurred to me to consider what business an English ship could have in that part of the world, since it was not the way to or from any part of the world where the English had any traffic; and I knew there had been no storms to drive them in there in distress; and that if they were really English it was most probable that they were here upon no good design.

I had not kept myself long in this posture till I saw the boat draw near the shore, as if they looked for a creek to thrust in at, for the convenience of landing. There were in all eleven men, whereof three of them I found were unarmed and, as I thought, bound; and when the first four or five of them were jumped on shore, they took those three out of the boat as prisoners: one of the three I could perceive using the most passionate gestures of entreaty, affliction, and despair, even to a kind of extravagance; the other two, I could perceive, lifted up their hands sometimes, and appeared concerned indeed, but not to such a degree as the first.

I HAD SOME SECRET DOUBTS HUNG ABOUT ME – BIDDING ME KEEP UPON MY GUARD.

All this while I had no thought of what the matter really was, but stood trembling with the horror of the sight, expecting every moment when the three prisoners should be killed; nay, once I saw one of the villains lift up his arm with a great cutlass, as the seamen call it, or sword, to strike one of the poor men; and I expected to see him fall every moment; at which all the blood in my body seemed to run chill in my veins. I wished heartily now for the Spaniard, and the savage that had gone with him, or that I had any way to have come undiscovered within shot of them, that I might have secured the three men, for I saw no firearms they had among them; but it fell out to my mind another way. After I had observed the outrageous usage of the three men by the insolent seamen, I observed the fellows run scattering about the island, as if they wanted to see the country. I observed that the three other men had liberty to go also where they pleased; but they sat down all three upon the ground, very pensive, and looked like men in despair. This put me in mind of the first time when I came on shore, and began to look about me; how I gave myself over for lost; how wildly I looked round me; what dreadful apprehensions I had; and how I lodged in the tree all night for fear of being devoured by wild beasts. As I knew nothing that night of the supply I was to receive by the providential driving of the ship nearer the land by the storms and tide, by which I have since been so long nourished and supported; so these three poor desolate men knew nothing how certain of deliverance and supply they were, how near it was to them, and how effectually and really they were in a condition of safety, at the same time that they thought themselves lost and their case desperate.

It was just at high-water when these people came on shore; and while they rambled about to see what kind of a place they were in, they had carelessly stayed till the tide was spent, and the water was ebbed considerably away, leaving their boat aground. They had left two men in the boat, who, as I found afterwards, having drunk a little too much brandy, fell asleep; however, one of them waking a little sooner than the other and finding the boat too fast aground for him to stir it, hallooed out for the rest, who were straggling about: upon which they all soon came to the boat: but it was past all their strength to launch her, the boat being very heavy, and the shore on that side being a soft oozy sand, almost like a quicksand. In this condition, like true seamen, who are, perhaps, the least of all mankind given to forethought,

And with that word knocked him down with the stock of his musket.

they gave it over, and away they strolled about the country again; and I heard one of them say aloud to another, calling them off from the boat, "Why, let her alone, Jack, can't you? she'll float next tide;" by which I was fully confirmed in the main inquiry of what countrymen they were. All this while I kept myself very close, not once daring to stir out of my castle any farther than to my place of observation near the top of the hill: and very glad I was to think how well it was fortified. I knew it was no less than ten hours before the boat could float again, and by that time it would be dark, and I might be at more liberty to see their motions, and to hear their discourse, if they had any. In the meantime I fitted myself up for a battle as before, though with more caution, knowing I had to do with another kind of enemy than I had at first. I ordered Friday also, whom I had made an excellent marksman with his gun, to load himself with arms. I took myself two fowling-pieces, and I gave him three muskets. My figure, indeed, was very fierce; I had my formidable goat-skin coat on, with the great cap I have mentioned, a naked sword by my side, two pistols in my belt, and a gun upon each shoulder.

"DO NOT BE SURPRISED AT ME; PERHAPS YOU MAY HAVE A FRIEND NEAR WHEN YOU DID NOT EXPECT IT."

It was my design, as I said above, not to have made any attempt till it was dark; but about two o'clock, being the heat of the day, I found that they were all gone straggling into the woods, and, as I thought, laid down to sleep. The three poor distressed men, too anxious for their condition to get any sleep, had, however, sat down under the shelter of a great tree, at about a quarter of a mile from me, and, as I thought, out of sight of any of the rest. Upon this I resolved to discover myself to them, and learn something of their condition; immediately I marched as above, my man Friday at a good distance behind me, as formidable for his arms as I, but not making quite so staring a spectre-like figure as I did. I came as near them undiscovered as I could, and then, before any of them saw me, I called aloud to them in Spanish, "What are ye, gentlemen?" They started up at the noise, but were ten times more confounded when they saw me, and the uncouth figure that I made. They made no answer at all, but I thought I perceived them just going to fly from me, when I spoke to them in English. "Gentlemen," said I, "do not be surprised at me; perhaps you may have a friend near when you did not expect it." "He must be sent directly from heaven then," said one of them very gravely to me, and pulling off his hat at the same time to me; "for our condition is past the help of man." "All help is from heaven, sir," said I, "but can you put a stranger in the way to help you? for you seem to be in some great distress. I saw you when you landed; and when you seemed to make application to the brutes that came with you, I saw one of them lift up his sword to kill you."

The poor man, with tears running down his face, and trembling, looking like one astonished, returned, "Am I talking to God or man? Is it a real man or an angel?" "Be in no fear about that, sir," said I; "if God had sent an angel to relieve you, he would have come better clothed, and armed after another manner than you see me; pray lay aside your fears; I am a man, an Englishman, and disposed to assist you; you see I have one servant only; we have arms and ammunition; tell us freely, can we serve you? What is your case?" "Our case, sir," said he, "is too long to tell you while our murderers are so near us; but, in short, sir, I was commander of that ship – my men have mutinied against me; they have been hardly prevailed on not to murder me, and, at last, have set me on shore in this desolate place, with these two men with me – one my mate, the other a passenger – where we expected to perish, believing the place to be uninhabited, and know not yet what to think of it." "Where are these brutes, your enemies?" said I; "do you know where they are gone?" "There they lie, sir," said he, pointing to a thicket of trees; "my heart trembles for fear they have seen us and heard you speak; if they have, they will certainly murder us all." "Have they any fire-arms?" said I. He answered, "They had only two pieces, one of which they left in the boat." "Well, then," said I, "leave the rest to me; I see they are all asleep; it is an easy thing to kill them all; but shall we rather take them prisoners?" He told me there were two desperate villains among them that it was scarce safe to show any mercy to; but if they were secured, he believed all the rest would return to their duty. I asked him which they were. He told me he could not at that distance distinguish them, but he would obey my orders in anything I would direct. "Well," says I, "let us retreat out of their view or hearing, lest they awake, and we will resolve further." So they willingly went back with me, till the woods covered us from them.

"Look you, sir," said I, "if I venture upon your deliverance, are you willing to make two conditions with me?" He anticipated my proposals by telling me that both he and the ship, if recovered, should be wholly directed and commanded by me in everything; and if the ship was not recovered, he would live and die with me in what part of the world soever I would send him; and the two other men said the same. "Well," says I, "my conditions are but two; first, that while you stay in this island with me, you will not pretend to any authority here; and if I put arms in your hands, you will, upon all occasions, give them up to me, and do no prejudice to me or mine upon this island, and in the meantime be governed by my orders; secondly, that if the ship is or may be recovered, you will carry me and my man to England passage free."

He gave me all the assurances that the invention or faith of man could devise that he would comply with these most reasonable demands, and besides would owe his life to me, and acknowledge it upon all occasions as long as he lived. "Well, then," said I, "here are three muskets for you, with powder and ball; tell me next what you think is proper to be done." He showed all the testimonies of his gratitude that he was able, but offered to be wholly guided by me. I told him I thought it was very hard venturing anything; but the best method I could think of was to fire on them at once as they lay, and if any were not killed at the first volley, and offered to submit, we might save them, and so put it wholly upon God's providence to direct the shot. He said, very modestly, that he was loath to kill them if he could help it; but that those two were incorrigible villains, and had been the authors of all the mutiny in the ship, and if they escaped, we should be undone still, for they would go on board and bring the whole ship's company, and destroy us all. "Well, then," says I, "necessity legitimates my advice, for it is the only way to save our lives." However, s eeing him still cautious of shedding blood, I told him they should go themselves, and manage as they found convenient.

In the middle of this discourse we heard some of them awake, and soon after we saw two of them on their feet. I asked him if either of them were the heads

"Am I talking to God or man? Is it a real man or an angel?"

of the mutiny? He said, "No." "Well, then," said I, "you may let them escape; and Providence seems to have awakened them on purpose to save themselves. Now," says I, "if the rest escape you, it is your fault." Animated with this, he took the musket I had given him in his hand, and a pistol in his belt, and his two comrades with him, with each a piece in his hand; the two men who were with him going first made some noise, at which one of the seamen who was awake turned about, and seeing them coming, cried out to the rest; but was too late then, for the moment he cried out they fired – I mean the two men, the captain wisely reserving his own piece. They had so well aimed their shot at the men they knew, that one of them was killed on the spot, and the other very much wounded; but not being dead, he started up on his feet, and called eagerly for help to the other; but the captain stepping to him, told him it was too late to cry for help, he should call upon God to forgive his villainy, and with that word knocked him down with the stock of his musket, so that he never spoke more; there were three more in the company, and one of them was slightly wounded. By this time I was come; and when they saw their danger, and that it was in vain to resist, they begged for mercy. The captain told them he would spare their lives if they would give him an assurance of their abhorrence of the treachery they had been guilty of, and would swear to be faithful to him in recovering the ship, and afterwards in carrying her back to Jamaica, from whence they came. They gave him all the protestations of their sincerity that could be desired; and he was willing to believe them, and spare their lives, which I was not against, only that I obliged him to keep them bound hand and foot while they were on the island. While this was doing, I sent Friday with the captain's mate to the boat with orders to secure her, and bring away the oars and sails, which they did; and by-and-by three straggling men, that were (happily for them) parted from the rest, came back upon hearing the guns fired; and seeing the captain, who was before their prisoner, now their conqueror, they submitted to be bound also; and so our victory was complete.

It now remained that the captain and I should inquire into one another's circumstances. I began first, and told him my whole history, which he heard with an attention even to amazement. After this communication was at an end, I carried him and his two men into my apartment, leading them in just where I came out, viz. at the top of the house, where I refreshed them with such provisions as I had, and showed them all the contrivances I had made during my long, long inhabiting that place.

WHEN THEY SAW THEIR DANGER, AND THAT IT WAS IN VAIN TO RESIST, THEY BEGGED FOR MERCY.

All I showed them, all I said to them, was perfectly amazing; but above all, the captain admired my fortification, and how perfectly I had concealed my retreat with a grove of trees, which having been now planted nearly twenty years. I told him this was my castle and my residence, but that I had a seat in the country, as most princes have, whither I could retreat upon occasion, and I would show him that too another time; but at present our business was to consider how to recover the ship. He agreed with me as to that, but told me he was perfectly at a loss what measures to take, for that there were still six-and-twenty hands on board, who, having entered into a cursed conspiracy, by which they had all forfeited their lives to the law, would be hardened in it now by desperation, and would carry it on, knowing that if they were subdued they would be brought to the gallows as soon as they came to England, or to any of the English colonies, and that, therefore, there would be no attacking them with so small a number as we were.

I mused for some time on what he had said, and found it was a very rational conclusion, and that therefore something was to be resolved on speedily, as well to draw the men on board into some snare for their surprise as to prevent their landing upon us, and destroying us. Upon this, it presently occurred to me that in a little while the ship's crew, wondering what was become of their comrades and of the boat, would certainly come on shore in their other boat to look for them, and that then, perhaps, they might come armed, and be too strong for us: this he allowed to be rational. Upon this, I told him the first thing we had to do was to stave the boat which lay upon the beach, so that they might not carry her off, and taking everything out of her, leave her so far useless as not to be fit to swim. Accordingly, we went on board, took the arms which were left on board out of her, and whatever else we found there – which was a bottle of brandy, and another of rum, a few biscuit-cakes, a horn of powder, and a great lump of sugar in a piece of canvas (the sugar was five or six pounds): all which was very welcome to me, especially the brandy and sugar, of which I had had none left for many years.

When we had carried all these things on shore (the oars, mast, sail, and rudder of the boat were carried away before), we knocked a great hole in her bottom, that if they had come strong enough to master us, yet they could not carry off the boat. Indeed, it was not much in my thoughts that we could be able to recover the ship; but my view was, that if they went away without the boat, I did not much question to make her again fit to carry as to the Leeward Islands, and call upon our friends the Spaniards in my way, for I had them still in my thoughts.

THE VESSEL RECLAIMED

We had, upon the first appearance of the boat's coming from the ship, considered of separating our prisoners; and we had, indeed, secured them effectually. Two of them, of whom the captain was less assured than ordinary, I sent with Friday, and one of the three delivered men, to my cave, where they were remote enough, and out of danger of being heard or discovered, or of finding their way out of the woods if they could have delivered themselves. Here they left them bound, but gave them provisions; and promised them, if they continued there quietly, to give them their liberty in a day or two; but that if they attempted their escape they should be put to death without mercy.

The other prisoners had better usage; two of them were kept pinioned, indeed, because the captain was not able to trust them; but the other two were taken into my service, upon the captain's recommendation, and upon their solemnly engaging to live and die with us; so with them and the three honest men we were seven men, well armed; and I made no doubt we should be able to deal well enough with the ten that were coming, considering that the captain had said there were three or four honest men among them also. As soon as they got to the place where their other boat lay, they ran their boat into the beach and came all on shore, hauling the boat up after them, which I was glad to see, for I was afraid they would rather have left the boat at an anchor some distance from the shore, with some hands in her to guard her, and so we should not be able to seize the boat. Being on shore, the first thing they did, they ran all to their other boat; and it was easy to see they were under a great surprise to find her stripped, as above, of all that was in her, and a great hole in her bottom. After they had mused a while upon this, they set up two or three great shouts, hallooing with all their might, to try if they could make their companions hear; but all was to no purpose. Then they came all close in a ring, and fired a volley of their small arms, which indeed we heard, and the echoes made the woods ring. But it was all one; those in the cave, we were sure, could not hear; and those in our keeping, though they heard it well enough, yet durst give no answer to them. They were so astonished at the surprise of this, that, as they told us afterwards, they resolved to go all on board again to their ship, and let them know that the men were all murdered, and the long-boat staved; accordingly, they immediately launched their boat again, and got all of them on board. The captain was terribly amazed, and even confounded, at this, believing they would go on board the ship again and set sail, giving their comrades over for lost, and so he should still lose the ship, which he was in hopes we should have recovered; but he was quickly as much frightened the other way. They had not been long put off with the boat, when we perceived them all coming on shore again; but with this new measure in their conduct, which it seems they consulted together upon, viz. to leave three men in the boat, and the rest to go on shore, and go up into the country to look for their fellows.

We had nothing now to do but to watch for them in the dark, and to fall upon them, so as to make sure work with them. It was several hours after Friday came back to me before they came back to their boat; and we could hear the foremost of them, long before they came quite up, calling to those behind to come along; and could also hear them answer, and complain how lame and tired they were, and not able to come any faster: which was very welcome news to us. At length they came up to the boat: but it is impossible to express their confusion when they found the boat fast aground in the creek, the tide ebbed out, and their two men gone. We could hear them call one to another in a most lamentable manner, telling one another they were got into an enchanted island; that either there were inhabitants in it, and they should all be murdered, or else there were devils and spirits in it, and they should be all carried away and devoured. They hallooed again, and called their two comrades by their names a great many times; but no answer. After some time we could see them, by the little light there was, run about, wringing their hands like men in despair, and sometimes they would go and sit down in the boat to rest themselves: then come ashore again, and walk about again, and so the same thing over again. My men would fain have had me give them leave to fall

THE VESSEL RECLAIMED

They had not been long put off with the boat, when we perceived them all coming on shore again.

upon them at once in the dark; but I was willing to take them at some advantage, so as to spare them, and kill as few of them as I could; and especially I was unwilling to hazard the killing of any of our men, knowing the others were very well armed. I resolved to wait, to see if they did not separate; and therefore, to make sure of them, I drew my ambuscade nearer, and ordered Friday and the captain to creep upon their hands and feet, as close to the ground as they could, that they might not be discovered, and get as near them as they could possibly before they offered to fire.

They had not been long in that posture when the boatswain, who was the principal ringleader of the mutiny, came walking towards them, with two more of the crew; the captain was so eager at having this principal rogue so much in his power, that he could hardly have patience to let him come so near as to be sure of him, for they only heard his tongue before: but when they came nearer, the captain and Friday, starting up on their feet, let fly at them. The boatswain was killed upon the spot: the next man was shot in the body, and fell just by him. At the noise of the fire I immediately advanced with my whole army, which was now eight men; myself, generalissimo; Friday, my lieutenant-general; the captain and his two men, and the three prisoners of war whom we had trusted with arms. We came upon them, indeed, in the dark, so that they could not see our number; and I made the man they had left in the boat, who was now one of us, to call them by name, to try if I could bring them to a parley, and so perhaps might reduce them to terms; which fell out just as we desired: for indeed it was easy to think, as their condition then was, they would be very willing to capitulate. So he calls out as loud as he could to one of them, "Tom Smith! Tom Smith!" Tom Smith answered immediately, "Is that Robinson?" for it seems he knew the voice. The other answered, "Ay, ay; for God's sake, Tom Smith, throw down your arms and yield, or you are all dead men this moment." "Who must we yield to? Where are they?" says Smith again. "Here they are," says he; "here's our captain and fifty men with him, have been hunting you these two hours; the boatswain is killed; Will Fry is wounded, and I am a prisoner; and if you do not yield you are all lost." "Will they give us quarter, then?" says Tom Smith, "and we will yield." "I'll go and ask, if you promise to yield," said Robinson: so he asked the captain, and the captain himself then calls out, "You, Smith, you know my voice; if you lay down your arms immediately and submit, you shall have your lives, all but Will Atkins." Upon this Will

Atkins cried out, "For God's sake, captain, give me quarter; what have I done? They have all been as bad as I:" which, by the way, was not true; for it seems this Will Atkins was the first man that laid hold of the captain when they first mutinied, and used him barbarously in tying his hands and giving him injurious language. However, the captain told him he must lay down his arms at discretion, and trust to the governor's mercy: by which he meant me, for they all called me governor. In a word, they all laid down their arms and begged their lives; and I sent the man that had parleyed with them, and two more, who bound them all.

Our next work was to repair the boat, and think of seizing the ship: and as for the captain, now he had leisure to parley with them, he expostulated with them upon the villainy of their practices with him, and upon the further wickedness of their design, and how certainly it must bring them to misery and distress in the end , and perhaps to the gallows.

They all appeared very penitent, and begged hard for their lives. As for that, he told them they were not his prisoners, but the commander's of the island; that they thought they had set him on shore in a barren, uninhabited island; but it had pleased God so to direct them that it was inhabited, and that the governor was an Englishman; that he might hang them all there, if he pleased; but as he had given them all quarter, he supposed he would send them to England, to be dealt with there as justice required, except Atkins, whom he was commanded by the governor to advise to prepare for death, for that he would be hanged in the morning.

Though this was all but a fiction of his own, yet it had its desired effect; Atkins fell upon his knees to beg the captain to intercede with the governor for his life; and all the rest begged of him, for God's sake, that they might not be sent to England. It now occurred to me that the time of our deliverance was come, and that it would be a most easy thing to bring these fellows in to be hearty in getting possession of the ship; so I retired in the dark from them, that they might not see what kind of a governor they had, and called the captain to me. Upon the captain coming to me, I told him my project for seizing the ship, which he liked wonderfully well, and resolved to put it in execution the next morning. But, in order to execute it with more art, and to be secure of success, I told him we must divide the prisoners, and that he should go and take Atkins, and two more of the worst of them, and send them pinioned to the cave where the others lay. This was committed to Friday and the two men who came on shore with the captain. They conveyed them to the cave as to a prison: and it was, indeed, a dismal place, especially to men in their condition. The others I ordered to my bower.

To these in the morning I sent the captain, who was to enter into a parley with them; in a word, to try them, and tell me whether he thought they might be trusted or not to go on board and surprise the ship. He talked to them of the injury done him, of the condition they were brought to, and that though the governor had given them quarter for their lives as to the present action, yet that if they were sent to England they would all be hanged in chains; but that if they would join in so just an attempt as to recover the ship, he would have the governor's engagement for their pardon.

Any one may guess how readily such a proposal would be accepted by men in their condition; they fell down on their knees to the captain, and promised, with the deepest imprecations, that they would be faithful to him to the last drop, and that they should owe their lives to him, and would go with him all over the world; that they would own him as a father to them as long as they lived. "Well," says the captain, "I must go and tell the governor what you say, and see what I can do to bring him to consent to it." So he brought me an account of the temper he found them in, and that he verily believed they would be faithful. However, that we might be very secure, I told him he should go back again and choose out those five, and tell them, that they might see he did not want men, that he would take out those five to be his assistants, and that the governor would keep the other two, and the three that were sent prisoners to the castle (my cave), as hostages for the fidelity of those five; and that if they proved unfaithful in the execution, the five hostages should be hanged in chains alive on the shore. This looked severe, and convinced them that the governor was in earnest; however, they had no way left them but to accept it; and it was now the business of the prisoners, as much as of the captain, to persuade the other five to do their duty.

IT NOW OCCURRED TO ME THAT THE TIME OF OUR DELIVERANCE WAS COME.

Our strength was now thus ordered for the expedition: first, the captain, his mate, and passenger; second, the two prisoners of the first gang, to whom, having their character from the captain, I had given their liberty, and trusted them with arms; third, the other two that I had kept till now in my bower, pinioned, but on the captain's motion had now released; fourth, these five released at last; so that there were twelve in all, besides five we kept prisoners in the cave for hostages. When I showed myself to the two hostages, it was with the captain, who told them I was the person the governor had ordered to look after them; and that it was the governor's pleasure they should not stir anywhere but by my direction; that if they did, they would be fetched into the castle, and be laid in irons: so that as we never suffered them to see me as governor, I now appeared as another person, and spoke of the governor, the garrison, the castle, and the like, upon all occasions.

The captain now had no difficulty before him, but to furnish his two boats, stop the breach of one, and man them. As soon as the ship was thus secured, the captain ordered seven guns to be fired, which was the signal agreed upon with me to give me notice of his success, which, you may be sure, I was very glad to hear, having sat watching upon the shore for it till near two o'clock in the morning. Having thus heard the signal plainly, I laid me down; and it having been a day of great fatigue to me, I slept very sound, till I was surprised with the noise of a gun; and presently starting up, I heard a man call me by the name of "Governor! Governor!" and presently I knew the captain's voice; when, climbing up to the top of the hill, there he stood, and, pointing to the ship, he embraced me in his arms, "My dear friend and deliverer," says he, "there's your ship; for she is all yours, and so are we, and all that belong to her."

I cast my eyes to the ship, and there she rode, within little more than half a mile of the shore; for they had weighed her anchor as soon as they were masters of her, and, the weather being fair, had brought her to an anchor just against the mouth of the little creek. I was at first ready to sink down with the surprise; for I saw my deliverance, indeed, visibly put into my hands, all things easy, and a large ship just ready to carry me away whither I pleased to go. He said a thousand kind and

Climbing up to the top of the hill, there he stood, and, pointing to the ship, he embraced me in his arms.

tender things to me, to compose and bring me to myself; but such was the flood of joy in my breast, that it put all my spirits into confusion: at last it broke out into tears, and in a little while after I recovered my speech; I then took my turn, and embraced him as my deliverer, and we rejoiced together. The captain told me he had brought me some little refreshment, such as the wretches that had been so long his masters had not plundered him of. Upon this, he called aloud to the boat, and bade his men bring the things ashore; and, indeed, it was a present as if I had been one that was not to be carried away with them, but as if I had been to dwell upon the island still. First, he had brought me a case of bottles full of excellent cordial waters, six large bottles of Madeira wine, two pounds of tobacco, twelve good pieces of the ship's beef, and six pieces of pork, a box of sugar, a box of flour, a bag full of lemons, and two bottles of lime-juice, and abundance of other things. But besides these, and what was a thousand times more useful to me, he brought me six new clean shirts, six very good neckcloths, two pair of gloves, one pair of shoes, a hat, and one pair of stockings, with a very good suit of clothes of his own.

We began to consult what was to be done with the prisoners; for it was worth considering whether we might venture to take them with us or no, especially two of them, whom he knew to be incorrigible and refractory to the last degree; and the captain said he knew they were such rogues that there was no obliging them, and if he did carry them away, it must be in irons, as malefactors, to be delivered over to justice at the first English colony he could come to; and I found that the captain himself was very anxious about it. I let them know that by my direction the ship had been seized; that she lay now in the road; and they might see by-and-by that their new captain had received the reward of his villainy, and that they would see him hanging at the yard-arm; that, as to them, I wanted to know what they had to say why I should not execute them as pirates taken in the fact.

One of them answered in the name of the rest, that they had nothing to say but this, that when they were taken the captain promised them their lives, and they humbly implored my mercy. But I told them I knew not what mercy to show them; for as for myself, I had resolved to quit the island with all my men, and had taken passage with the captain to go to England; and as for the captain, he could not carry them to England other than as prisoners in irons, to be tried for mutiny and running away with the ship; the consequence of which, they must needs know, would be the gallows; so that I could not tell what was best for them, unless they had a mind to take their fate in the island. If they desired that, as I had liberty to leave the island, I had some inclination to give them their lives, if they thought they could shift on shore. They seemed very thankful for it, and said they would much rather venture to stay there than be carried to England to be hanged. So I left it on that issue.

I told them I thought they had made a right choice; that if the captain had carried them away they would certainly be hanged. I showed them the new captain hanging at the yard-arm of the ship, and told them they had nothing less to expect. When they had all declared their willingness to stay, I then told them I would let them into the story of my living there, and put them into the way of making it easy to them. Accordingly, I gave them the whole history of the place, and of my coming to it; showed them my fortifications, the way I made my bread, planted my corn, cured my grapes; and, in a word, all that was necessary to make them easy. I told them the story also of the seventeen Spaniards that were to be expected, for whom I left a letter, and made them promise to treat them in common with themselves.

RETURN TO ENGLAND

And thus I left the island, the 19th of December, as I found by the ship's account, in the year 1686, after I had been upon it eight-and-twenty years, two months, and nineteen days; being delivered from this second captivity the same day of the month that I first made my escape in the long-boat from among the Moors of Sallee. In this vessel, after a long voyage, I arrived in England the 11th of June, in the year 1687, having been thirty-five years absent.

RETURN TO ENGLAND

When I came to England I was as perfect a stranger to all the world as if I had never been known there. My benefactor and faithful steward, whom I had left my money in trust with, was alive, but had had great misfortunes in the world; was become a widow the second time, and very low in the world. I made her very easy as to what she owed me, assuring her I would give her no trouble; but, on the contrary, in gratitude for her former care and faithfulness to me, I relieved her as my little stock would afford; which at that time would, indeed, allow me to do but little for her; but I assured her I would never forget her former kindness to me; nor did I forget her when I had sufficient to help her, as shall be observed in its proper place. I went down afterwards into Yorkshire; but my father was dead, and my mother and all the family extinct, except that I found two sisters, and two of the children of one of my brothers; and as I had been long ago given over for dead, there had been no provision made for me; so that, in a word, I found nothing to relieve or assist me; and that the little money I had would not do much for me as to settling in the world.

I met with one piece of gratitude indeed, which I did not expect; and this was, that the master of the ship, whom I had so happily delivered, and by the same means saved the ship and cargo, having given a very handsome account to the owners of the manner how I had saved the lives of the men and the ship, they invited me to meet them and some other merchants concerned, and all together made me a very handsome compliment upon the subject, and a present of almost £200 sterling.

But after making several reflections upon the circumstances of my life, and how little way this would go towards settling me in the world, I resolved to go to Lisbon, and see if I might not come at some information of the state of my plantation in the Brazils, and of what was become of my partner, who, I had reason to suppose, had some years past given me over for dead. With this view I took shipping for Lisbon, where I arrived in April following, my man Friday accompanying me very honestly in all these ramblings, and proving a most faithful servant upon all occasions. When I came to Lisbon, I found out, by inquiry, and to my particular satisfaction, my old friend, the captain of the ship who first took me up at sea off the shore of Africa. He was now grown old, and had left off going to sea, having put his son, who was far from a young man, into his ship, and who still used the Brazil trade. The old man did not know me, and indeed I hardly knew him. But I soon brought him to my remembrance, and as soon brought myself to his remembrance, when I told him who I was.

AND AS I HAD BEEN LONG AGO GIVEN OVER FOR DEAD, THERE HAD BEEN NO PROVISION MADE FOR ME.

After some passionate expressions of the old acquaintance between us, I inquired, you may be sure, after my plantation and my partner. The old man told me he had not been in the Brazils for about nine years; but that he could assure me that when he came away my partner was living, but the trustees whom I had joined with him to take cognisance of my part were both dead: that, however, he believed I would have a

The old man did not know me, and indeed I hardly knew him. But I soon brought him to my remembrance.

very good account of the improvement of the plantation; for that, upon the general belief of my being cast away and drowned, my trustees had given in the account of the produce of my part of the plantation to the procurator-fiscal, who had appropriated it, in case I never came to claim it, one-third to the king, and two-thirds to the monastery of St. Augustine, to be expended for the benefit of the poor, and for the conversion of the Indians to the Catholic faith: but that, if I appeared, or any one for me, to claim the inheritance, it would be restored; only that the improvement, or annual production, being distributed to charitable uses, could not be restored: but he assured me that the steward of the king's revenue from lands, and the providore, or steward of the monastery, had taken great care all along that the incumbent, that is to say my partner, gave every year a faithful account of the produce, of which they had duly received my moiety. I asked him if he knew to what height of improvement he had brought the plantation, and whether he thought it might be worth looking after; or whether, on my going thither, I should meet with any obstruction to my possessing my just right in the moiety. He told me he could not tell exactly to what degree the plantation was improved; but this he knew, that my partner was grown exceeding rich upon the enjoying his part of it; and that, to the best of his remembrance, he had heard that the king's third of my part, which was, it seems, granted away to some other monastery or religious house, amounted to above two hundred moidores a year: that as to my being restored to a quiet possession of it, there was no question to be made of that, my partner being alive to witness my title, and my name being also enrolled in the register of the country; also he told me that the survivors of my two trustees were very fair, honest people, and very wealthy; and he believed I would not only have their assistance for putting me in possession, but would find a very considerable sum of money in their hands for my account, being the produce of the farm while their fathers held the trust, and before it was given up, as above; which, as he remembered, was for about twelve years.

After a few days' further conference with this ancient friend, he brought me an account of the first six years' income of my plantation, signed by my partner and the merchant-trustees, being always delivered in goods, viz. tobacco in roll, and sugar in chests, besides rum, molasses, &c., which is the consequence of a sugar-work; and I found by this account, that every year the income considerably increased; but, as above, the disbursements being large, the sum at first was small: however, the old man let me see that he was debtor to me four hundred and seventy moidores of gold, besides sixty chests of sugar and fifteen double rolls of tobacco, which were lost in his ship; he having been shipwrecked coming home to Lisbon, about eleven years after my having the place. The good man then began to complain of his misfortunes, and how he had been obliged to make use of my money to recover his losses, and buy him a share in a new ship. "However, my old friend," says he, "you shall not want a supply in your necessity; and as soon as my son returns you shall be fully satisfied." Upon this he pulls out an old pouch, and gives me one hundred and sixty Portugal moidores in gold; and giving the writings of his title to the ship, which his son was gone to the Brazils in, of which he was quarter-part owner, and his son another, he puts them both into my hands for security of the rest.

I had now to consider which way to steer my course next, and what to do with the estate that Providence had thus put into my hands; and, indeed, I had more care upon my head now than I had in my state of life in the island where I wanted nothing but what I had, and had nothing but what I wanted; whereas I had now a great charge upon me, and my business was how to secure it. I had not a cave now to hide my money in, or a place where it might lie without lock or key, till it grew mouldy and tarnished before anybody would meddle with it; on the contrary, I knew not where to put it, or whom to trust with it. My old patron, the captain, indeed, was honest, and that was the only refuge I had. In the next place, my interest in the Brazils seemed to summon me thither; but now I could not tell how to think of going thither till I had settled my affairs, and left my effects in some safe hands behind me. At first I thought of my old friend the widow, who I knew was honest, and would be just to me; but then she was in years, and but poor, and, for aught I knew, might be in debt: so that, in a word, I had no way but to go back to England myself and take my effects with me.

I HAD NOW TO CONSIDER WHICH WAY TO STEER MY COURSE NEXT.

In this manner I set out from Lisbon; and our company being very well mounted and armed, we made a little troop, whereof they did me the honour to call me captain, as well because I was the oldest man, as because I had two servants, and, indeed, was the origin of the whole journey.

As I have troubled you with none of my sea journals, so I shall trouble you now with none of my land journals; but some adventures that happened to us in this tedious and difficult journey I must not omit.

The night was coming on, and the light began to be dusky, which made it worse on our side; but the noise increasing, we could easily perceive that it was the howling and yelling of those hellish creatures; and on a sudden we perceived three troops of wolves, one on our left, one behind us, and one in our front, so that we seemed to be surrounded with them: however, as they did not fall upon us, we kept our way forward, as fast as we could make our horses go, which, the way being very rough, was only a good hard trot. In this manner, we came in view of the entrance of a wood, through which we were to pass, at the farther side of the plain; but we were greatly surprised, when coming nearer

And this fury of theirs, it seems, was principally occasioned by their seeing our horses behind us.

the lane or pass, we saw a confused number of wolves standing just at the entrance. On a sudden, at another opening of the wood, we heard the noise of a gun, and looking that way, out rushed a horse, with a saddle and a bridle on him, flying like the wind, and sixteen or seventeen wolves after him, full speed: the horse had the advantage of them; but as we supposed that he could not hold it at that rate, we doubted not but they would get up with him at last: no question but they did.

But here we had a most horrible sight; for riding up to the entrance where the horse came out, we found the carcasses of another horse and of two men, devoured by the ravenous creatures; and one of the men was no doubt the same whom we heard fire the gun, for there lay a gun just by him fired off; but as to the man, his head and the upper part of his body was eaten up. This filled us with horror, and we knew not what course to take; but the creatures resolved us soon, for they gathered about us presently, in hopes of prey; and I verily believe there were three hundred of them. It happened, very much to our advantage, that at the entrance into the wood, but a little way from it, there lay some large timber-trees, which had been cut down the summer before, and I suppose lay there for carriage. I drew my little troop in among those trees, and placing ourselves in a line behind one long tree, I advised them all to alight, and keeping that tree before us for a breastwork, to stand in a triangle, or three fronts, enclosing our horses in the centre. We did so, and it was well we did; for never was a more furious charge than the creatures made upon us in this place. They came on with a growling kind of noise, and mounted the piece of timber, which, as I said, was our breastwork, as if they were only rushing upon their prey; and this fury of theirs, it seems, was principally occasioned by their seeing our horses behind us. I ordered our men to fire as before, every other man; and they took their aim so sure that they killed several of the wolves at the first volley; but there was a necessity to keep a continual firing, for they came on like devils, those behind pushing on those before.

When we had fired a second volley of our fusees, we thought they stopped a little, and I hoped they would have gone off, but it was but a moment, for others came forward again; so we fired two volleys of our pistols; and I believe in these four firings we had killed seventeen or eighteen of them, and lamed twice as many, yet they came on again. I was loth to spend our shot too hastily; so I called my servant, not my man Friday, for he was better employed, for, with the greatest dexterity imaginable, he had charged my fusee and his own while we were engaged – but, as I said, I called my other man, and giving him a horn of powder, I had him lay a train all along the piece of timber, and let it be a large train. He did so, and had but just time to get away, when the wolves came up to it, and some got upon it, when I, snapping an unchanged pistol close to the powder, set it on fire; those that were upon the timber were scorched with it, and six or seven of them fell; or rather jumped in among us with the force and fright of the fire; we despatched these in an instant, and the rest were so frightened with the light, which the night – for it was now very near dark – made more terrible that they drew back a little; upon which I ordered our last pistols to be fired off in one volley, and after that we gave a shout; upon this the wolves turned tail, and we sallied immediately upon near twenty lame ones that we found struggling on the ground, and fell to cutting them with our swords, which answered our expectation, for the crying and howling they made was better understood by their fellows; so that they all fled and left us.

The field of battle being thus cleared, , we made forward again, for we had still near a league to go. I have nothing uncommon to take notice of in my passage through France – nothing but what other travellers have given an account of with much more advantage than I can. I travelled from Toulouse to Paris, and without any considerable stay came to Calais, and landed safe at Dover the 14th of January, after having had a severe cold season to travel in. I was now come to the centre of my travels, and had in a little time all my new-discovered estate safe about me, the bills of exchange which I brought with me having been currently paid. My principal guide and privy-counsellor was my good ancient widow, who, in gratitude for the money I had sent her, thought no pains too much nor care too great to employ for me; and I trusted her so entirely that I was perfectly easy as to the security of my effects; and, indeed, I was very happy from the beginning, and now to the end, in the unspotted integrity of this good gentlewoman.

I COULD NOT KEEP THAT COUNTRY OUT OF MY HEAD, AND HAD A GREAT MIND TO BE UPON THE WING AGAIN.

And now, having resolved to dispose of my plantation in the Brazils, I wrote to my old friend at Lisbon, who, having offered it to the two merchants, the survivors of my trustees, who lived in the Brazils, they accepted the offer, and remitted thirty-three thousand pieces of eight to a correspondent of theirs at Lisbon to pay for it.

In return, I signed the instrument of sale in the form which they sent from Lisbon, and sent it to my old man, who sent me the bills of exchange for thirty-two thousand eight hundred pieces of eight for the estate, reserving the payment of one hundred moidores a year to him (the old man) during his life, and fifty moidores afterwards to his son for his life, which I had promised them, and which the plantation was to make good as a rent-charge. And thus I have given the first part of a life of fortune and adventure – a life of Providence's chequer-work, and of a variety which the world will seldom be able to show the like of; beginning foolishly, but closing much more happily than any part of it ever gave me leave so much as to hope for.

Any one would think that in this state of complicated good fortune I was past running any more hazards – and so, indeed, I had been, if other circumstances had concurred; but I was inured to a wandering life, had no family, nor many relations; nor, however rich, had I contracted fresh acquaintance; and though I had sold my estate in the Brazils, yet I could not keep that country out of my head, and had a great mind to be upon the wing again; especially I could not resist the strong inclination I had to see my island, and to know if the poor Spaniards were in being there. My true friend, the widow, earnestly dissuaded me from it, and so far prevailed with me, that for almost seven years she prevented my running abroad, during which time I took my two nephews, the children of one of my brothers, into my care; the eldest, having something of his own, I bred up as a gentleman, and gave him a settlement of some addition to his estate after my decease. The other I placed with the captain of a ship; and after five years, finding him a sensible, bold, enterprising young fellow,

I put him into a good ship, and sent him to sea; and this young fellow afterwards drew me in, as old as I was, to further adventures myself.

In the meantime, I in part settled myself here; for, first of all, I married, and that not either to my disadvantage or dissatisfaction, and had three children, two sons and one daughter; but my wife dying, and my nephew coming home with good success from a voyage to Spain, my inclination to go abroad, and his importunity, prevailed, and engaged me to go in his ship as a private trader to the East Indies; this was in the year 1694.

In this voyage I visited my new colony in the island, saw my successors the Spaniards, had the old story of their lives and of the villains I left there; how at first they insulted the poor Spaniards, how they afterwards agreed, disagreed, united, separated, and how at last the Spaniards were obliged to use violence with them; how they were subjected to the Spaniards, how honestly the Spaniards used them – a history, if it were entered into, as full of variety and wonderful accidents as my own part – particularly, also, as to their battles with the Caribbeans, who landed several times upon the island, and as to the improvement they made upon the island itself, and how five of them made an attempt upon the mainland, and brought away eleven men and five women prisoners, by which, at my coming, I found about twenty young children on the island.

Here I stayed about twenty days, left them supplies of all necessary things, and particularly of arms, powder, shot, clothes, tools, and two workmen, which I had brought from England with me, viz. a carpenter and a smith.

Besides this, I shared the lands into parts with them, reserved to myself the property of the whole, but gave them such parts respectively as they agreed on; and having settled all things with them, and engaged them not to leave the place, I left them there.

THE MYSTERIOUS ISLAND

Jules Verne, 1875
Illustrations by Newell Convers Wyeth, Zdeněk Burian, and Jules Férat

Originally published as serialized fiction in French and American magazines in the 1870s and issued immediately afterward as a novel in both countries, Jules Verne's arresting *L'Île mystérieuse* (*The Mysterious Island*) is foremost a male castaway story set in 1865–69, long after the Golden Age of Piracy. It relates the adventures of four persons from northern states of the United States, where slavery had been long ended, and an ex-slave trapped in the besieged Confederate capital of Richmond, Virginia near the end of the American Civil War. Desperate to flee Richmond, they steal a Confederate gas balloon and fly away with a dog in the midst of a vicious hurricane, only to be blown days later on to a seemingly uninhabited island in the Pacific Ocean. They get along famously there, and manage to establish a sustainable society with domesticated animals, crops, a flour mill, and even a telegraph line; they also cope resourcefully with a succession of dangers and mishaps, culminating in the destruction of their island by natural forces and their survival, after which they return to a post-Civil War America. The tale is also a sequel to Verne's famous science-fiction novel *Twenty Thousand Leagues Under the Seas*, and was obviously intended to attract readers of that tale about Captain Nemo and his submarine *Nautilus*. The captain and his vessel are lurking just off-shore in an undersea cavern all the time the balloonists are stranded on their island, and Nemo is secretly and repeatedly intervening to help them escape tight situations. Sub-titles of different early editions of *The Mysterious Island* published in English referred to it being, in one version, "The Modern Robinson Crusoe", and in another, a sequel to *Twenty Thousand Leagues*. Pirates wait until well into the narrative to make their appearance: They fly a generic "black flag" aboard their brig, *The Speedy*, and little is learned about their earlier lives or shipboard customs, other than their drinking and singing. Verne's pirates are mercilessly murderous ex-convicts from Australia, led by a man called Bob Harvey who is bent on depriving the five heroic "settlers" of their domain.

DESCENT

"Are we rising again?" – "No. On the contrary." –
"Are we descending?" – "Worse than that, captain! We are falling!" –
"For Heaven's sake heave out the ballast!" – "There! The last sack is empty!" –
"Does the balloon rise?" – "No!" – "I hear a noise like the dashing of waves.
The sea is below the car! It cannot be more than 500 feet from us!" –
"Overboard with every weight! ... everything!"

DESCENT

Such were the loud and startling words which resounded through the air, above the vast watery desert of the Pacific, about four o'clock in the evening of the 23rd of March, 1865.

Few can possibly have forgotten the terrible storm from the northeast, in the middle of the equinox of that year. The tempest raged without intermission from the 18th to the 26th of March. Its ravages were terrible in America, Europe, and Asia, covering a distance of eighteen hundred miles, and extending obliquely to the equator from the thirty-fifth north parallel to the fortieth south parallel. Towns were overthrown, forests uprooted, coasts devastated by the mountains of water which were precipitated on them, vessels cast on the shore, which the published accounts numbered by hundreds, whole districts levelled by waterspouts which destroyed everything they passed over, several thousand people crushed on land or drowned at sea; such were the traces of its fury, left by this devastating tempest. It surpassed in disasters those which so frightfully ravaged Havana and Guadalupe, one on the 25th of October, 1810, the other on the 26th of July, 1825.

But while so many catastrophes were taking place on land and at sea, a drama not less exciting was being enacted in the agitated air.

In fact, a balloon, as a ball might be carried on the summit of a waterspout, had been taken into the circling movement of a column of air and had traversed space at the rate of ninety miles an hour, turning round and round as if seized by some aerial maelstrom.

Beneath the lower point of the balloon swung a car, containing five passengers, scarcely visible in the midst of the thick vapour mingled with spray which hung over the surface of the ocean.

Whence, it may be asked, had come that plaything of the tempest? From what part of the world did it rise? It surely could not have started during the storm. But the storm had raged five days already, and the first symptoms were manifested on the 18th. It cannot be doubted that the balloon came from a great distance, for it could not have travelled less than two thousand miles in twenty-four hours.

At any rate the passengers, destitute of all marks for their guidance, could not have possessed the means of reckoning the route traversed since their departure. It was a remarkable fact that, although in the very midst of the furious tempest, they did not suffer from it. They were thrown about and whirled round and round without feeling the rotation in the slightest degree, or being sensible that they were removed from a horizontal position.

Their eyes could not pierce through the thick mist which had gathered beneath the car. Dark vapour was all around them. Such was the density of the atmosphere that they could not be certain whether it was day or night. No reflection of light, no sound from inhabited land, no roaring of the ocean could have reached them, through the obscurity, while suspended in those elevated zones. Their rapid descent alone had informed them of the dangers which they ran from the waves. However, the balloon, lightened of heavy articles, such as ammunition, arms, and provisions, had risen into the higher layers of the atmosphere, to a height of 4,500 feet. The voyagers, after having discovered that the sea extended beneath them, and thinking the dangers above less dreadful than those below, did not hesitate to throw overboard even their most useful articles, while they endeavoured to lose no more of that fluid, the life of their enterprise, which sustained them above the abyss.

The night passed in the midst of alarms which would have been death to less energetic souls. Again the day appeared and with it the tempest began to

Half plunged into the sea, they were beaten by the furious waves.

moderate. From the beginning of that day, the 24th of March, it showed symptoms of abating. At dawn, some of the lighter clouds had risen into the more lofty regions of the air. In a few hours the wind had changed from a hurricane to a fresh breeze, that is to say, the rate of the transit of the atmospheric layers was diminished by half. It was still what sailors call "a close-reefed topsail breeze," but the commotion in the elements had none the less considerably diminished.

Towards eleven o'clock, the lower region of the air was sensibly clearer. The atmosphere threw off that chilly dampness which is felt after the passage of a great meteor. The storm did not seem to have gone farther to the west. It appeared to have exhausted itself. Could it have passed away in electric sheets, as is sometimes the case with regard to the typhoons of the Indian Ocean?

But at the same time, it was also evident that the balloon was again slowly descending with a regular movement. It appeared as if it were, little by little, collapsing, and that its case was lengthening and extending, passing from a spherical to an oval form. Towards midday the balloon was hovering above the sea at a height of only 2,000 feet. It contained 50,000 cubic feet of gas, and, thanks to its capacity, it could maintain itself a long time in the air, although it should reach a great altitude or might be thrown into a horizontal position.

Perceiving their danger, the passengers cast away the last articles which still weighed down the car, the few provisions they had kept, everything, even to their pocket-knives, and one of them, having hoisted himself on to the circles which united the cords of the net, tried to secure more firmly the lower point of the balloon.

It was, however, evident to the voyagers that the gas was failing, and that the balloon could no longer be sustained in the higher regions. They must infallibly perish!

There was not a continent, nor even an island, visible beneath them. The watery expanse did not present a single speck of land, not a solid surface upon which their anchor could hold.

It was the open sea, whose waves were still dashing with tremendous violence! It was the ocean, without any visible limits, even for those whose gaze, from their commanding position, extended over a radius of forty miles. The vast liquid plain, lashed without mercy by the storm, appeared as if covered with herds of furious chargers, whose white and dishevelled crests were streaming in the wind. No land was in sight, not a solitary ship could be seen. It was necessary at any cost to arrest their downward course, and to prevent the balloon from being engulfed in the waves. The voyagers directed all their energies to this urgent work. But, notwithstanding their efforts, the balloon still fell, and at the same time shifted with the greatest rapidity, following the direction of the wind, that is to say, from the northeast to the southwest.

NO HUMAN EFFORTS COULD SAVE THEM NOW.

Frightful indeed was the situation of these unfortunate men. They were evidently no longer masters of the machine. All their attempts were useless. The case of the balloon collapsed more and more. The gas escaped without any possibility of retaining it. Their descent was visibly accelerated, and soon after midday the car hung within 600 feet of the ocean.

It was impossible to prevent the escape of gas, which rushed through a large rent in the silk. By lightening the car of all the articles which it contained, the passengers had been able to prolong their suspension in the air for a few hours. But the inevitable catastrophe could only be retarded, and if land did not appear before night, voyagers, car, and balloon must to a certainty vanish beneath the waves.

They now resorted to the only remaining expedient. They were truly dauntless men, who knew how to look death in the face. Not a single murmur escaped from their lips. They were determined to struggle to the last minute, to do anything to retard their fall. The car was only a sort of willow basket, unable to float, and there was not the slightest possibility of maintaining it on the surface of the sea.

Two more hours passed and the balloon was scarcely 400 feet above the water.

At that moment a loud voice, the voice of a man whose heart was inaccessible to fear, was heard. To this voice responded others not less determined. "Is everything thrown out?" – "No, here are still 2,000 dollars in gold." A heavy bag immediately plunged into the sea. "Does the balloon rise?" – "A little, but it will not be long before it falls again." – "What still remains to be thrown out?" – "Nothing." – "Yes! The car!" – "Let us catch hold of the net, and into the sea with the car."

This was, in fact, the last and only mode of lightening the balloon. The ropes which held the car were cut, and the balloon, after its fall, mounted 2,000 feet. The five voyagers had hoisted themselves into the net, and clung to the meshes, gazing at the abyss.

The delicate sensibility of balloons is well known. It is sufficient to throw out the lightest article to produce a difference in its vertical position. The apparatus in the air is like a balance of mathematical precision. It can be thus easily understood that when it is lightened of any considerable weight its movement will be impetuous and sudden. So it happened on this occasion. But after being suspended for an instant aloft, the balloon began to redescend, the gas escaping by the rent which it was impossible to repair.

The men had done all that men could do. No human efforts could save them now. They must trust to the mercy of Him who rules the elements. At four o'clock the balloon was only 500 feet above the surface of the water. A loud barking was heard. A dog accompanied the voyagers, and was held pressed close to his master in the meshes of the net.

"Top has seen something," cried one of the men. Then immediately a loud voice shouted, "Land! Land!" The balloon, which the wind still drove towards the southwest, had since daybreak gone a considerable distance, which might be reckoned by hundreds of miles, and a tolerably high land had, in fact, appeared in that direction. But this land was still thirty miles off. It would not take less than an hour to get to it, and then there was the chance of falling to leeward.

An hour! Might not the balloon before that be emptied of all the fluid it yet retained? Such was the terrible question! The voyagers could distinctly see that solid spot which they must reach at any cost. They were ignorant of what it was, whether an island or a continent, for they did not know to what part of the world the hurricane had driven them. But they must reach this land, whether inhabited or desolate, whether hospitable or not.

It was evident that the balloon could no longer support itself! Several times already had the crests of the enormous billows licked the bottom of the net, making it still heavier, and the balloon only half rose, like a bird with a wounded wing. Half an hour later the land was not more than a mile off, but the balloon, exhausted, flabby, hanging in great folds, had gas in its upper part alone. The voyagers, clinging to the net, were still too heavy for it, and soon, half plunged into the sea, they were beaten by the furious waves. The balloon-case bulged out again, and the wind, taking it, drove it along like a vessel. Might it not possibly thus reach the land?

But, when only two fathoms off, terrible cries resounded from four pairs of lungs at once. The balloon, which had appeared as if it would never again rise, suddenly made an unexpected bound, after having been struck by a tremendous sea. As if it had been at that instant relieved of a new part of its weight, it mounted to a height of 1,500 feet, and here it met a current of wind, which instead of taking it directly to the coast, carried it in a nearly parallel direction.

At last, two minutes later, it reproached obliquely, and finally fell on a sandy beach, out of the reach of the waves. The voyagers, aiding each other, managed to disengage themselves from the meshes of the net. The balloon, relieved of their weight, was taken by the wind, and like a wounded bird which revives for an instant, disappeared into space.

But the car had contained five passengers, with a dog, and the balloon only left four on the shore.

The missing person had evidently been swept off by the sea, which had just struck the net, and it was owing to this circumstance that the lightened balloon rose the last time, and then soon after reached the land. Scarcely had the four castaways set foot on firm ground, than they all, thinking of the absent one, simultaneously exclaimed, "Perhaps he will try to swim to land! Let us save him! Let us save him!"

A tolerably high land had, in fact, appeared in that direction.

THE ESCAPE

Those whom the hurricane had just thrown on this coast were neither aeronauts by profession nor amateurs. They were prisoners of war whose boldness had induced them to escape in this extraordinary manner. A hundred times they had almost perished! A hundred times had they almost fallen from their torn balloon into the depths of the ocean. But Heaven had reserved them for a strange destiny, and after having, on the 20th of March, escaped from Richmond, besieged by the troops of General Ulysses Grant, they found themselves seven thousand miles from the capital of Virginia, which was the principal stronghold of the South, during the terrible War of Secession. Their aerial voyage had lasted five days.

THE ESCAPE

The curious circumstances which led to the escape of the prisoners were as follows:

That same year, in the month of February, 1865, in one of the coups de main by which General Grant attempted, though in vain, to possess himself of Richmond, several of his officers fell into the power of the enemy and were detained in the town. One of the most distinguished was Captain Cyrus Harding. He was a native of Massachusetts, a first-class engineer, to whom the government had confided, during the war, the direction of the railways, which were so important at that time. A true Northerner, thin, bony, lean, about forty-five years of age; his close-cut hair and his beard, of which he only kept a thick moustache, were already getting grey. He had one of those finely-developed heads which appear made to be struck on a medal, piercing eyes, a serious mouth, the physiognomy of a clever man of the military school. He was one of those engineers who began by handling the hammer and pickaxe, like generals who first act as common soldiers. A man of action as well as a man of thought, all he did was without effort to one of his vigorous and sanguine temperament. Learned, clear-headed, and practical, he fulfilled in all emergencies those three conditions which united ought to insure human success – activity of mind and body, impetuous wishes, and powerful will. Cyrus Harding was courage personified. He had been in all the battles of that war. After having begun as a volunteer at Illinois, under Ulysses Grant, he fought everywhere and valiantly, a soldier worthy of the general who said, "I never count my dead!" And hundreds of times Captain Harding had almost been among those who were not counted by the terrible Grant; but in these combats where he never spared himself, fortune favoured him till the moment when he was wounded and taken prisoner on the field of battle near Richmond. At the same time and on the same day another important personage fell into the hands of the Southerners. This was no other than Gideon Spilett, a reporter for the *New York Herald*, who had been ordered to follow the changes of the war in the midst of the Northern armies.

HE WAS ONE OF THOSE INTREPID OBSERVERS WHO WRITE UNDER FIRE, "REPORTING" AMONG BULLETS.

Gideon Spilett was one of that race of indomitable English or American chroniclers, like Stanley and others, who stop at nothing to obtain exact information, and transmit it to their journal in the shortest possible time. The newspapers of the Union, such as the *New York Herald*, are genuine powers, and their reporters are men to be reckoned with. Gideon Spilett ranked among the first of those reporters: a man of great merit, energetic, prompt and ready for anything, full of ideas, having travelled over the whole world, soldier and artist, enthusiastic in council, resolute in action, caring neither for trouble, fatigue, nor danger, when in pursuit of information, for himself first, and then for his journal, a perfect treasury of knowledge on all sorts of curious subjects, of the unpublished, of the unknown, and of the impossible. He was one of those intrepid observers who write under fire, "reporting" among bullets, and to whom every danger is welcome.

He also had been in all the battles, in the first rank, revolver in one hand, note-book in the other; grape-shot never made his pencil tremble. He did not fatigue the wires with incessant telegrams, like those who speak when they have nothing to say, but each of his notes, short, decisive, and clear, threw light on some important point.

The two Americans had from the first determined to seize every chance; but although they were allowed to wander at liberty in the town, Richmond was so strictly guarded, that escape appeared impossible. In the meanwhile Captain Harding was rejoined by a servant who was devoted to him in life and in death. This intrepid fellow was a Negro born on the engineer's estate, of a slave father and mother, but to whom Cyrus, who was an Abolitionist from conviction and heart, had long since given his freedom. The once slave, though free, would not leave his master. He would have died for him. He was a man of about thirty, vigorous, active, clever, intelligent, gentle, and calm, sometimes naive, always merry, obliging, and honest. His name was Nebuchadnezzar, but he only answered to the familiar abbreviation of Neb.

When Neb heard that his master had been made prisoner, he left Massachusetts without hesitating an instant, arrived before Richmond, and by dint of stratagem and shrewdness, after having risked his life twenty times over, managed to penetrate into the besieged town. The pleasure of Harding on seeing his servant, and the joy of Neb at finding his master, can scarcely be described. But though Neb had been able to make his way into Richmond, it was quite another thing to get out again, for the Northern prisoners were very strictly watched. Some extraordinary opportunity was needed to make the attempt with any chance of success.

The reporter, to whom his tedious captivity did not offer a single incident worthy of note, could stand it no longer. His usually active mind was occupied with one sole thought – how he might get out of Richmond at any cost. Several times had he even made the attempt, but was stopped by some insurmountable obstacle. However, the siege continued; and if the prisoners were anxious to escape and join Grant's army, certain of the besieged were no less anxious to join the Southern forces. Among them was one Jonathan Forster, a determined Southerner. The truth was, that if the prisoners of the Secessionists could not leave the town, neither could the Secessionists themselves while the Northern army invested it. Thus Jonathan Forster accordingly conceived the idea of rising in a balloon, so as to pass over the besieging lines, and in that way reach the Secessionist camp.

The Governor authorized the attempt. A balloon was manufactured and placed at the disposal of Forster, who was to be accompanied by five other persons. They were furnished with arms in case they might have to defend themselves when they alighted, and provisions in the event of their aerial voyage being prolonged.

The balloon, inflated on the great square of Richmond, was ready to depart on the first abatement of the wind, and, as may be supposed, the impatience among the besieged to see the storm moderate was very great. On that day the engineer, Cyrus Harding, was accosted in one of the streets of Richmond by a person whom he did not in the least know. This was a sailor named Pencroft, a man of about thirty-five or forty years of age, strongly built, very sunburnt, and possessed of a pair of bright sparkling eyes and a remarkably good physiognomy. Pencroft was an Ame-rican from the North, who had sailed all the ocean over. It is needless to say that he was a bold, dashing fellow, ready to dare anything and was astonished at nothing. Pencroft at the beginning of the year had gone to Richmond on business, with a

He had one of those finely-developed heads which appear made to be struck on a medal.

young boy of fifteen from New Jersey, son of a former captain, an orphan, whom he loved as if he had been his own child. Not having been able to leave the town before the first operations of the siege, he found himself shut up, to his great disgust; but, not accustomed to succumb to difficulties, he resolved to escape by some means or other. He knew the engineer-officer by reputation; he knew with what impatience that determined man chafed under his restraint. On this day he did not, therefore, hesitate to accost him, saying, without circumlocution, "Have you had enough of Richmond, captain?"

The engineer looked fixedly at the man who spoke, and who added, in a low voice, "Captain Harding, will you try to escape?"

"When?" asked the engineer quickly, and it was evident that this question was uttered without consideration, for he had not yet examined the stranger who addressed him. But after having with a penetrating eye observed the open face of the sailor, he was convinced that he had before him an honest man.

"Who are you?" he asked briefly. Pencroft made himself known.

"Well," replied Harding, "and in what way do you propose to escape?"

"By that lazy balloon which is left there doing nothing, and which looks to me as if it was waiting on purpose for us – "

There was no necessity for the sailor to finish his sentence. The engineer understood him at once.

The sailor developed his project, which was indeed extremely simple. The plan was feasible, though, it must be confessed, dangerous in the extreme. In the night, in spite of their guards, they might approach the balloon, slip into the car, and then cut the cords which held it.

It would be a terrible journey. The engineer only feared one thing; it was that the balloon, held to the ground and dashed about by the wind, would be torn into shreds. For several hours he roamed round the nearly-deserted square, surveying the apparatus. Pencroft did the same on his side, his hands in his pockets, yawning now and then like a man who did not know how to kill the time, but really dreading, like his friend, either the escape or destruction of the balloon. Evening arrived. The night was dark in the extreme. Thick mists passed like clouds close to the ground. Rain fell mingled with snow, it was very cold. A mist hung over Richmond. It seemed as if the violent storm had produced a truce between the besiegers and the besieged, and that the cannon were

What was their disappointment, when, after trudging nearly two miles, having reached an elevated point composed of slippery rocks, they found themselves again stopped by sea.

silenced by the louder detonations of the storm. The streets of the town were deserted. It had not even appeared necessary in that horrible weather to place a guard in the square, in the midst of which plunged the balloon. Everything favoured the departure of the prisoners.

WHEN DAY BROKE, EVEN A GLIMPSE OF THE EARTH BELOW WAS INTERCEPTED BY FOG.

At half-past nine, Harding and his companions glided from different directions into the square. The five prisoners met by the car. Without speaking a word, Harding, Spilett, Neb, and Herbert took their places, while Pencroft by the engineer's order detached successively the bags of ballast. It was the work of a few minutes only, and the sailor rejoined his companions. The balloon was then only held by the cable, and the engineer had nothing to do but to give the word.

At that moment a dog sprang with a bound into the car. It was Top, a favourite of the engineer. The faithful creature, having broken his chain, had followed his master. He, however, fearing that its additional weight might impede their ascent, wished to send away the animal.

"One more will make but little difference, poor beast!" exclaimed Pencroft, heaving out two bags of sand, and as he spoke letting go the cable; the balloon ascending in an oblique direction.

Then, indeed, the full rage of the hurricane was exhibited to the voyagers. During the night the engineer could not dream of descending, and when day broke, even a glimpse of the earth below was intercepted by fog. Five days had passed when a partial clearing allowed them to see the wide extending ocean beneath their feet, now lashed into the maddest fury by the gale. Our readers will recollect what befell these five daring individuals who set out on their hazardous expedition in the balloon on the 20th of March. Five days afterwards four of them were thrown on a desert coast, seven thousand miles from their country! But one of their number was missing, the man who was to be their guide, their leading spirit, the engineer, Captain Harding! The instant they had recovered their feet, they all hurried to the beach in the hopes of rendering him assistance.

The engineer, the meshes of the net having given way, had been carried off by a wave. His dog also had disappeared. The faithful animal had voluntarily leaped out to help his master. "Forward," cried the reporter; and all four, Spilett, Herbert, Pencroft, and Neb, forgetting their fatigue, began their search. Poor Neb shed bitter tears, giving way to despair at the thought of having lost the only being he loved on earth. Only two minutes had passed from the time when Cyrus Harding disappeared to the moment when his companions set foot on the ground. They had hopes therefore of arriving in time to save him.

After walking for twenty minutes, the four castaways were suddenly brought to a standstill by the sight of foaming billows close to their feet. The solid ground ended here. They found themselves at the

After walking for twenty minutes, the four castaways were suddenly brought to a standstill by the sight of foaming billows close to their feet.

extremity of a sharp point on which the sea broke furiously.

"It is a promontory," said the sailor; "we must retrace our steps, holding towards the right, and we shall thus gain the mainland."

"But if he is there," said Neb, pointing to the ocean, whose waves shone of a snowy white in the darkness. "Well, let us call again," and all uniting their voices, they gave a vigorous shout, but there came no reply. They waited for a lull, then began again; still no reply. The castaways accordingly returned, following the opposite side of the promontory, over a soil equally sandy and rugged. However, Pencroft observed that the shore was more equal, that the ground rose, and he declared that it was joined by a long slope to a hill, whose massive front he thought that he could see looming indistinctly through the mist. The birds were less numerous on this part of the shore; the sea was also less tumultuous, the noise of the surf was scarcely heard. This side of the promontory evidently formed a semicircular bay, which the sharp point sheltered from the breakers of the open sea. After a walk of a mile and a half, the shore presented no curve which would permit them to return to the north. This promontory, of which they had turned the point, must be attached to the mainland. The castaways, although their strength was nearly exhausted, still marched courageously forward, hoping every moment to meet with a sudden angle which would set them in the first direction. What was their disappointment, when, after trudging nearly two miles, having reached an elevated point composed of slippery rocks, they found themselves again stopped by the sea.

"We are on an islet," said Pencroft, "and we have surveyed it from one extremity to the other." The sailor was right; they had been thrown, not on a continent, not even on an island, but on an islet which was not more than two miles in length, with even a less breadth.

Was this barren spot the desolate refuge of sea-birds, strewn with stones and destitute of vegetation, attached to a more important archipelago? It was impossible to say. When the voyagers from their car saw the land through the mist, they had not been able to reconnoitre it sufficiently. However, Pencroft, accustomed with his sailor eyes to pierce through the gloom, was almost certain that he could clearly distinguish in the west confused masses which indicated an elevated coast. But they could not in the dark determine whether it was a single island, or connected with others. They could not leave it either, as the sea surrounded them; they must therefore put off till the next day their search for the engineer, from whom, alas! Not a single cry had reached them to show that he was still in existence.

"The silence of our friend proves nothing," said the reporter. "Perhaps he has fainted or is wounded, and unable to reply directly, so we will not despair."

The night passed away. Towards five o'clock in the morning of the 25th of March, the sky began to lighten; the horizon still remained dark, but with daybreak a thick mist rose from the sea, so that the eye could scarcely penetrate beyond twenty feet or so from where they stood. At length the fog gradually unrolled itself in great heavily moving waves.

While the gaze of the reporter and Neb were cast upon the ocean, the sailor and Herbert looked eagerly for the coast in the west. But not a speck of land was visible. About half-past six, three-quarters of an hour after sunrise, the mist became more transparent. It grew thicker above, but cleared away below. Soon the isle appeared as if it had descended from a cloud, then the sea showed itself around them, spreading far away towards the east, but bounded on the west by an abrupt and precipitous coast.

Yes! The land was there. Their safety was at least provisionally insured. The islet and the coast were separated by a channel about half a mile in breadth, through which rushed an extremely rapid current.

Opposite the islet, the beach consisted first of sand, covered with black stones, which were now appearing little by little above the retreating tide. The second level was separated by a perpendicular granite cliff. On the upper plateau of the coast not a tree appeared, however, verdure was not wanting to the right beyond the precipice. They could easily distinguish a confused mass of great trees, which extended beyond the limits of their view. This verdure relieved the eye, so long wearied by the continued ranges of granite. Lastly, beyond and above the plateau, in a northwesterly direction and at a distance of at least seven miles, glittered a white summit which reflected the sun's rays. It was that of a lofty mountain, capped with snow. On beholding the convulsed masses heaped up on the left, no geologist would have hesitated to give them a volcanic origin, for they were unquestionably the work of subterranean convulsions.

Gideon Spilett, Pencroft, and Herbert attentively examined this land.

"Well," asked Herbert, "what do you say, Pencroft?"

"There is some good and some bad, as in everything," replied the sailor. "We shall see. But now the ebb is evidently making. In three hours we will attempt the passage, and once on the other side, we will try to get out of this scrape, and I hope may find the captain." Pencroft was not wrong in his anticipations. Three hours later at low tide, the greater part of the sand forming the bed of the channel was uncovered. Between the islet and the coast there only remained a narrow channel which would no doubt be easy to cross.

About ten o'clock, Gideon Spilett and his companions stripped themselves of their clothes and ventured into the water, which was not more than five feet deep. All three arrived without difficulty on the opposite shore. Quickly drying themselves in the sun, they put on their clothes, which they had preserved from contact with the water, and sat down to take counsel together what to do next. All at once the reporter sprang up, and telling the sailor that he would rejoin them at that same place, he climbed the cliff in the direction which the Negro Neb had taken a few hours before. Herbert wished to accompany him.

Two hundred paces farther they arrived at the cutting, through which, as Pencroft had guessed, ran a stream of water. At this place the wall appeared to have been separated by some violent subterranean force. At its base was hollowed out a little creek, the farthest part of which formed a tolerably sharp angle. The watercourse at that part measured one hundred feet in breadth, and its two banks on each side were scarcely twenty feet high. The river became strong almost directly between the two walls of granite; it then suddenly turned and disappeared beneath a wood of stunted trees half a mile off.

"Here is the water, and yonder is the wood we require!" said Pencroft. "Well, Herbert, now we only want the house."

The water of the river was limpid. The sailor ascertained that at this time – that is to say, at low tide, when the rising floods did not reach it – it was sweet. This important point established, Herbert looked for some cavity which would serve them as a retreat, but in vain; everywhere the wall appeared smooth, plain, and perpendicular. However, at the mouth of the watercourse and above the reach of the high tide, the convulsions of nature had formed, not a grotto, but a pile of enormous rocks, such as are often met with in granite countries and which bear the name of "Chimneys."

THE SEARCH

Gideon Spilett was standing motionless on the shore, his arms crossed, gazing over the sea, the horizon of which was lost towards the east in a thick black cloud which was spreading rapidly towards the zenith. The wind was already strong, and increased with the decline of day. The whole sky was of a threatening aspect, and the first symptoms of a violent storm were clearly visible.

hat astonishes me," rejoined the reporter, "while admitting that our companion has perished, is that Top has also met his death, and that neither the body of the dog nor of his master has been cast on the shore!"

"It is not astonishing, with such a heavy sea," replied the sailor. "Besides, it is possible that currents have carried them farther down the coast."

"Then, it is your opinion that our friend has perished in the waves?" again asked the reporter.

"That is my opinion."

"My own opinion," said Gideon Spilett, "with due deference to your experience, Pencroft, is that in the double fact of the absolute disappearance of Cyrus and Top, living or dead, there is something unaccountable and unlikely."

Meanwhile the night advanced, and it was perhaps two hours from morning, when Pencroft, then sound asleep, was vigorously shaken.

"What's the matter?" he cried, rousing himself, and collecting his ideas with the promptitude usual to seamen.

"Listen, Pencroft, listen!" The sailor strained his ears, but could hear no noise beyond those caused by the storm.

"It is the wind," said he. "No," replied Gideon Spilett, listening again, "I thought I heard – "

"What?" – "The barking of a dog!" – "A dog!" cried Pencroft, springing up. "Yes – barking – "

"It's not possible!" replied the sailor. "And besides, how, in the roaring of the storm – "

"Stop – listen – " said the reporter.

Pencroft listened more attentively, and really thought he heard, during a lull, distant barking.

"Well!" said the reporter, pressing the sailor's hand.

"Yes – yes!" replied Pencroft.

"It is Top! It is Top!" cried Herbert, who had just awoke; and all three rushed towards the opening of the Chimneys. They had great difficulty in getting out. The wind drove them back. But at last they succeeded, and could only remain standing by leaning against the rocks. They looked about, but could not speak. The darkness was intense. The sea, the sky, the land were all mingled in one black mass. Not a speck of light was visible.

It was indeed Top, a magnificent Anglo-Norman, who derived from these two races crossed the swiftness of foot and the acuteness of smell which are the preeminent qualities of coursing dogs. It was the dog of the engineer, Cyrus Harding. But he was alone! Neither Neb nor his master accompanied him!

How was it that his instinct had guided him straight to the Chimneys, which he did not know? It appeared inexplicable, above all, in the midst of this black night and in such a tempest! But what was still more inexplicable was that Top was neither tired, nor exhausted, nor even soiled with mud or sand! Herbert had drawn him towards him, and was patting his head, the dog rubbing his neck against the lad's hands.

"If the dog is found, the master will be found also!" said the reporter.

"God grant it!" responded Herbert. "Let us set off! Top will guide us!"

Pencroft did not make any objection. He felt that Top's arrival contradicted his conjectures. "Come along then!" said he.

Pencroft carefully covered the embers on the hearth. He placed a few pieces of wood among them, so as to keep in the fire until their return. Then, preceded by the dog, who seemed to invite them by short barks to come with him, and followed by the reporter and

The body was that of the engineer, Cyrus Harding.

the boy, he dashed out, after having put up in his handkerchief the remains of the supper.

The storm was then in all its violence, and perhaps at its height. Not a single ray of light from the moon pierced through the clouds. To follow a straight course was difficult. It was best to rely on Top's instinct. They did so. The reporter and Herbert walked behind the dog, and the sailor brought up the rear. It was impossible to exchange a word. The rain was not very heavy, but the wind was terrific.

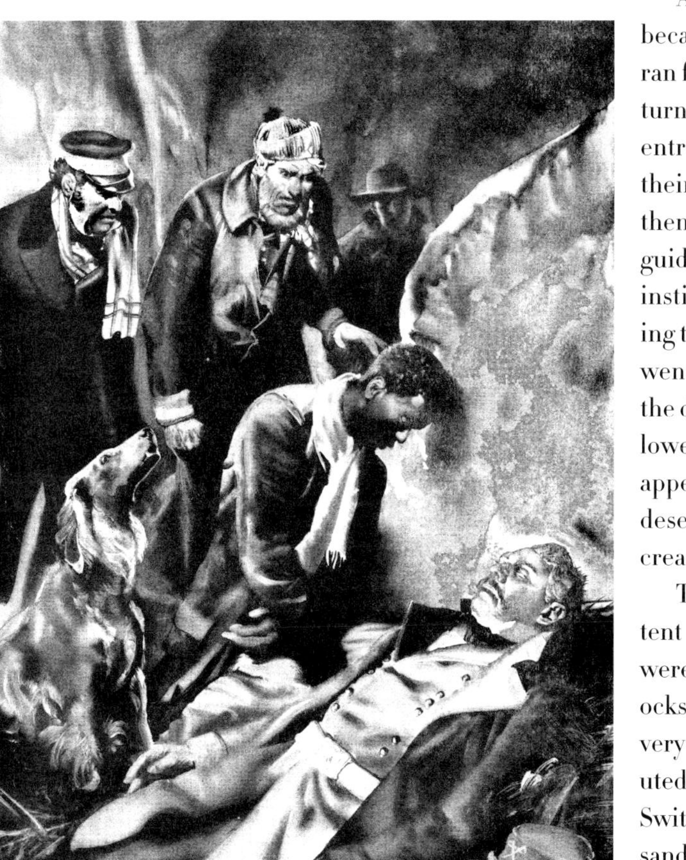

After having passed the precipice, Herbert, the reporter, and Pencroft prudently stepped aside to stop and take breath. The turn of the rocks sheltered them from the wind, and they could breathe after this walk or rather run of a quarter of an hour.

They could now hear and reply to each other, and the lad having pronounced the name of Cyrus Harding, Top gave a few short barks, as much as to say that his master was saved.

At six o'clock day had broken. The clouds rapidly lifted. The seaman and his companions were then about six miles from the Chimneys. They were following a very flat shore bounded by a reef of rocks, whose heads scarcely emerged from the sea, for they were in deep water.

At this moment, Top became very excited. He ran forward, then returned, and seemed to entreat them to hasten their steps. The dog then left the beach, and guided by his wonderful instinct, without showing the least hesitation, went straight in among the downs. They followed him. The country appeared an absolute desert. Not a living creature was to be seen.

The downs, the extent of which was large, were composed of hillocks and even of hills, very irregularly distributed. They resembled a Switzerland modelled in sand, and only an amazing instinct could have possibly recognized the way.

Five minutes after having left the beach, the reporter and his two companions arrived at a sort of excavation, hollowed out at the back of a high mound. There Top stopped, and gave a loud, clear bark. Spilett, Herbert, and Pencroft dashed

The litter was brought; the transverse branches had been crossed with leaves and long grass. Harding was laid on it, and they started towards the coast.

into the cave. Neb was there, kneeling beside a body extended on a bed of grass. The body was that of the engineer, Cyrus Harding.

Neb did not move. Pencroft only uttered one word.

"Living?" he cried.

Neb did not reply. Spilett and the sailor turned pale. Herbert clasped his hands, and remained motionless. The poor Negro, absorbed in his grief, evidently had neither seen his companions nor heard the sailor speak.

A MINUTE – AN AGE! – PASSED, DURING WHICH HE ENDEAVOURED TO CATCH THE FAINTEST THROB OF THE HEART.

The reporter knelt down beside the motionless body, and placed his ear to the engineer's chest, having first torn open his clothes. A minute – an age! – passed, during which he endeavoured to catch the faintest throb of the heart. Neb had raised himself a little and gazed without seeing. Despair had completely changed his countenance. He could scarcely be recognized, exhausted with fatigue, broken with grief. He believed his master was dead.

Gideon Spilett at last rose, after a long and attentive examination.

"He lives!" said he.

The reporter then told him all that had occurred. He recounted all the events with which Cyrus was unacquainted, as well as many other matters.

"But," asked Harding, in a still feeble voice, "you did not, then, pick me up on the beach?"

"No," replied the reporter. "And did you not bring me to this cave?" – "No." – "At what distance is this cave from the sea?" – "About a mile," replied Pencroft; "and if you are astonished, captain, we are not less surprised ourselves at seeing you in this place!"

"Indeed," said the engineer, who was recovering gradually, and who took great interest in these details, "indeed it is very singular!"

"But," resumed the sailor, "can you tell us what happened after you were carried off by the sea?"

Cyrus Harding considered. He knew very little. The wave had torn him from the balloon net. He sank at first several fathoms. On returning to the surface, in the half light, he felt a living creature struggling near him. It was Top, who had sprung to his help. He saw nothing of the balloon, which, lightened both of his weight and that of the dog, had darted away like an arrow.

There he was, in the midst of the angry sea, at a distance which could not be less than half a mile from the shore. He attempted to struggle against the billows by swimming vigorously. Top held him up by his clothes; but a strong current seized him and drove him towards the north, and after half an hour of exertion, he sank, dragging Top with him into the depths. From that moment to the moment in which he recovered to find himself in the arms of his friends he remembered nothing.

"However," remarked Pencroft, "you must have been thrown on to the beach, and you must have had strength to walk here, since Neb found your footmarks!"

"Yes... of course," replied the engineer, thoughtfully; "and you found no traces of human beings on this coast?"

"Not a trace," replied the reporter; "besides, if by chance you had met with some deliverer there, just in

the nick of time, why should he have abandoned you after having saved you from the waves?"

"You are right, my dear Spilett. Tell me, Neb," added the engineer, turning to his servant, "it was not you who... you can't have had a moment of unconsciousness... during which, no, that's absurd.... Do any of the footsteps still remain?" asked Harding.

"Yes, master," replied Neb; "here, at the entrance, at the back of the mound, in a place sheltered from the rain and wind. The storm has destroyed the others."

"Pencroft," said Cyrus Harding, "will you take my shoe and see if it fits exactly to the footprints?"

The sailor did as the engineer requested. While he and Herbert, guided by Neb, went to the place where the footprints were to be found, Cyrus remarked to the reporter,

"It is a most extraordinary thing!"

"Perfectly inexplicable!" replied Gideon Spilett.

"But do not dwell upon it just now, my dear Spilett, we will talk about it by-and-by."

A moment after the others entered.

There was no doubt about it. The engineer's shoe fitted exactly to the footmarks. It was therefore Cyrus Harding who had left them on the sand.

"Come," said he, "I must have experienced this unconsciousness which I attributed to Neb. I must have walked like a somnambulist, without any knowledge of my steps, and Top must have guided me here, after having dragged me from the waves... Come, Top! Come, old dog!"

The magnificent animal bounded barking to his master, and caresses were lavished on him. It was agreed that there was no other way of accounting for the rescue of Cyrus Harding, and that Top deserved all the honour of the affair.

Towards twelve o'clock, Pencroft having asked the engineer if they could now remove him, Harding, instead of replying, and by an effort which exhibited the most energetic will, got up. But he was obliged to lean on the sailor, or he would have fallen.

"Well done!" cried Pencroft; "bring the captain's litter." The litter was brought; the transverse branches had been covered with leaves and long grass. Harding was laid on it, and Pencroft, having taken his place at one end and Neb at the other, they started towards the coast. There was a distance of eight miles to be accomplished; but, as they could not go fast, and it would perhaps be necessary to stop frequently, they reckoned that it would take at least six hours to reach the Chimneys. The wind was still strong, but fortunately it did not rain. Although lying down, the engineer, leaning on his elbow, observed the coast, particularly inland. He did not speak, but he gazed; and, no doubt, the appearance of the country, with its inequalities of ground, its forests, its various productions, were impressed on his mind. However, after traveling for two hours, fatigue overcame him, and he slept.

At half-past five the little band arrived at the precipice, and a short time after at the Chimneys. They stopped, and the litter was placed on the sand; Cyrus Harding was sleeping profoundly, and did not awake.

Pencroft, to his extreme surprise, found that the terrible storm had quite altered the aspect of the place. The sea had penetrated to the end of the passages, and everything was overthrown and destroyed in the interior of the Chimneys!

Night had closed in, and the temperature, which had modified when the wind shifted to the northwest, again became extremely cold. Also, the sea having destroyed the partitions which Pencroft had put up in certain

places in the passages, the Chimneys, on account of the draughts, had become scarcely habitable. The engineer's condition would, therefore, have been bad enough, if his companions had not carefully covered him with their coats and waistcoats.

Next day, the 28th of March, when the engineer awoke, about eight in the morning, he saw his companions around him watching his sleep. Herbert, Neb, and Pencroft did the same, while Top slept at his master's feet. This time, the hunters, instead of following the course of the river, plunged straight into the heart of the forest. They had scarcely entered the bushes when they saw Top engaged in a struggle with an animal which he was holding by the ear. This quadruped was a sort of pig nearly two feet and a half long, of a blackish brown colour, lighter below, having hard scanty hair; its toes, then strongly fixed in the ground, seemed to be united by a membrane. Herbert recognized in this animal the capybara.

Meanwhile, the capybara did not struggle against the dog. It stupidly rolled its eyes, deeply buried in a thick bed of fat. In a few minutes the animal appeared on the surface of the water. Top was upon it in a bound, and kept it from plunging again. An instant later the capybara, dragged to the bank, was killed by a blow from Neb's stick. Pencroft hoisted the capybara on his shoulders, and judging by the height of the sun that it was about two o'clock, he gave the signal to return.

Pencroft soon made a raft of wood, as he had done before, though if there was no fire it would be a useless task, and the raft following the current, they returned towards the Chimneys. But the sailor had not gone fifty paces when he stopped, and again uttering a tremendous hurrah, pointed towards the angle of the cliff,

"Herbert! Neb! Look!" he shouted.

Smoke was escaping and curling up among the rocks. In a few minutes the three hunters were before a crackling fire. The captain and the reporter were there. Pencroft looked from one to the other, his capybara in his hand, without saying a word.

"Well, yes, my brave fellow," cried the reporter. "Fire, real fire, which will roast this splendid pig perfectly, and we will have a feast presently!"

"But who lighted it?" asked Pencroft. – "The sun!"

Gideon Spilett was quite right in his reply. It was the sun which had furnished the heat which so astonished Pencroft. The sailor could scarcely believe his eyes, and he was so amazed that he did not think of questioning the engineer.

"Had you a burning-glass, sir?" asked Herbert of Harding. "No, my boy," replied he, "but I made one."

And he showed the apparatus which served for a burning-glass. It was simply two glasses which he had taken from his own and the reporter's watches. Having filled them with water and rendered their edges adhesive by means of a little clay, he thus fabricated a regular burning-glass, which, concentrating the solar rays on some very dry moss, soon caused it to blaze.

The sailor considered the apparatus; then he gazed at the engineer without saying a word, only a look plainly expressed his opinion that if Cyrus Harding was not a magician, he was certainly no ordinary man.

Cyrus Harding and his companions remained an hour at the top of the mountain. The island was displayed under their eyes, like a plan in relief with different tints, green for the forests, yellow for the sand, blue for the water. They viewed it in its *tout-ensemble*.

THE SEARCH

Cyrus Harding and his companions remained an hour at the top of the mountain. The island was displayed under their eyes.

The exploration of the island was finished, its shape determined, its features made out, its extent calculated, the water and mountain systems ascertained. The disposition of the forests and plains had been marked in a general way on the reporter's plan. They had now only to descend the mountain slopes again, and explore the soil, in the triple point of view, of its mineral, vegetable, and animal resources.

But before giving his companions the signal for departure, Cyrus Harding said to them in a calm, grave voice, "Here, my friends, is the small corner of land upon which the hand of the Almighty has thrown us. We are going to live here; a long time, perhaps. Perhaps, too, unexpected help will arrive, if some ship passes by chance. I say by chance, because this is an unimportant island; there is not even a port in which ships could anchor, and it is to be feared that it is situated out of the route usually followed, that is to say, too much to the south for the ships which frequent the archipelagoes of the Pacific, and too much to the north for those which go to Australia by doubling Cape Horn. I wish to hide nothing of our position from you – "

"And you are right, my dear Cyrus," replied the reporter, with animation. "You have to deal with men. They have confidence in you, and you can depend upon them. Is it not so, my friends?"

"I will obey you in everything, captain," said Herbert, seizing the engineer's hand.

"My master always, and everywhere!" cried Neb.

"As for me," said the sailor, "if I ever grumble at work, my name's not Jack Pencroft, and if you like, captain, we will make a little America of this island! We will build towns, we will establish railways, start telegraphs, and one fine day, when it is quite changed, quite put in order and quite civilized, we will go and offer it to the government of the Union. Only, I ask one thing."

"What is that?" said the reporter.

"It is, that we do not consider ourselves castaways, but colonists, who have come here to settle." Harding could not help smiling, and the sailor's idea was adopted. He then thanked his companions, and added that he would rely on their energy and on the aid of Heaven.

"Well, now let us set off to the Chimneys!" cried Pencroft.

"One minute, my friends," said the engineer. "It seems to me it would be a good thing to give a name to this island, as well as to the capes, promontories, and watercourses, which we can see.

"Very good," said the reporter. "In the future, that will simplify the instructions which we shall have to give and follow."

"Indeed," said the sailor, "already it is something to be able to say where one is going, and where one has come from. At least, it looks like somewhere."

"The Chimneys, for example," said Herbert.

"Exactly!" replied Pencroft. "That name was the most convenient, and it came to me quite of myself. Shall we keep the name of the Chimneys for our first encampment, captain?"

"Yes, Pencroft, since you have so christened it."

"Good! As for the others, that will be easy," returned the sailor, who was in high spirits. "Let us give them names, as the Robinsons did, whose story Herbert has often read to me; Providence Bay, Whale Point, Cape Disappointment!"

"Or, rather, the names of Captain Harding," said Herbert, "of Mr. Spilett, of Neb! – "

"My name!" cried Neb, showing his sparkling white teeth.

"Why not?" replied Pencroft. "Port Neb, that would do very well! And Cape Gideon!"

"I should prefer borrowing names from our country," said the reporter, "which would remind us of America."

"Yes, for the principal ones," then said Cyrus Harding; "for those of the bays and seas, I admit it willingly. We might give to that vast bay on the east the name of Union Bay, for example; to that large hollow on the south, Washington Bay; to the mountain upon which we are standing, that of Mount Franklin; to that lake which is extended under our eyes, that of Lake Grant; nothing could be better, my friends. These names will recall our country, and those of the great citizens who have honoured it; but for the rivers, gulfs, capes, and promontories, which we perceive from the top of this mountain, rather let us choose names which will recall their particular shape. The shape of the island is so strange that we shall not be troubled to imagine what it resembles. What do you think, my friends?"

The engineer's proposal was unanimously agreed to. The island was spread out under their eyes like a map, and they had only to give names to all its angles and points. Gideon Spilett would write them down, and the geographical nomenclature of the island would be definitely adopted. First, they named the two bays and the mountain as the engineer had suggested.

"Now," said the reporter, "to this peninsula at the southwest, I propose to give the name of Serpentine Peninsula, and that of Reptile End to the bent tail which terminates it, for it is just like a reptile's tail."

"Adopted," said the engineer.

"Now," said Herbert, pointing to the other extremity of the island, "let us call this gulf which is so singularly like a pair of open jaws, Shark Gulf."

"Capital!" cried Pencroft, "and we can complete the resemblance by naming the two parts of the jaws Mandible Cape."

"But there are two capes," observed the reporter.

"Well," replied Pencroft, "we can have North Mandible Cape and South Mandible Cape."

"They are inscribed," said Spilett.

"There is only the point at the southeastern extremity of the island to be named," said Pencroft.

"That is, the extremity of Union Bay?" asked Herbert.

"Claw Cape," cried Neb directly, who also wished to be godfather to some part of his domain.

Neb had found an excellent name, for this cape was very like the powerful claw of the fantastic animal which this singularly-shaped island represented. The settlers had only to descend Mount Franklin to return to the Chimneys, when Pencroft cried out,

"Well! We are preciously stupid!"

"Why?" asked Gideon Spilett, who had closed his notebook and risen to depart.

"Why! Our island! We have forgotten to christen it!"

Herbert was going to propose to give it the engineer's name and all his companions would have applauded him, when Cyrus Harding said simply,

"Let us give it the name of a great citizen, my friend; of him who now struggles to defend the unity of the American Republic! Let us call it Lincoln Island!"

The engineer's proposal was replied to by three hurrahs. And that evening, before sleeping, the new colonists talked of their absent country; they spoke of the terrible war which stained it with blood; they could not doubt that the South would soon be subdued, and that the cause of the North, the cause of justice, would triumph, thanks to Grant, thanks to Lincoln!

Now this happened the 30th of March, 1865. They little knew that sixteen days afterwards a frightful crime would be committed in Washington, and that on Good Friday Abraham Lincoln would fall by the hand of a fanatic.

THE CHEST

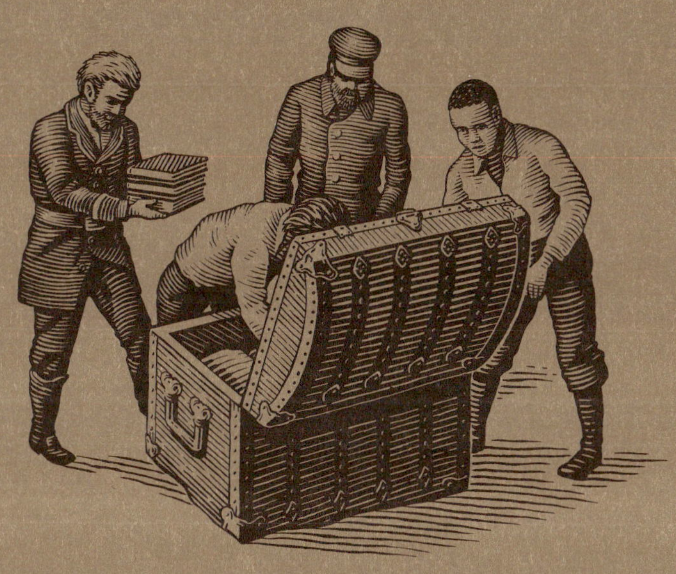

The settlers were now following the eastern bank of the lake, and they would not be long in reaching the part which they already knew. The engineer was much surprised at not seeing any indication of the discharge of water. The reporter and the sailor talked with him, and he could not conceal his astonishment.

Neb, his iron-tipped spear in his hand, wished to go to Top's help, and attack the dangerous animal in its own element.

At this moment Top, who had been very quiet till then, gave signs of agitation. The intelligent animal went backwards and forwards on the shore, stopped suddenly, and looked at the water, one paw raised, as if he was pointing at some invisible game; then he barked furiously, and was suddenly silent.

Neither Cyrus Harding nor his companions had at first paid any attention to Top's behaviour; but the dog's barking soon became so frequent that the engineer noticed it.

"What is there, Top?" he asked.

The dog bounded towards his master, seeming to be very uneasy, and then rushed again towards the bank. Then, all at once, he plunged into the lake.

"Here, Top!" cried Cyrus Harding, who did not like his dog to venture into the treacherous water.

"What's happening down there?" asked Pencroft, examining the surface of the lake.

"Top smells some amphibious creature," replied Herbert.

"An alligator, perhaps," said the reporter.

"I do not think so," replied Harding. "Alligators are only met with in regions less elevated in latitude."

Meanwhile Top had returned at his master's call, and had regained the shore: but he could not stay quiet; he plunged in among the tall grass, and guided by instinct, he appeared to follow some invisible being which was slipping along under the surface of the water. However the water was calm; not a ripple disturbed its surface. Several times the settlers stopped on the bank, and observed it attentively. Nothing appeared. There was some mystery there.

The engineer was puzzled.

"Let us pursue this exploration to the end," said he.

Half an hour after they had all arrived at the south-east angle of the lake, on Prospect Heights. At this point the examination of the banks of the lake was considered finished, and yet the engineer had not been able to discover how and where the waters were discharged. "There is no doubt this overflow exists," he repeated, "and since it is not visible it must go through the granite cliff at the west!"

"But what importance do you attach to knowing that, my dear Cyrus?" asked Gideon Spilett.

"Considerable importance," replied the engineer; "for if it flows through the cliff there is probably some cavity, which it would be easy to render habitable after turning away the water."

"But is it not possible, captain, that the water flows away at the bottom of the lake," said Herbert, "and that it reaches the sea by some subterranean passage?"

"That might be," replied the engineer, "and should it be so we shall be obliged to build our house ourselves, since nature has not done it for us."

The colonists were about to begin to traverse the plateau to return to the Chimneys when Top gave new signs of agitation. He barked with fury, and before his master could restrain him, he had plunged a second time into the lake.

All ran towards the bank. The dog was already more than twenty feet off, and Cyrus was calling him back, when an enormous head emerged from the water, which did not appear to be deep in that place.

Herbert recognized directly the species of amphibian to which the tapering head, with large eyes, and adorned with long silky moustaches, belonged.

"A lamantin!" he cried.

It was not a lamantin, but one of that species of the order of cetaceans, which bear the name of the "dugong," for its nostrils were open at the upper part of its snout. The enormous animal rushed on the dog, who

tried to escape by returning towards the shore. His master could do nothing to save him, and before Gideon Spilett or Herbert thought of bending their bows, Top, seized by the dugong, had disappeared beneath the water.

Neb, his iron-tipped spear in his hand, wished to go to Top's help, and attack the dangerous animal in its own element.

"No, Neb," said the engineer, restraining his courageous servant.

Meanwhile, a struggle was going on beneath the water, an inexplicable struggle, for in his situation Top could not possibly resist; and judging by the bubbling of the surface it must be also a terrible struggle, and could not but terminate in the death of the dog! But suddenly, in the middle of a foaming circle, Top reappeared. Thrown in the air by some unknown power, he rose ten feet above the surface of the lake, fell again into the midst of the agitated waters, and then soon gained the shore, without any severe wounds, miraculously saved.

THROWN IN THE AIR BY SOME UNKNOWN POWER, HE ROSE TEN FEET ABOVE THE SURFACE OF THE LAKE.

Cyrus Harding and his companions could not understand it. What was not less inexplicable was that the struggle still appeared to be going on. Doubtless, the dugong, attacked by some powerful animal, after having released the dog, was fighting on its own account. But it did not last long. The water became red with blood, and the body of the dugong, emerging from the sheet of scarlet which spread around, soon stranded on a little beach at the south angle of the lake. The colonists ran towards it. The dugong was dead. It was an enormous animal, fifteen or sixteen feet long, and must have weighed from three to four thousand pounds. At its neck was a wound, which appeared to have been produced by a sharp blade.

What could the amphibious creature have been, who, by this terrible blow had destroyed the formidable dugong? No one could tell, and much interested in this incident, Harding and his companions returned to the Chimneys.

On the 9th of October the bark canoe was entirely finished. Pencroft had kept his promise, and a light boat, the shell of which was joined together by the flexible twigs of the crejimba, had been constructed in five days. A seat in the stern, a second seat in the middle to preserve the equilibrium, a third seat in the bows, rowlocks for the two oars, a scull to steer with, completed the little craft, which was twelve feet long, and did not weigh more than two hundred pounds. The operation of launching it was extremely simple. The canoe was carried to the beach and laid on the sand before Granite House, and the rising tide floated it. Pencroft, who leaped in directly, manoeuvred it with the scull and declared it to be just the thing for the purpose to which they wished to put it.

In the meantime, after a voyage of three-quarters of an hour, the canoe reached the extremity of the point, and Pencroft was preparing to return, when Herbert, rising, pointed to a black object, saying,

THE CHEST

"What do I see down there on the beach?"

All eyes turned towards the point indicated.

"Why," said the reporter, "there is something. It looks like part of a wreck half buried in the sand."

"Ah!" cried Pencroft, "I see what it is!" – "What?" asked Neb. "Barrels, barrels, which perhaps are full," replied the sailor. "Pull to the shore, Pencroft!" said Cyrus.

A few strokes of the oar brought the canoe into a little creek, and its passengers leaped on shore.

Pencroft was not mistaken. Two barrels were there, half buried in the sand, but still firmly attached to a large chest, which, sustained by them, had floated to the moment when it stranded on the beach.

"There has been a wreck, then, in some part of the island," said Herbert.

"Evidently," replied Spilett.

"But what's in this chest?" cried Pencroft, with very natural impatience. "What's in this chest? It is shut up, and nothing to open it with! Well, perhaps a stone – "

And the sailor, raising a heavy block, was about to break in one of the sides of the chest, when the engineer arrested his hand.

"Pencroft," said he, "can you restrain your impatience for one hour only?"

"But, captain, just think! Perhaps there is everything we want in there!"

"We shall find that out, Pencroft," replied the engineer; "but trust to me, and do not break the chest, which may be useful to us. We must convey it to Granite House, where we can open it easily, and without breaking it. It is quite prepared for a voyage; and since it has floated here, it may just as well float to the mouth of the river."

The chest was heavy, and the barrels were scarcely sufficient to keep it above water. The sailor also feared every instant that it would get loose and sink to the bottom of the sea. But happily his fears were not realized, and an hour and a half after they set out – all that time had been taken up in going a distance of three miles – the boat touched the beach below Granite House.

Canoe and chest were then hauled up on the sands; and as the tide was then going out, they were soon left high and dry. Neb, hurrying home, brought back some tools with which to open the chest in such a way that it might be injured as little as possible, and they proceeded to its inventory.

The covering of zinc was torn off and thrown back over the sides of the chest, and by degrees numerous articles of very varied character were produced and strewn about on the sand. At each new object Pencroft uttered fresh hurrahs, Herbert clapped his hands, and Neb danced up and down. There were books which made Herbert wild with joy, and cooking utensils which Neb covered with kisses!

"It must be allowed," said the reporter, after the inventory had been made, "that the owner of this chest was a practical man! Tools, weapons, instruments, clothes, utensils, books – nothing is wanting! It might really be said that he expected to be wrecked, and had prepared for it beforehand."

Each article was carefully examined, especially the books, instruments and weapons. Neither the weapons nor the instruments, contrary to the usual custom, bore the name of the maker; they were, besides, in a perfect state, and did not appear to have been used. The same peculiarity marked the tools and utensils; all were new, which proved that the articles had not been taken by chance and thrown into the chest, but, on the contrary, that the choice of things had been well considered and arranged with care. This was also indicated by the second case of metal which had preserved them from damp, and which could not have been soldered in a

Pencroft was not mistaken. Two barrels were there, half buried in the sand, but still firmly attached to a large chest.

moment of haste. As to the dictionaries of natural science and Polynesian idioms, both were English; but they neither bore the name of the publisher nor the date of publication. The same with the Bible printed in English, in quarto, remarkable from a typographic point of view, and which appeared to have been often used.

The atlas was a magnificent work, comprising maps of every country in the world, and several planispheres arranged upon Mercator's projection, and of which the nomenclature was in French – but which also bore neither date nor name of publisher. Herbert fetched the atlas, and the map of the Pacific was opened, and the engineer, compass in hand, prepared to determine their position.

Suddenly the compasses stopped, and he exclaimed,

"But an island exists in this part of the Pacific already!"

"An island?" cried Pencroft.

"Tabor Island."

"An important island?"

"No, an islet lost in the Pacific, and which perhaps has never been visited."

"Well, we will visit it," said Pencroft.

There was nothing, therefore, on these different articles by which they could be traced, and nothing consequently of a nature to show the nationality of the vessel which must have recently passed these shores.

But, wherever the chest might have come from, it was a treasure to the settlers on Lincoln Island. Till then, by making use of the productions of nature, they had created everything for themselves, and, thanks to their intelligence, they had managed without difficulty. But did it not appear as if Providence had wished to reward them by sending them these productions of human industry? Their thanks rose unanimously to Heaven.

No one could help laughing at this speech of the sailor's. But the result of this discovery of the chest was that it was now more than ever necessary to explore the island thoroughly. It was therefore agreed that the next morning at break of day they should set out, by ascending the Mercy so as to reach the western shore. If any castaways had landed on the coast, it was to be feared they were without resources, and it was therefore the more necessary to carry help to them without delay.

During the day the different articles were carried to Granite House, where they were methodically arranged in the great hall. This day – the 29th of October – happened to be a Sunday, and, before going to bed, Herbert asked the engineer if he would not read them something from the Gospel.

"Willingly," replied Cyrus Harding.

He took the sacred volume, and was about to open it, when Pencroft stopped him, saying, "Captain, I am superstitious. Open at random and read the first verse which your eye falls upon. We will see if it applies to our situation."

Cyrus Harding smiled at the sailor's idea, and, yielding to his wish, he opened exactly at a place where the leaves were separated by a marker.

Immediately his eyes were attracted by a cross which, made with a pencil, was placed against the eighth verse of the seventh chapter of the Gospel of St. Matthew. He read the verse, which was this: –

"For every one that asketh receiveth; and he that seeketh findeth."

B 15

A NEW MEMBER

Cyrus Harding stood still, without saying a word. His companions searched in the darkness on the wall, in case the wind should have moved the ladder, and on the ground, thinking that it might have fallen down... But the ladder had quite disappeared. As to ascertaining if a squall had blown it on the landing-place, half way up, that was impossible in the dark.

A NEW MEMBER

Someone had entered Granite House – there could be no more doubt about that.

The upper ladder, which generally hung from the door to the landing, was in its place, but the lower ladder was drawn up and raised to the threshold. It was evident that the intruders had wished to guard themselves against a surprise.

Pencroft hailed again.

No reply.

"The beggars," exclaimed the sailor. "There they are sleeping quietly as if they were in their own house. Hallo there, you pirates, brigands, robbers, sons of John Bull!"

Cyrus Harding, Gideon Spilett, Pencroft, and Neb drew back, so as to see if anything appeared at the windows. The reporter lifted his gun to his shoulder and covered the door.

The bow was bent, the arrow flew, taking the cord with it, and passed between the two last rungs.

The operation had succeeded.

Herbert immediately seized the end of the cord, but, at that moment when he gave it a pull to bring down the ladder, an arm, thrust suddenly out between the wall and the door, grasped it and dragged it inside Granite House.

"The rascals!" shouted the sailor. "If a ball can do anything for you, you shall not have long to wait for it."

"But who was it?" asked Neb. – "Who was it? Didn't you see?" – "No." – "It was a monkey, a sapajou, an orangoutang, a baboon, a gorilla, a sagoin. Our dwelling has been invaded by monkeys, who climbed up the ladder during our absence."

And, at this moment, as if to bear witness to the truth of the sailor's words, two or three quadrumana showed themselves at the windows, from which they had pushed back the shutters, and saluted the real proprietors of the place with a thousand hideous grimaces.

"I knew that it was only a joke," cried Pencroft; "but one of the jokers shall pay the penalty for the rest."

So saying, the sailor, raising his piece, took a rapid aim at one of the monkeys and fired. All disappeared, except one who fell mortally wounded on the beach. This monkey, which was of a large size, evidently belonged to the first order of the quadrumana. Whether this was a chimpanzee, an orangoutang, or a gorilla, he took rank among the anthropoid apes, who are so called from their resemblance to the human race. However, Herbert declared it to be an orangoutang.

"What a magnificent beast!" cried Neb.

"Magnificent, if you like," replied Pencroft; "but still I do not see how we are to get into our house."

"Herbert is a good marksman," said the reporter, "and his bow is here. He can try again."

"Why, these apes are so cunning," returned Pencroft; "they won't show themselves again at the windows and so we can't kill them; and when I think of the mischief they may do in the rooms and storehouse – "

"Have patience," replied Harding; "these creatures cannot keep us long at bay."

It was already past twelve o'clock when the colonists, well armed and provided with picks and spades, left the Chimneys, passed beneath the windows of Granite House and began to ascend the left bank of the Mercy, so as to reach Prospect Heights.

But they had not made fifty steps in this direction, when they heard the dog barking furiously. And all rushed down the bank again. Arrived at the turning, they saw that the situation had changed.

In fact, the apes, seized with a sudden panic, from some unknown cause, were trying to escape. Two or

They threw themselves on the orang, who defended himself gallantly, but was soon overpowered and bound.

three ran and clambered from one window to another with the agility of acrobats. They were not even trying to replace the ladder, by which it would have been easy to descend; perhaps in their terror they had forgotten this way of escape. The colonists, now being able to take aim without difficulty, fired. Some, wounded or killed, fell back into the rooms, uttering piercing cries. The rest, throwing themselves out, were dashed to pieces in their fall, and in a few minutes, so far as they knew, there was not a living quadrumana in Granite House.

"Well now, and the ladder," cried the sailor; "who can the gentleman have been who sent us that down?"

But at that moment a cry was heard, and a great orang, who had hidden himself in the passage, rushed into the room, pursued by Neb.

"Ah, the robber!" cried Pencroft.

And hatchet in hand, he was about to cleave the head of the animal, when Cyrus Harding seized his arm, saying, "Spare him, Pencroft." – "Pardon this rascal?" – "Yes! It was he who threw us the ladder!"

And the engineer said this in such a peculiar voice that it was difficult to know whether he spoke seriously or not.

Nevertheless, they threw themselves on the orang, who defended himself gallantly, but was soon overpowered and bound.

The one which had been seized in the hall of Granite House was a great fellow, six feet high, with an admirably proportioned frame, a broad chest, head of a moderate size, the facial angle reaching sixty-five degrees, round skull, projecting nose, skin covered with soft glossy hair, in short, a fine specimen of the anthropoids. His eyes, rather smaller than human eyes, sparkled with intelligence; his white teeth glittered under his moustache, and he wore a little curly brown beard.

"A handsome fellow!" said Pencroft; "if we only knew his language, we could talk to him."

"But, master," said Neb, "are you serious? Are we going to take him as a servant?"

"Yes, Neb," replied the engineer, smiling. "But you must not be jealous."

"And I hope he will make an excellent servant," added Herbert. "He appears young, and will be easy to educate, and we shall not be obliged to use force to subdue him, nor draw his teeth. He will soon grow fond of his masters if they are kind to him."

"And they will be," replied Pencroft, who had forgotten all his rancour against "the jokers."

Then, approaching the orang, "Well, old boy!" he asked, "how are you?"

The orang replied by a little grunt which did not show any anger. "You wish to join the colony?" again asked the sailor. "You are going to enter the service of Captain Cyrus Harding?"

Another respondent grunt was uttered by the ape.

"And you will be satisfied with no other wages than your food?"

Third affirmative grunt.

"This conversation is slightly monotonous," observed Gideon Spilett.

"So much the better," replied Pencroft; "the best servants are those who talk the least. And then, no wages, do you hear, my boy? We will give you no wages at first, but we will double them afterwards if we are pleased with you."

Thus the colony was increased by a new member. As to his name the sailor begged that in memory of another ape which he had known he might be called Jupiter, and Jup for short.

And so, without more ceremony, Master Jup was installed in Granite House.

SIGN OF LIFE

An incident must here be related, not only as interesting in itself, but because it was the first attempt made by the colonists to communicate with the rest of mankind. Gideon Spilett had already several times pondered whether to throw into the sea a letter enclosed in a bottle, which currents might perhaps carry to an inhabited coast, or to confide it to pigeons. But how could it be seriously hoped that either pigeons or bottles could cross the distance of twelve hundred miles which separated the island from any inhabited land? It would have been pure folly.

SIGN OF LIFE

Page 189
Liberty was given to this swift courier of the air, and it was not without some emotion that the colonists watched it disappear.

Left
The sail was hoisted, the Lincolnian flag floated from the masthead, and the "Bonadventure," steered by Pencroft, stood out to sea.

But on the 30th of June the capture was effected, not without difficulty, of an albatross, which a shot from Herbert's gun had slightly wounded in the foot. It was a magnificent bird, measuring ten feet from wing to wing, and which could traverse seas as wide as the Pacific.

Herbert would have liked to keep this superb bird, as its wound would soon heal, and he thought he could tame it; but Spilett explained to him that they should not neglect this opportunity of attempting to communicate by this messenger with the lands of the Pacific; for if the albatross had come from some inhabited region, there was no doubt but that it would return there so soon as it was set free.

Perhaps in his heart Gideon Spilett, in whom the journalist sometimes came to the surface, was not sorry to have the opportunity of sending forth to take its chance an exciting article relating the adventures of the settlers in Lincoln Island. What a success for the authorized reporter of the *New York Herald*, and for the number which should contain the article, if it should ever reach the address of its editor, the Honourable James Bennett!

Gideon Spilett then wrote out a concise account, which was placed in a strong waterproof bag, with an earnest request to whoever might find it to forward it to the office of the *New York Herald*. This little bag was fastened to the neck of the albatross, and not to its foot, for these birds are in the habit of resting on the surface of the sea; then liberty was given to this swift courier of the air, and it was not without some emotion that the colonists watched it disappear in the misty west.

With the month of September the winter ended, and the works were again eagerly commenced. The building of the vessel advanced rapidly, she was already completely decked over, and all the inside parts of the hull were firmly united with ribs bent by means of steam, which answered all the purposes of a mould. As there was no want of wood, Pencroft proposed to the engineer to give a double lining to the hull, to insure the strength of the vessel.

On the 10th of October the vessel was launched. Pencroft was radiant with joy, the operation was perfectly successful; the boat completely rigged, having been pushed on rollers to the water's edge, was floated by the rising tide, amid the cheers of the colonists, particularly of Pencroft, who showed no modesty on this occasion. Besides his importance was to last beyond the finishing of the vessel, since, after having built her, he was to command her. The grade of captain was bestowed upon him with the approbation of all. To satisfy Captain Pencroft, it was now necessary to give a name to the vessel, and, after many propositions had been discussed, the votes were all in favour of the "Bonadventure". As soon as the "Bonadventure" had been lifted by the rising tide, it was seen that she lay evenly in the water, and would be easily navigated. However, the trial trip was to be made that very day, by an excursion off the coast.

Cyrus Harding was equally anxious to try the vessel, the model of which had originated with him, although on the sailor's advice he had altered some parts of it, but he did not share Pencroft's confidence in her, and as the latter had not again spoken of the voyage to Tabor Island, Harding hoped he had given it up. He would have indeed great reluctance in letting two or three of his companions venture so far in so small a boat, which was not of more than fifteen tons' burden.

They saw the lad thrown on the ground and in the grasp of a savage being, apparently a gigantic ape, who was about to do him some great harm.

At half-past ten everybody was on board, even Top and Jup, and Herbert weighed the anchor, which was fast in the sand near the mouth of the Mercy. The sail was hoisted, the Lincolnian flag floated from the mast-head, and the "Bonadventure," steered by Pencroft, stood out to sea. All hands were enchanted, they had a good vessel, which, in case of need, would be of great service to them, and with fine weather and a fresh breeze the voyage promised to be charming.

They were not more than half a mile from the coast, and it was necessary to tack to beat against the wind. The "Bonadventure" was then going at a very moderate rate, as the breeze, partly intercepted by the high land, scarcely swelled her sails, and the sea, smooth as glass, was only rippled now and then by passing gusts.

Herbert had stationed himself in the bows that he might indicate the course to be followed among the channels, when all at once he shouted,

"Luff, Pencroft, luff!" – "What's the matter," replied the sailor; "a rock?" – "No – wait," said Herbert; "I don't quite see. Luff again – right – now." So saying, Herbert, leaning over the side, plunged his arm into the water, and pulled it out, exclaiming, "A bottle!"

He held in his hand a corked bottle which he had just seized a few cables' length from the shore.

Cyrus Harding took the bottle. Without uttering a single word he drew the cork, and took from it a damp paper, on which were written these words: "Castaway... Tabor island: 153deg W. long., 37deg 11' S. lat."

And there was no reason to doubt that this was Tabor Island, since according to the most recent charts there was no island in this part of the Pacific between New Zealand and the American Coast.

There was not a trace of a habitation in any part, not the print of a human foot on the shore of the island, which after four hours' walking had been gone completely round.

"Let us go on board, and tomorrow we will begin again," said the reporter.

This was the wisest course, and it was about to be followed when Herbert, pointing to a confused mass among the trees, exclaimed,

"A hut!"

All three immediately ran towards the dwelling. In the twilight it was just possible to see that it was built of planks and covered with a thick tarpaulin.

The half-closed door was pushed open by Pencroft, who entered with a rapid step.

The hut was empty!

Day dawned; Pencroft and his companions immediately proceeded to survey the dwelling. It had certainly been built in a favourable situation, at the back of a little hill, sheltered by five or six magnificent gum-trees. Before its front and through the trees the axe had prepared a wide clearing, which allowed the view to extend to the sea. Beyond a lawn, surrounded by a wooden fence falling to pieces, was the shore, on the left of which was the mouth of the stream.

The hut had been built of planks, and it was easy to see that these planks had been obtained from the hull or deck of a ship. It was probable that a disabled vessel had been cast on the coast of the island, that one at least of the crew had been saved, and that by means of the wreck this man, having tools at his disposal, had built the dwelling. And this became still more evident when Gideon Spilett, after having walked around the hut, saw on a plank, probably one of those which had formed the armour of the wrecked vessel, these letters already half effaced: BR – TAN – A

The sailor was of Herculean strength, the reporter also very powerful, and in spite of the monster's resistance he was firmly tied so that he could not even move.

"Britannia," exclaimed Pencroft, whom the reporter had called; "it is a common name for ships, and I could not say if she was English or American!"

"It matters very little, Pencroft!"

"Very little indeed," answered the sailor, "and we will save the survivor of her crew if he is still living, to whatever country he may belong. But before beginning our search again let us go on board the 'Bonadventure'."

They returned on board, breakfasted, so that it should not be necessary to dine until very late; then the repast being ended, the exploration was continued and conducted with the most minute care.

"We won't waste time," returned Pencroft. "You, Herbert, go and gather the seeds, which you know better than we do. While you do that, Mr. Spilett and I will go and have a pig hunt, and even without Top I hope we shall manage to catch a few!"

Herbert accordingly took the path which led towards the cultivated part of the islet, while the sailor and the reporter entered the forest.

Many specimens of the porcine race fled before them, and these animals, which were singularly active, did not appear to be in a humour to allow themselves to be approached.

However, after an hour's chase, the hunters had just managed to get hold of a couple lying in a thicket, when cries were heard resounding from the north part of the island. With the cries were mingled terrible yells, in which there was nothing human. Pencroft and Gideon Spilett were at once on their feet, and the pigs by this movement began to run away, at the moment when the sailor was getting ready the rope to bind them.

"That's Herbert's voice," said the reporter.

"Run!" exclaimed Pencroft.

And the sailor and Spilett immediately ran at full speed towards the spot from whence the cries proceeded. They did well to hasten, for at a turn of the path near a clearing they saw the lad thrown on the ground and in the grasp of a savage being, apparently a gigantic ape, who was about to do him some great harm.

To rush on this monster, throw him on the ground in his turn, snatch Herbert from him, then bind him securely, was the work of a minute for Pencroft and

Gideon Spilett. The sailor was of Herculean strength, the reporter also very powerful, and in spite of the monster's resistance he was firmly tied so that he could not even move.

"You are not hurt, Herbert?" asked Spilett. – "No, no!" – "Oh, if this ape had wounded him!" exclaimed Pencroft.

"But he is not an ape," answered Herbert.

At these words Pencroft and Gideon Spilett looked at the singular being who lay on the ground. Indeed it was not an ape; it was a human being, a man. But what a man! A savage in all the horrible acceptation of the word, and so much the more frightful that he seemed fallen to the lowest degree of brutishness!

Shaggy hair, untrimmed beard descending to the chest, the body almost naked except a rag round the waist, wild eyes, enormous hands with immensely long nails, skin the colour of mahogany, feet as hard as if made of horn, such was the miserable creature who yet had a claim to be called a man. But it might justly be asked if there were yet a soul in this body, or if the brute instinct alone survived in it!

"Are you quite sure that this is a man, or that he has ever been one?" said Pencroft to the reporter.

"Alas! There is no doubt about it," replied Spilett.

"Then this must be the castaway?" asked Herbert.

"Yes," replied Gideon Spilett, "but the unfortunate man has no longer anything human about him!"

The reporter spoke the truth. It was evident that if the castaway had ever been a civilized being, solitude had made him a savage, or worse, perhaps a regular man of the woods. Hoarse sounds issued from his throat between his teeth, which were sharp as the teeth of a wild beast made to tear raw flesh.

Memory must have deserted him long before, and for a long time also he had forgotten how to use his gun and tools, and he no longer knew how to make a fire! It could be seen that he was active and powerful, but the physical qualities had been developed in him to the injury of the moral qualities. Gideon Spilett spoke to him. He did not appear to understand or even to hear. And yet on looking into his eyes, the reporter thought he could see that all reason was not extinguished in him. However, the prisoner did not struggle, nor even attempt to break his bonds. Was he overwhelmed by the presence of men whose fellow he had once been? Had he found in some corner of his brain a fleeting remembrance which recalled him to humanity? If free, would he attempt to fly, or would he remain? They could not tell, but they did not make the experiment; and after gazing attentively at the miserable creature,

"Whoever he may be," remarked Gideon Spilett, "whoever he may have been, and whatever he may become, it is our duty to take him with us to Lincoln Island."

"Yes, yes!" replied Herbert, "and perhaps with care we may arouse in him some gleam of intelligence."

"The soul does not die," said the reporter, "and it would be a great satisfaction to rescue one of God's creatures from brutishness."

Pencroft shook his head doubtfully.

"We must try at any rate," returned the reporter; "humanity commands us."

SIX AGAINST FIFTY

It was now two years and a half since the castaways from the balloon had been thrown on Lincoln Island, and during that period there had been no communication between them and their fellow-creatures. Once the reporter had attempted to communicate with the inhabited world by confiding to a bird a letter which contained the secret of their situation, but that was a chance on which it was impossible to reckon seriously. Ayrton, alone, under the circumstances which have been related, had come to join the little colony. Now, suddenly, on this day, the 17th of October, other men had unexpectedly appeared in sight of the island, on that deserted sea!

SIX AGAINST FIFTY

There could be no doubt about it! A vessel was there! But would she pass on, or would she put into port? In a few hours the colonists would definitely know what to expect.

Was it simple chance which brought it to that part of the Pacific, where the maps mentioned no land except Tabor Island, which itself was out of the route usually followed by vessels from the Polynesian Archipelagoes, from New Zealand, and from the American coast? To this question, which each one asked himself, a reply was suddenly made by Herbert.

"Can it be the 'Duncan'?" he cried.

The "Duncan," as has been said, was Lord Glenarvan's yacht, which had left the castaway Ayrton on the islet, and which was to return there someday to fetch him.

"We must tell Ayrton," said Gideon Spilett, "and send for him immediately. He alone can say if it is the 'Duncan.'"

This was the opinion of all, and the reporter, going to the telegraphic apparatus which placed the corral in communication with Granite House, sent this telegram: – "Come with all possible speed."

In a few minutes the bell sounded.

"I am coming," replied Ayrton.

Then the settlers continued to watch the vessel.

"If it is the 'Duncan,'" said Herbert, "Ayrton will recognize her without difficulty, since he sailed on board her for some time."

"And if he recognizes her," added Pencroft, "it will agitate him exceedingly!"

"Yes," answered Cyrus Harding; "but now Ayrton is worthy to return on board the 'Duncan,' and pray Heaven that it is indeed Lord Glenarvan's yacht, for I should be suspicious of any other vessel. These are ill-famed seas, and I have always feared a visit from Malay pirates to our island."

"We could defend it," cried Herbert.

"No doubt, my boy," answered the engineer smiling, "but it would be better not to have to defend it."

"A useless observation," said Spilett. "Lincoln Island is unknown to navigators, since it is not marked even on the most recent maps. Do you think, Cyrus, that that is a sufficient motive for a ship, finding herself unexpectedly in sight of new land, to try and visit rather than avoid it?"

"Certainly," replied Pencroft.

"I think so too," added the engineer. "It may even be said that it is the duty of a captain to come and survey any land or island not yet known, and Lincoln Island is in this position."

A VESSEL WAS THERE! BUT WOULD SHE PASS ON, OR WOULD SHE PUT INTO PORT?

"Well," said Pencroft, "suppose this vessel comes and anchors there a few cables-lengths from our island, what shall we do?"

This sudden question remained at first without any reply. But Cyrus Harding, after some moments' thought, replied in the calm tone which was usual to him,

"What we shall do, my friends? What we ought to do is this: – we will communicate with the ship, we will take our passage on board her, and we will leave our island, after having taken possession of it in the name of the United States. Then we will return with any who may wish to follow us to colonize it definitely, and endow the American Republic with a useful station in this part of the Pacific Ocean!"

"Hurrah!" exclaimed Pencroft, "and that will be no small present which we shall make to our country! The colonization is already almost finished; names are given to every part of the island; there is a natural port, fresh water, roads, a telegraph, a dockyard, and manufactories; and there will be nothing to be done but to inscribe Lincoln Island on the maps!"

For an hour it was impossible to say with any certainty whether the vessel was or was not standing towards Lincoln Island. Towards four o'clock – an hour after he had been sent for – Ayrton arrived at Granite House. He entered the dining-room saying, "At your service, gentlemen."

Cyrus Harding gave him his hand, as was his custom to do, and, leading him to the window,

"Ayrton," said he, "we have begged you to come here for an important reason. A ship is in sight of the island."

Ayrton at first paled slightly, and for a moment his eyes became dim; then, leaning out the window, he surveyed the horizon, but could see nothing.

"Take this telescope," said Spilett, "and look carefully, Ayrton, for it is possible that this ship may be the 'Duncan' come to these seas for the purpose of taking you home again."

"No," said he, "no! It cannot be the 'Duncan'!"

"Look, Ayrton," then said the engineer, "for it is necessary that we should know beforehand what to expect."

Ayrton took the glass and pointed it in the direction indicated. During some minutes he examined the horizon without moving, without uttering a word. Then,

"It is indeed a vessel," said he, "but I do not think she is the 'Duncan.'"

"Why do you not think so?" asked Gideon Spilett.

"Because the 'Duncan' is a steam-yacht, and I cannot perceive any trace of smoke either above or near that vessel."

The brig's ensign hung in folds, and it became more and more difficult to observe it.

"It is not the American flag," said Pencroft from time to time, "nor the English, the red of which could be easily seen, nor the French or German colours, nor the white flag of Russia, nor the yellow of Spain. One would say it was all one colour. Let's see: in these seas, what do we generally meet with?"

At that moment the breeze blew out the unknown flag. Ayrton seizing the telescope which the sailor had put down, put it to his eye, and in a hoarse voice,

"The black flag!" he exclaimed.

Had the engineer, then, been right in his presentiments? Was this a pirate vessel? Did she scour the Pacific, competing with the Malay proas which still infest it? For what had she come to look at the shores of Lincoln Island? Was it to them an unknown island, ready to become a magazine for stolen cargoes? Had she come to find on the coast a sheltered port for the winter months? Was the settlers' honest domain destined to be transformed into an infamous refuge – the headquarters of the piracy of the Pacific?

"My friends," said Cyrus Harding, "perhaps this vessel only wishes to survey the coast of the island. Perhaps her crew will not land. There is a chance of it. However that may be, we ought to do everything we can to hide our presence here."

The engineer's orders were immediately executed. Neb and Ayrton ascended the plateau, and took the necessary precautions to conceal any indication of a settlement. While they were thus occupied, their companions went to the border of Jacamar Wood, and brought back a large quantity of branches and creepers, which would at some distance appear as natural foliage, and thus disguise the windows in the granite cliff. At the same time, the ammunition and guns were placed ready so as to be at hand in case of an unexpected attack.

"My friends," said Harding, and his voice betrayed some emotion, "if the wretches endeavour to seize Lincoln Island, we shall defend it – shall we not?"

"Yes, Cyrus," replied the reporter, "and if necessary we will die to defend it!"

The engineer extended his hand to his companions, who pressed it warmly.

Night fell. The new moon had disappeared. Profound darkness enveloped the island and the sea. No light could pierce through the heavy piles of clouds on the horizon.

"Well! Who knows?" said Pencroft. "Perhaps that cursed craft will stand off during the night, and we shall see nothing of her at daybreak."

As if in reply to the sailor's observation, a bright light flashed in the darkness, and a cannon-shot was heard.

The vessel was still there and had guns on board.

Six seconds elapsed between the flash and the report. Therefore the brig was about a mile and a quarter from the coast.

At the same time, the chains were heard rattling through the hawse-holes. The vessel had just anchored in sight of Granite House!

There was no longer any doubt as to the pirates' intentions. They had dropped anchor at a short distance from the island, and it was evident that the next day by means of their boats they purposed to land on the beach!

Cyrus Harding and his companions were ready to act, but, determined though they were, they must not forget to be prudent. Perhaps their presence might still be concealed in the event of the pirates contenting themselves with landing on the shore without examining the interior of the island.

But why was that flag hoisted at the brig's peak? What was that shot fired for? Pure bravado doubtless, unless it was a sign of the act of taking possession. Harding knew now that the vessel was well armed. And what had the colonists of Lincoln Island to reply to the pirates' guns? A few muskets only.

"However," observed Cyrus Harding, "here we are in an impregnable position. The enemy cannot discover the mouth of the outlet, now that it is hidden under reeds and grass, and consequently it would be impossible for them to penetrate into Granite House."

"Are they numerous? that is the question," said the reporter. "If they are not more than a dozen, we shall be able to stop them, but forty, fifty, more perhaps!"

"Captain Harding," then said Ayrton, advancing towards the engineer, "will you give me leave?"

"For what, my friend?"

"To go to that vessel to find out the strength of her crew."

"But Ayrton – " answered the engineer, hesitating, "you will risk your life – "

"Why not, sir?"

"That is more than your duty."

"I have more than my duty to do," replied Ayrton.

"Will you go to the ship in the boat?" asked Gideon Spilett.

"No, sir, but I will swim. A boat would be seen where a man may glide between wind and water."

"Do you know that the brig is a mile and a quarter from the shore?" said Herbert.

"I am a good swimmer, Mr. Herbert."

"I tell you it is risking your life," said the engineer.

"Indeed," returned the sailor, "I only propose to

He took breath, then, hoisting himself up, he managed to reach the extremity of the cutwater.

accompany Ayrton as far as the islet. It may be, although it is scarcely possible, that one of these villains has landed, and in that case two men will not be too many to hinder him from giving the alarm. I will wait for Ayrton on the islet, and he shall go alone to the vessel, since he has proposed to do so."

Ayrton and Pencroft, followed by their companions, descended to the beach. Ayrton undressed and rubbed himself with grease, so as to suffer less from the temperature of the water, which was still cold. He might, indeed, be obliged to remain in it for several hours.

Half an hour afterwards, Ayrton, without having been either seen or heard, arrived at the ship and caught hold of the main-chains. He took breath, then, hoisting himself up, he managed to reach the extremity of the cutwater. There were drying several pairs of sailors' trousers. He put on a pair. Then settling himself firmly, he listened. They were not sleeping on board the brig. On the contrary, they were talking, singing, laughing. And these were the sentences, accompanied with oaths, which principally struck Ayrton:

"Our brig is a famous acquisition."

"She sails well, and merits her name of the 'Speedy.'"

"She would show all the navy of Norfolk a clean pair of heels."

"Hurrah for her captain!"

"Hurrah for Bob Harvey!"

What Ayrton felt when he overheard this fragment of conversation may be understood when it is known that in this Bob Harvey he recognized one of his old Australian companions, a daring sailor, who had continued his criminal career. Bob Harvey had seized, on the shores of Norfolk Island, this brig, which was loaded with arms, ammunition, utensils, and tools of all sorts, destined for one of the Sandwich Islands. All his gang had gone on board, and pirates after having been convicts, these wretches, more ferocious than the Malays themselves, scoured the Pacific, destroying vessels, and massacring their crews.

The conversation still continued amid shouts and libations. Ayrton learned that chance alone had brought the "Speedy" in sight of Lincoln Island; Bob Harvey had never yet set foot on it; but, as Cyrus Harding had conjectured, finding this unknown land in his course, its position being marked on no chart, he had formed the project of visiting it, and, if he found it suitable, of making it the brig's headquarters.

As to the black flag hoisted at the "Speedy's" peak, and the gun which had been fired, in imitation of men-of-war when they lower their colours, it was pure piratical bravado. It was in no way a signal, and no communication yet existed between the convicts and Lincoln Island.

The settlers' domain was now menaced with terrible danger. Evidently the island, with its water, its harbour, its resources of all kinds so increased in value by the colonists, and the concealment afforded by Granite House, could not but be convenient for the convicts; in their hands it would become an excellent place of refuge, and, being unknown, it would assure them, for a long time perhaps, impunity and security. Evidently, also, the lives of the settlers would not be respected, and Bob Harvey and his accomplices' first care would be to massacre them without mercy. Harding and his companions had, therefore, not even the choice of flying and hiding themselves in the island, since the convicts intended to reside there, and since, in the event of the "Speedy" departing on an expedition, it was probable that some of the crew would remain on shore, so as to settle themselves there. Therefore, it would be necessary to fight, to destroy every one of these

He soon extricated himself from their grasp. He fired his revolver, and two of the convicts fell.

scoundrels, unworthy of pity, and against whom any means would be right.

But was resistance and, in the last place, victory possible? That would depend on the equipment of the brig, and the number of men which she carried.

This Ayrton resolved to learn at any cost, and as an hour after his arrival the vociferations had begun to die away, and as a large number of the convicts were already buried in a drunken sleep, Ayrton did not hesitate to venture onto the "Speedy's" deck, which the extinguished lanterns now left in total darkness. He hoisted himself onto the cutwater, and by the bowsprit arrived at the forecastle. Then, gliding among the convicts stretched here and there, he made the round of the ship, and found that the "Speedy" carried four guns, which would throw shot of from eight to ten pounds in weight. He found also, on touching them that these guns were breech-loaders. They were, therefore, of modern make, easily used, and of terrible effect.

As to the men lying on the deck, they were about ten in number, but it was to be supposed that more were sleeping down below. Besides, by listening to them, Ayrton had understood that there were fifty on board. That was a large number for the six settlers of Lincoln Island to contend with! But now, thanks to Ayrton's devotion, Cyrus Harding would not be surprised, he would know the strength of his adversaries, and would make his arrangements accordingly.

There was nothing more for Ayrton to do but to return, and render to his companions an account of the mission with which he had charged himself, and he prepared to regain the bows of the brig, so that he might let himself down into the water.

But to this man, whose wish was, as he had said, to do more than his duty, there came an heroic thought. This was to sacrifice his own life, but save the island and the colonists. Ayrton did not hesitate. There would be no want of powder in a vessel which followed such a trade, and a spark would be enough to destroy it in an instant.

Ayrton stole carefully along the between-decks, strewn with numerous sleepers, overcome more by drunkenness than sleep. A lantern was lighted at the foot of the mainmast, round which was hung a gun-rack, furnished with weapons of all sorts.

Ayrton took a revolver from the rack, and assured himself that it was loaded and primed. Nothing more was needed to accomplish the work of destruction. He then glided towards the stern, so as to arrive under the brig's poop at the powder-magazine.

It was difficult to proceed along the dimly lighted deck without stumbling over some half-sleeping convict, who retorted by oaths and kicks. Ayrton was, therefore, more than once obliged to halt. But at last he arrived at the partition dividing the aftercabin, and found the door opening into the magazine itself.

Ayrton, compelled to force it open, set to work. It was a difficult operation to perform without noise, for he had to break a padlock. But under his vigorous hand, the padlock broke, and the door was open.

At that moment a hand was laid on Ayrton's shoulder.

"What are you doing here?" asked a tall man, in a harsh voice, who, standing in the shadow, quickly threw the light of a lantern in Ayrton's face.

Ayrton drew back. In the rapid flash of the lantern, he had recognized his former accomplice, Bob Harvey, who could not have known him, as he must have thought Ayrton long since dead.

"What are you doing here?" again said Bob Harvey, seizing Ayrton by the waistband.

But Ayrton, without replying, wrenched himself from his grasp and attempted to rush into the

A fifth shot from Ayrton laid one low, and the others drew back, not understanding what was going on.

magazine. A shot fired into the midst of the powder-casks, and all would be over!

"Help, lads!" shouted Bob Harvey.

At his shout two or three pirates awoke, jumped up, and, rushing on Ayrton, endeavoured to throw him down. He soon extricated himself from their grasp. He fired his revolver, and two of the convicts fell, but a blow from a knife which he could not ward off made a gash in his shoulder.

Ayrton perceived that he could no longer hope to carry out his project. Bob Harvey had reclosed the door of the powder-magazine, and a movement on the deck indicated a general awakening of the pirates. Ayrton must reserve himself to fight at the side of Cyrus Harding. There was nothing for him but flight!

But was flight still possible? It was doubtful, yet Ayrton resolved to dare everything in order to rejoin his companions.

Four barrels of the revolver were still undischarged. Two were fired – one, aimed at Bob Harvey, did not wound him, or at any rate only slightly, and Ayrton, profiting by the momentary retreat of his adversaries, rushed towards the companion-ladder to gain the deck. Passing before the lantern, he smashed it with a blow from the butt of his revolver. A profound darkness ensued, which favoured his flight. Two or three pirates, awakened by the noise, were descending the ladder at the same moment.

A fifth shot from Ayrton laid one low, and the others drew back, not understanding what was going on. Ayrton was on deck in two bounds, and three seconds later, having discharged his last barrel in the face of a pirate who was about to seize him by the throat, he leaped over the bulwarks into the sea. Ayrton had not made six strokes before shots were splashing around him like hail.

All immediately took refuge in the Chimneys. There Ayrton recounted all that had passed, even to his plan for blowing up the brig, which he had attempted to put into execution.

All hands were extended to Ayrton, who did not conceal from them that their situation was serious.

SIX AGAINST FIFTY

The pirates had been alarmed. They knew that Lincoln Island was inhabited. They would land upon it in numbers and well armed. They would respect nothing. Should the settlers fall into their hands, they must expect no mercy!

"Well, we shall know how to die!" said the reporter.

"Let us go in and watch," answered the engineer.

"Have we any chance of escape, captain?" asked the sailor.

"Yes, Pencroft."

"Hum! Six against fifty!"

"Yes! six! Without counting – "

"Who?" asked Pencroft.

Cyrus did not reply, but pointed upwards.

It was half-past six in the morning. Soon the fog began to clear away, and the topmasts of the brig issued from the vapour.

The "Speedy" now appeared in full view, with a spring on her cable, her head to the north, presenting her larboard side to the island. Just as Harding had calculated, she was not more than a mile and a quarter from the coast. The sinister black flag floated from the peak.

The engineer, with his telescope, could see that the four guns on board were pointed at the island. They were evidently ready to fire at a moment's notice.

In the meanwhile the "Speedy" remained silent. About thirty pirates could be seen moving on the deck. A few more on the poop; two others posted in the shrouds, and armed with spyglasses, were attentively surveying the island.

At eight o'clock, however, the colonists observed a movement on board the "Speedy." A boat was lowered, and seven men jumped into her. They were armed with muskets; one took the yoke-lines, four others the oars, and the two others, kneeling in the bows, ready to fire, reconnoitred the island. Their object was no doubt to make an examination but not to land, for in the latter case they would have come in larger numbers.

Pencroft and Ayrton, each hidden in a narrow cleft of the rock, saw them coming directly towards them, and waited till they were within range.

The boat advanced with extreme caution. The oars only dipped into the water at long intervals. It could now be seen that one of the convicts held a lead-line in his hand, and that he wished to fathom the depth of the channel hollowed out by the current of the Mercy. This showed that it was Bob Harvey's intention to bring his brig as near as possible to the coast. About thirty pirates, scattered in the rigging, followed every movement of the boat, and took the bearings of certain landmarks which would allow them to approach without danger.

At that moment two shots were heard. Smoke curled up from among the rocks of the islet. The man at the helm and the man with the lead-line fell backwards into the boat. Ayrton's and Pencroft's balls had struck them both at the same moment. Almost immediately a louder report was heard, a cloud of smoke issued from the brig's side, and a ball, striking the summit of the rock which sheltered Ayrton and Pencroft, made it fly in splinters, but the two marksmen remained unhurt.

Horrible imprecations burst from the boat, which immediately continued its way. The man who had been at the tiller was replaced by one of his comrades, and the oars were rapidly plunged into the water. However, instead of returning on board as might have been expected, the boat coasted along the islet, so as to round its southern point. The pirates pulled

Pencroft and Ayrton, each hidden in a narrow cleft of the rock, saw them coming direclty towards them, and waited till they were within range.

vigorously at their oars that they might get out of range of the bullets.

Twenty minutes after the first shots were fired, the boat was less than two cables-lengths off the Mercy. As the tide was beginning to rise with its accustomed violence, caused by the narrowness of the straits, the pirates were drawn towards the river, and it was only by dint of hard rowing that they were able to keep in the middle of the channel. But, as they were passing within good range of the mouth of the Mercy, two balls saluted them, and two more of their number were laid in the bottom of the boat. Neb and Spilett had not missed their aim.

The brig immediately sent a second ball on the post betrayed by the smoke, but without any other result than that of splintering the rock. The boat now contained only three able men. Carried on by the current, it shot through the channel with the rapidity of an arrow, passed before Harding and Herbert, who, not thinking it within range, withheld their fire, then, rounding the northern point of the islet with the two remaining oars, they pulled towards the brig.

Hitherto the settlers had nothing to complain of. Their adversaries had certainly had the worst of it. The latter already counted four men seriously wounded if not dead; they, on the contrary, unwounded, had not

missed a shot. If the pirates continued to attack them in this way, if they renewed their attempt to land by means of a boat, they could be destroyed one by one.

Half an hour passed before the boat, having to pull against the current, could get alongside the "Speedy." Frightful cries were heard when they returned on board with the wounded, and two or three guns were fired with no results.

But now about a dozen other convicts, maddened with rage, and possibly by the effect of the evening's potations, threw themselves into the boat. A second boat was also lowered, in which eight men took their places, and while the first pulled straight for the islet, to dislodge the colonists from thence, the second manoeuvred so as to force the entrance of the Mercy.

The situation was evidently becoming very dangerous for Pencroft and Ayrton, and they saw that they must regain the mainland.

However, they waited till the first boat was within range, when two well-directed balls threw its crew into disorder. Then, Pencroft and Ayrton, abandoning their posts, under fire from the dozen muskets, ran across the islet at full speed, jumped into their boat, crossed the channel at the moment the second boat reached the southern end, and ran to hide themselves in the Chimneys.

They had scarcely rejoined Cyrus Harding and Herbert, before the islet was overrun with pirates in every direction. Almost at the same moment, fresh reports resounded from the Mercy station, to which the second boat was rapidly approaching. Two, out of the eight men who manned her, were mortally wounded by Gideon Spilett and Neb, and the boat herself, carried irresistibly onto the reefs, was stove in at the mouth of the Mercy. But the six survivors, holding their muskets above their heads to preserve them from contact with the water, managed to land on the right bank of the river. Then, finding they were exposed to the fire of the ambush there, they fled in the direction of Flotsam Point, out of range of the balls.

THE ISLET WAS OVERRUN WITH PIRATES IN EVERY DIRECTION.

The actual situation was this: on the islet were a dozen convicts, of whom some were no doubt wounded, but who had still a boat at their disposal; on the island were six, but who could not by any possibility reach Granite House, as they could not cross the river, all the bridges being raised.

In the meanwhile, the pirates who occupied the islet had gradually advanced to the opposite shore, and were now only separated from the mainland by the channel.

Being armed with muskets alone, they could do no harm to the settlers, in ambush at the Chimneys and the mouth of the Mercy; but, not knowing the latter to be supplied with long-range rifles, they on their side did not believe themselves to be exposed. Quite uncovered, therefore, they surveyed the islet, and examined the shore.

Their illusion was of short duration. Ayrton's and Gideon Spilett's rifles then spoke, and no doubt imparted some very disagreeable intelligence to two of the convicts, for they fell backwards.

Then there was a general helter-skelter. The ten others, not even stopping to pick up their dead or wounded companions, fled to the other side of the islet,

Ayrton's and Gideon Spilett's rifles then spoke.

tumbled into the boat which had brought them, and pulled away with all their strength.

"Eight less!" exclaimed Pencroft. "Really, one would have thought that Mr. Spilett and Ayrton had given the word to fire together!"

"Gentlemen," said Ayrton, as he reloaded his gun, "this is becoming more serious. The brig is making sail!"

"The anchor is weighed!" exclaimed Pencroft.

"Yes, and she is already moving."

In fact, they could distinctly hear the creaking of the windlass. The "Speedy" was at first held by her anchor; then, when that had been raised, she began to drift towards the shore.

Soon the "Speedy" reached the point of the islet; she rounded it with ease; the mainsail was braced up, and the brig hugging the wind, stood across the mouth of the Mercy.

"The scoundrels! they are coming!" said Pencroft.

At that moment, Cyrus Harding, Ayrton, the sailor, and Herbert, were rejoined by Neb and Gideon Spilett. The reporter and his companion had judged it best to abandon the post at the Mercy, from which they could do nothing against the ship, and they had acted wisely.

"Have you formed any plan, Cyrus?" asked the reporter.

"We must take refuge in Granite House while there is still time, and the convicts cannot see us."

There was not a moment to be lost. The colonists left the Chimneys. A bend of the cliff prevented them from being seen by those in the brig, but two or three reports, and the crash of bullets on the rock, told them that the "Speedy" was at no great distance.

To spring into the lift, hoist themselves up to the door of Granite House, where Top and Jup had been shut up since the evening before, to rush into the large room, was the work of a minute only.

It was quite time, for the settlers, through the branches, could see the "Speedy," surrounded with smoke, gliding up the channel. The firing was incessant, and shot from the four guns struck blindly, both on the Mercy post, although it was not occupied, and on the Chimneys. The rocks were splintered, and cheers accompanied each discharge. However, they were hoping that Granite House would be spared, thanks to Harding's precaution of concealing the windows when a shot, piercing the door, penetrated into the passage.

"We are discovered!" exclaimed Pencroft.

The colonists had not, perhaps, been seen, but it was certain that Bob Harvey had thought proper to send a ball through the suspected foliage which concealed that part of the cliff. Soon he redoubled his attack, when another ball having torn away the leafy screen, disclosed a gaping aperture in the granite.

The colonists' situation was desperate. Their retreat was discovered. They could not oppose any obstacle to these missiles, nor protect the stone, which flew in splinters around them. There was nothing to be done but to take refuge in the upper passage of Granite House, and leave their dwelling to be devastated, when a deep roar was heard, followed by frightful cries!

Cyrus Harding and his companions rushed to one of the windows –

The brig, irresistibly raised on a sort of water-spout, had just split in two, and in less than ten seconds she was swallowed up with all her criminal crew!

"She has blown up!" cried Herbert. "Yes! Blown up, just as if Ayrton had set fire to the powder!" returned Pencroft, throwing himself into the lift together with Neb and the lad. "But what has happened?" asked Gideon Spilett, quite stunned by this unexpected catastrophe. "Oh! This time, we shall know – " answered the engineer quickly.

A week after the catastrophe – or, rather, after the fortunate, though inexplicable, event to which the colony owed its preservation – nothing more could be seen of the vessel, even at low tide. The wreck had disappeared, and Granite House was enriched by nearly all it had contained.

THE COLONISTS' SITUATION WAS DESPERATE. THEIR RETREAT WAS DISCOVERED.

"My friends, then," said Cyrus Harding, "we can no longer be in doubt as to the presence of a mysterious being, a castaway like us, perhaps, abandoned on our island, and I say this in order that Ayrton may be acquainted with all the strange events which have occurred during these two years. Who this beneficent stranger is, whose intervention has, so fortunately for us, been manifested on many occasions, I cannot imagine. But his services are not the less real, and are of such a nature that only a man possessed of prodigious power could render them. Ayrton is indebted to him as much as we are, for, if it was the stranger who saved me from the waves after the fall from the balloon, evidently it was he who wrote the document, who placed the bottle in the channel, and who has made known to us the situation of our companion. I will add that it was he who guided that chest, provided with everything we wanted, and stranded it on Flotsam Point; that it was he who lighted that fire on the heights of the island, which permitted you to land, that it was he who fired that bullet found in the body of the peccary; that it was he who plunged that torpedo into the channel. We have contracted a debt, and I hope that we shall one day pay it."

In a few seconds, before he had even time to fire his second barrel, he fell, struck to the heart by Harding's dagger, more sure even than his gun.

However, the chief business of the colonists was to make that complete exploration of the island which had been decided upon, and which would have two objects: to discover the mysterious being whose existence was now indisputable, and at the same time to find out what had become of the pirates, what retreat they had chosen, what sort of life they were leading, and what was to be feared from them.

Moreover, it was necessary for Ayrton to return to the corral, where the domesticated animals required his care. It was decided that he should spend two days there, and return to Granite House after having liberally supplied the stables.

That evening a telegram was sent to Ayrton, requesting him to bring from the corral a couple of goats, which Neb wished to acclimatize to the plateau. Singularly enough, Ayrton did not acknowledge the receipt of the despatch, as he was accustomed to do. The colonists waited, therefore, for Ayrton to appear on Prospect Heights. Neb and Herbert even watched at the bridge so as to be ready to lower it the moment their companion presented himself. But up to ten in the evening, there were no signs of Ayrton. It was, therefore, judged best to send a fresh despatch, requiring an immediate reply.

The bell of the telegraph at Granite House remained mute. The colonists' uneasiness was great. What had happened? Was Ayrton no longer at the corral, or if he was still there, had he no longer control over his movements? Could they go to the corral in this dark night?

They consulted. Some wished to go, the others to remain.

"But," said Herbert, "perhaps some accident has happened to the telegraphic apparatus, so that it works no longer?"

"That may be," said the reporter.

"Wait till tomorrow," replied Cyrus Harding. "It is possible, indeed, that Ayrton has not received our despatch, or even that we have not received his."

They waited, of course not without some anxiety. At dawn of day, the 11th of November, Harding again sent the electric current along the wire and received no reply. He tried again: the same result.

He tried again: the same result.

"Off to the corral," said he.

"And well armed!" added Pencroft.

The colonists were now half way between Granite House and the corral, having still two miles and a half to go. They pressed forward with redoubled speed. Indeed, it was to be feared that some serious accident had occurred in the corral.

At last the palisade appeared through the trees. No trace of any damage could be seen. The gate was shut as usual. Deep silence reigned in the corral. Neither the accustomed bleating of the sheep nor Ayrton's voice could be heard.

"Let us enter," said Cyrus Harding.

And the engineer advanced, while his companions, keeping watch about twenty paces behind him, were ready to fire at a moment's notice.

Harding raised the inner latch of the gate and was about to push it back, when Top barked loudly. A report sounded and was responded to by a cry of pain. Herbert, struck by a bullet, lay stretched on the ground.

At Herbert's cry, Pencroft, letting his gun fall, rushed towards him. "They have killed him!" he cried. "My boy! They have killed him!" Cyrus Harding and Gideon Spilett ran to Herbert. The reporter listened to ascertain if the poor lad's heart was still beating. "He lives," said he, "but he must be carried – "

"To Granite House? that is impossible!" replied the engineer.

"Into the corral, then!" said Pencroft.

"In a moment," said Harding.

And he ran round the left corner of the palisade. There he found a convict, who aiming at him, sent a ball through his hat. In a few seconds, before he had even time to fire his second barrel, he fell, struck to the heart by Harding's dagger, more sure even than his gun.

During this time, Gideon Spilett and the sailor hoisted themselves over the palisade, leaped into the enclosure, threw down the props which supported the inner door, ran into the empty house, and soon, poor Herbert was lying on Ayrton's bed. In a few moments, Harding was by his side.

On seeing Herbert senseless, the sailor's grief was terrible. He sobbed, he cried, he tried to beat his head against the wall.

Neither the engineer nor the reporter could calm him. They themselves were choked with emotion. They could not speak.

However, they knew that it depended on them to rescue from death the poor boy who was suffering beneath their eyes. Gideon Spilett had not passed through the many incidents by which his life had been checkered without acquiring some slight knowledge of medicine. He knew a little of everything, and several times he had been obliged to attend to wounds produced either by a sword-bayonet or shot. Assisted by Cyrus Harding, he proceeded to render the aid Herbert required. The reporter was immediately struck by the complete stupor in which Herbert lay, a stupor owing either to the hemorrhage, or to the shock, the ball having struck a bone with sufficient force to produce a violent concussion.

Herbert was deadly pale, and his pulse so feeble that Spilett only felt it beat at long intervals, as if it was on the point of stopping. These symptoms were very serious.

Herbert's chest was laid bare, and the blood having been stanched with handkerchiefs, it was bathed with cold water.

The contusion, or rather the contused wound appeared – an oval below the chest between the third and fourth ribs. It was there that Herbert had been hit by the bullet.

Cyrus Harding and Gideon Spilett then turned the poor boy over; as they did so, he uttered a moan so feeble that they almost thought it was his last sigh.

Herbert's back was covered with blood from another contused wound, by which the ball had immediately escaped.

"God be praised!" said the reporter, "the ball is not in the body, and we shall not have to extract it."

"But the heart?" asked Harding.

"The heart has not been touched; if it had been, Herbert would be dead!"

"Dead!" exclaimed Pencroft, with a groan.

The sailor had only heard the last words uttered by the reporter.

"No, Pencroft," replied Cyrus Harding, "no! He is not dead. His pulse still beats. He has even uttered a moan. But for your boy's sake, calm yourself. We have need of all our self-possession."

"Do not make us lose it, my friend."

Pencroft was silent, but a reaction set in, and great tears rolled down his cheeks. Herbert's life hung on a thread, and this thread might break at any moment. The next day, the 12th of November, the hopes of Harding and his companions slightly revived. Herbert had come out of his long stupor. He opened his eyes, he recognized Cyrus Harding, the reporter, and Pencroft. He uttered two or three words. He did not know what had happened. They told him, and Spilett begged him to remain perfectly still, telling him that his life was not in danger, and that his wounds would heal in a few days. However, Herbert scarcely suffered at all, and the cold water with which they were constantly bathed prevented any inflammation of the wounds. The suppuration was established in a regular way, the fever did not increase, and it might now be hoped that this terrible wound would not involve any catastrophe. Pencroft felt the swelling of his heart gradually subside. He was like a sister of mercy, like a mother by the bed of her child. Herbert dozed again, but his sleep appeared more natural.

"Tell me again that you hope, Mr. Spilett," said Pencroft. "Tell me again that you will save Herbert!"

"Yes, we will save him!" replied the reporter. "The wound is serious, and, perhaps, even the ball has traversed the lungs, but the perforation of this organ is not fatal."

"God bless you!" answered Pencroft.

As may be believed, during the four-and-twenty hours they had been in the corral, the colonists had no other thought than that of nursing Herbert. They did not think either of the danger which threatened them should the convicts return, or of the precautions to be taken for the future.

But on this day, while Pencroft watched by the sick-bed, Cyrus Harding and the reporter consulted as to what it would be best to do.

First of all they examined the corral. There was not a trace of Ayrton. Had the unhappy man been dragged away by his former accomplices? Had he resisted, and been overcome in the struggle? This last supposition was only too probable. Gideon Spilett, at the moment he scaled the palisade, had clearly seen some one of the convicts running along the southern spur of Mount Franklin, towards whom Top had sprung. It was one of those whose object had been so completely defeated by the rocks at the mouth of the Mercy. Besides, the one killed by Harding, and whose body was found outside the enclosure, of course belonged to Bob Harvey's crew.

As to the corral, it had not suffered any damage. The gates were closed, and the animals had not been able to disperse in the forest. Nor could they see traces of any struggle, any devastation, either in the hut, or in the palisade. The ammunition only, with which Ayrton had been supplied, had disappeared with him.

THE ENIGMA UNVEILED

Of the convicts, the dangers which menaced Granite House, the ruins with which the plateau was covered, the colonists thought no longer. Herbert's critical state outweighed all other considerations. Would the removal prove fatal to him by causing some internal injury? The reporter could not affirm it, but he and his companions almost despaired of the result. The cart was brought to the bend of the river. There some branches, disposed as a liner, received the mattress on which lay the unconscious Herbert. Ten minutes after, Cyrus Harding, Spilett, and Pencroft were at the foot of the cliff, leaving Neb to take the cart on to the plateau of Prospect Heights. The lift was put in motion, and Herbert was soon stretched on his bed in Granite House.

THE ENIGMA UNVEILED

What cares were lavished on him to bring him back to life! He smiled for a moment on finding himself in his room, but could scarcely even murmur a few words, so great was his weakness. Gideon Spilett examined his wounds. He feared to find them reopened, having been imperfectly healed. There was nothing of the sort. From whence, then, came this prostration? why was Herbert so much worse? The lad then fell into a kind of feverish sleep, and the reporter and Pencroft remained near the bed.

The night was frightful. In his delirium Herbert uttered words which went to the hearts of his companions. He struggled with the convicts, he called to Ayrton, he poured forth entreaties to that mysterious being – that powerful unknown protector – whose image was stamped upon his mind; then he again fell into a deep exhaustion which completely prostrated him. Several times Gideon Spilett thought that the poor boy was dead.

The next day, the 8th of December, was but a succession of the fainting fits. Herbert's thin hands clutched the sheets. They had administered further doses of pounded bark, but the reporter expected no result from it.

"If before tomorrow morning we have not given him a more energetic febrifuge," said the reporter, "Herbert will be dead."

Night arrived – the last night, it was too much to be feared, of the good, brave, intelligent boy, so far in advance of his years, and who was loved by all as their own child. The only remedy which existed against this terrible malignant fever, the only specific which could overcome it, was not to be found in Lincoln Island.

During the night, Herbert was seized by a more violent delirium. His liver was fearfully congested, his brain affected, and already it was impossible for him to recognize anyone.

Towards three o'clock in the morning Herbert uttered a piercing cry. He seemed to be torn by a supreme convulsion. Neb, who was near him, terrified, ran into the next room where his companions were watching.

It was five in the morning. The rays of the rising sun began to shine in at the windows of Granite House. It promised to be a fine day, and this day was to be poor Herbert's last!

A ray glanced on the table placed near the bed.

Suddenly Pencroft, uttering a cry, pointed to the table.

On it lay a little oblong box, of which the cover bore these words: "SULPHATE OF QUININE."

Gideon Spilett took the box and opened it. It contained nearly two hundred grains of a white powder, a few particles of which he carried to his lips. The extreme bitterness of the substance precluded all doubt; it was certainly the precious extract of quinine, that pre-eminent antifebrile.

This powder must be administered to Herbert without delay. How it came there might be discussed later.

"Some coffee!" said Spilett.

In a few moments Neb brought a cup of the warm infusion. Gideon Spilett threw into it about eighteen grains of quinine, and they succeeded in making Herbert drink the mixture.

The hopes of all had now revived. The mysterious influence had been again exerted, and in a critical moment, when they had despaired of it.

In a few hours Herbert was much calmer. The colonists could now discuss this incident. The intervention of the stranger was more evident than ever. But how had he been able to penetrate during the night into Granite House? It was inexplicable, and, in truth, the proceedings of the genius of the island were not less mysterious than was that genius himself. During this day the sulphate of quinine was administered to Herbert every three hours.

The next day some improvement in Herbert's condition was apparent. Certainly, he was not out of danger, intermittent fevers being subject to frequent and dangerous relapses, but the most assiduous care was bestowed on him. And the hearts of all were animated by returning hope.

This hope was not disappointed. Ten days after, on the 20th of December, Herbert's convalescence commenced.

Pencroft was as a man who has been drawn up from the bottom of an abyss. Fits of joy approaching delirium seized him. When the time for the third attack had passed by, he nearly suffocated the reporter in his embrace. Since then, he always called him Dr. Spilett.

The real doctor, however, remained undiscovered.

"We will find him!" repeated the sailor.

Certainly, this man, whoever he was, might expect a somewhat too energetic embrace from the worthy Pencroft!

The month of December ended, and with it the year 1867, during which the colonists of Lincoln Island had of late been so severely tried. They commenced the year 1868 with magnificent weather, great heat, and a tropical temperature, delightfully cooled by the sea-breeze. Herbert's recovery progressed, and from his bed, placed near one of the windows of Granite House, he could inhale the fresh air, charged with ozone, which could not fail to restore his health.

During all this time, the convicts did not once appear in the vicinity of Granite House. There was no news of Ayrton, and though the engineer and Herbert still had some hopes of finding him again, their companions did not doubt but that the unfortunate man had perished. However, this uncertainty could not last, and when once the lad should have recovered, the expedition, the result of which must be so important, would be undertaken.

The necessary preparations for this exploration were now commenced, and were important, for the colonists had sworn not to return to Granite House until their twofold object had been achieved; on the one hand, to exterminate the convicts, and rescue Ayrton, if he was still living; on the other, to discover who it was that presided so effectually over the fortunes of the colony. The engineer's plan was this: To minutely survey the valley forming the bed of the river, and to cautiously approach the neighbourhood of the corral; if the corral was occupied, to seize it by force; if it was not, to entrench themselves there and make it the centre of the operations.

AND THE HEARTS OF ALL WERE ANIMATED BY RETURNING HOPE.

This thirty feet, which it was necessary to cross from the wood to the palisade, constituted the dangerous zone, to borrow a ballistic term: in fact, one or more bullets fired from behind the palisade might knock over anyone who ventured on to this zone. In a few moments they were near the closed door of the house. Harding signed to his companions not to stir, and approached the window, then feebly lighted by the inner light. On the table burned a lantern. Near the table was the bed formerly used by Ayrton.

THE ENIGMA UNVEILED

Suddenly Cyrus Harding drew back, and in a hoarse voice, "Ayrton!" he exclaimed.

Immediately the door was forced rather than opened, and the colonists rushed into the room. But, at that moment, Top, breaking loose, began to bark furiously and rush to the back of the corral, to the right of the house. The colonists followed him, and reached the borders of the little stream, shaded by large trees. And there, in the bright moonlight, what did they see? Five corpses, stretched on the bank! They were those of the convicts who, four months previously, had landed on Lincoln Island!

Ayrton – bound, gagged, and closely watched – had lived in this cave for four months.

Sometimes, however, when the conversation bore on some interesting subject the hour for sleep was delayed for a time. The colonists then spoke of the future, and talked willingly of the changes which a voyage in the schooner to inhabited lands would make in their situation. But always, in the midst of these plans, prevailed the thought of a subsequent return to Lincoln Island. Never would they abandon this colony, founded with so much labour and with such success, and to which a communication with America would afford a fresh impetus.

One evening on the 15th of October, the conversation was prolonged later than usual. It was nine o'clock. Already, long badly concealed yawns gave warning of the hour of rest, and Pencroft was proceeding to his bed when the electric bell, placed in the dining-room, suddenly rang.

All were there, Cyrus Harding, Gideon Spilett, Herbert, Ayrton, Pencroft, Neb. Therefore none of the colonists were at the corral.

Cyrus Harding rose. His companions stared at each other, scarcely believing their ears.

"What does that mean?" cried Neb. "Was it the devil who rang it?"

No one answered.

"The weather is stormy," observed Herbert. "Might not its influence of electricity – "

Herbert did not finish his phrase. The engineer, towards whom all eyes were turned, shook his head negatively.

"We must wait," said Gideon Spilett. "If it is a signal, whoever it may be who has made it, he will renew it."

"But who do you think it is?" cried Neb.

"Who?" answered Pencroft, "but he – "

The sailor's sentence was cut short by a new tinkle of the bell.

Harding went to the apparatus, and sent this question to the corral:

"What do you want?"

A few moments later the needle, moving on the alphabetic dial, gave this reply to the tenants of Granite House:

"Come to the corral immediately."

"At last!" exclaimed Harding.

Yes! At last! The mystery was about to be unveiled. The colonists' fatigue had disappeared before the tremendous interest which was about to urge them to the corral, and all wish for rest had ceased. Without having uttered a word, in a few moments they had left Granite House, and were standing on the beach.

The night was black. As Herbert had observed, great stormy clouds formed a lowering and heavy vault, preventing any star rays. A few lightning flashes, reflections from a distant storm, illuminated the horizon.

They walked at a good pace, a prey to the liveliest emotions. There was no doubt but that they were now going to learn the long-searched-for answer to the enigma, the name of that mysterious being, so deeply concerned in their life, so generous in his influence, so powerful in his action! Must not this stranger have indeed mingled with their existence, have known the smallest details, have heard all that was said in Granite House, to have been able always to act in the very nick of time?

In a minute the corral was crossed, and Harding stood before the hut. Probably the house was occupied by the stranger, since it was from thence that the telegram had been sent. However, no light shone through the window.

The engineer knocked at the door. No answer.

Cyrus Harding opened the door, and the settlers entered the room, which was perfectly dark. A light was struck by Neb, and in a few moments the lantern was lighted and the light thrown into every corner of the room.

There was no one there. Everything was in the state in which it had been left.

"Have we been deceived by an illusion?" murmured Cyrus Harding.

No! That was not possible! The telegram had clearly said,

"Come to the corral immediately."

They approached the table specially devoted to the use of the wire. Everything was in order – the pile on the box containing it, as well as all the apparatus.

"Ah! A note!" cried Herbert, pointing to a paper lying on the table.

On this paper were written these words in English:

"Follow the new wire."

"Forward!" cried Harding, who understood that the despatch had not been sent from the corral, but from the mysterious retreat, communicating directly with Granite House by means of a supplementary wire joined to the old one.

Neb took the lighted lantern, and all left the corral. The storm then burst forth with tremendous violence.

There was no telegraphic communication in any part of the corral between the house and the palisade; but the engineer, running straight to the first post, saw by the light of a flash a new wire hanging from the isolator to the ground.

"There it is!" said he.

This wire appeared to pass through the wood and the southern spurs of the mountain, and consequently it ran towards the west.

At last the wire touched the rocks on the beach. The colonists had reached the bottom of the basalt cliff.

There appeared a narrow ridge, running horizontally and parallel with the sea. The settlers followed the wire along it. They had not gone a hundred paces when the ridge by a moderate incline sloped down to the level of the sea.

"Follow it!" said Cyrus Harding.

And the settlers immediately pressed forward, guided by the wire.

The engineer seized the wire and found that it disappeared beneath the waves. His companions were stupefied. A cry of disappointment, almost a cry of despair, escaped them! Must they then plunge beneath the water and seek there for some submarine cavern? In their excited state they would not have hesitated to do it. The engineer stopped them. He led his companions to a hollow in the rocks, and there –

"We must wait," said he. "The tide is high. At low water the way will be open."

"But what can make you think – " asked Pencroft.

"He would not have called us if the means had been wanting to enable us to reach him!"

All the prisms, all the peaks, were flooded with the electric fluid, so that the brilliancy belonged to them.

At midnight, Harding carrying the lantern, descended to the beach to reconnoitre.

The engineer was not mistaken. The beginning of an immense excavation could be seen under the water. There the wire, bending at a right angle, entered the yawning gulf. Cyrus Harding returned to his companions, and said simply,

"In an hour the opening will be practicable."

"It is there, then?" said Pencroft.

"Did you doubt it?" returned Harding.

"But this cavern must be filled with water to a certain height," observed Herbert.

"Either the cavern will be completely dry," replied Harding, "and in that case we can traverse it on foot, or it will not be dry, and some means of transport will be put at our disposal."

An hour passed. All climbed down through the rain to the level of the sea. There was now eight feet of the opening above the water. It was like the arch of a bridge, under which rushed the foaming water. Leaning forward, the engineer saw a black object floating on the water. He drew it towards him. It was a boat, moored to some interior projection of the cave.

"Jump in!" said Harding.

In a moment the settlers were in the boat. Neb and Ayrton took the oars, Pencroft the rudder. Cyrus Harding in the bows, with the lantern, lighted the way. Solemn silence reigned in this basaltic cavern. On they

went for another quarter of an hour, and a distance of half-a-mile must have been cleared from the mouth of the cave, when Harding's voice was again heard. The boat stopped, and the colonists perceived a bright light illuminating the vast cavern, so deeply excavated in the bowels of the island, of which nothing had ever led them to suspect the existence.

THEN, FALLING BACK ON THE SEAT, HE MURMURED A NAME WHICH GIDEON SPILETT ALONE COULD HEAR.

At this place the breadth of the sheet of water measured nearly 350 feet, and beyond the dazzling centre could be seen an enormous basaltic wall, blocking up any issue on that side. The cavern widened here considerably, the sea forming a little lake. But the roof, the side walls, the end cliff, all the prisms, all the peaks, were flooded with the electric fluid, so that the brilliancy belonged to them, and as if the light issued from them. In the centre of the lake a long cigar-shaped object floated on the surface of the water, silent, motionless. The brilliancy which issued from it escaped from its sides as from two kilns heated to a white heat. This apparatus, similar in shape to an enormous whale, was about 250 feet long, and rose about ten or twelve above the water. The boat slowly approached it, Cyrus Harding stood up in the bows. He gazed, a prey to violent excitement. Then, all at once, seizing the reporter's arm,

"It is he! It can only be he!" he cried, "he! – "

Then, falling back on the seat, he murmured a name which Gideon Spilett alone could hear. The reporter evidently knew this name, for it had a wonderful effect upon him, and he answered in a hoarse voice,

"He! An outlawed man!"

"He!" said Harding.

At the engineer's command the boat approached this singular floating apparatus. The boat touched the left side, from which escaped a ray of light. Harding and his companions mounted on the platform. An open hatchway was there. All darted down the opening. At the bottom of the ladder was a deck, lighted by electricity. At the end of this deck was a door, which Harding opened. A richly-ornamented room, quickly traversed by the colonists, was joined to a library, over which a luminous ceiling shed a flood of light. At the end of the library a large door, also shut, was opened by the engineer. An immense saloon – a sort of museum, in which were heaped up, with all the treasures of the mineral world, works of art, marvels of industry – appeared before the eyes of the colonists, who almost thought themselves suddenly transported into a land of enchantment.

Stretched on a rich sofa they saw a man, who did not appear to notice their presence. Then Harding raised his voice, and to the extreme surprise of his companions, he uttered these words,

"Captain Nemo, you asked for us! We are here."

CAPTAIN NEMO

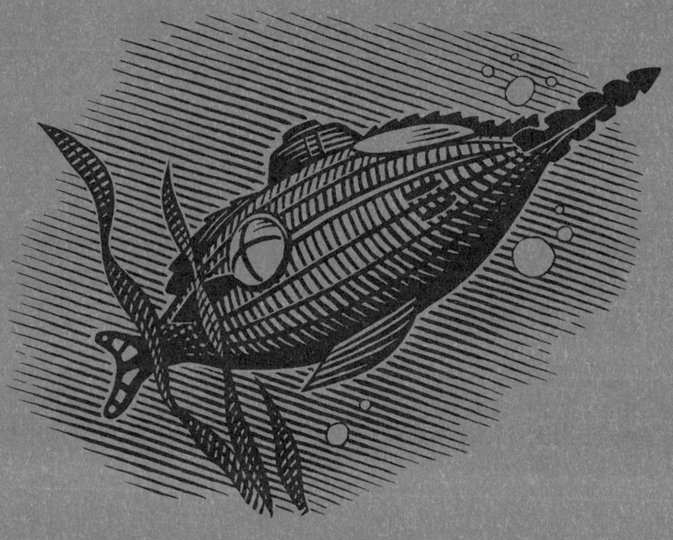

At these words the reclining figure rose, and the electric light fell upon his countenance; a magnificent head, the forehead high, the glance commanding, beard white, hair abundant and falling over the shoulders.

His hand rested upon the cushion of the divan from which he had just risen. He appeared perfectly calm. It was evident that his strength had been gradually undermined by illness, but his voice seemed yet powerful, as he said in English, and in a tone which evinced extreme surprise,

"Sir, I have no name."

"Nevertheless, I know you!" replied Cyrus Harding.

Captain Nemo fixed his penetrating gaze upon the engineer, as though he were about to annihilate him.

Then, falling back amid the pillows of the divan,

"After all, what matters now?" he murmured; "I am dying!"

All regarded him with profound emotion. Before them they beheld that being whom they had styled the "genius of the island," the powerful protector whose intervention, in so many circumstances, had been so efficacious, the benefactor to whom they owed such a debt of gratitude! Their eyes beheld a man only, and a man at the point of death, where Pencroft and Neb had expected to find an almost supernatural being!

But how happened it that Cyrus Harding had recognized Captain Nemo? why had the latter so suddenly risen on hearing this name uttered, a name which he had believed known to none?

The captain had resumed his position on the divan, and leaning on his arm, he regarded the engineer, seated near him.

"You know the name I formerly bore, sir?" he asked.

"I do," answered Cyrus Harding, "and also that of this wonderful submarine vessel – "

"The 'Nautilus'?" said the captain, with a faint smile.

"The 'Nautilus.'" – "But do you – do you know who I am?" – "I do." – "It is nevertheless many years since I have held any communication with the inhabited world; three long years have I passed in the depth of the sea, the only place where I have found liberty! Who then can have betrayed my secret?"

"A man who was bound to you by no tie, Captain Nemo, and who, consequently, cannot be accused of treachery."

"The Frenchman who was cast on board my vessel by chance sixteen years since?" – "The same." – "He and his two companions did not then perish in the maelstrom, in the midst of which the 'Nautilus' was struggling?"

"They escaped, and a book has appeared under the title of 'Twenty Thousand Leagues Under the Sea,' which contains your history."

"The history of a few months only of my life!" interrupted the captain impetuously.

"It is true," answered Cyrus Harding, "but a few months of that strange life have sufficed to make you known."

"As a great criminal, doubtless!" said Captain Nemo, a haughty smile curling his lips. "Yes, a rebel, perhaps an outlaw against humanity!"

The engineer was silent.

"Well, sir?"

"It is not for me to judge you, Captain Nemo," answered Cyrus Harding, "at any rate as regards your past life. I am, with the rest of the world, ignorant of the motives which induced you to adopt this strange mode of existence, and I cannot judge of effects without knowing their causes; but what I do know is, that a beneficent hand has constantly protected us since our arrival on Lincoln Island, that we all owe our lives to a good, generous, and powerful being, and that this being so powerful, good and generous, Captain Nemo, is yourself!"

"It is I," answered the captain simply.

The engineer and the reporter rose. Their companions had drawn near, and the gratitude with which their hearts were charged was about to express itself in their gestures and words.

Captain Nemo stopped them by a sign, and in a voice which betrayed more emotion than he doubtless intended to show.

"Wait till you have heard all," he said.

And the captain, in a few concise sentences, ran over the events of his life.

CAPTAIN NEMO FIXED HIS PENETRATING GAZE UPON THE ENGINEER, AS THOUGH HE WERE ABOUT TO ANNIHILATE HIM.

His narrative was short, yet he was obliged to summon up his whole remaining energy to arrive at the end. He was evidently contending against extreme weakness.

Captain Nemo was an Indian, the Prince Dakkar, son of a rajah of the then independent territory of Bundelkund. His father sent him, when ten years of age, to Europe, in order that he might receive an education in all respects complete, and in the hopes that by his talents and knowledge he might one day take a leading part in raising his long degraded and heathen country to a level with the nations of Europe.

From the age of ten years to that of thirty Prince Dakkar, endowed by Nature with her richest gifts of intellect, accumulated knowledge of every kind, and in science, literature, and art his researches were extensive and profound.

He travelled over the whole of Europe. His rank and fortune caused him to be everywhere sought after; but the pleasures of the world had for him no attractions. Though young and possessed of every personal advantage, he was ever grave – sombre even – devoured by an unquenchable thirst for knowledge.

Prince Dakkar returned to Bundelkund in the year 1849. He married a noble Indian lady, who was imbued with an ambition not less ardent than that by which he was inspired. Two children were born to them, whom they tenderly loved.

Instigated by princes equally ambitious and less sagacious and more unscrupulous than he was, the people of India were persuaded that they might successfully rise against their English rulers, In 1857, the great sepoy revolt broke out. Prince Dakkar, under the belief that he should thereby have the opportunity of attaining the object of his long-cherished ambition, was easily drawn into it. He forthwith devoted his talents and wealth to the service of this cause. He aided it in person; he fought in the front ranks; but at length the sanguinary rebels were utterly defeated, and the atrocious mutiny was brought to an end.

Where, then, did he seek that liberty denied him upon the inhabited earth? Under the waves, in the depths of the ocean, where none could follow. For a long time after this, Captain Nemo continued to live thus, traversing every sea. But one by one his companions died, and found their last resting-place in their cemetery of coral, in the bed of the Pacific. At last Captain Nemo remained the solitary survivor of all those who had taken refuge with him in the depths of the ocean.

The electric light fell upon his countenance; a magnificent head, the forehead high, the glance commanding, beard white, hair abundant and falling over the shoulders.

He was now sixty years of age. Although alone, he succeeded in navigating the "Nautilus" towards one of those submarine caverns which had sometimes served him as a harbour.

One of these ports was hollowed beneath Lincoln Island, and at this moment furnished an asylum to the "Nautilus."

He observed these men thrown without resources upon a desert island, but had no wish to be himself discovered by them. He learned from them the tremendous conflict of America with America itself, for the abolition of slavery. Yes, these men were worthy to reconcile Captain Nemo with that humanity which they represented so nobly in the island.

Captain Nemo had saved Cyrus Harding. It was he also who had brought back the dog to the Chimneys, who rescued Top from the waters of the lake, who caused to fall at Flotsam Point the case containing so many things useful to the colonists, who conveyed the canoe back into the stream of the Mercy, who cast the cord from the top of Granite House at the time of the attack by the baboons, who made known the presence of Ayrton upon Tabor Island, by means of the document enclosed in the bottle, who caused the explosion of the brig by the shock of a torpedo placed at the bottom of the canal, who saved Herbert from certain death by bringing the sulphate of quinine; and finally, it was he who had killed the convicts with the electric balls, of which he possessed the secret, and which he employed in the chase of submarine creatures. Thus were explained so many apparently supernatural occurrences, and which all proved the generosity and power of the captain.

The captain concluded the narrative of his life. Cyrus Harding then spoke; he recalled all the incidents which had exercised so beneficent an influence upon the colony, and in the names of his companions and himself thanked the generous being to whom they owed so much.

But Captain Nemo paid little attention; his mind appeared to be absorbed by one idea, and without taking the proffered hand of the engineer,

"Now, sir," said he, "now that you know my history, your judgement! What think you of my life, gentlemen?"

Cyrus Harding extended his hand to the former prince and replied gravely, "Sir, your error was in supposing that the past can be resuscitated, and in contending against inevitable progress. It is one of those errors which some admire, others blame; which God alone can judge. He who is mistaken in an action which he sincerely believes to be right may be an enemy, but retains our esteem. Your error is one that we may admire, and your name has nothing to fear from the judgement of history, which does not condemn heroic folly, but its results."

The old man's breast swelled with emotion, and raising his hand to heaven,

"Was I wrong, or in the right?" he murmured.

Cyrus Harding replied, "All great actions return to God, from whom they are derived. Captain Nemo, we, whom you have succoured, shall ever mourn your loss."

Herbert, who had drawn near the captain, fell on his knees and kissed his hand.

A tear glistened in the eyes of the dying man. "My child," he said, "may God bless you!"

An extreme exhaustion now overcame Captain Nemo, who had fallen back upon the divan. It was useless to contemplate removing him to Granite House, for he had expressed his wish to remain in the midst of those marvels of the "Nautilus" which millions could not have purchased, and to wait there for that death which was swiftly approaching.

An extreme exhaustion now overcame Captain Nemo, who had fallen back upon the divan.

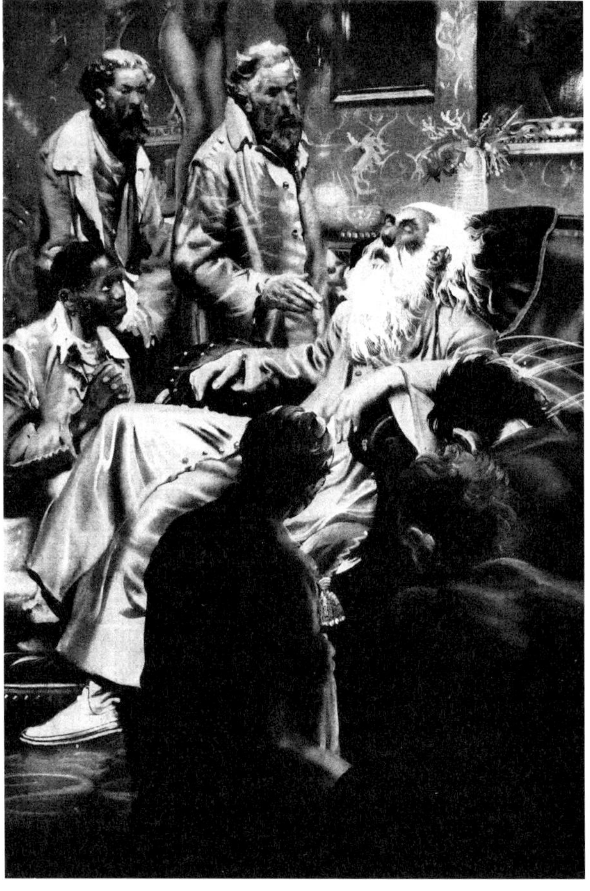

During a long interval of prostration, which rendered him almost unconscious, Cyrus Harding and Gideon Spilett attentively observed the condition of the dying man. His strength was gradually diminishing. That frame, once so robust, was now but the fragile tenement of a departing soul. All of life was concentrated in the heart and head.

The engineer and reporter consulted in whispers. Was it possible to render any aid to the dying man? Might his life, if not saved, be prolonged for some days? He himself had said that no remedy could avail, and he awaited with tranquility that death which had for him no terrors.

"We can do nothing," said Gideon Spilett.

"But of what is he dying?" asked Pencroft.

"Life is simply fading out," replied the reporter.

"Nevertheless," said the sailor, "if we move him into the open air, and the light of the sun, he might perhaps recover."

"No, Pencroft," answered the engineer, "it is useless to attempt it. Besides, Captain Nemo would never consent to leave his vessel. He has lived for a dozen years on board the 'Nautilus,' and on board the 'Nautilus' he desires to die."

Without doubt Captain Nemo heard Cyrus Harding's reply, for he raised himself slightly, and in a voice more feeble, but always intelligible,

"You are right, sir," he said. "I shall die here – it is my wish; and therefore I have a request to make of you."

The colonists listened reverently to the words of the dying man.

"Tomorrow, after my death, Mr. Harding," continued the captain, "yourself and companions will leave the 'Nautilus,' for all the treasures it contains must perish with me. One token alone will remain with you of Prince Dakkar, with whose history you are now acquainted. That coffer yonder contains diamonds of the value of many millions, most of them mementoes of the time when, husband and father, I thought happiness possible for me, and a collection of pearls gathered by my friends and myself in the depths of the ocean. Of this treasure at a future day, you may make good use. In the hands of such men as yourself and your comrades, Captain Harding, money will never be a source of danger. From on high I shall still participate in your enterprises, and I fear not but that they will prosper."

After a few moments' repose, necessitated by his extreme weakness, Captain Nemo continued,

"Tomorrow you will take the coffer, you will leave the saloon, of which you will close the door; then you will ascend on to the deck of the 'Nautilus,' and you will lower the mainhatch so as entirely to close the vessel."

"It shall be done, captain," answered Cyrus Harding.

"Good. You will then embark in the canoe which brought you hither; but, before leaving the 'Nautilus,' go to the stern and there open two large stop-cocks which you will find upon the water-line. The water will penetrate into the reservoirs, and the 'Nautilus' will gradually sink beneath the water to repose at the bottom of the abyss."

And comprehending a gesture of Cyrus Harding, the captain added,

"Fear nothing! You will but bury a corpse!"

Neither Cyrus Harding nor his companions ventured to offer any observation to Captain Nemo. He had expressed his last wishes, and they had nothing to do but to conform to them.

"I have your promise, gentlemen?" added Captain Nemo.

"You have, captain," replied the engineer.

The captain thanked the colonists by a sign, and requested them to leave him for some hours. Gideon Spilett wished to remain near him, in the event of a crisis coming on, but the dying man refused, saying, "I shall live until tomorrow, sir."

All left the saloon, passed through the library and the dining-room, and arrived forward, in the machine-room where the electrical apparatus was established, which supplied not only heat and light, but the mechanical power of the "Nautilus."

"What a man!" said Pencroft. "Is it possible that he can have lived at the bottom of the sea? And it seems to me that perhaps he has not found peace there any more than elsewhere!"

"The 'Nautilus,'" observed Ayrton, "might have enabled us to leave Lincoln Island and reach some inhabited country."

"Good Heavens!" exclaimed Pencroft, "I for one would never risk myself in such a craft. To sail on the seas, good, but under the seas, never!"

"I believe, Pencroft," answered the reporter, "that the navigation of a submarine vessel such as the 'Nautilus' ought to be very easy, and that we should soon become accustomed to it. There would be no storms, no lee-shore to fear. At some feet beneath the surface the waters of the ocean are as calm as those of a lake."

"That may be," replied the sailor, "but I prefer a gale of wind on board a well-found craft. A vessel is built to sail on the sea, and not beneath it."

"My friends," said the engineer, "it is useless, at any rate as regards the 'Nautilus,' to discuss the question of submarine vessels. The 'Nautilus' is not ours, and we have not the right to dispose of it. Moreover, we could in no case avail ourselves of it. Independently of the fact that it would be impossible to get it out of this cavern, whose entrance is now closed by the uprising of the basaltic rocks, Captain Nemo's wish is that it shall be buried with him. His wish is our law, and we will fulfil it."

After a somewhat prolonged conversation, Cyrus Harding and his companions again descended to the interior of the "Nautilus." There they took some refreshment and returned to the saloon.

Captain Nemo had somewhat rallied from the prostration which had overcome him, and his eyes shone with their wonted fire. A faint smile even curled his lips.

The colonists drew around him.

"Gentlemen," said the captain, "you are brave and honest men. You have devoted yourselves to the common weal. Often have I observed your conduct. I have esteemed you – I esteem you still! Your hand, Mr. Harding."

Cyrus Harding gave his hand to the captain, who clasped it affectionately.

"It is well!" he murmured.

He resumed,

"But enough of myself. I have to speak concerning yourselves, and this Lincoln Island, upon which you have taken refuge. You now desire to leave it?"

"To return, captain!" answered Pencroft quickly.

"To return, Pencroft?" said the captain, with a smile. "I know, it is true, your love for this island. You have helped to make it what it now is, and it seems to you a paradise!"

"Our project, captain," interposed Cyrus Harding, "is to annex it to the United States, and to establish for our shipping a port so fortunately situated in this part of the Pacific."

"Your thoughts are with your country, gentlemen," continued the captain; "your toils are for her prosperity and glory. You are right. One's native land! – There should one live! There die! And I die far from all I loved!"

"You have some last wish to transmit," said the engineer with emotion, "some souvenir to send to those friends you have left in the mountains of India?"

"No, Captain Harding; no friends remain to me! I am the last of my race, and to all whom I have known I have long been as are the dead. But to return to yourselves. Solitude, isolation, are painful things, and beyond human endurance. I die of having thought it possible to live alone! You should, therefore, dare all in the attempt to leave Lincoln Island, and see once more the land of your birth. I am aware that those wretches have destroyed the vessel you have built."

The day closed without change. The colonists did not quit the "Nautilus" for a moment. Night arrived, although it was impossible to distinguish it from day in the cavern.

Captain Nemo suffered no pain, but he was visibly sinking. His noble features, paled by the approach of death, were perfectly calm. Inaudible words escaped at intervals from his lips, bearing upon various incidents of his checkered career. Life was evidently ebbing slowly and his extremities were already cold.

Once or twice more he spoke to the colonists who stood around him, and smiled on them with that last smile which continues after death.

At length, shortly after midnight, Captain Nemo by a supreme effort succeeded in folding his arms across his breast, as if wishing in that attitude to compose himself for death.

By one o'clock his glance alone showed signs of life. A dying light gleamed in those eyes once so brilliant. Then, murmuring the words, "God and my country!" he quietly expired.

Cyrus Harding, bending low, closed the eyes of him who had once been the Prince Dakkar, and was now not even Captain Nemo.

THE LAST HOPE

A frightful sound was heard. The colonists at first thought the island was rent asunder, and rushed out of Granite House. This occurred about two o'clock in the morning. The sky appeared on fire. The superior cone, a mass of rock a thousand feet in height, and weighing thousands of millions of pounds, had been thrown down upon the island, making it tremble to its foundation. Fortunately, this cone inclined to the north, and had fallen upon the plain of sand and tufa stretching between the volcano and the sea. The aperture of the crater being thus enlarged projected towards the sky a glare so intense that by the simple effect of reflection the atmosphere appeared red-hot.

Already they were stretched on the rock, inanimate, and no longer conscious of what passed around them.

At the same time a torrent of lava, bursting from the new summit, poured out in long cascades, like water escaping from a vase too full, and a thousand tongues of fire crept over the sides of the volcano. An hour afterwards the boiling lava filled the corral, converting into vapour the water of the little rivulet which ran through it, burning up the house like dry grass, and leaving not even a post of the palisade to mark the spot where the corral once stood.

To contend against this disaster would have been folly – nay, madness. In presence of Nature's grand convulsions man is powerless.

It was now daylight – the 24th of January. Cyrus Harding and his companions, before returning to Granite House, desired to ascertain the probable direction this inundation of lava was about to take. The soil sloped gradually from Mount Franklin to the east coast, and it was to be feared that, in spite of the thick Jacamar Wood, the torrent would reach the plateau of Prospect Heights.

"The lake will cover us," said Gideon Spilett.

"I hope so!" was Cyrus Harding's only reply.

The colonists were desirous of reaching the plain upon which the superior cone of Mount Franklin had fallen, but the lava arrested their progress. There was no possibility of crossing the torrent of lava; on the contrary, the colonists were obliged to retreat before it. The volcano, without its crown, was no longer recognizable, terminated as it was by a sort of flat table which replaced the ancient crater. From two openings in its southern and eastern sides an unceasing flow of lava poured forth, thus forming two distinct streams. Above the new crater a cloud of smoke and ashes, mingled with those of the atmosphere, massed over the island. Loud peals of thunder broke, and could scarcely be distinguished from the rumblings of the mountain, whose mouth vomited forth ignited rocks, which, hurled to more than a thousand feet, burst in the air like shells. Flashes of lightning rivalled in intensity the volcano's eruption.

It was the 20th of February. Yet another month must elapse before the vessel would be ready for sea. Would the island hold together till then? The intention of Pencroft and Cyrus Harding was to launch the vessel as soon as the hull should be complete. The deck, the upperworks, the interior woodwork and the rigging might be finished afterwards, but the essential point was that the colonists should have an assured refuge away from the island. Perhaps it might be even better to conduct the vessel to Port Balloon, that is to say, as far as possible from the centre of eruption, for at the mouth of the Mercy, between the islet and the wall of granite, it would run the risk of being crushed in the event of any convulsion. All the exertions of the voyagers were therefore concentrated upon the completion of the hull.

FLASHES OF LIGHTNING RIVALLED IN INTENSITY THE VOLCANO'S ERUPTION.

During the first week of March appearances again became menacing. Thousands of threads like glass, formed of fluid lava, fell like rain upon the island. The crater was again boiling with lava which overflowed the back of the volcano. And they worked away without losing a moment. This last blow to the work of the colonists was terrible. The mill, the buildings of the inner court, the stables, were all destroyed. The colonists

were driven to their last entrenchment, and although the upper seams of the vessel were not yet caulked, they decided to launch her at once.

Pencroft and Ayrton therefore set about the necessary preparations for the launching, which was to take place the morning of the next day, the 9th of March. But during the night of the 8th an enormous column of vapour escaping from the crater rose with frightful explosions to a height of more than three thousand feet. The wall of Dakkar Grotto had evidently given way under the pressure of gases, and the sea, rushing through the central shaft into the igneous gulf, was at once converted into vapour. But the crater could not afford a sufficient outlet for this vapour. An explosion, which might have been heard at a distance of a hundred miles, shook the air. Fragments of mountains fell into the Pacific, and, in a few minutes, the ocean rolled over the spot where Lincoln Island once stood.

An isolated rock, thirty feet in length, twenty in breadth, scarcely ten from the water's edge, such was the only solid point which the waves of the Pacific had not engulfed. It was all that remained of the structure of Granite House! The wall had fallen headlong and been then shattered to fragments, and a few of the rocks of the large room were piled one above another to form this point. All around had disappeared in the abyss; the inferior cone of Mount Franklin, rent asunder by the explosion; the lava jaws of Shark Gulf, the plateau of Prospect Heights, Safety Islet, the granite rocks of Port Balloon, the basalts of Dakkar Grotto, the long Serpentine Peninsula, so distant nevertheless from the centre of the eruption. All that could now be seen of Lincoln Island was the narrow rock which now served as a refuge to the six colonists and their dog Top.

The animals had also perished in the catastrophe; the birds, as well as those representing the fauna of the island – all either crushed or drowned, and the unfortunate Jup himself had, alas! Found his death in some crevice of the soil. If Cyrus Harding, Gideon Spilett, Herbert, Pencroft, Neb, and Ayrton had survived, it was because, assembled under their tent, they had been hurled into the sea at the instant when the fragments of the island rained down on every side.

When they reached the surface they could only perceive, at half a cable's length, this mass of rocks, towards which they swam and on which they found footing.

On this barren rock they had now existed for nine days. A few provisions taken from the magazine of Granite House before the catastrophe, a little fresh water from the rain, was all that the unfortunate colonists possessed. Their last hope, the vessel, had been shattered to pieces. They had no means of quitting the reef; no fire, nor any means of obtaining it. It seemed that they must inevitably perish. This day, the 18th of March, there remained only provisions for two days, although they limited their consumption to the bare necessaries of life. All their science and intelligence could avail them nothing in their present position. They were in the hand of God. Cyrus Harding was calm, Gideon Spilett more nervous, and Pencroft, a prey to sullen anger, walked to and fro on the rock. Herbert did not for a moment quit the engineer's side, as if demanding from him that assistance he had no power to give. Neb and Ayrton were resigned to their fate.

"Ah, what a misfortune! What a misfortune!" often repeated Pencroft. "If we had but a walnut-shell to take us to Tabor Island! But we have nothing, nothing!"

"Captain Nemo did right to die," said Neb.

During the five ensuing days Cyrus Harding and his unfortunate companions husbanded their provisions with the most extreme care, eating only what would prevent them from dying of starvation. Their weakness was extreme. Herbert and Neb began to show symptoms of delirium. Under these circumstances was it possible for them to retain even the shadow of a hope? No! What was their sole remaining chance? That a vessel should appear in sight of the rock? But they knew only too well from experience that no ships ever visited this part of the Pacific. Could they calculate that, by a truly providential coincidence, the Scotch yacht would arrive precisely at this time in search of Ayrton at Tabor Island? It was scarcely probable; and, besides, supposing she should come there, as the colonists had not been able to deposit a notice pointing out Ayrton's change of abode, the commander of the yacht, after having explored Tabor Island without results, would again set sail and return to lower latitudes. No! No hope of being saved could be retained, and a horrible death, death from hunger and thirst, awaited them upon this rock.

HE RAISED HIMSELF, AT FIRST ON HIS KNEES, THEN UPRIGHT, AND HIS HAND SEEMED TO MAKE A SIGNAL.

Already they were stretched on the rock, inanimate, and no longer conscious of what passed around them. Ayrton alone, by a supreme effort, from time to time raised his head, and cast a despairing glance over the desert ocean. But on the morning of the 24th of March Ayrton's arms were extended toward a point in the horizon; he raised himself, at first on his knees, then upright, and his hand seemed to make a signal. A sail was in sight off the rock. She was evidently not without an object. The reef was the mark for which she was making in a direct line, under all steam, and the unfortunate colonists might have made her out some hours before if they had had the strength to watch the horizon.

"The 'Duncan'!" murmured Ayrton – and fell back without sign of life.

When Cyrus Harding and his companions recovered consciousness, thanks to the attention lavished upon them, they found themselves in the cabin of a steamer, without being able to comprehend how they had escaped death. A word from Ayrton explained everything.

"The 'Duncan'!" he murmured.

"The 'Duncan'!" exclaimed Cyrus Harding. And raising his hand to Heaven, he said, "Oh! Almighty God! mercifully hast Thou preserved us!"

It was, in fact, the "Duncan," Lord Glenarvan's yacht, now commanded by Robert, son of Captain Grant, who had been despatched to Tabor Island to find Ayrton, and bring him back to his native land after twelve years of expiation. The colonists were not only saved, but already on the way to their native country.

"Captain Grant," asked Cyrus Harding, "who can have suggested to you the idea, after having left Tabor Island, where you did not find Ayrton, of coming a hundred miles farther northeast?"

"Captain Harding," replied Grant, "it was in order to find, not only Ayrton, but yourself and your companions."

"My companions and myself?" – "Doubtless, at Lincoln Island." – "At Lincoln Island!" exclaimed in

An explosion, which might have been heard at a distance of a hundred miles, shook the air.

a breath Gideon Spilett, Herbert, Neb, and Pencroft, in the highest degree astonished.

"How could you be aware of the existence of Lincoln Island?" inquired Cyrus Harding, "it is not even named in the charts."

"I knew of it from a document left by you on Tabor Island," answered Robert Grant.

"A document!" cried Gideon Spilett.

"Without doubt, and here it is," answered Robert Grant, producing a paper which indicated the longitude and latitude of Lincoln Island, "the present residence of Ayrton and five American colonists."

"YOU LEFT BEHIND YOU A CRIMINAL; YOU FIND IN HIS PLACE A MAN WHO HAS BECOME HONEST BY PENITENCE."

"It is Captain Nemo!" cried Cyrus Harding, after having read the notice, and recognized that the handwriting was similar to that of the paper found at the corral.

"Ah!" said Pencroft, "it was then he who took our 'Bonadventure' and hazarded himself alone to go to Tabor Island!"

"In order to leave this notice," added Herbert.

"I was then right in saying," exclaimed the sailor, "that even after his death the captain would render us a last service."

"My friends," said Cyrus Harding, in a voice of the profoundest emotion, "may the God of mercy have had pity on the soul of Captain Nemo, our benefactor."

The colonists uncovered themselves at these last words of Cyrus Harding, and murmured the name of Captain Nemo. Then Ayrton, approaching the engineer, said simply, "Where should this coffer be deposited?"

It was the coffer which Ayrton had saved at the risk of his life, at the very instant that the island had been engulfed, and which he now faithfully handed to the engineer.

"Ayrton! Ayrton!" said Cyrus Harding, deeply touched. Then, addressing Robert Grant, "Sir," he added, "you left behind you a criminal; you find in his place a man who has become honest by penitence, and whose hand I am proud to clasp in mine."

Robert Grant was now made acquainted with the strange history of Captain Nemo and the colonists of Lincoln Island. Then, observation being taken of what remained of this shoal, the order was given to make all sail. A few weeks afterwards the colonists landed in America, and found their country once more at peace after the terrible conflict in which right and justice had triumphed. Of the treasures contained in the coffer left by Captain Nemo to the colonists of Lincoln Island, the larger portion was employed in the purchase of a vast territory in the State of Iowa. One pearl alone, the finest, was reserved from the treasure and sent to Lady Glenarvan in the name of the castaways restored to their country by the "Duncan."

There, to conclude, all were happy, united in the present as they had been in the past; but never could they forget that island upon which they had arrived poor and friendless, which, during four years had supplied all their wants, and of which there remained but a fragment of granite washed by the waves of the Pacific, the tomb of him who had borne the name of Captain Nemo.

TREASURE ISLAND

Robert Louis Stevenson, 1883
Illustrations by George Varian, George Roux, Newell Convers Wyeth, and Louis Rhead

Published originally in *Young Folks*, a U.S. children's magazine, between October 1881 and January 1882, *Treasure Island* was the first full-length fiction work of the Scottish author Robert Louis Stevenson. Set in unspecified years in the 1700s, the tale relates the seaborne adventures of a boy in his early teens named Jim Hawkins. Jim joins a quest to recover the buried treasure of a famously brutal (and invented) pirate captain named Flint on the "Isle of Treasure", after a map turns up in the effects of the pirate Billy Bones who dies at Jim's father's inn. Undoubtedly, the fact that Stevenson came from a family involved in lighthouse construction around the coasts of Scotland benefited his meticulous descriptions in *Treasure Island* of ship construction, harbors, the Bristol (England) dock scene, nautical life, and the lingo of seamen. But Stevenson obviously also absorbed what was currently known about pirates before writing his book. Although his portrait of pirate life was rife with imagined elements, he also knew, for instance, about Execution Dock in London where pirates were hanged, and that pirates sometimes marooned captives and disaffected crew members instead of killing them. Allusions to both these elements appear at intervals in the narrative. Stevenson also recognized that pirates operated according to formal rules of their own. One of the book's most intriguing passages occurs when the pirate leader Long John Silver, about to be deposed by rebellious accomplices, reminds the dissidents that their principles of conduct require them first to present him with their grievances and give him the opportunity to respond. What should readers make of Stevenson's characterization of the multi-dimensional, sometimes chameleon-like, and always conniving Silver? Is his intention to humanize pirates? And what is to be made, in this tale admittedly crafted by Stevenson with boy readers in mind, of his portrait of his central character and main narrator, voluntarily serving as cabin boy on a vessel – the *Hispaniola* – that unbeknownst to him (at first) is manned by a mostly pirate crew? No naive victim of fate, Jim Hawkins achieves more than sufficient agency to outwit and outfight the hard-drinking, ruthless, mutinous pirates. He spies on them, dissembles, cuts deals, sets their ship adrift, shoots the pirate coxswain to death, and with astounding audacity boasts to Silver *when he is Silver's captive* that he has been responsible for virtually all the pirates' mishaps since they arrived at Treasure Island: "The laugh's on my side; I've had the top of this business from the first; I no more fear you than I fear a fly." But if Silver will spare his life, Jim will intervene to save the pirate's neck from hanging after he is inevitably taken captive by English authorities!

THE OLD SEA-DOG
AT THE "ADMIRAL BENBOW"

Squire Trelawney, Dr. Livesey, and the rest of these gentlemen having asked me to write down the whole particulars about Treasure Island, from the beginning to the end, keeping nothing back but the bearings of the island, and that only because there is still treasure not yet lifted, I take up my pen in the year of grace 17-- and go back to the time when my father kept the Admiral Benbow inn and the brown old seaman with the sabre cut first took up his lodging under our roof.

THE OLD SEA-DOG AT THE "ADMIRAL BENBOW"

I remember him as if it were yesterday, as he came plodding to the inn door, his sea-chest following behind him in a hand-barrow – a tall, strong, heavy, nut-brown man, his tarry pigtail falling over the shoulder of his soiled blue coat, his hands ragged and scarred, with black, broken nails, and the sabre cut across one cheek, a dirty, livid white. I remember him looking round the cover and whistling to himself as he did so, and then breaking out in that old sea-song that he sang so often afterwards:

"Fifteen men on the dead man's chest
Yo-ho-ho, and a bottle of rum!"

in the high, old tottering voice that seemed to have been tuned and broken at the capstan bars. Then he rapped on the door with a bit of stick like a handspike that he carried, and when my father appeared, called roughly for a glass of rum. This, when it was brought to him, he drank slowly, like a connoisseur, lingering on the taste and still looking about him at the cliffs and up at our signboard.

"This is a handy cove," says he at length; "and a pleasant sittyated grog-shop. Much company, mate?"

My father told him no, very little company, the more was the pity.

"Well, then," said he, "this is the berth for me. Here you, matey," he cried to the man who trundled the barrow; "bring up alongside and help up my chest. I'll stay here a bit," he continued. "I'm a plain man; rum and bacon and eggs is what I want, and that head up there for to watch ships off. What you mought call me? You mought call me captain. Oh, I see what you're at – there"; and he threw down three or four gold pieces on the threshold. "You can tell me when I've worked through that," says he, looking as fierce as a commander.

And indeed bad as his clothes were and coarsely as he spoke, he had none of the appearance of a man who sailed before the mast, but seemed like a mate or skipper accustomed to be obeyed or to strike. The man who came with the barrow told us the mail had set him down the morning before at the Royal George, that he had inquired what inns there were along the coast, and hearing ours well spoken of, I suppose, and described as lonely, had chosen it from the others for his place of residence. And that was all we could learn of our guest.

He was a very silent man by custom. All day he hung round the cove or upon the cliffs with a brass telescope; all evening he sat in a corner of the parlour next the fire and drank rum and water very strong. Mostly he would not speak when spoken to, only look up sudden and fierce and blow through his nose like a fog-horn; and we and the people who came about our house soon learned to let him be. Every day when he came back from his stroll he would ask if any seafaring men had gone by along the road. At first we thought it was the want of company of his own kind that made him ask this question, but at last we began to see he was desirous to avoid them. When a seaman did put up at the Admiral Benbow (as now and then some did, making by the coast road for Bristol) he would look in at him through the curtained door before he entered the parlour; and he was always sure to be as silent as a mouse when any such was present. For me, at least, there was no secret about the matter, for I was, in a way, a sharer in his alarms. He had taken me aside one day and promised me a silver fourpenny on the first of every month if I would only keep my "weather-eye open for a seafaring man with one leg" and let him know the moment he appeared. Often enough when the first of the month came round and I applied to him for my wage, he would only blow through his nose at me and stare me down, but before the week was out he was sure to think better of it, bring me my four-penny piece, and repeat his orders to look out for "the seafaring man with one leg."

How that personage haunted my dreams, I need scarcely tell you. On stormy nights, when the wind shook the four corners of the house and the surf roared along the cove and up the cliffs, I would see him in a thousand forms, and with a thousand diabolical expressions. Now the leg would be cut off at the knee, now at the hip; now he was a monstrous kind of a creature who had never had but the one leg, and that in the middle of his body. To see him leap and run and pursue me over hedge and ditch was the worst of nightmares. And altogether I paid pretty dear for my monthly four-penny piece, in the shape of these abominable fancies.

HIS STORIES WERE WHAT FRIGHTENED PEOPLE WORST OF ALL.

But though I was so terrified by the idea of the seafaring man with one leg, I was far less afraid of the captain himself than anybody else who knew him. There were nights when he took a deal more rum and water than his head would carry; and then he would sometimes sit and sing his wicked, old, wild sea-songs, minding nobody; but sometimes he would call for glasses round and force all the trembling company to listen to his stories or bear a chorus to his singing. Often I have heard the house shaking with "Yo-ho-ho, and a bottle of rum," all the neighbours joining in for dear life, with the fear of death upon them, and each singing louder than the other to avoid remark. For in these fits he was the most overriding companion ever known; he would slap his hand on the table for silence all round; he would fly up in a passion of anger at a question, or sometimes because none was put, and so he judged the company was not following his story. Nor would he allow anyone to leave the inn till he had drunk himself sleepy and reeled off to bed.

His stories were what frightened people worst of all. Dreadful stories they were – about hanging, and walking the plank, and storms at sea, and the Dry Tortugas, and wild deeds and places on the Spanish Main. By his own account he must have lived his life among some of the wickedest men that God ever allowed upon the sea, and the language in which he told these stories shocked our plain country people almost as much as the crimes that he described. My father was always saying the inn would be ruined, for people would soon cease coming there to be tyrannized over and put down, and sent shivering to their beds; but I really believe his presence did us good. People were frightened at the time, but on looking back they rather liked it; it was a fine excitement in a quiet country life, and there was even a party of the younger men who pretended to admire him, calling him a "true sea-dog" and a "real old salt" and such like names, and saying there was the sort of man that made England terrible at sea.

In one way, indeed, he bade fair to ruin us, for he kept on staying week after week, and at last month after month, so that all the money had been long exhausted, and still my father never plucked up the heart to insist on having more. If ever he mentioned it, the captain blew through his nose so loudly that you might say he roared, and stared my poor father out of the room. I have seen him wringing his hands after such a rebuff, and I am sure the annoyance and the terror

THE OLD SEA-DOG AT THE "ADMIRAL BENBOW"

He sprang to his feet, drew and opened a sailor's clasp-knife, and threatened to pin the doctor to the wall.

he lived in must have greatly hastened his early and unhappy death.

All the time he lived with us the captain made no change whatever in his dress but to buy some stockings from a hawker. One of the cocks of his hat having fallen down, he let it hang from that day forth, though it was a great annoyance when it blew. I remember the appearance of his coat, which he patched himself upstairs in his room, and which, before the end, was nothing but patches. He never wrote or received a letter, and he never spoke with any but the neighbours, and with these, for the most part, only when drunk on rum. The great sea-chest none of us had ever seen open.

He was only once crossed, and that was towards the end, when my poor father was far gone in a decline that took him off. Dr. Livesey came late one afternoon to see the patient, took a bit of dinner from my mother, and went into the parlour to smoke a pipe until his horse should come down from the hamlet, for we had no stabling at the old Benbow. I followed him in, and I remember observing the contrast the neat, bright doctor, with his powder as white as snow and his bright, black eyes and pleasant manners, made with the coltish country folk, and above all, with that filthy, heavy, bleared scarecrow of a pirate of ours, sitting, far gone in rum, with his arms on the table. Suddenly he – the captain, that is – began to pipe up his eternal song:

"Fifteen men on the
dead man's chest –
Yo-ho-ho, and a
bottle of rum!
Drink and the devil
had done for the rest –
Yo-ho-ho, and a
bottle of rum!"

At first I had supposed "the dead man's chest" to be that identical big box of his upstairs in the front room, and the thought had been mingled in my nightmares with that of the one-legged seafaring man. But by this time we had all long ceased to pay any particular notice to the song; it was new, that night, to nobody but Dr. Livesey, and on him I observed it did not produce an agreeable effect, for he looked up for a moment quite angrily before he went on with his

All day he hung round the cove or upon the cliffs with a brass telescope.

talk to old Taylor, the gardener, on a new cure for the rheumatics. In the meantime, the captain gradually brightened up at his own music, and at last flapped his hand upon the table before him in a way we all knew to mean silence. The voices stopped at once, all but Dr. Livesey's; he went on as before speaking clear and kind and drawing briskly at his pipe between every word or two. The captain glared at him for a while, flapped his hand again, glared still harder, and at last broke out with a villainous, low oath, "Silence, there, between decks!"

"Were you addressing me, sir?" says the doctor; and when the ruffian had told him, with another oath, that this was so, "I have only one thing to say to you, sir," replies the doctor, "that if you keep on drinking rum, the world will soon be quit of a very dirty scoundrel!"

The old fellow's fury was awful. He sprang to his feet, drew and opened a sailor's clasp-knife, and balancing it open on the palm of his hand, threatened to pin the doctor to the wall.

The doctor never so much as moved. He spoke to him as before, over his shoulder and in the same tone of voice, rather high, so that all the room might hear, but perfectly calm and steady: "If you do not put that knife this instant in your pocket, I promise, upon my honour, you shall hang at the next assizes."

Then followed a battle of looks between them, but the captain soon knuckled under, put up his weapon, and resumed his seat, grumbling like a beaten dog.

"And now, sir," continued the doctor, "since I now know there's such a fellow in my district, you may count I'll have an eye upon you day and night. I'm not a doctor only; I'm a magistrate; and if I catch a breath of complaint against you, if it's only for a piece of incivility like tonight's, I'll take effectual means to have you hunted down and routed out of this. Let that suffice."

Soon after, Dr. Livesey's horse came to the door and he rode away, but the captain held his peace that evening, and for many evenings to come.

BLACK DOG
APPEARS AND DISAPPEARS

It was not very long after this that there occurred the first of the mysterious events that rid us at last of the captain, though not, as you will see, of his affairs.

BLACK DOG APPEARS AND DISAPPEARS

It was a bitter cold winter, with long, hard frosts and heavy gales; and it was plain from the first that my poor father was little likely to see the spring. He sank daily, and my mother and I had all the inn upon our hands, and were kept busy enough without paying much regard to our unpleasant guest.

It was one January morning, very early – a pinching, frosty morning – the cove all grey with hoar-frost, the ripple lapping softly on the stones, the sun still low and only touching the hilltops and shining far to seaward. The captain had risen earlier than usual and set out down the beach, his cutlass swinging under the broad skirts of the old blue coat, his brass telescope under his arm, his hat tilted back upon his head. I remember his breath hanging like smoke in his wake as he strode off, and the last sound I heard of him as he turned the big rock was a loud snort of indignation, as though his mind was still running upon Dr. Livesey.

Well, mother was upstairs with father and I was laying the breakfast-table against the captain's return when the parlour door opened and a man stepped in on whom I had never set my eyes before. He was a pale, tallowy creature, wanting two fingers of the left hand, and though he wore a cutlass, he did not look much like a fighter. I had always my eye open for seafaring men, with one leg or two, and I remember this one puzzled me. He was not sailorly, and yet he had a smack of the sea about him too.

I asked him what was for his service, and he said he would take rum; but as I was going out of the room to fetch it, he sat down upon a table and motioned me to draw near. I paused where I was, with my napkin in my hand.

"Come here, sonny," says he. "Come nearer here."

I took a step nearer.

"Is this here table for my mate Bill?" he asked with a kind of leer.

I told him I did not know his mate Bill, and this was for a person who stayed in our house whom we called the captain.

"Well," said he, "my mate Bill would be called the captain, as like as not. He has a cut on one cheek and a mighty pleasant way with him, particularly in drink, has my mate Bill. We'll put it, for argument like, that your captain has a cut on one cheek – and we'll put it, if you like, that that cheek's the right one. Ah, well! I told you. Now, is my mate Bill in this here house?"

I REMEMBER HIS BREATH HANGING LIKE SMOKE IN HIS WAKE.

I told him he was out walking.

"Which way, sonny? Which way is he gone?"

And when I had pointed out the rock and told him how the captain was likely to return, and how soon, and answered a few other questions, "Ah," said he, "this'll be as good as drink to my mate Bill."

The expression of his face as he said these words was not at all pleasant, and I had my own reasons for thinking that the stranger was mistaken, even supposing he meant what he said. But it was no affair of mine, I thought; and besides, it was difficult to know what to do. The stranger kept hanging about just inside the inn door, peering round the corner like a cat waiting for a mouse. Once I stepped out myself into the road, but he immediately called me back, and as I did not obey quick enough for his fancy, a most horrible change

The next instant I saw Black Dog in full flight, and the captain hotly pursuing, both with drawn cutlasses.

came over his tallowy face, and he ordered me in with an oath that made me jump. As soon as I was back again he returned to his former manner, half fawning, half sneering, patted me on the shoulder, told me I was a good boy and he had taken quite a fancy to me. "I have a son of my own," said he, "as like you as two blocks, and he's all the pride of my 'art. But the great thing for boys is discipline, sonny – discipline. Now, if you had sailed along of Bill, you wouldn't have stood there to be spoke to twice – not you. That was never Bill's way, nor the way of sich as sailed with him. And here, sure enough, is my mate Bill, with a spy-glass under his arm, bless his old 'art, to be sure. You and me'll just go back into the parlour, sonny, and get behind the door, and we'll give Bill a little surprise – bless his 'art, I say again."

HE CLEARED THE HILT OF HIS CUTLASS AND LOOSENED THE BLADE IN THE SHEATH.

So saying, the stranger backed along with me into the parlour and put me behind him in the corner so that we were both hidden by the open door. I was very uneasy and alarmed, as you may fancy, and it rather added to my fears to observe that the stranger was certainly frightened himself. He cleared the hilt of his cutlass and loosened the blade in the sheath; and all the time we were waiting there he kept swallowing as if he felt what we used to call a lump in the throat.

At last in strode the captain, slammed the door behind him, without looking to the right or left, and marched straight across the room to where his breakfast awaited him.

"Bill," said the stranger in a voice that I thought he had tried to make bold and big.

The captain spun round on his heel and fronted us; all the brown had gone out of his face, and even his nose was blue; he had the look of a man who sees a ghost, or the evil one, or something worse, if anything can be; and upon my word, I felt sorry to see him all in a moment turn so old and sick.

"Come, Bill, you know me; you know an old shipmate, Bill, surely," said the stranger.

The captain made a sort of gasp.

"Black Dog!" said he.

"And who else?" returned the other, getting more at his ease. "Black Dog as ever was, come for to see his old shipmate Billy, at the Admiral Benbow inn. Ah, Bill, Bill, we have seen a sight of times, us two, since I lost them two talons," holding up his mutilated hand.

"Now, look here," said the captain; "you've run me down; here I am; well, then, speak up; what is it?"

"That's you, Bill," returned Black Dog, "you're in the right of it, Billy. I'll have a glass of rum from this dear child here, as I've took such a liking to; and we'll sit down, if you please, and talk square, like old shipmates."

When I returned with the rum, they were already seated on either side of the captain's breakfast-table – Black Dog next to the door and sitting sideways so as to have one eye on his old shipmate and one, as I thought, on his retreat.

He bade me go and leave the door wide open. "None of your keyholes for me, sonny," he said; and I left them together and retired into the bar.

For a long time, though I certainly did my best to listen, I could hear nothing but a low gattling; but at last

N.C. WYETH
'11

the voices began to grow higher, and I could pick up a word or two, mostly oaths, from the captain.

"No, no, no, no; and an end of it!" he cried once. And again, "If it comes to swinging, swing all, say I."

Then all of a sudden there was a tremendous explosion of oaths and other noises – the chair and table went over in a lump, a clash of steel followed, and then a cry of pain, and the next instant I saw Black Dog in full flight, and the captain hotly pursuing, both with drawn cutlasses, and the former streaming blood from the left shoulder. Just at the door the captain aimed at the fugitive one last tremendous cut, which would certainly have split him to the chine had it not been intercepted by our big signboard of Admiral Benbow. You may see the notch on the lower side of the frame to this day.

That blow was the last of the battle. Once out upon the road, Black Dog, in spite of his wound, showed a wonderful clean pair of heels and disappeared over the edge of the hill in half a minute. The captain, for his part, stood staring at the signboard like a bewildered man. Then he passed his hand over his eyes several times and at last turned back into the house.

"Jim," says he, "rum"; and as he spoke, he reeled a little, and caught himself with one hand against the wall.

"Are you hurt?" cried I.

"Rum," he repeated. "I must get away from here. Rum! Rum!"

I ran to fetch it, but I was quite unsteadied by all that had fallen out, and I broke one glass and fouled the tap, and while I was still getting in my own way, I heard a loud fall in the parlour, and running in, beheld the captain lying full length upon the floor. At the same instant my mother, alarmed by the cries and fighting, came running downstairs to help me. Between us we raised his head. He was breathing very loud and hard, but his eyes were closed and his face a horrible colour.

"Dear, deary me," cried my mother, "what a disgrace upon the house! And your poor father sick!"

In the meantime, we had no idea what to do to help the captain, nor any other thought but that he had got his death-hurt in the scuffle with the stranger. I got the rum, to be sure, and tried to put it down his throat, but his teeth were tightly shut and his jaws as strong as iron. It was a happy relief for us when the door opened and Doctor Livesey came in, on his visit to my father.

HE WAS BREATHING VERY LOUD AND HARD, BUT HIS EYES WERE CLOSED AND HIS FACE A HORRIBLE COLOUR.

"Oh, doctor," we cried, "what shall we do? Where is he wounded?"

"Wounded? A fiddle-stick's end!" said the doctor. "No more wounded than you or I. The man has had a stroke, as I warned him. Now, Mrs. Hawkins, just you run upstairs to your husband and tell him, if possible, nothing about it. For my part, I must do my best to save this fellow's trebly worthless life; Jim, you get me a basin."

When I got back with the basin, the doctor had already ripped up the captain's sleeve and exposed his great sinewy arm. It was tattooed in several places. "Here's luck," "A fair wind," and "Billy Bones his fancy," were very neatly and clearly executed on the forearm; and up near the shoulder there was a sketch of a gallows and a man hanging from it – done, as I thought, with great spirit.

"Prophetic," said the doctor, touching this picture with his finger. "And now, Master Billy Bones, if that be your name, we'll have a look at the colour of your blood. Jim," he said, "are you afraid of blood?"

"No, sir," said I.

"Well, then," said he, "you hold the basin"; and with that he took his lancet and opened a vein.

A great deal of blood was taken before the captain opened his eyes and looked mistily about him. First he recognized the doctor with an unmistakable frown; then his glance fell upon me, and he looked relieved. But suddenly his colour changed, and he tried to raise himself, crying, "Where's Black Dog?"

"There is no Black Dog here," said the doctor, "except what you have on your own back. You have been drinking rum; you have had a stroke, precisely as I told you; and I have just, very much against my own will, dragged you headforemost out of the grave. Now, Mr. Bones – "

"That's not my name," he interrupted.

"Much I care," returned the doctor. "It's the name of a buccaneer of my acquaintance; and I call you by it for the sake of shortness, and what I have to say to you is this; one glass of rum won't kill you, but if you take one you'll take another and another, and I stake my wig if you don't break off short, you'll die – do you understand that? – die, and go to your own place, like the man in the Bible. Come, now, make an effort. I'll help you to your bed for once."

Between us, with much trouble, we managed to hoist him upstairs, and laid him on his bed, where his head fell back on the pillow as if he were almost fainting.

"Now, mind you," said the doctor, "I clear my conscience – the name of rum for you is death."

And with that he went off to see my father, taking me with him by the arm.

"This is nothing," he said as soon as he had closed the door. "I have drawn blood enough to keep him quiet awhile; he should lie for a week where he is – that is the best thing for him and you; but another stroke would settle him."

THE BLACK SPOT

About noon I stopped at the captain's door with some cooling drinks and medicines. He was lying very much as we had left him, only a little higher, and he seemed both weak and excited.

THE BLACK SPOT

"Jim," he said, "you're the only one here that's worth anything, and you know I've been always good to you. Never a month but I've given you a silver fourpenny for yourself. And now you see, mate, I'm pretty low, and deserted by all; and Jim, you'll bring me one noggin of rum, now, won't you, matey?"

"The doctor – " I began.

But he broke in cursing the doctor, in a feeble voice but heartily. "Doctors is all swabs," he said; "and that doctor there, why, what do he know about seafaring men? I been in places hot as pitch, and mates dropping round with Yellow Jack, and the blessed land a-heaving like the sea with earthquakes – what do the doctor know of lands like that? – and I lived on rum, I tell you. It's been meat and drink, and man and wife, to me; and if I'm not to have my rum now I'm a poor old hulk on a lee shore, my blood'll be on you, Jim, and that doctor swab"; and he ran on again for a while with curses. "Look, Jim, how my fingers fidges," he continued in the pleading tone. "I can't keep 'em still, not I. I haven't had a drop this blessed day. That doctor's a fool, I tell you. If I don't have a dram o' rum, Jim, I'll have the horrors; I seen some on 'em already. I seen old Flint in the corner there, behind you; as plain as print, I seen him; and if I get the horrors, I'm a man that has lived rough, and I'll raise Cain. Your doctor hisself said one glass wouldn't hurt me. I'll give you a golden guinea for a noggin, Jim."

He was growing more and more excited, and this alarmed me for my father, who was very low that day and needed quiet; besides, I was reassured by the doctor's words, now quoted to me, and rather offended by the offer of a bribe.

"I want none of your money," said I, "but what you owe my father. I'll get you one glass, and no more."

When I brought it to him, he seized it greedily and drank it out.

"Aye, aye," said he, "that's some better, sure enough. And now, matey, did that doctor say how long I was to lie here in this old berth?"

"A week at least," said I.

"Thunder!" he cried. "A week! I can't do that; they'd have the black spot on me by then. The lubbers is going about to get the wind of me this blessed moment; lubbers as couldn't keep what they got, and want to nail what is another's. Is that seamanly behaviour, now, I want to know? But I'm a saving soul. I never wasted good money of mine, nor lost it neither; and I'll trick 'em again. I'm not afraid on 'em. I'll shake out another reef, matey, and daddle 'em again."

As he was thus speaking, he had risen from bed with great difficulty, holding to my shoulder with a grip that almost made me cry out, and moving his legs like so much dead weight. His words, spirited as they were in meaning, contrasted sadly with the weakness of the voice in which they were uttered. He paused when he had got into a sitting position on the edge.

"That doctor's done me," he murmured. "My ears is singing. Lay me back."

Before I could do much to help him he had fallen back again to his former place, where he lay for a while silent.

"Jim," he said at length, "you saw that seafaring man today?"

"Black Dog?" I asked.

"Ah! Black Dog," says he. "He's a bad un; but there's worse that put him on. Now, if I can't get away nohow, and they tip me the black spot, mind you, it's my old sea-chest they're after; you get on a horse – you can, can't you? Well, then, you get on a horse, and go to – well, yes, I will! – to that eternal doctor swab, and tell him to pipe

He was hunched, as if with age or weakness, and wore a huge old tattered sea-cloak with a hood that made him appear positively deformed.

all hands – magistrates and sich – and he'll lay 'em aboard at the Admiral Benbow – all old Flint's crew, man and boy, all on 'em that's left. I was first mate, I was, old Flint's first mate, and I'm the on'y one as knows the place. He gave it me at Savannah, when he lay a-dying, like as if I was to now, you see. But you won't peach unless they get the black spot on me, or unless you see that Black Dog again or a seafaring man with one leg, Jim – him above all."

"But what is the black spot, captain?" I asked.

"That's a summons, mate. I'll tell you if they get that. But you keep your weather-eye open, Jim, and I'll share with you equals, upon my honour."

He wandered a little longer, his voice growing weaker; but soon after I had given him his medicine, which he took like a child, with the remark, "If ever a seaman wanted drugs, it's me," he fell at last into a heavy, swoon-like sleep, in which I left him. What I should have done had all gone well I do not know. Probably I should have told the whole story to the doctor, for I was in mortal fear lest the captain should repent of his confessions and make an end of me. But as things fell out, my poor father died quite suddenly that evening, which put all other matters on one side. Our natural distress, the visits of the neighbours, the arranging of the funeral, and all the work of the inn to be carried on in the meanwhile kept me so busy that I had scarcely time to think of the captain, far less to be afraid of him.

He got downstairs next morning, to be sure, and had his meals as usual, though he ate little and had more, I am afraid, than his usual supply of rum. On the night before the funeral he was as drunk as ever; and it was shocking, in that house of mourning, to hear him singing away at his ugly old sea-song; but weak as he was, we were all in the fear of death for him, and the doctor was suddenly taken up with a case many miles away and was never near the house after my father's death.

So things passed until, the day after the funeral, and about three o'clock of a bitter, foggy, frosty afternoon, I was standing at the door for a moment, full of sad thoughts about my father, when I saw someone drawing slowly near along the road. He was plainly blind, for he tapped before him with a stick and wore a great green shade over his eyes and nose; and he was hunched, as if with age or weakness, and wore a huge old tattered sea-cloak with a hood that made him appear positively deformed. I never saw in my life a more dreadful-looking figure. He stopped a little from the inn, and raising his voice in an odd sing-song, addressed the air in front of him, "Will any kind friend inform a poor blind man, who has lost the precious sight of his eyes in the gracious defence of his native country, England – and God bless King George! – where or in what part of this country he may now be?"

"You are at the Admiral Benbow, Black Hill Cove, my good man," said I.

"I hear a voice," said he, "a young voice. Will you give me your hand, my kind young friend, and lead me in?"

I held out my hand, and the horrible, soft-spoken, eyeless creature gripped it in a moment like a vise. I was so much startled that I struggled to withdraw, but the blind man pulled me close up to him with a single action of his arm.

"Now, boy," he said, "take me in to the captain." – "Sir," said I, "upon my word I dare not." – "Oh," he sneered, "that's it! Take me in straight or I'll break your arm." And he gave it, as he spoke, a wrench that made me cry out.

"Sir," said I, "it is for yourself I mean. The captain is not what he used to be. He sits with a drawn cutlass. Another gentleman – "

"Come, now, march," interrupted he; and I never heard a voice so cruel, and cold, and ugly as that blind man's. It cowed me more than the pain, and I began to obey him at once, walking straight in at the door and towards the parlour, where our sick old buccaneer was sitting, dazed with rum. The blind man clung close to me, holding me in one iron fist and leaning almost more of his weight on me than I could carry. "Lead me straight up to him, and when I'm in view, cry out, 'Here's a friend for you, Bill.' If you don't, I'll do this," and with that he gave me a twitch that I thought would have made me faint. Between this and that, I was so utterly terrified of the blind beggar that I forgot my terror of the captain, and as I opened the parlour door, cried out the words he had ordered in a trembling voice.

The poor captain raised his eyes, and at one look the rum went out of him and left him staring sober. The expression of his face was not so much of terror as of mortal sickness. He made a movement to rise, but I do not believe he had enough force left in his body.

"Now, Bill, sit where you are," said the beggar. "If I can't see, I can hear a finger stirring. Business is business. Hold out your left hand. Boy, take his left hand by the wrist and bring it near to my right."

We both obeyed him to the letter, and I saw him pass something from the hollow of the hand that held his stick into the palm of the captain's, which closed upon it instantly.

"And now that's done," said the blind man; and at the words he suddenly left hold of me, and with incredible accuracy and nimbleness, skipped out of the parlour and into the road, where, as I still stood motionless, I could hear his stick go tap-tap-tapping into the distance.

It was some time before either I or the captain seemed to gather our senses, but at length, and about at the same moment, I released his wrist, which I was still holding, and he drew in his hand and looked sharply into the palm.

But there he remained behind, tapping up and down the road in a frenzy, and groping and calling for his comrades.

"Ten o'clock!" he cried. "Six hours. We'll do them yet," and he sprang to his feet.

Even as he did so, he reeled, put his hand to his throat, stood swaying for a moment, and then, with a peculiar sound, fell from his whole height face foremost to the floor.

I ran to him at once, calling to my mother. But haste was all in vain. The captain had been struck dead by thundering apoplexy. It is a curious thing to understand, for I had certainly never liked the man, though of late I had begun to pity him, but as soon as I saw that he was dead, I burst into a flood of tears. It was the second death I had known, and the sorrow of the first was still fresh in my heart.

I lost no time, of course, in telling my mother all that I knew, and perhaps should have told her long before, and we saw ourselves at once in a difficult and dangerous position. Some of the man's money – if he had any – was certainly due to us, but it was not likely that our captain's shipmates, above all the two specimens seen by me, Black Dog and the blind beggar, would be inclined to give up their booty in payment of the dead man's debts. It was like any other seaman's chest on the outside. "Give me the key," said my mother; and though the lock was very stiff, she had turned it and thrown back the lid in a twinkling. "Mother," said I, "take the whole and let's be going." But my mother, frightened as she was, would not consent to take a fraction more than was due to her and was obstinately unwilling to be content with less, and she was still arguing with me when a little low whistle sounded a good way off upon the hill. That was enough, and more than enough, for both of us.

"I'll take what I have," she said, jumping to her feet.

"And I'll take this to square the count," said I, picking up the oilskin packet.

We had not started a moment too soon. "My dear," said my mother suddenly, "take the money and run on. I am going to faint." We were just at the little bridge, by good fortune; and I helped her, tottering as she was, to the edge of the bank, where, sure enough, she gave a sigh and fell on my shoulder. I do not know how I found the strength to do it at all, and I am afraid it was roughly done, but I managed to drag her down the bank and a little way under the arch.

My curiosity, in a sense, was stronger than my fear, for I could not remain where I was, but crept back to the bank again, whence, sheltering my head behind a bush of broom, I might command the road before our door. I was scarcely in position ere my enemies began to arrive, seven or eight of them, running hard, their feet beating out of time along the road and the man with the lantern some paces in front. Three men ran together, hand in hand; and I made out, even through the mist, that the middle man of this trio was the blind beggar. The next moment his voice showed me that I was right.

"Down with the door!" he cried.

"Aye, aye, sir!" answered two or three; and a rush was made upon the Admiral Benbow, the lantern-bearer following; and then I could see them pause, and hear speeches passed in a lower key, as if they were surprised to find the door open. But the pause was brief, for the blind man again issued his commands. His voice sounded louder and higher, as if he were afire with eagerness and rage.

"In, in, in!" he shouted, and cursed them for their delay.

Four or five of them obeyed at once, two remaining on the road with the formidable beggar. There was a

N C WYETH
1911

pause, then a cry of surprise, and then a voice shouting from the house, "Bill's dead."

But the blind man swore at them again for their delay.

"Search him, some of you shirking lubbers, and the rest of you aloft and get the chest," he cried.

I could hear their feet rattling up our old stairs, so that the house must have shook with it. Promptly afterwards, fresh sounds of astonishment arose; the window of the captain's room was thrown open with a slam and a jingle of broken glass, and a man leaned out into the moonlight, head and shoulders, and addressed the blind beggar on the road below him.

"Pew," he cried, "they've been before us. Someone's turned the chest out alow and aloft."

"Is it there?" roared Pew. – "The money's there." – The blind man cursed the money. – "Flint's fist, I mean," he cried. – "We don't see it here nohow," returned the man. – "Here, you below there, is it on Bill?" cried the blind man again.

At that another fellow, probably him who had remained below to search the captain's body, came to the door of the inn. "Bill's been overhauled a'ready," said he; "nothin' left."

"It's these people of the inn – it's that boy. I wish I had put his eyes out!" cried the blind man, Pew. "There were no time ago – they had the door bolted when I tried it. Scatter, lads, and find 'em."

"Sure enough, they left their glim here," said the fellow from the window.

"Scatter and find 'em! Rout the house out!" reiterated Pew, striking with his stick upon the road.

Then there followed a great to-do through all our old inn, heavy feet pounding to and fro, furniture thrown over, doors kicked in, until the very rocks re-echoed and the men came out again, one after another, on the road and declared that we were nowhere to be found. And just the same whistle that had alarmed my mother and myself over the dead captain's money was once more clearly audible through the night, but this time twice repeated. I had thought it to be the blind man's trumpet, so to speak, summoning his crew to the assault, but I now found that it was a signal from the hillside towards the hamlet, and from its effect upon the buccaneers, a signal to warn them of approaching danger.

"There's Dirk again," said one. "Twice! We'll have to budge, mates."

"Budge, you skulk!" cried Pew. "Dirk was a fool and a coward from the first – you wouldn't mind him. They must be close by; they can't be far; you have your hands on it. Scatter and look for them, dogs! Oh, shiver my soul," he cried, "if I had eyes!"

This appeal seemed to produce some effect, for two of the fellows began to look here and there among the lumber, but half-heartedly, I thought, and with half an eye to their own danger all the time, while the rest stood irresolute on the road.

"You have your hands on thousands, you fools, and you hang a leg! You'd be as rich as kings if you could find it, and you know it's here, and you stand there skulking. There wasn't one of you dared face Bill, and I did it – a blind man! And I'm to lose my chance for you! I'm to be a poor, crawling beggar, sponging for rum, when I might be rolling in a coach! If you had the pluck of a weevil in a biscuit you would catch them still."

"Hang it, Pew, we've got the doubloons!" grumbled one.

"They might have hid the blessed thing," said another. "Take the Georges, Pew, and don't stand here squalling."

Squalling was the word for it; Pew's anger rose so high at these objections till at last he struck at them right and left in his blindness and his stick sounded heavily on more than one.

These, in their turn, cursed back at the blind miscreant, threatened him in horrid terms, and tried in vain to catch the stick and wrest it from his grasp.

This quarrel was the saving of us, for while it was still raging, another sound came from the top of the hill on the side of the hamlet – the tramp of horses galloping. Almost at the same time a pistol-shot, flash and report, came from the hedge side. And that was plainly the last signal of danger, for the buccaneers turned at once and ran, separating in every direction, one seaward along the cove, one slant across the hill, and so on, so that in half a minute not a sign of them remained but Pew. Him they had deserted, whether in sheer panic or out of revenge for his ill words and blows I know not; but there he remained behind, tapping up and down the road in a frenzy, and groping and calling for his comrades. Finally he took a wrong turn and ran a few steps past me, towards the hamlet, crying, "Johnny, Black Dog, Dirk," and other names, "you won't leave old Pew, mates – not old Pew!"

Just then the noise of horses topped the rise, and four or five riders came in sight in the moonlight and swept at full gallop down the slope.

At this Pew saw his error, turned with a scream, and ran straight for the ditch, into which he rolled. But he was on his feet again in a second and made another dash, now utterly bewildered, right under the nearest of the coming horses. The rider tried to save him, but in vain. Down went Pew with a cry that rang high into the night; and the four hoofs trampled and spurned him and passed by. He fell on his side, then gently collapsed upon his face and moved no more.

I leaped to my feet and hailed the riders. They were pulling up, at any rate, horrified at the accident; and I soon saw what they were. One, tailing out behind the rest, was a lad that had gone from the hamlet to Dr. Livesey's; the rest were revenue officers, whom he had met by the way, and with whom he had had the intelligence to return at once. Some news of the lugger in Kitt's Hole had found its way to Supervisor Dance and set him forth that night in our direction, and to that circumstance my mother and I owed our preservation from death.

DOWN WENT PEW WITH A CRY THAT RANG HIGH INTO THE NIGHT.

Mr. Dance could make nothing of the scene.

"They got the money, you say? Well, then, Hawkins, what in fortune were they after? More money, I suppose?" – "No, sir; not money, I think," replied I. "In fact, sir, I believe I have the thing in my breast pocket; and to tell you the truth, I should like to get it put in safety."

"To be sure, boy; quite right," said he. "I'll take it, if you like."

"I thought perhaps Dr. Livesey – " I began.

"Perfectly right," he interrupted very cheerily, "perfectly right – a gentleman and a magistrate. And, now I come to think of it, I might as well ride round there myself and report to him or squire. Master Pew's dead, when all's done; not that I regret it, but he's dead, you see, and people will make it out against an officer of his Majesty's revenue, if make it out they can. Now, I'll tell you, Hawkins, if you like, I'll take you along."

THE VOYAGE

We rode hard all the way till we drew up before Dr. Livesey's door. The house was all dark to the front. Mr. Dance told me to jump down and knock, and Dogger gave me a stirrup to descend by. The door was opened almost at once by the maid.

"Is Dr. Livesey in?" I asked.

No, she said, he had come home in the afternoon but had gone up to the hall to dine and pass the evening with the squire.

"So there we go, boys," said Mr. Dance.

This time, as the distance was short, I did not mount, but ran with Dogger's stirrup-leather to the lodge gates and up the long, leafless, moonlit avenue to where the white line of the hall buildings looked on either hand on great old gardens. Here Mr. Dance dismounted, and taking me along with him, was admitted at a word into the house.

The servant led us down a matted passage and showed us at the end into a great library, all lined with bookcases and busts upon the top of them, where the squire and Dr. Livesey sat, pipe in hand, on either side of a bright fire.

I had never seen the squire so near at hand. He was a tall man, over six feet high, and broad in proportion, and he had a bluff, rough-and-ready face, all roughened and reddened and lined in his long travels. His eyebrows were very black, and moved readily, and this gave him a look of some temper, not bad, you would say, but quick and high.

"Come in, Mr. Dance," says he, very stately and condescending.

"Good evening, Dance," says the doctor with a nod. "And good evening to you, friend Jim. What good wind brings you here?"

The supervisor stood up straight and stiff and told his story like a lesson; and you should have seen how the two gentlemen leaned forward and looked at each other, and forgot to smoke in their surprise and interest. When they heard how my mother went back to the inn, Dr. Livesey fairly slapped his thigh, and the squire cried "Bravo!" and broke his long pipe against the grate. Long before it was done, Mr. Trelawney (that, you will remember, was the squire's name) had got up from his seat and was striding about the room, and the doctor, as if to hear the better, had taken off his powdered wig and sat there looking very strange indeed with his own close-cropped black poll.

At last Mr. Dance finished the story.

"Mr. Dance," said the squire, "you are a very noble fellow. And as for riding down that black, atrocious miscreant, I regard it as an act of virtue, sir, like stamping on a cockroach. This lad Hawkins is a trump, I perceive. Hawkins, will you ring that bell? Mr. Dance must have some ale."

"And so, Jim," said the doctor, "you have the thing that they were after, have you?"

"Here it is, sir," said I, and gave him the oilskin packet.

The doctor looked it all over, as if his fingers were itching to open it; but instead of doing that, he put it quietly in the pocket of his coat.

"Squire," said he, "when Dance has had his ale he must, of course, be off on his Majesty's service; but I mean to keep Jim Hawkins here to sleep at my house, and with your permission, I propose we should have up the cold pie and let him sup."

"As you will, Livesey," said the squire; "Hawkins has earned better than cold pie."

So a big pigeon pie was brought in and put on a sidetable, and I made a hearty supper, for I was as hungry as a hawk, while Mr. Dance was further complimented and at last dismissed.

"And now, squire," said the doctor.

"And now, Livesey," said the squire in the same breath.

"One at a time, one at a time," laughed Dr. Livesey. "You have heard of this Flint, I suppose?"

And there fell out the map of an island, with latitude and longitude, soundings, names of hills and bays and inlets.

"Heard of him!" cried the squire. "Heard of him, you say! He was the bloodthirstiest buccaneer that sailed. Blackbeard was a child to Flint. The Spaniards were so prodigiously afraid of him that, I tell you, sir, I was sometimes proud he was an Englishman. I've seen his top-sails with these eyes, off Trinidad, and the cowardly son of a rum-puncheon that I sailed with put back – put back, sir, into Port of Spain."

"Well, I've heard of him myself, in England," said the doctor. "But the point is, had he money?"

"Money!" cried the squire. "Have you heard the story? What were these villains after but money? What do they care for but money? For what would they risk their rascal carcasses but money?"

"That we shall soon know," replied the doctor. "But you are so confoundedly hot-headed and exclamatory that I cannot get a word in. What I want to know is this: Supposing that I have here in my pocket some clue to where Flint buried his treasure, will that treasure amount to much?"

"Amount, sir!" cried the squire. "It will amount to this: If we have the clue you talk about, I fit out a ship in Bristol dock, and take you and Hawkins here along, and I'll have that treasure if I search a year."

"Very well," said the doctor. "Now, then, if Jim is agreeable, we'll open the packet"; and he laid it before him on the table.

The bundle was sewn together, and the doctor had to get out his instrument case and cut the stitches with his medical scissors. It contained two things – a book and a sealed paper.

The paper had been sealed in several places with a thimble by way of seal; the very thimble, perhaps, that I had found in the captain's pocket. The doctor opened the seals with great care, and there fell out the map of an island, with latitude and longitude, soundings, names of hills and bays and inlets, and every particular that would be needed to bring a ship to a safe anchorage upon its shores. It was about nine miles long and five across, shaped, you might say, like a fat dragon standing up, and had two fine land-locked harbours, and a hill in the centre part marked "The Spy-glass." There were several additions of a later date, but above all, three crosses of red ink – two on the north part of the island, one in the southwest – and beside this last, in the same red ink, and in a small, neat hand, very different from the captain's tottery characters, these words: "Bulk of treasure here."

Over on the back the same hand had written this further information:

Tall tree, Spy-glass shoulder, bearing a point to the N. of N.N.E.
Skeleton Island E.S.E. and by E.
Ten feet.
The bar silver is in the north cache; you can find it by the trend of the east hummock, ten fathoms south of the black crag with the face on it.
The arms are easy found, in the sand-hill, N. point of north inlet cape, bearing E. and a quarter N. J.F.

That was all; but brief as it was, and to me incomprehensible, it filled the squire and Dr. Livesey with delight.

"Livesey," said the squire, "you will give up this wretched practice at once. Tomorrow I start for Bristol. In three weeks' time – three weeks! – two weeks – ten days – we'll have the best ship, sir, and the choicest crew in England. Hawkins shall come as cabin-boy. You'll make a famous cabin-boy, Hawkins. You, Livesey, are ship's doctor; I am admiral. We'll take Redruth, Joyce, and Hunter. We'll have favourable winds, a quick

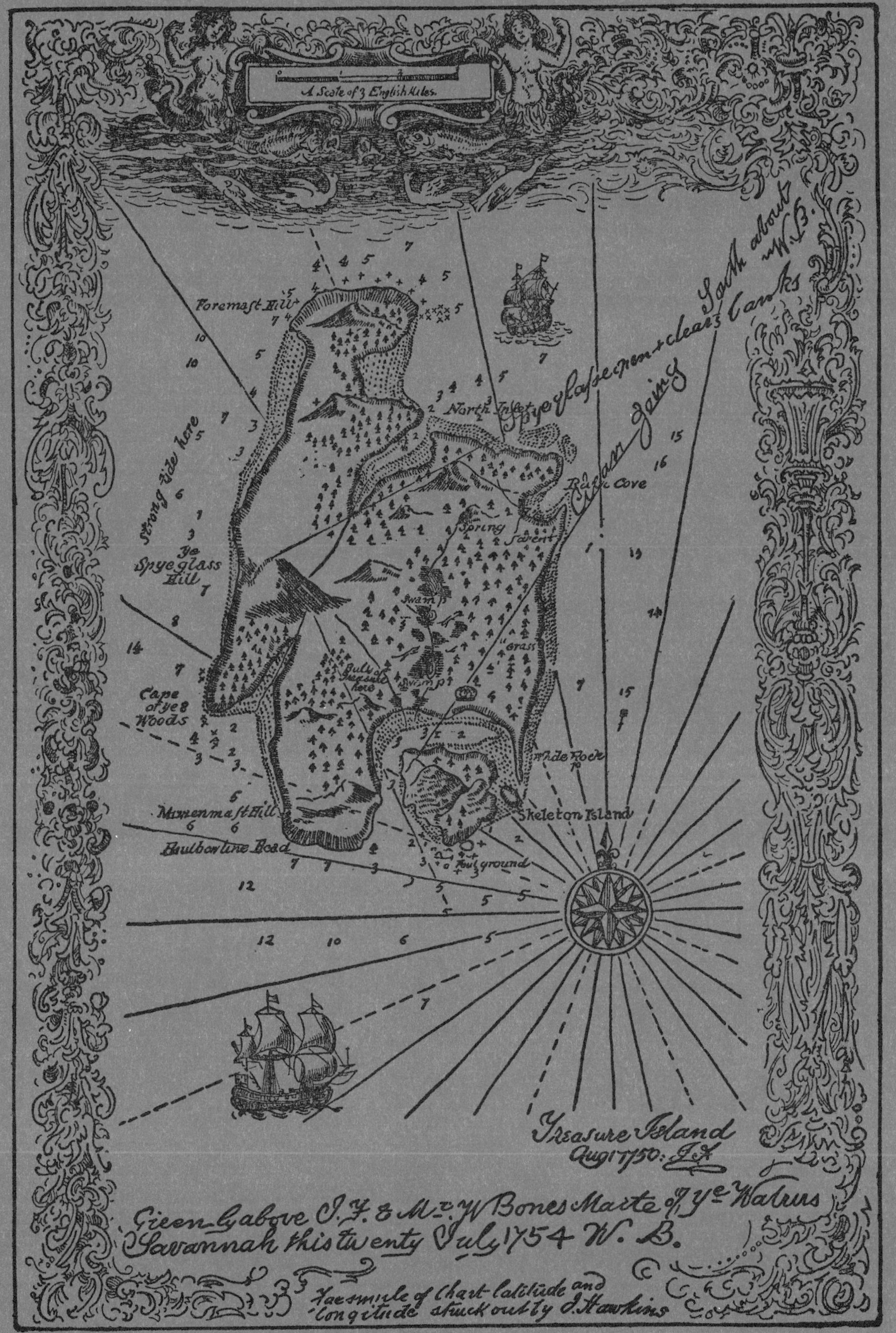

A Scale of 3 English Miles
Foremast Hill
Strong tide here
Ye Spyeglass Hill
North Inlet
Spring
Swamp
Grass
Bulk of treasure here
Cape of ye Woods
Mizzenmast Hill
Haulbowline Head
Foul ground
Skeleton Island
White Rock
Treasure Island Augt 1750 J.F.
Given by above J. F. & Mr W Bones Maste of ye Walrus
Savannah this twenty July 1754 W. B.
Facsimile of Chart latitude and longitude struck out by J. Hawkins

To me he was unweariedly kind, and always glad to see me in the galley.

passage, and not the least difficulty in finding the spot, and money to eat, to roll in, to play duck and drake with ever after."

"Trelawney," said the doctor, "I'll go with you; and I'll go bail for it, so will Jim, and be a credit to the undertaking. There's only one man I'm afraid of."

"And who's that?" cried the squire. "Name the dog, sir!"

"You," replied the doctor; "for you cannot hold your tongue. We are not the only men who know of this paper. These fellows who attacked the inn tonight – bold, desperate blades, for sure – and the rest who stayed aboard that lugger, and more, I dare say, not far off, are, one and all, through thick and thin, bound that they'll get that money. We must none of us go alone till we get to sea. Jim and I shall stick together in the meanwhile; you'll take Joyce and Hunter when you ride to Bristol, and from first to last, not one of us must breathe a word of what we've found."

"Livesey," returned the squire, "you are always in the right of it. I'll be as silent as the grave."

The *Hispaniola* lay some way out, and we went under the figureheads and round the sterns of many other ships, and their cables sometimes grated underneath our keel, and sometimes swung above us. At last, however, we got alongside, and were met and saluted as we stepped aboard by the mate, Mr. Arrow, a brown old sailor with earrings in his ears and a squint.

All that night we were in a great bustle getting things stowed in their place, and boatfuls of the squire's friends, Mr. Blandly and the like, coming off to wish him a good voyage and a safe return. We never had a night at the Admiral Benbow when I had half the work; and I was dog-tired when, a little before dawn, the boatswain sounded his pipe and the crew began to man the capstan-bars. I might have been twice as weary, yet I would not have left the deck, all was so new and interesting to me – the brief commands, the shrill note of the whistle, the men bustling to their places in the glimmer of the ship's lanterns.

"Now, Barbecue, tip us a stave," cried one voice.

"The old one," cried another.

"Aye, aye, mates," said Long John, who was standing by, with his crutch under his arm, and at once broke out in the air and words I knew so well:

"Fifteen men on the dead man's chest – "

And then the whole crew bore chorus:

"Yo-ho-ho, and a bottle of rum!"

And at the third "Ho!" drove the bars before them with a will.

Even at that exciting moment it carried me back to the old Admiral Benbow in a second, and I seemed to hear the voice of the captain piping in the chorus. But soon the anchor was short up; soon it was hanging dripping at the bows; soon the sails began to draw, and the land and shipping to flit by on either side; and before I could lie down to snatch an hour of slumber the *Hispaniola* had begun her voyage to the Isle of Treasure.

I am not going to relate that voyage in detail. It was fairly prosperous. The ship proved to be a good ship, the crew were capable seamen, and the captain thoroughly understood his business. But before we came the length of Treasure Island, two or three things had happened which require to be known.

Mr. Arrow, first of all, turned out even worse than the captain had feared. He had no command among the men, and people did what they pleased with him. But that was by no means the worst of it, for after a day or two at sea he began to appear on deck with hazy eye, red cheeks, stuttering tongue, and other marks of drunkenness. Time after time he was ordered below in disgrace. Sometimes he fell and cut himself; sometimes he lay all day long in his little bunk at one side of the companion; sometimes for a day or two he would be almost sober and attend to his work at least passably.

SOON THE SAILS BEGAN TO DRAW, AND THE LAND AND SHIPPING TO FLIT BY ON EITHER SIDE.

In the meantime, we could never make out where he got the drink. That was the ship's mystery. Watch him as we pleased, we could do nothing to solve it; and when we asked him to his face, he would only laugh if he were drunk, and if he were sober deny solemnly that he ever tasted anything but water.

He was not only useless as an officer and a bad influence amongst the men, but it was plain that at this rate he must soon kill himself outright, so nobody was much surprised, nor very sorry, when one dark night, with a head sea, he disappeared entirely and was seen no more.

"Overboard!" said the captain. "Well, gentlemen, that saves the trouble of putting him in irons."

But there we were, without a mate; and it was necessary, of course, to advance one of the men. The boatswain, Job Anderson, was the likeliest man aboard, and though he kept his old title, he served in a way as mate. Mr. Trelawney had followed the sea, and his knowledge made him very useful, for he often took a watch himself in easy weather. And the coxswain, Israel Hands, was a careful, wily, old, experienced seaman who could be trusted at a pinch with almost anything.

He was a great confidant of Long John Silver, and so the mention of his name leads me on to speak of our ship's cook, Barbecue, as the men called him.

Aboard ship he carried his crutch by a lanyard round his neck, to have both hands as free as possible. It was something to see him wedge the foot of the crutch against a bulkhead, and propped against it, yielding to every movement of the ship, get on with his cooking like someone safe ashore. Still more strange was it to see him in the heaviest of weather cross the deck. He had a line or two rigged up to help him across the widest spaces – Long John's earrings, they were called; and he would hand himself from one place to another, now using the crutch, now trailing it alongside by the lanyard, as quickly as another man could walk. Yet some of the men who had sailed with him before expressed their pity to see him so reduced.

"He's no common man, Barbecue," said the coxswain to me. "He had good schooling in his young days and can speak like a book when so minded; and brave – a lion's nothing alongside of Long John! I seen him grapple four and knock their heads together – him unarmed."

All the crew respected and even obeyed him. He had a way of talking to each and doing everybody some particular service. To me he was unweariedly kind, and always glad to see me in the galley, which he kept as clean as a new pin, the dishes hanging up burnished and his parrot in a cage in one corner.

"Come away, Hawkins," he would say; "come and have a yarn with John. Nobody more welcome than yourself, my son. Sit you down and hear the news. Here's Cap'n Flint – I calls my parrot Cap'n Flint, after the famous buccaneer – here's Cap'n Flint predicting success to our v'yage. Wasn't you, cap'n?"

And the parrot would say, with great rapidity, "Pieces of eight! Pieces of eight! Pieces of eight!" till you wondered that it was not out of breath, or till John threw his handkerchief over the cage.

"Now, that bird," he would say, "is, maybe, two hundred years old, Hawkins – they live forever mostly; and if anybody's seen more wickedness, it must be the devil himself. She's sailed with England, the great Cap'n England, the pirate. She's been at Madagascar, and at Malabar, and Surinam, and Providence, and Portobello. She was at the fishing up of the wrecked plate ships. It's there she learned 'Pieces of eight,' and little wonder; three hundred and fifty thousand of 'em, Hawkins! She was at the boarding of the viceroy of the Indies out of Goa, she was; and to look at her you would think she was a babby. But you smelt powder – didn't you, cap'n?"

"Stand by to go about," the parrot would scream.

"Ah, she's a handsome craft, she is," the cook would say, and give her sugar from his pocket, and then the bird would peck at the bars and swear straight on, passing belief for wickedness. "There," John would add, "you can't touch pitch and not be mucked, lad. Here's this poor old innocent bird o' mine swearing blue fire, and none the wiser, you may lay to that. She would swear the same, in a manner of speaking, before chaplain." And John would touch his forelock with a solemn way he had that made me think he was the best of men.

In the meantime, the squire and Captain Smollett were still on pretty distant terms with one another. The squire made no bones about the matter; he despised the captain. The captain, on his part, never spoke but when he was spoken to, and then sharp and short and dry, and not a word wasted. He owned, when driven into a corner, that he seemed to have been wrong about the crew, that some of them were as brisk as he wanted to see and all had behaved fairly well. As for the ship, he had taken a downright fancy to her. "She'll lie a point nearer the wind than a man has a right to expect of his own married wife, sir. But," he would add, "all I say is, we're not home again, and I don't like the cruise."

The squire, at this, would turn away and march up and down the deck, chin in air.

"A trifle more of that man," he would say, "and I shall explode."

We had some heavy weather, which only proved the qualities of the *Hispaniola*. Every man on board seemed well content, and they must have been hard to please if they had been otherwise, for it is my belief there was never a ship's company so spoiled since Noah put to sea. Double grog was going on the least excuse; there was duff on odd days, as, for instance, if the squire heard it was any man's birthday, and always a barrel of apples standing broached in the waist for anyone to help himself that had a fancy.

"Never knew good come of it yet," the captain said to Dr. Livesey. "Spoil forecastle hands, make devils. That's my belief."

But good did come of the apple barrel, as you shall hear, for if it had not been for that, we should have had no note of warning and might all have perished by the hand of treachery.

This was how it came about.

We had run up the trades to get the wind of the island we were after – I am not allowed to be more plain – and now we were running down for it with a bright lookout day and night. It was about the last day of our outward voyage by the largest computation; some time that night, or at latest before noon of the morrow, we should sight the Treasure Island. We were heading S.S.W. and had a steady breeze abeam and a quiet sea. The *Hispaniola* rolled steadily, dipping her bowsprit now and then with a whiff of spray. All was drawing alow and aloft; everyone was in the bravest spirits because we were now so near an end of the first part of our adventure.

Now, just after sundown, when all my work was over and I was on my way to my berth, it occurred to me that I should like an apple. I ran on deck. The watch was all forward looking out for the island. The man at the helm was watching the luff of the sail and whistling away gently to himself, and that was the only sound excepting the swish of the sea against the bows and around the sides of the ship.

In I got bodily into the apple barrel, and found there was scarce an apple left; but sitting down there in the dark, what with the sound of the waters and the rocking movement of the ship, I had either fallen asleep or was on the point of doing so when a heavy man sat down with rather a clash close by. The barrel shook as he leaned his shoulders against it, and I was just about to jump up when the man began to speak. It was Silver's voice, and before I had heard a dozen words, I would not have shown myself for all the world, but lay there, trembling and listening, in the extreme of fear and curiosity, for from these dozen words I understood that the lives of all the honest men aboard depended upon me alone.

"No, not I," said Silver. "Flint was cap'n; I was quartermaster, along of my timber leg. The same broadside I lost my leg, old Pew lost his deadlights. It was a master surgeon, him that ampytated me – out of college and all – Latin by the bucket, and what not; but he was hanged like a dog, and sun-dried like the rest, at Corso Castle. That was Roberts' men, that was, and comed of changing names to their ships – *Royal Fortune* and so on. Now, what a ship was christened, so let her stay, I says. So it was with the *Cassandra*, as brought us all safe home from Malabar, after England took the viceroy of the Indies; so it was with the old *Walrus*, Flint's old ship, as I've seen amuck with the red blood and fit to sink with gold."

"Ah!" cried another voice, that of the youngest hand on board, and evidently full of admiration. "He was the flower of the flock, was Flint!"

"Davis was a man too, by all accounts," said Silver. "I never sailed along of him; first with England, then with Flint, that's my story; and now here on my own account, in a manner of speaking. I laid by nine hundred safe, from England, and two thousand after Flint. That ain't bad for a man before the mast – all safe in bank. 'Tain't earning now, it's saving does it, you may lay to that. Where's all England's men now? I dunno. Where's Flint's? Why, most on 'em aboard here, and glad to get the duff – been begging before that, some on 'em. Old Pew, as had lost his sight, and might have thought shame, spends twelve hundred pound in a year, like a lord in Parliament. Where is he now? Well, he's dead now and under hatches; but for two year before that, shiver my timbers, the man was starving! He begged, and he stole, and he cut throats, and starved at that, by the powers!"

"Well, it ain't much use, after all," said the young seaman.

"'Tain't much use for fools, you may lay to it – that, nor nothing," cried Silver. "But now, you look here: you're young, you are, but you're as smart as paint. I see that when I set my eyes on you, and I'll talk to you like a man."

You may imagine how I felt when I heard this abominable old rogue addressing another in the very same words of flattery as he had used to myself. I think, if I had been able, that I would have killed him through the barrel. Meantime, he ran on, little supposing he was overheard.

"Here it is about gentlemen of fortune. They lives rough, and they risk swinging, but they eat and drink

It was Silver's voice, and before I had heard a dozen words, I would not have shown myself for all the world.

like fighting-cocks, and when a cruise is done, why, it's hundreds of pounds instead of hundreds of farthings in their pockets. Now, the most goes for rum and a good fling, and to sea again in their shirts. But that's not the course I lay. I puts it all away, some here, some there, and none too much anywheres, by reason of suspicion. I'm fifty, mark you; once back from this cruise, I set up gentleman in earnest. Time enough too, says you. Ah, but I've lived easy in the meantime, never denied myself o' nothing heart desires, and slep' soft and ate dainty all my days but when at sea. And how did I begin? Before the mast, like you!"

"Well," said the other, "but all the other money's gone now, ain't it? You daren't show face in Bristol after this."

"Why, where might you suppose it was?" asked Silver derisively.

"At Bristol, in banks and places," answered his companion.

"It were," said the cook; "it were when we weighed anchor. But my old missis has it all by now. And the Spy-glass is sold, lease and goodwill and rigging; and the old girl's off to meet me. I would tell you where, for I trust you, but it'd make jealousy among the mates."

"And can you trust your missis?" asked the other.

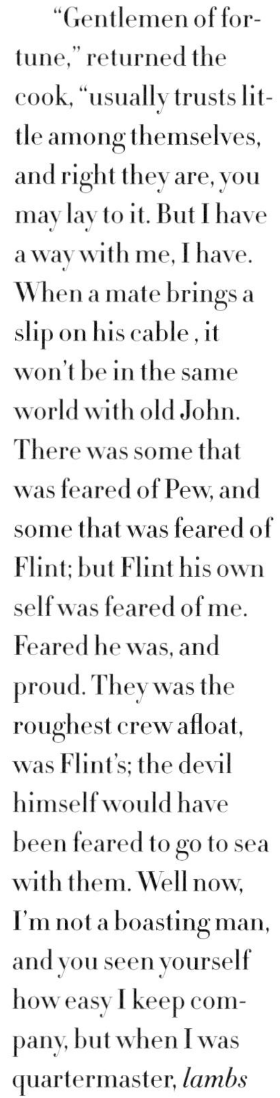

"Gentlemen of fortune," returned the cook, "usually trusts little among themselves, and right they are, you may lay to it. But I have a way with me, I have. When a mate brings a slip on his cable , it won't be in the same world with old John. There was some that was feared of Pew, and some that was feared of Flint; but Flint his own self was feared of me. Feared he was, and proud. They was the roughest crew afloat, was Flint's; the devil himself would have been feared to go to sea with them. Well now, I'm not a boasting man, and you seen yourself how easy I keep company, but when I was quartermaster, *lambs* wasn't the word for Flint's old buccaneers. Ah, you may be sure of yourself in old John's ship."

"Well, I tell you now," replied the lad, "I didn't half a quarter like the job till I had this talk with you, John;

but there's my hand on it now." – "And a brave lad you were, and smart too," answered Silver, shaking hands so heartily that all the barrel shook, "and a finer figure-head for a gentleman of fortune I never clapped my eyes on."

By this time I had begun to understand the meaning of their terms. By a "gentleman of fortune" they plainly meant neither more nor less than a common pirate, and the little scene that I had overheard was the last act in the corruption of one of the honest hands – perhaps of the last one left aboard. But on this point I was soon to be relieved, for Silver giving a little whistle, a third man strolled up and sat down by the party.

"Dick's square," said Silver.

"Oh, I know'd Dick was square," returned the voice of the coxswain, Israel Hands. "He's no fool, is Dick." And he turned his quid and spat. "But look here," he went on, "here's what I want to know, Barbecue: how long are we a-going to stand off and on like a blessed bumboat? I've had a'most enough o' Cap'n Smollett; he's hazed me long enough, by thunder! I want to go into that cabin, I do. I want their pickles and wines, and that."

"Israel," said Silver, "your head ain't much account, nor ever was. But you're able to hear, I reckon; leastways, your ears is big enough. Now, here's what I say: you'll berth forward, and you'll live hard, and you'll speak soft, and you'll keep sober till I give the word; and you may lay to that, my son."

"Well, I don't say no, do I?" growled the coxswain. "What I say is, when? That's what I say."

"When! By the powers!" cried Silver. "Well now, if you want to know, I'll tell you when. The last moment I can manage, and that's when. Here's a first-rate seaman, Cap'n Smollett, sails the blessed ship for us. Here's this squire and doctor with a map and such – I don't know where it is, do I? No more do you, says you. Well then, I mean this squire and doctor shall find the stuff, and help us to get it aboard, by the powers. Then we'll see. If I was sure of you all, sons of double Dutchmen, I'd have Cap'n Smollett navigate us half-way back again before I struck."

"Why, we're all seamen aboard here, I should think," said the lad Dick.

"We're all forecastle hands, you mean," snapped Silver. "We can steer a course, but who's to set one? That's what all you gentlemen split on, first and last. If I had my way, I'd have Cap'n Smollett work us back into the trades at least; then we'd have no blessed miscalculations and a spoonful of water a day. But I know the sort you are. I'll finish with 'em at the island, as soon's the blunt's on board, and a pity it is. But you're never happy till you're drunk. Split my sides, I've a sick heart to sail with the likes of you!"

"Easy all, Long John," cried Israel. "Who's a-crossin' of you?"

"Why, how many tall ships, think ye, now, have I seen laid aboard? And how many brisk lads drying in the sun at Execution Dock?" cried Silver. "And all for this same hurry and hurry and hurry. You hear me? I seen a thing or two at sea, I have. If you would on'y lay your course, and a p'int to windward, you would ride in carriages, you would. But not you! I know you. You'll have your mouthful of rum tomorrow, and go hang."

"Everybody knowed you was a kind of a chapling, John; but there's others as could hand and steer as well as you," said Israel. "They liked a bit o' fun, they did. They wasn't so high and dry, nohow, but took their fling, like jolly companions every one."

"So?" says Silver. "Well, and where are they now? Pew was that sort, and he died a beggar-man. Flint was, and he died of rum at Savannah. Ah, they was a sweet crew, they was! On'y, where are they?"

"But," asked Dick, "when we do lay 'em athwart, what are we to do with 'em, anyhow?"

"THIS TIME IT'S SERIOUS. DOOTY IS DOOTY, MATES. I GIVE MY VOTE – DEATH."

"There's the man for me!" cried the cook admiringly. "That's what I call business. Well, what would you think? Put 'em ashore like maroons? That would have been England's way. Or cut 'em down like that much pork? That would have been Flint's, or Billy Bones's."

"Billy was the man for that," said Israel. "'Dead men don't bite,' says he. Well, he's dead now hisself; he knows the long and short on it now; and if ever a rough hand come to port, it was Billy."

"Right you are," said Silver; "rough and ready. But mark you here, I'm an easy man – I'm quite the gentleman, says you; but this time it's serious. Dooty is dooty, mates. I give my vote – death. When I'm in Parlyment and riding in my coach, I don't want none of these sea-lawyers in the cabin a-coming home, unlooked for, like the devil at prayers. Wait is what I say; but when the time comes, why, let her rip!"

"John," cries the coxswain, "you're a man!"

"You'll say so, Israel, when you see," said Silver. "Only one thing I claim – I claim Trelawney. I'll wring his calf's head off his body with these hands, Dick!" he added, breaking off. "You just jump up, like a sweet lad, and get me an apple, to wet my pipe like."

You may fancy the terror I was in! I should have leaped out and run for it if I had found the strength, but my limbs and heart alike misgave me. I heard Dick begin to rise, and then someone seemingly stopped him, and the voice of Hands exclaimed, "Oh, stow that! Don't you get sucking of that bilge, John. Let's have a go of the rum."

"Dick," said Silver, "I trust you. I've a gauge on the keg, mind. There's the key; you fill a pannikin and bring it up."

Terrified as I was, I could not help thinking to myself that this must have been how Mr. Arrow got the strong waters that destroyed him.

Dick was gone but a little while, and during his absence Israel spoke straight on in the cook's ear. It was but a word or two that I could catch, and yet I gathered some important news, for besides other scraps that tended to the same purpose, this whole clause was audible: "Not another man of them'll jine." Hence there were still faithful men on board.

When Dick returned, one after another of the trio took the pannikin and drank – one "To luck," another with a "Here's to old Flint," and Silver himself saying, in a kind of song, "Here's to ourselves, and hold your luff, plenty of prizes and plenty of duff."

Just then a sort of brightness fell upon me in the barrel, and looking up, I found the moon had risen and was silvering the mizzen-top and shining white on the luff of the fore-sail; and almost at the same time the voice of the lookout shouted, "Land ho!"

HOW MY SHORE ADVENTURE BEGAN

We brought up just where the anchor was in the chart, about a third of a mile from each shore, the mainland on one side and Skeleton Island on the other. The bottom was clean sand. The plunge of our anchor sent up clouds of birds wheeling and crying over the woods, but in less than a minute they were down again and all was once more silent.

Page 271
It was so decided; loaded pistols were served out to all the sure men.

Silver was the captain, and a mighty rebellious crew he had of it.

The place was entirely land-locked, buried in woods, the trees coming right down to high-water mark, the shores mostly flat, and the hilltops standing round at a distance in a sort of amphitheatre, one here, one there. Two little rivers, or rather two swamps, emptied out into this pond, as you might call it; and the foliage round that part of the shore had a kind of poisonous brightness. From the ship we could see nothing of the house or stockade, for they were quite buried among trees; and if it had not been for the chart on the companion, we might have been the first that had ever anchored there since the island arose out of the seas.

There was not a breath of air moving, nor a sound but that of the surf booming half a mile away along the beaches and against the rocks outside. A peculiar stagnant smell hung over the anchorage – a smell of sodden leaves and rotting tree trunks. I observed the doctor sniffing and sniffing, like someone tasting a bad egg.

"I don't know about treasure," he said, "but I'll stake my wig there's fever here."

If the conduct of the men had been alarming in the boat, it became truly threatening when they had come aboard. They lay about the deck growling together in talk. The slightest order was received with a black look and grudgingly and carelessly obeyed. Even the honest hands must have caught the infection, for there was not one man aboard to mend another. Mutiny, it was plain, hung over us like a thunder-cloud.

And it was not only we of the cabin party who perceived the danger. Long John was hard at work going from group to group, spending himself in good advice, and as for example no man could have shown a better. He fairly outstripped himself in willingness and civility; he was all smiles to everyone. If an order were given, John would be on his crutch in an instant, with the cheeriest "Aye, aye, sir!" in the world; and when there was nothing else to do, he kept up one song after another, as if to conceal the discontent of the rest.

Of all the gloomy features of that gloomy afternoon, this obvious anxiety on the part of Long John appeared the worst.

We held a council in the cabin.

"Sir," said the captain, "if I risk another order, the whole ship'll come about our ears by the run. You see, sir, here it is. I get a rough answer, do I not? Well, if I speak back, pikes will be going in two shakes; if I don't, Silver will see there's something under that, and the game's up. Now, we've only one man to rely on."

"And who is that?" asked the squire.

"Silver, sir," returned the captain; "he's as anxious as you and I to smother things up. This is a tiff; he'd soon talk 'em out of it if he had the chance, and what I propose to do is to give him the chance. Let's allow the men an afternoon ashore. If they all go, why we'll fight the ship. If they none of them go, well then, we hold the cabin, and God defend the right. If some go, you mark my words, sir, Silver'll bring 'em aboard again as mild as lambs."

It was so decided; loaded pistols were served out to all the sure men; Hunter, Joyce, and Redruth were taken into our confidence and received the news with less surprise and a better spirit than we had looked for, and then the captain went on deck and addressed the crew.

"My lads," said he, "we've had a hot day and are all tired and out of sorts. A turn ashore'll hurt nobody – the boats are still in the water; you can take the gigs, and as many as please may go ashore for the afternoon. I'll fire a gun half an hour before sundown."

I believe the silly fellows must have thought they would break their shins over treasure as soon as they were landed, for they all came out of their sulks in a moment and gave a cheer that started the echo in a faraway hill and sent the birds once more flying and squalling round the anchorage.

The captain was too bright to be in the way. He whipped out of sight in a moment, leaving Silver to arrange the party, and I fancy it was as well he did so. Had he been on deck, he could no longer so much as have pretended not to understand the situation. It was as plain as day. Silver was the captain, and a mighty rebellious crew he had of it. The honest hands – and I was soon to see it proved that there were such on board – must have been very stupid fellows. Or rather, I suppose the truth was this, that all hands were disaffected by the example of the ringleaders – only some more, some less; and a few, being good fellows in the main, could neither be led nor driven any further. It is one thing to be idle and skulk and quite another to take a ship and murder a number of innocent men.

At last, however, the party was made up. Six fellows were to stay on board, and the remaining thirteen, including Silver, began to embark.

Then it was that there came into my head the first of the mad notions that contributed so much to save our lives. If six men were left by Silver, it was plain our party could not take and fight the ship; and since only six were left, it was equally plain that the cabin party had no present need of my assistance. It occurred to me at once to go ashore. In a jiffy I had slipped over the side and curled up in the fore-sheets of the nearest boat, and almost at the same moment she shoved off.

No one took notice of me, only the bow oar saying, "Is that you, Jim? Keep your head down." But Silver, from the other boat, looked sharply over and called out to know if that were me; and from that moment I began to regret what I had done.

I was so pleased at having given the slip to Long John that I began to enjoy myself and look around me with some interest on the strange land that I was in.

From the side of the hill, which was here steep and stony, a spout of gravel was dislodged and fell rattling and bounding through the trees. My eyes turned instinctively in that direction, and I saw a figure leap with great rapidity behind the trunk of a pine. What it was, whether bear or man or monkey, I could in no wise tell. It seemed dark and shaggy; more I knew not. But the terror of this new apparition brought me to a stand. I was now, it seemed, cut off upon both sides; behind me the murderers, before me this lurking nondescript.

N.C. WYETH

I saw a figure leap with great rapidity behind the trunk of a pine.

And immediately I began to prefer the dangers that I knew to those I knew not. Silver himself appeared less terrible in contrast with this creature of the woods, and I turned on my heel, and looking sharply behind me over my shoulder, began to retrace my steps in the direction of the boats.

Instantly the figure reappeared, and making a wide circuit, began to head me off. I was tired, at any rate; but had I been as fresh as when I rose, I could see it was in vain for me to contend in speed with such an adversary. From trunk to trunk the creature flitted like a deer, running manlike on two legs, but unlike any man that I had ever seen, stooping almost double as it ran. Yet a man it was, I could no longer be in doubt about that.

I began to recall what I had heard of cannibals. I was within an ace of calling for help. But the mere fact that he was a man, however wild, had somewhat reassured me, and my fear of Silver began to revive in proportion. I stood still, therefore, and cast about for some method of escape; and as I was so thinking, the recollection of my pistol flashed into my mind. As soon as I remembered I was not defenceless, courage glowed again in my heart and I set my face resolutely for this man of the island and walked briskly towards him.

He was concealed by this time behind another tree trunk; but he must have been watching me closely, for as soon as I began to move in his direction he reappeared and took a step to meet me. Then he hesitated, drew back, came forward again, and at last, to my wonder and confusion, threw himself on his knees and held out his clasped hands in supplication.

At that I once more stopped.

"Who are you?" I asked.

"Ben Gunn," he answered, and his voice sounded hoarse and awkward, like a rusty lock. "I'm poor Ben Gunn, I am; and I haven't spoke with a Christian these three years."

I could now see that he was a white man like myself and that his features were even pleasing. His skin, wherever it was exposed, was burnt by the sun; even his lips were black, and his fair eyes looked quite startling in so dark a face. Of all the beggar-men that I had seen or fancied, he was the chief for raggedness. He was clothed with tatters of old ship's canvas and old sea-cloth, and this extraordinary patchwork was all held together by a system of the most various and incongruous fastenings, brass buttons, bits of stick, and loops of tarry gaskin. About his waist he wore an old brass-buckled leather belt, which was the one thing solid in his whole accoutrement.

"Three years!" I cried. "Were you shipwrecked?"

"Nay, mate," said he; "marooned."

I had heard the word, and I knew it stood for a horrible kind of punishment common enough among the buccaneers, in which the offender is put ashore with a little powder and shot and left behind on some desolate and distant island.

AS SOON AS I REMEMBERED I WAS NOT DEFENCELESS, COURAGE GLOWED AGAIN IN MY HEART.

"Marooned three years agone," he continued, "and lived on goats since then, and berries, and oysters. Wherever a man is, says I, a man can do for himself. But, mate, my heart is sore for Christian diet. You mightn't happen to have a piece of cheese about you, now? No?

Well, many's the long night I've dreamed of cheese – toasted, mostly – and woke up again, and here I were."

"If ever I can get aboard again," said I, "you shall have cheese by the stone."

All this time he had been feeling the stuff of my jacket, smoothing my hands, looking at my boots, and generally, in the intervals of his speech, showing a childish pleasure in the presence of a fellow creature. But at my last words he perked up into a kind of startled slyness.

"If ever you can get aboard again, says you?" he repeated. "Why, now, who's to hinder you?"

"Not you, I know," was my reply.

"And right you was," he cried. "Now you – what do you call yourself, mate?"

"Jim," I told him.

"Jim, Jim," says he, quite pleased apparently. "Well, now, Jim, I've lived that rough as you'd be ashamed to hear of. Now, for instance, you wouldn't think I had had a pious mother – to look at me?" he asked.

"Why, no, not in particular," I answered.

"Ah, well," said he, "but I had – remarkable pious. And I was a civil, pious boy, and could rattle off my catechism that fast, as you couldn't tell one word from another. And here's what it come to, Jim, and it begun with chuck-farthen on the blessed grave-stones! That's what it begun with, but it went further'n that; and so my mother told me, and predicked the whole, she did, the pious woman! But it were Providence that put me here. I've thought it all out in this here lonely island, and I'm back on piety. You don't catch me tasting rum so much, but just a thimbleful for luck, of course, the first chance I have. I'm bound I'll be good, and I see the way to. And, Jim" – looking all round him and lowering his voice to a whisper – "I'm rich."

I now felt sure that the poor fellow had gone crazy in his solitude, and I suppose I must have shown the feeling in my face, for he repeated the statement hotly: "Rich! Rich! I says. And I'll tell you what: I'll make a man of you, Jim. Ah, Jim, you'll bless your stars, you will, you was the first that found me!"

And at this there came suddenly a lowering shadow over his face, and he tightened his grasp upon my hand and raised a forefinger threateningly before my eyes.

"Now, Jim, you tell me true: that ain't Flint's ship?" he asked.

HE TIGHTENED HIS GRASP UPON MY HAND AND RAISED A FOREFINGER THREATENINGLY.

At this I had a happy inspiration. I began to believe that I had found an ally, and I answered him at once.

"It's not Flint's ship, and Flint is dead; but I'll tell you true, as you ask me – there are some of Flint's hands aboard; worse luck for the rest of us."

"Not a man – with one – leg?" he gasped. – "Silver?" I asked. – "Ah, Silver!" says he. "That were his name." – "He's the cook, and the ringleader too."

He was still holding me by the wrist, and at that he give it quite a wring.

"If you was sent by Long John," he said, "I'm as good as pork, and I know it. But where was you, do you suppose?"

I had made my mind up in a moment, and by way of answer told him the whole story of our voyage and the predicament in which we found ourselves. He

He hesitated, drew back, and at last, to my wonder and confusion, threw himself on his knees and held out his clasped hands in supplication.

heard me with the keenest interest, and when I had done he patted me on the head.

"You're a good lad, Jim," he said; "and you're all in a clove hitch, ain't you? Well, you just put your trust in Ben Gunn – Ben Gunn's the man to do it. Would you think it likely, now, that your squire would prove a liberal-minded one in case of help – him being in a clove hitch, as you remark?"

I told him the squire was the most liberal of men.

"Aye, but you see," returned Ben Gunn, "I didn't mean giving me a gate to keep, and a suit of livery clothes, and such; that's not my mark, Jim. What I mean is, would he be likely to come down to the toon of, say one thousand pounds out of money that's as good as a man's own already?"

"I am sure he would," said I. "As it was, all hands were to share."

"*And* a passage home?" he added with a look of great shrewdness.

"Why," I cried, "the squire's a gentleman. And besides, if we got rid of the others, we should want you to help work the vessel home." – "Ah," said he, "so you would." And he seemed very much relieved.

"Now, I'll tell you what," he went on. "So much I'll tell you, and no more. I were in Flint's ship when he buried the treasure; he and six along – six strong seamen. They was ashore nigh on a week, and us standing off and on in the old *Walrus*. One fine day up went the signal, and here come Flint by himself in a little boat, and his head done up in a blue scarf. The sun was getting up, and mortal white he looked about the cutwater. But, there he was, you mind, and the six all dead – dead and buried. How he done it, not a man aboard us could make out. It was battle, murder, and sudden death, leastways – him against six. Billy Bones was the mate; Long John, he was quartermaster; and they asked him where the treasure was. 'Ah,' says he, 'you can go ashore, if you like, and stay,' he says; 'but as for the ship, she'll beat up for more, by thunder!' That's what he said.

"Well, I was in another ship three years back, and we sighted this island. 'Boys,' said I, 'here's Flint's treasure; let's land and find it.' The cap'n was displeased at that, but my messmates were all of a mind and landed. Twelve days they looked for it, and every day they had the worse word for me, until one fine morning all

I beheld the Union Jack flutter in the air above a wood.

hands went aboard. 'As for you, Benjamin Gunn,' says they, 'here's a musket,' they says, 'and a spade, and pick-axe. You can stay here and find Flint's money for yourself,' they says.

"Well, Jim, three years have I been here, and not a bite of Christian diet from that day to this. But now, you look here; look at me. Do I look like a man before the mast? No, says you. Nor I weren't, neither, I says."

And with that he winked and pinched me hard.

"Just you mention them words to your squire, Jim," he went on. "Nor he weren't, neither – that's the words. Three years he were the man of this island, light and dark, fair and rain; and sometimes he would maybe think upon a prayer (says you), and sometimes he would maybe think of his old mother, so be as she's alive (you'll say); but the most part of Gunn's time (this is what you'll say) – the most part of his time was took up with another matter. And then you'll give him a nip, like I do."

And he pinched me again in the most confidential manner.

"Then," he continued, "then you'll up, and you'll say this: Gunn is a good man (you'll say), and he puts a precious sight more confidence – a precious sight, mind that – in a gen'leman born than in these gen'lemen of fortune, having been one hisself."

"Well," I said, "I don't understand one word that you've been saying. But that's neither here nor there; for how am I to get on board?"

"Ah," said he, "that's the hitch, for sure. Well, there's my boat, that I made with my two hands. I keep her under the white rock. If the worst come to the worst, we might try that after dark. Hi!" he broke out. "What's that?"

For just then, although the sun had still an hour or two to run, all the echoes of the island awoke and bellowed to the thunder of a cannon.

"They have begun to fight!" I cried. "Follow me."

And I began to run towards the anchorage, my terrors all forgotten, while close at my side the marooned man in his goatskins trotted easily and lightly.

The cannon-shot was followed after a considerable interval by a volley of small arms.

Another pause, and then, not a quarter of a mile in front of me, I beheld the Union Jack flutter in the air above a wood.

As soon as Ben Gunn saw the colours he came to a halt, stopped me by the arm, and sat down.

"Now," said he, "there's your friends, sure enough."

"Far more likely it's the mutineers," I answered.

"That!" he cried. "Why, in a place like this, where nobody puts in but gen'lemen of fortune, Silver would fly the Jolly Roger, you don't make no doubt of that. No, that's your friends."

Then I skirted among the woods until I had regained the rear, or shoreward side, of the stockade, and was soon warmly welcomed by the faithful party.

N.C. WYETH

THE ATTACK

"Now," resumed Silver, "here it is. You give us the chart to get the treasure by, and drop shooting poor seamen and stoving of their heads in while asleep. You do that, and we'll offer you a choice. Either you come aboard along of us, once the treasure shipped, and then I'll give you my affy-davy, upon my word of honour, to clap you somewhere safe ashore." "Very good," said the captain. "Now you'll hear me: You can't find the treasure. You can't sail the ship. You can't fight us. I stand here and tell you so; and they're the last good words you'll get from me, for in the name of heaven, I'll put a bullet in your back when next I meet you."

As soon as Silver disappeared, the captain, who had been closely watching him, turned towards the interior of the house and found not a man of us at his post but Gray. It was the first time we had ever seen him angry.

"Quarters!" he roared. And then, as we all slunk back to our places, "Gray," he said, "I'll put your name in the log; you've stood by your duty like a seaman. Mr. Trelawney, I'm surprised at you, sir. Doctor, I thought you had worn the king's coat! If that was how you served at Fontenoy, sir, you'd have been better in your berth."

The doctor's watch were all back at their loopholes, the rest were busy loading the spare muskets, and everyone with a red face, you may be certain, and a flea in his ear, as the saying is.

The captain looked on for a while in silence. Then he spoke.

"My lads," said he, "I've given Silver a broadside. I pitched it in red-hot on purpose; and before the hour's out, as he said, we shall be boarded. We're outnumbered, I needn't tell you that, but we fight in shelter. I've no manner of doubt that we can drub them, if you choose."

Then he went the rounds and saw, as he said, that all was clear.

On the two short sides of the house, east and west, there were only two loopholes; on the south side where the porch was, two again; and on the north side, five. There was a round score of muskets for the seven of us; the firewood had been built into four piles – tables, you might say – one about the middle of each side, and on each of these tables some ammunition and four loaded muskets were laid ready to the hand of the defenders. In the middle, the cutlasses lay ranged.

"Toss out the fire," said the captain; "the chill is past, and we mustn't have smoke in our eyes."

The iron fire-basket was carried bodily out by Mr. Trelawney, and the embers smothered among sand.

"Hawkins hasn't had his breakfast. Hawkins, help yourself, and back to your post to eat it," continued Captain Smollett. "Lively, now, my lad; you'll want it before you've done. Hunter, serve out a round of brandy to all hands."

And while this was going on, the captain completed, in his own mind, the plan of the defence.

"Doctor, you will take the door," he resumed. "See, and don't expose yourself; keep within, and fire through the porch. Hunter, take the east side, there. Joyce, you stand by the west, my man. Mr. Trelawney, you are the best shot – you and Gray will take this long north side, with the five loopholes; it's there the danger is. If they can get up to it and fire in upon us through our own ports, things would begin to look dirty. Hawkins, neither you nor I are much account at the shooting; we'll stand by to load and bear a hand."

AND WE STOOD THERE, EACH AT HIS POST, IN A FEVER OF HEAT AND ANXIETY.

As the captain had said, the chill was past. As soon as the sun had climbed above our girdle of trees, it fell with all its force upon the clearing and drank up the vapours at a draught. Soon the sand was baking and the resin melting in the logs of the block house. Jackets and coats were flung aside, shirts thrown open at the neck and rolled up to the shoulders; and we stood there,

The boarders swarmed over the fence like monkeys.

each at his post, in a fever of heat and anxiety. An hour passed away.

"Hang them!" said the captain. "This is as dull as the doldrums. Gray, whistle for a wind."

And just at that moment came the first news of the attack.

"If you please, sir," said Joyce, "if I see anyone, am I to fire?"

"I told you so!" cried the captain.

"Thank you, sir," returned Joyce with the same quiet civility.

Nothing followed for a time, but the remark had set us all on the alert, straining ears and eyes – the musketeers with their pieces balanced in their hands, the captain out in the middle of the block house with his mouth very tight and a frown on his face.

So some seconds passed, till suddenly Joyce whipped up his musket and fired. The report had scarcely died away ere it was repeated and repeated from without in a scattering volley, shot behind shot, like a string of geese, from every side of the enclosure. Several bullets struck the log-house, but not one entered; and as the smoke cleared away and vanished, the stockade and the woods around it looked as quiet and empty as before. Not a bough waved, not the gleam of a musket-barrel betrayed the presence of our foes.

"Did you hit your man?" asked the captain.

"No, sir," replied Joyce. "I believe not, sir."

"Next best thing to tell the truth," muttered Captain Smollett. "Load his gun, Hawkins. How many should say there were on your side, doctor?"

"I know precisely," said Dr. Livesey. "Three shots were fired on this side. I saw the three flashes – two close together – one farther to the west."

"Three!" repeated the captain. "And how many on yours, Mr. Trelawney?"

But this was not so easily answered. There had come many from the north – seven by the squire's computation, eight or nine according to Gray. From the east and west only a single shot had been fired. It was plain, therefore, that the attack would be developed from the north and that on the other three sides we were only to be annoyed by a show of hostilities. But Captain Smollett made no change in his arrangements. If the mutineers succeeded in crossing the stockade, he argued, they would take possession of any unprotected loophole and shoot us down like rats in our own stronghold.

BUT THE REMARK HAD SET US ALL ON THE ALERT, STRAINING EARS AND EYES.

Nor had we much time left to us for thought. Suddenly, with a loud huzza, a little cloud of pirates leaped from the woods on the north side and ran straight on the stockade. At the same moment, the fire was once more opened from the woods.

The boarders swarmed over the fence like monkeys. Squire and Gray fired again and yet again; three men fell, one forwards into the enclosure, two back on the outside. But of these, one was evidently more frightened than hurt, for he was on his feet again in a crack and instantly disappeared among the trees.

Two had bit the dust, one had fled, four had made good their footing inside our defences, while from the shelter of the woods seven or eight men, each evidently supplied with several muskets, kept up a hot though useless fire on the log-house.

N C WYETH
11

THE ATTACK

Cries and confusion, the flashes and reports of pistol-shots, and one loud groan rang in my ears.

The four who had boarded made straight before them for the building, shouting as they ran. Several shots were fired, but such was the hurry of the marksmen that not one appears to have taken effect. In a moment, the four pirates had swarmed up the mound and were upon us.

The head of Job Anderson, the boatswain, appeared at the middle loophole.

"At 'em, all hands – all hands!" he roared in a voice of thunder.

At the same moment, another pirate grasped Hunter's musket by the muzzle, wrenched it from his hands, plucked it through the loophole, and with one stunning blow, laid the poor fellow senseless on the floor. Meanwhile a third, running unharmed all around the house, appeared suddenly in the doorway and fell with his cutlass on the doctor.

Our position was utterly reversed. A moment since we were firing, under cover, at an exposed enemy; now it was we who lay uncovered and could not return a blow. The log-house was full of smoke, to which we owed our comparative safety. Cries and confusion, the flashes and reports of pistol-shots, and one loud groan rang in my ears.

"Out, lads, out, and fight 'em in the open! Cutlasses!" cried the captain.

Mechanically, I obeyed, turned eastwards, and with my cutlass raised, ran round the corner of the house. Next moment I was face to face with Anderson. He roared aloud, and his hanger went up above his head, flashing in the sunlight. I had not time to be afraid, but as the blow still hung impending, leaped in a trice upon one side, and missing my foot in the soft sand, rolled headlong down the slope.

When I had first sallied from the door, the other mutineers had been already swarming up the palisade to make an end of us. One man, in a red night-cap, with his cutlass in his mouth, had even got upon the top and thrown a leg across. Well, so short had been the interval that when I found my feet again all was in the same posture, the fellow with the red night-cap still half-way over, another still just showing his head above the top of the stockade. And yet, in this breath of time, the fight was over and the victory was ours.

Gray, following close behind me, had cut down the big boatswain ere he had time to recover from his last blow. Another had been shot at a loophole in the very act of firing into the house and now lay in agony, the pistol still smoking in his hand. A third, as I had seen, the doctor had disposed of at a blow. Of the four who had scaled the palisade, one only remained unaccounted for, and he, having left his cutlass on the field, was now clambering out again with the fear of death upon him.

"Fire – fire from the house!" cried the doctor. "And you, lads, back into cover."

But his words were unheeded, no shot was fired, and the last boarder made good his escape and disappeared with the rest into the wood. In three seconds nothing remained of the attacking party but the five who had fallen, four on the inside and one on the outside of the palisade.

The doctor and Gray and I ran full speed for shelter. The survivors would soon be back where they had left their muskets, and at any moment the fire might recommence. The house was by this time somewhat cleared of smoke, and we saw at a glance the price we had paid for victory. Hunter lay beside his loophole, stunned; Joyce by his, shot through the head, never to move again; while right in the centre, the squire was supporting the captain, one as pale as the other.

"The captain's wounded," said Mr. Trelawney.

"Have they run?" asked Mr. Smollett.

"All that could, you may be bound," returned the doctor; "but there's five of them will never run again."

There was no return of the mutineers – not so much as another shot out of the woods. They had "got their rations for that day," as the captain put it, and we had the place to ourselves and a quiet time to overhaul the wounded and get dinner. Squire and I cooked outside in spite of the danger, and even outside we could hardly tell what we were at, for horror of the loud groans that reached us from the doctor's patients. Out of the eight men who had fallen in the action, only three still breathed – that one of the pirates who had been shot at the loophole, Hunter, and Captain Smollett; and of these, the first two were as good as dead; the mutineer indeed died under the doctor's knife, and Hunter, do what we could, never recovered consciousness in this world. He lingered all day, breathing loudly like the old buccaneer at home in his apoplectic fit, but the bones of his chest had been crushed by the blow and his skull fractured in falling, and some time in the following night, without sign or sound, he went to his Maker.

As for the captain, his wounds were grievous indeed, but not dangerous. No organ was fatally injured. Anderson's ball – for it was Job that shot him first – had broken his shoulder-blade and touched the lung, not badly; the second had only torn and displaced some muscles in the calf. He was sure to recover, the doctor said, but in the meantime, and for weeks to come, he must not walk nor move his arm, nor so much as speak when he could help it.

My own accidental cut across the knuckles was a flea-bite. Doctor Livesey patched it up with plaster and pulled my ears for me into the bargain.

After dinner the squire and the doctor sat by the captain's side awhile in consultation; and when they had talked to their hearts' content, it being then a little past noon, the doctor took up his hat and pistols, girt on a cutlass, put the chart in his pocket, and with a musket over his shoulder crossed the palisade on the north side and set off briskly through the trees.

Gray and I were sitting together at the far end of the block house, to be out of earshot of our officers consulting; and Gray took his pipe out of his mouth and fairly forgot to put it back again, so thunder-struck he was at this occurrence.

"Why, in the name of Davy Jones," said he, "is Dr. Livesey mad?" – "Why no," says I. "He's about the last of this crew for that, I take it." – "Well, shipmate," said Gray, "mad he may not be; but if *he's* not, you mark my words, I am." – "I take it," replied I, "the doctor has his idea; and if I am right, he's going now to see Ben Gunn."

I was right, as appeared later; but in the meantime, the house being stifling hot and the little patch of sand inside the palisade ablaze with midday sun, I began to get another thought into my head, which was not by any means so right. What I began to do was to envy the doctor walking in the cool shadow of the woods with the birds about him and the pleasant smell of the pines, while I sat grilling, with my clothes stuck to the hot resin, and so much blood about me and so many poor dead bodies lying all around that I took a disgust of the place that was almost as strong as fear.

All the time I was washing out the block house, and then washing up the things from dinner, this disgust and envy kept growing stronger and stronger, till at last, being near a bread-bag, and no one then observing me, I took the first step towards my escapade and filled both pockets of my coat with biscuit.

THE ATTACK

I was a fool, if you like, and certainly I was going to do a foolish, over-bold act; but I was determined to do it with all the precautions in my power.

The next thing I laid hold of was a brace of pistols, and as I already had a powder-horn and bullets, I felt myself well supplied with arms.

As for the scheme I had in my head, it was not a bad one in itself. I was to go down the sandy spit that divides the anchorage on the east from the open sea, find the white rock I had observed last evening, and ascertain whether it was there or not that Ben Gunn had hidden his boat, a thing quite worth doing, as I still believe.

Well, as things at last fell out, I found an admirable opportunity. The squire and Gray were busy helping the captain with his bandages, the coast was clear, I made a bolt for it over the stockade and into the thickest of the trees, and before my absence was observed I was out of cry of my companions.

This was my second folly, far worse than the first, as I left but two sound men to guard the house; but like the first, it was a help towards saving all of us.

I took my way straight for the east coast of the island, for I was determined to go down the sea side of the spit to avoid all chance of observation from the anchorage. It was already late in the afternoon, although still warm and sunny. As I continued to thread the tall woods, I could hear from far before me not only the continuous thunder of the surf, but a certain tossing of foliage and grinding of boughs which showed me the sea breeze had set in higher than usual. Soon cool draughts of air began to reach me, and a few steps farther I came forth into the open borders of the grove, and saw the sea lying blue and sunny to the horizon and the surf tumbling and tossing its foam along the beach.

I have never seen the sea quiet round Treasure Island. The sun might blaze overhead, the air be without a breath, the surface smooth and blue, but still these great rollers would be running along all the external coast, thundering and thundering by day and night; and I scarce believe there is one spot in the island where a man would be out of earshot of their noise. I walked along beside the surf with great enjoyment, till, thinking I was now got far enough to the south, I took the cover of some thick bushes and crept warily up to the ridge of the spit.

Behind me was the sea, in front the anchorage. The *Hispaniola,* in that unbroken mirror, was exactly portrayed from the truck to the waterline, the Jolly Roger hanging from her peak.

Alongside lay one of the gigs, Silver in the sternsheets – him I could always recognize – while a couple of men were leaning over the stern bulwarks, one of them with a red cap – the very rogue that I had seen some hours before stride-legs upon the palisade. Apparently they were talking and laughing, though at that distance – upwards of a mile – I could, of course, hear no word of what was said. All at once there began the most horrid, unearthly screaming, which at first startled me badly, though I had soon remembered the voice of Captain Flint and even thought I could make out the bird by her bright plumage as she sat perched upon her master's wrist.

Soon after, the jolly-boat shoved off and pulled for shore, and the man with the red cap and his comrade went below by the cabin companion.

Just about the same time, the sun had gone down behind the Spy-glass, and as the fog was collecting rapidly, it began to grow dark in earnest. I saw I must lose no time if I were to find the boat that evening.

The white rock, visible enough above the brush, was still some eighth of a mile further down the spit, and it took me a goodish while to get up with it,

Next moment I was face to face with Anderson. He roared aloud, and his hanger went above his head, flashing in the sunlight.

crawling, often on all fours, among the scrub. Night had almost come when I laid my hand on its rough sides. Right below it there was an exceedingly small hollow of green turf, hidden by banks and a thick underwood about knee-deep, that grew there very plentifully; and in the centre of the dell, sure enough, a little tent of goat-skins. I dropped into the hollow, lifted the side of the tent, and there was Ben Gunn's boat.

I had not then seen a coracle, such as the ancient Britons made, but I have seen one since, and I can give you no fairer idea of Ben Gunn's boat than by saying it was like the first and the worst coracle ever made by man. But the great advantage of the coracle it certainly possessed, for it was exceedingly light and portable.

Well, now that I had found the boat, you would have thought I had had enough of truantry for once, but in the meantime I had taken another notion and become so obstinately fond of it that I would have carried it out, I believe, in the teeth of Captain Smollett himself. This was to slip out under cover of the night, cut the *Hispaniola* adrift, and let her go ashore where she fancied. I had quite made up my mind that the mutineers, after their repulse of the morning, had nothing nearer their hearts than to up anchor and away to sea; this, I thought, it would be a fine thing to prevent, and now that I had seen how they left their watchmen unprovided with a boat, I thought it might be done with little risk.

The ebb had already run some time, and I had to wade through a long belt of swampy sand, where I sank several times above the ankle, before I came to the edge of the retreating water, and wading a little way in, with some strength and dexterity, set my coracle, keel downwards, on the surface.

The *Hispaniola* loomed before me like a blot of something yet blacker than darkness, then her spars and hull began to take shape, and the next moment, as it seemed (for, the farther I went, the brisker grew the current of the ebb), I was alongside of her hawser and had laid hold.

At last the breeze came; the schooner sidled and drew nearer in the dark; I felt the hawser slacken once more, and with a good, tough effort, cut the last fibres through.

I SAW I MUST LOSE NO TIME IF I WERE TO FIND THE BOAT THAT EVENING.

I had scarce time to think – scarce time to act and save myself. I was on the summit of one swell when the schooner came stooping over the next. The bowsprit was over my head. I sprang to my feet and leaped, stamping the coracle under water. With one hand I caught the jib-boom, while my foot was lodged between the stay and the brace; and as I still clung there panting, a dull blow told me that the schooner had charged down upon and struck the coracle and that I was left without retreat on the *Hispaniola*.

The breeze had but little action on the coracle, and I was almost instantly swept against the bows of the *Hispaniola*. At the same time, the schooner began to turn upon her heel, spinning slowly, end for end, across the current.

ISRAEL HANDS

I walked aft until I reached the main-mast. "Come aboard, Mr. Hands," I said ironically. He rolled his eyes round heavily, but he was too far gone to express surprise. "And where mought you have come from?" – "Well," said I, "I've come aboard to take possession of this ship, Mr. Hands; and you'll please regard me as your captain until further notice." – "I reckon," he said at last, "I reckon, Cap'n Hawkins, you'll kind of want to get ashore now. S'pose we talks." – "I'll tell you one thing," says I: "I'm not going back to Captain Kidd's anchorage. I mean to get into North Inlet and beach her quietly there."

ISRAEL HANDS

The wind, serving us to a desire, now hauled into the west. We could run so much the easier from the north-east corner of the island to the mouth of the North Inlet. Only, as we had no power to anchor and dared not beach her till the tide had flowed a good deal farther, time hung on our hands. The coxswain told me how to lay the ship to; after a good many trials I succeeded, and we both sat in silence over another meal.

"Cap'n," said he at length with that same uncomfortable smile, "here's my old shipmate, O'Brien; s'pose you was to heave him overboard. I ain't partic'lar as a rule, and I don't take no blame for settling his hash, but I don't reckon him ornamental now, do you?"

"I'm not strong enough, and I don't like the job; and there he lies, for me," said I.

"This here's an unlucky ship, this *Hispaniola*, Jim," he went on, blinking. "There's a power of men been killed in this *Hispaniola* – a sight o' poor seamen dead and gone since you and me took ship to Bristol. I never seen sich dirty luck, not I. There was this here O'Brien now – he's dead, ain't he? Well now, I'm no scholar, and you're a lad as can read and figure, and to put it straight, do you take it as a dead man is dead for good, or do he come alive again?"

"You can kill the body, Mr. Hands, but not the spirit; you must know that already," I replied. "O'Brien there is in another world, and may be watching us."

"Ah!" says he. "Well, that's unfort'nate – appears as if killing parties was a waste of time. Howsomever, sperrits don't reckon for much, by what I've seen. I'll chance it with the sperrits, Jim. And now, you've spoke up free, and I'll take it kind if you'd step down into that there cabin and get me a – well, a – shiver my timbers! I can't hit the name on 't; well, you get me a bottle of wine, Jim – this here brandy's too strong for my head."

Now, the coxswain's hesitation seemed to be unnatural, and as for the notion of his preferring wine to brandy, I entirely disbelieved it. The whole story was a pretext. He wanted me to leave the deck – so much was plain; but with what purpose I could in no way imagine. His eyes never met mine; they kept wandering to and fro, up and down, now with a look to the sky, now with a flitting glance upon the dead O'Brien. All the time he kept smiling and putting his tongue out in the most guilty, embarrassed manner, so that a child could have told that he was bent on some deception. I was prompt with my answer, however, for I saw where my advantage lay and that with a fellow so densely stupid I could easily conceal my suspicions to the end.

A CHILD COULD HAVE TOLD THAT HE WAS BENT ON SOME DECEPTION.

"Some wine?" I said. "Far better. Will you have white or red?" – "Well, I reckon it's about the blessed same to me, shipmate," he replied; "so it's strong, and plenty of it, what's the odds?"

"All right," I answered. "I'll bring you port, Mr. Hands. But I'll have to dig for it."

With that I scuttled down the companion with all the noise I could, slipped off my shoes, ran quietly along the sparred gallery, mounted the forecastle ladder, and popped my head out of the fore companion. I knew he would not expect to see me there, yet I took every precaution possible, and certainly the worst of my suspicions proved too true.

And I put the helm hard up, and the Hispaniola *swung round rapidly and ran stem on for the low, wooded shore.*

He had risen from his position to his hands and knees, and though his leg obviously hurt him pretty sharply when he moved – for I could hear him stifle a groan – yet it was at a good, rattling rate that he trailed himself across the deck. In half a minute he had reached the port scuppers and picked, out of a coil of rope, a long knife, or rather a short dirk, discoloured to the hilt with blood. He looked upon it for a moment, thrusting forth his under jaw, tried the point upon his hand, and then, hastily concealing it in the bosom of his jacket, trundled back again into his old place against the bulwark.

This was all that I required to know. Israel could move about, he was now armed, and if he had been at so much trouble to get rid of me, it was plain that I was meant to be the victim. What he would do afterwards – whether he would try to crawl right across the island from North Inlet to the camp among the swamps or whether he would fire Long Tom, trusting that his own comrades might come first to help him – was, of course, more than I could say.

Yet I felt sure that I could trust him in one point, since in that our interests jumped together, and that was in the disposition of the schooner. We both desired to have her stranded safe enough, in a sheltered place, and so that, when the time came, she could be got off again with as little labour and danger as might be; and until that was done I considered that my life would certainly be spared.

While I was thus turning the business over in my mind, I had not been idle with my body. I had stolen back to the cabin, slipped once more into my shoes, and laid my hand at random on a bottle of wine, and now, with this for an excuse, I made my reappearance on the deck.

Hands lay as I had left him, all fallen together in a bundle and with his eyelids lowered as though he were too weak to bear the light. He looked up, however, at my coming, knocked the neck off the bottle like a man who had done the same thing often, and took a good swig, with his favourite toast of "Here's luck!" Then he lay quiet for a little, and then, pulling out a stick of tobacco, begged me to cut him a quid.

"Cut me a junk o' that," says he, "for I haven't no knife and hardly strength enough, so be as I had. Ah, Jim, Jim, I reckon I've missed stays! Cut me a quid, as'll likely be the last, lad, for I'm for my long home, and no mistake."

"Well," said I, "I'll cut you some tobacco, but if I was you and thought myself so badly, I would go to my prayers like a Christian man."

"Why?" said he. "Now, you tell me why."

"Why?" I cried. "You were asking me just now about the dead. You've broken your trust; you've lived in sin and lies and blood; there's a man you killed lying at your feet this moment, and you ask me why! For God's mercy, Mr. Hands, that's why."

I spoke with a little heat, thinking of the bloody dirk he had hidden in his pocket and designed, in his ill thoughts, to end me with. He, for his part, took a great draught of the wine and spoke with the most unusual solemnity.

"For thirty years," he said, "I've sailed the seas and seen good and bad, better and worse, fair weather and foul, provisions running out, knives going, and what not. Well, now I tell you, I never seen good come o' goodness yet. Him as strikes first is my fancy; dead men don't bite; them's my views – amen, so be it. And now, you look here," he added, suddenly changing his tone, "we've had about enough of this foolery. The tide's made good enough by now. You just take my orders, Cap'n Hawkins, and we'll sail slap in and be done with it."

Scarcely had we passed the heads before the land closed around us. The shores of North Inlet were as thickly wooded as those of the southern anchorage, but the space was longer and narrower and more like, what in truth it was, the estuary of a river. Right before us, at the southern end, we saw the wreck of a ship in the last stages of dilapidation. It had been a great vessel of three masts but had lain so long exposed to the injuries of the weather that it was hung about with great webs of dripping seaweed, and on the deck of it shore bushes had taken root and now flourished thick with flowers. It was a sad sight, but it showed us that the anchorage was calm.

I SPOKE WITH A LITTLE HEAT, THINKING OF THE BLOODY DIRK HE HAD HIDDEN IN HIS POCKET.

"Now," said Hands, "look there; there's a pet bit for to beach a ship in. Fine flat sand, never a cat's paw, trees all around of it, and flowers a-blowing like a garding on that old ship."

"And once beached," I inquired, "how shall we get her off again?"

"Why, so," he replied: "you take a line ashore there on the other side at low water, take a turn about one of them big pines; bring it back, take a turn around the capstan, and lie to for the tide. Come high water, all hands take a pull upon the line, and off she comes as sweet as natur'. And now, boy, you stand by. We're near the bit now, and she's too much way on her. Starboard a little – so – steady – starboard – larboard a little – steady – steady!"

So he issued his commands, which I breathlessly obeyed, till, all of a sudden, he cried, "Now, my hearty, luff!" And I put the helm hard up, and the *Hispaniola*

Then, with a pistol in either hand, I addressed him. "One more step, Mr. Hands," said I, "and I'll blow your brains out!"

swung round rapidly and ran stem on for the low, wooded shore.

The excitement of these last manoeuvres had somewhat interfered with the watch I had kept hitherto, sharply enough, upon the coxswain. Even then I was still so much interested, waiting for the ship to touch, that I had quite forgot the peril that hung over my head and stood craning over the starboard bulwarks and watching the ripples spreading wide before the bows. I might have fallen without a struggle for my life had not a sudden disquietude seized upon me and made me turn my head. Perhaps I had heard a creak or seen his shadow moving with the tail of my eye; perhaps it was an instinct like a cat's; but, sure enough, when I looked round, there was Hands, already half-way towards me, with the dirk in his right hand.

We must both have cried out aloud when our eyes met, but while mine was the shrill cry of terror, his was a roar of fury like a charging bully's. At the same instant, he threw himself forward and I leapt sideways towards the bows. As I did so, I let go of the tiller, which sprang sharp to leeward, and I think this saved my life, for it struck Hands across the chest and stopped him, for the moment, dead.

Before he could recover, I was safe out of the corner where he had me trapped, with all the deck to dodge about. Just forward of the main-mast I stopped, drew a pistol from my pocket, took a cool aim, though he had already turned and was once more coming directly after me, and drew the trigger. The hammer fell, but there followed neither flash nor sound; the priming was useless with sea-water. I cursed myself for my neglect. Why had not I, long before, reprimed and reloaded my only weapons? Then I should not have been as now, a mere fleeing sheep before this butcher.

Wounded as he was, it was wonderful how fast he could move, his grizzled hair tumbling over his face, and his face itself as red as a red ensign with his haste and fury. I had no time to try my other pistol, nor indeed much inclination, for I was sure it would be useless. One thing I saw plainly: I must not simply retreat before him, or he would speedily hold me boxed into the bows, as a moment since he had so nearly boxed me in the stern. Once so caught, and nine or ten inches of the blood-stained dirk would be my last experience on this side of eternity. I placed my palms against the main-mast, which was of a goodish bigness, and waited, every nerve upon the stretch.

I HAD NO TIME TO TRY MY OTHER PISTOL, FOR I WAS SURE IT WOULD BE USELESS.

Seeing that I meant to dodge, he also paused; and a moment or two passed in feints on his part and corresponding movements upon mine. It was such a game as I had often played at home about the rocks of Black Hill Cove, but never before, you may be sure, with such a wildly beating heart as now. Still, as I say, it was a boy's game, and I thought I could hold my own at it against an elderly seaman with a wounded thigh. Indeed my courage had begun to rise so high that I allowed myself a few darting thoughts on what would be the end of the affair, and while I saw certainly that I could spin it out for long, I saw no hope of any ultimate escape.

Well, while things stood thus, suddenly the *Hispaniola* struck, staggered, ground for an instant in the sand, and then, swift as a blow, canted over to the

port side till the deck stood at an angle of forty-five degrees and about a puncheon of water splashed into the scupper holes and lay, in a pool, between the deck and bulwark.

THERE STOOD ISRAEL HANDS WITH HIS MOUTH OPEN AND HIS FACE UPTURNED TO MINE.

We were both of us capsized in a second, and both of us rolled, almost together, into the scuppers, the dead red-cap, with his arms still spread out, tumbling stiffly after us. So near were we, indeed, that my head came against the coxswain's foot with a crack that made my teeth rattle. Blow and all, I was the first afoot again, for Hands had got involved with the dead body. The sudden canting of the ship had made the deck no place for running on; I had to find some new way of escape, and that upon the instant, for my foe was almost touching me. Quick as thought, I sprang into the mizzen shrouds, rattled up hand over hand, and did not draw a breath till I was seated on the cross-trees.

I had been saved by being prompt; the dirk had struck not half a foot below me as I pursued my upward flight; and there stood Israel Hands with his mouth open and his face upturned to mine, a perfect statue of surprise and disappointment.

Now that I had a moment to myself, I lost no time in changing the priming of my pistol, and then, having one ready for service, and to make assurance doubly sure, I proceeded to draw the load of the other and recharge it afresh from the beginning.

My new employment struck Hands all of a heap; he began to see the dice going against him, and after an obvious hesitation, he also hauled himself heavily into the shrouds, and with the dirk in his teeth, began slowly and painfully to mount. It cost him no end of time and groans to haul his wounded leg behind him, and I had quietly finished my arrangements before he was much more than a third of the way up. Then, with a pistol in either hand, I addressed him.

"One more step, Mr. Hands," said I, "and I'll blow your brains out! Dead men don't bite, you know," I added with a chuckle. He stopped instantly. I could see by the working of his face that he was trying to think, and the process was so slow and laborious that, in my new-found security, I laughed aloud. At last, with a swallow or two, he spoke, his face still wearing the same expression of extreme perplexity. In order to speak he had to take the dagger from his mouth, but in all else he remained unmoved.

"Jim," says he, "I reckon we're fouled, you and me, and we'll have to sign articles. I'd have had you but for that there lurch, but I don't have no luck, not I; and I reckon I'll have to strike, which comes hard, you see, for a master mariner to a ship's younker like you, Jim."

I was drinking in his words and smiling away, as conceited as a cock upon a wall, when, all in a breath, back went his right hand over his shoulder. Something sang like an arrow through the air; I felt a blow and then a sharp pang, and there I was pinned by the shoulder to the mast. In the horrid pain and surprise of the moment – I scarce can say it was by my own volition, and I am sure it was without a conscious aim – both my pistols went off, and both escaped out of my hands. They did not fall alone; with a choked cry, the coxswain loosed his grasp upon the shrouds and plunged head first into the water.

"PIECES OF EIGHT"

I was now alone upon the ship; the tide had just turned. The sun was within so few degrees of setting that already the shadow of the pines upon the western shore began to reach right across the anchorage and fall in patterns on the deck. The evening breeze had sprung up, and though it was well warded off by the hill with the two peaks upon the east, the cordage had begun to sing a little softly to itself and the idle sails to rattle to and fro.

I scrambled forward and looked over. It seemed shallow enough, and holding the cut hawser in both hands for a last security, I let myself drop softly overboard. The water scarcely reached my waist; the sand was firm and covered with ripple marks, and I waded ashore in great spirits, leaving the *Hispaniola* on her side, with her main-sail trailing wide upon the surface of the bay. About the same time, the sun went fairly down and the breeze whistled low in the dusk among the tossing pines.

At least, and at last, I was off the sea, nor had I returned thence empty-handed. There lay the schooner, clear at last from buccaneers and ready for our own men to board and get to sea again. I had nothing nearer my fancy than to get home to the stockade and boast of my achievements. Possibly I might be blamed a bit for my truantry, but the recapture of the *Hispaniola* was a clenching answer, and I hoped that even Captain Smollett would confess I had not lost my time.

Gradually the night fell blacker; it was all I could do to guide myself even roughly towards my destination; the double hill behind me and the Spy-glass on my right hand loomed faint and fainter; the stars were few and pale; and in the low ground where I wandered I kept tripping among bushes and rolling into sandy pits.

The moon was climbing higher and higher, its light began to fall here and there in masses through the more open districts of the wood, and right in front of me a glow of a different colour appeared among the trees. It was red and hot, and now and again it was a little darkened – as it were, the embers of a bonfire smouldering.

For the life of me I could not think what it might be. At last I came right down upon the borders of the clearing. The western end was already steeped in moonshine; the rest, and the block house itself, still lay in a black shadow chequered with long silvery streaks of light. On the other side of the house an immense fire had burned itself into clear embers and shed a steady, red reverberation, contrasted strongly with the mellow paleness of the moon. There was not a soul stirring nor a sound beside the noises of the breeze.

I stopped, with much wonder in my heart, and perhaps a little terror also. It had not been our way to build great fires; we were, indeed, by the captain's orders, somewhat niggardly of firewood, and I began to fear that something had gone wrong while I was absent.

I stole round by the eastern end, keeping close in shadow, and at a convenient place, where the darkness was thickest, crossed the palisade.

To make assurance surer, I got upon my hands and knees and crawled, without a sound, towards the corner of the house. As I drew nearer, my heart was suddenly and greatly lightened. It is not a pleasant noise in itself, and I have often complained of it at other times, but just then it was like music to hear my friends snoring together so loud and peaceful in their sleep. The sea-cry of the watch, that beautiful "All's well," never fell more reassuringly on my ear.

In the meantime, there was no doubt of one thing; they kept an infamous bad watch. If it had been Silver and his lads that were now creeping in on them, not a soul would have seen daybreak. That was what it was, thought I, to have the captain wounded; and again I blamed myself sharply for leaving them in that danger with so few to mount guard.

By this time I had got to the door and stood up. All was dark within, so that I could distinguish nothing by the eye. With my arms before me I walked steadily in. I should lie down in my own place and enjoy their faces when they found me in the morning. And then,

"PIECES OF EIGHT"

By this time I had got to the door and stood up. All was dark within, so that I could distinguish nothing by the eye.

all of a sudden, a shrill voice broke forth out of the darkness:

"Pieces of eight! Pieces of eight! Pieces of eight! Pieces of eight! Pieces of eight!" and so forth, without pause or change, like the clacking of a tiny mill.

Silver's green parrot, Captain Flint! At the sharp, clipping tone of the parrot, the sleepers awoke and sprang up; and with a mighty oath, the voice of Silver cried, "Who goes?"

I turned to run, struck violently against one person, recoiled, and ran full into the arms of a second, who for his part closed upon and held me tight.

"Bring a torch, Dick," said Silver when my capture was thus assured.

And one of the men left the log-house and presently returned with a lighted brand.

The red glare of the torch, lighting up the interior of the block house, showed me the worst of my apprehensions realized. The pirates were in possession of the house and stores: there was the cask of cognac, there were the pork and bread, as before, and what tenfold increased my horror, not a sign of any prisoner. I could only judge that all had perished, and my heart smote me sorely that I had not been there to perish with them.

There were six of the buccaneers, all told; not another man was left alive. Five of them were on their feet, flushed and swollen, suddenly called out of the first sleep of drunkenness. The sixth had only risen upon his elbow; he was deadly pale, and the blood-stained bandage round his head told that he had recently been wounded, and still more recently dressed. I remembered the man who had been shot and had run back among the woods in the great attack, and doubted not that this was he.

The parrot sat, preening her plumage, on Long John's shoulder. He himself, I thought, looked somewhat paler and more stern than I was used to. He still wore the fine broadcloth suit in which he had fulfilled his mission, but it was bitterly the worse for wear, daubed with clay and torn with the sharp briers of the wood.

"So," said he, "here's Jim Hawkins, shiver my timbers! Dropped in, like, eh? Well, come, I take that friendly."

And thereupon he sat down across the brandy cask and began to fill a pipe.

And thereupon he sat down across the brandy cask and began to fill a pipe.

"Give me a loan of the link, Dick," said he; and then, when he had a good light, "That'll do, lad," he added; "stick the glim in the wood heap; and you, gentlemen, bring yourselves to! You needn't stand up for Mr. Hawkins; *he'll* excuse you, you may lay to that. And so, Jim" – stopping the tobacco – "here you were, and quite a pleasant surprise for poor old John. I see you were smart when first I set my eyes on you, but this here gets away from me clean, it do."

To all this, as may be well supposed, I made no answer. They had set me with my back against the wall, and I stood there, looking Silver in the face, pluckily enough, I hope, to all outward appearance, but with black despair in my heart.

Silver took a whiff or two of his pipe with great composure and then ran on again.

"Now, you see, Jim, so be as you *are* here," says he, "I'll give you a piece of my mind. I've always liked you, I have, for a lad of spirit, and the picter of my own self when I was young and handsome. I always wanted you to jine and take your share, and die a gentleman, and now, my cock, you've got to. Cap'n Smollett's a fine seaman, as I'll own up to any day, but stiff on discipline. 'Dooty is dooty,' says he, and right he is. Just you keep clear of the cap'n. The doctor himself is gone dead again you – 'ungrateful scamp' was what he said; and the short and the long of the whole story is about here: you can't go back to your own lot, for they won't have you; and without you start a third ship's company all by yourself, which might be lonely, you'll have to jine with Cap'n Silver."

So far so good. My friends, then, were still alive, and though I partly believed the truth of Silver's statement, that the cabin party were incensed at me for my desertion, I was more relieved than distressed by what I heard.

"I don't say nothing as to your being in our hands," continued Silver, "though there you are, and you may lay to it. I'm all for argyment; I never seen good come out o' threatening. If you like the service, well, you'll jine; and if you don't, Jim, why, you're free to answer no – free and welcome, shipmate; and if fairer can be said by mortal seaman, shiver my sides!"

"Am I to answer, then?" I asked with a very tremulous voice. Through all this sneering talk, I was made to feel the threat of death that overhung me, and my cheeks burned and my heart beat painfully in my breast.

"Ax your pardon, sir," returned one of the men; "you're pretty free with some of the rules; maybe you'll kindly keep an eye upon the rest. This crew's dissatisfied; this crew don't vally bullying a marlin-spike; this crew has its rights like other crews, I'll make so free as that; and by your own rules, I take it we can talk together. I ax your pardon, sir, acknowledging you for to be captaing at this present; but I claim my right, and steps outside for a council."

And with an elaborate sea-salute, this fellow, a long, ill-looking, yellow-eyed man of five and thirty, stepped coolly towards the door and disappeared out of the house. One after another the rest followed his example, each making a salute as he passed.

The sea-cook instantly removed his pipe.

"Now, look you here, Jim Hawkins," he said in a steady whisper that was no more than audible, "you're within half a plank of death, and what's a long sight worse, of torture. They're going to throw me off. But, you mark, I stand by you through thick and thin. I didn't mean to; no, not till you spoke up. I was about desperate to lose that much blunt, and be hanged into the bargain. But I see you was the right sort. I says to myself, you stand by Hawkins, John, and Hawkins'll stand by you. You're his last card, and by the living thunder, John, he's yours! Back to back, says I. You save your witness, and he'll save your neck!"

I began dimly to understand.

"You mean all's lost?" I asked.

"Aye, by gum, I do!" he answered. "Ship gone, neck gone – that's the size of it. Once I looked into that bay, Jim Hawkins, and seen no schooner – well, I'm tough, but I gave out. As for that lot and their council, mark me, they're outright fools and cowards. I'll save your life – if so be as I can – from them. But, see here, Jim – tit for tat – you save Long John from swinging."

I was bewildered; it seemed a thing so hopeless he was asking – he, the old buccaneer, the ringleader throughout.

"What I can do, that I'll do," I said.

"It's a bargain!" cried Long John. "You speak up plucky, and by thunder, I've a chance!"

He hobbled to the torch, where it stood propped among the firewood, and took a fresh light to his pipe.

"Understand me, Jim," he said, returning. "I've a head on my shoulders, I have. I'm on squire's side now. I know you've got that ship safe somewheres. How you done it, I don't know, but safe it is. I guess Hands and O'Brien turned soft. I never much believed in neither of *them*. Now you mark me. I ask no questions, nor I won't let others. I know when a game's up, I do; and I know a lad that's staunch. Ah, you that's young – you and me might have done a power of good together!"

He drew some cognac from the cask into a tin cannikin.

"Will you taste, messmate?" he asked; and when I had refused: "Well, I'll take a dram myself, Jim," said he. "I need a caulker, for there's trouble on hand. And talking o' trouble, why did that doctor give me the chart, Jim?"

My face expressed a wonder so unaffected that he saw the needlessness of further questions.

"Ah, well, he did, though," said he. "And there's something under that, no doubt – something, surely, under that, Jim – bad or good."

And he took another swallow of the brandy, shaking his great fair head like a man who looks forward to the worst.

THE BLACK SPOT AGAIN

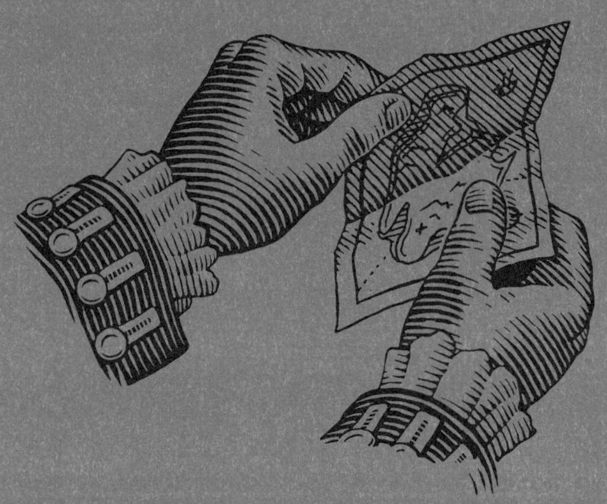

The council of buccaneers had lasted some time, when one of them re-entered the house, and with a repetition of the same salute, which had in my eyes an ironical air, begged for a moment's loan of the torch. Silver briefly agreed, and this emissary retired again, leaving us together in the dark.

Page 303
I could just make out that he had a book as well as a knife in his hand.

"There's a breeze coming, Jim," said Silver, who had by this time adopted quite a friendly and familiar tone.

I turned to the loophole nearest me and looked out. The embers of the great fire had so far burned themselves out and now glowed so low and duskily that I understood why these conspirators desired a torch. About half-way down the slope to the stockade, they were collected in a group; one held the light, another was on his knees in their midst, and I saw the blade of an open knife shine in his hand with varying colours in the moon and torch-light. The rest were all somewhat stooping, as though watching the manoeuvres of this last. I could just make out that he had a book as well as a knife in his hand, and was still wondering how anything so incongruous had come in their possession when the kneeling figure rose once more to his feet and the whole party began to move together towards the house.

"Here they come," said I; and I returned to my former position, for it seemed beneath my dignity that they should find me watching them.

"Well, let 'em come, lad – let 'em come," said Silver cheerily. "I've still a shot in my locker."

The door opened, and the five men, standing huddled together just inside, pushed one of their number forward. In any other circumstances it would have been comical to see his slow advance, hesitating as he set down each foot, but holding his closed right hand in front of him.

"Step up, lad," cried Silver. "I won't eat you. Hand it over, lubber. I know the rules, I do; I won't hurt a depytation."

Thus encouraged, the buccaneer stepped forth more briskly, and having passed something to Silver, from hand to hand, slipped yet more smartly back again to his companions. The sea-cook looked at what had been given him.

"The black spot! I thought so," he observed. "Where might you have got the paper? Why, hillo! Look here, now; this ain't lucky! You've gone and cut this out of a Bible. What fool's cut a Bible?"

"Ah, there!" said Morgan. "There! Wot did I say? No good'll come o' that, I said."

"Well, you've about fixed it now, among you," continued Silver. "You'll all swing now, I reckon. What soft-headed lubber had a Bible?"

"It was Dick," said one.

"Dick, was it? Then Dick can get to prayers," said Silver. "He's seen his slice of luck, has Dick, and you may lay to that."

But here the long man with the yellow eyes struck in.

"Belay that talk, John Silver," he said. "This crew has tipped you the black spot in full council, as in dooty bound; just you turn it over, as in dooty bound, and see what's wrote there. Then you can talk."

"Thanky, George," replied the sea-cook. "You always was brisk for business, and has the rules by heart, George, as I'm pleased to see. Well, what is it, anyway? Ah! 'Deposed' – that's it, is it? Very pretty wrote, to be sure; like print, I swear. Your hand o' write, George? Why, you was gettin' quite a leadin' man in this here crew. You'll be cap'n next, I shouldn't wonder. Just oblige me with that torch again, will you? This pipe don't draw."

"Come, now," said George, "you don't fool this crew no more. You're a funny man, by your account; but you're over now, and you'll maybe step down off that barrel and help vote."

"I thought you said you knowed the rules," returned Silver contemptuously. "Leastways, if you don't, I do; and I wait here – and I'm still your cap'n, mind – till you outs with your grievances and I reply; in the meantime, your black spot ain't worth a biscuit. After that, we'll see."

THEY LEAPED UPON IT LIKE CATS UPON A MOUSE.

And he cast down upon the floor a paper that I instantly recognized—none other than the chart on yellow paper, with the three red crosses, that I had found in the oilcloth at the bottom of the captain's chest. Why the doctor had given it to him was more than I could fancy.

But if it were inexplicable to me, the appearance of the chart was incredible to the surviving mutineers. They leaped upon it like cats upon a mouse.

"You lost the ship; I found the treasure. Who's the better man at that? And now I resign, by thunder! Elect whom you please to be your cap'n now; I'm done with it."

"Silver!" they cried. "Barbecue forever! Barbecue for cap'n!"

That was the end of the night's business. Soon after, with a drink all round, we lay down to sleep, and the outside of Silver's vengeance was to put George Merry up for sentinel and threaten him with death if he should prove unfaithful.

I was wakened – indeed, we were all wakened, for I could see even the sentinel shake himself together from where he had fallen against the door-post – by a clear, hearty voice hailing us from the margin of the wood:

"Block house, ahoy!" it cried. "Here's the doctor."

And the doctor it was. Although I was glad to hear the sound, yet my gladness was not without admixture. I remembered with confusion my insubordinate and stealthy conduct, and when I saw where it had brought me – among what companions and surrounded by what dangers – I felt ashamed to look him in the face.

He must have risen in the dark, for the day had hardly come; and when I ran to a loophole and looked out, I saw him standing, like Silver once before, up to the mid-leg in creeping vapour.

"You, doctor! Top o' the morning to you, sir!" cried Silver, broad awake and beaming with good nature in a moment. "Bright and early, to be sure; and it's the early bird, as the saying goes, that gets the rations. George, shake up your timbers, son, and help Dr. Livesey over the ship's side. All a-doin' well, your patients was – all well and merry."

So he pattered on, standing on the hilltop with his crutch under his elbow and one hand upon the side of the log-house – quite the old John in voice, manner, and expression.

"We've quite a surprise for you too, sir," he continued. "We've a little stranger here – he! he! A noo boarder and lodger, sir, and looking fit and taut as a fiddle; slep' like a supercargo, he did, right alongside of John – stem to stem we was, all night."

Dr. Livesey was by this time across the stockade and pretty near the cook, and I could hear the alteration in his voice as he said, "Not Jim?"

"The very same Jim as ever was," says Silver.

The doctor stopped outright, although he did not speak, and it was some seconds before he seemed able to move on.

They were collected in a group; one held the light, another was on his knees in their midst, and I saw the blade of an open knife shine in his hand.

"Well, well," he said at last, "duty first and pleasure afterwards, as you might have said yourself, Silver. Let us overhaul these patients of yours."

A moment afterwards he had entered the block house and with one grim nod to me proceeded with his work among the sick. He seemed under no apprehension, though he must have known that his life, among these treacherous demons, depended on a hair; and he rattled on to his patients as if he were paying an ordinary professional visit in a quiet English family. His manner, I suppose, reacted on the men, for they behaved to him as if nothing had occurred, as if he were still ship's doctor and they still faithful hands before the mast.

"You're doing well, my friend," he said to the fellow with the bandaged head, "and if ever any person had a close shave, it was you; your head must be as hard as iron. Well, George, how goes it? You're a pretty colour, certainly; why, your liver, man, is upside down. Did you take that medicine? Did he take that medicine, men?"

"Aye, aye, sir, he took it, sure enough," returned Morgan.

"Because, you see, since I am mutineers' doctor, or prison doctor as I prefer to call it," says Doctor Livesey, "I make it a point of honour not to lose a man for King George (God bless him!) and the gallows."

The rogues looked at each other but swallowed the home-thrust in silence.

"Dick don't feel well, sir," said one.

"Don't he?" replied the doctor. "Well, step up here, Dick, and let me see your tongue. No, I should be surprised if he did! The man's tongue is fit to frighten the French. Another fever."

"Ah, there," said Morgan, "that comed of sp'iling Bibles."

"That comes – as you call it – of being arrant asses," retorted the doctor, "and not having sense enough to know honest air from poison, and the dry land from a vile, pestiferous slough. I think it most probable – though of course it's only an opinion – that you'll all have the deuce to pay before you get that malaria out of your systems. Camp in a bog, would you? Silver, I'm surprised at you. You're less of a fool than many, take you all round; but you don't appear to me to have the rudiments of a notion of the rules of health.

"Well," he added after he had dosed them round and they had taken his prescriptions, with really laughable humility, more like charity schoolchildren than blood-guilty mutineers and pirates – "well, that's done for today. And now I should wish to have a talk with that boy, please."

IT SEEMED TO ME SO OBVIOUS, IN THIS CASE, THAT I COULD NOT IMAGINE HOW HE WAS TO TURN THEIR ANGER.

And he nodded his head in my direction carelessly.

"Then, doctor," said Silver, "you just step outside o' that stockade, and once you're there I'll bring the boy down on the inside, and I reckon you can yarn through the spars. Good day to you, sir, and all our dooties to the squire and Cap'n Smollett."

The explosion of disapproval, which nothing but Silver's black looks had restrained, broke out immediately the doctor had left the house. Silver was roundly accused of playing double – of trying to make a separate peace for himself, of sacrificing the interests of his

accomplices and victims, and, in one word, of the identical, exact thing that he was doing. It seemed to me so obvious, in this case, that I could not imagine how he was to turn their anger. But he was twice the man the rest were, and his last night's victory had given him a huge preponderance on their minds. He called them all the fools and dolts you can imagine, said it was necessary I should talk to the doctor, fluttered the chart in their faces, asked them if they could afford to break the treaty the very day they were bound a-treasure-hunting.

"No, by thunder!" he cried. "It's us must break the treaty when the time comes; and till then I'll gammon that doctor, if I have to ile his boots with brandy."

HIS CHEEKS SEEMED TO HAVE FALLEN IN, HIS VOICE TREMBLED.

And then he bade them get the fire lit, and stalked out upon his crutch, with his hand on my shoulder, leaving them in a disarray, and silenced by his volubility rather than convinced.

"Slow, lad, slow," he said. "They might round upon us in a twinkle of an eye if we was seen to hurry."

Very deliberately, then, did we advance across the sand to where the doctor awaited us on the other side of the stockade, and as soon as we were within easy speaking distance Silver stopped.

"You'll make a note of this here also, doctor," says he, "and the boy'll tell you how I saved his life, and were deposed for it too, and you may lay to that. Doctor, when a man's steering as near the wind as me – playing chuck-farthing with the last breath in his body, like – you wouldn't think it too much, mayhap, to give him one good word? You'll please bear in mind it's not my life only now – it's that boy's into the bargain; and you'll speak me fair, doctor, and give me a bit o' hope to go on, for the sake of mercy."

Silver was a changed man once he was out there and had his back to his friends and the block house; his cheeks seemed to have fallen in, his voice trembled; never was a soul more dead in earnest.

"So, Jim," said the doctor sadly, "here you are. As you have brewed, so shall you drink, my boy. Heaven knows, I cannot find it in my heart to blame you, but this much I will say, be it kind or unkind: when Captain Smollett was well, you dared not have gone off; and when he was ill and couldn't help it, by George, it was downright cowardly!"

I will own that I here began to weep. "Doctor," I said, "you might spare me. I have blamed myself enough; my life's forfeit anyway, and I should have been dead by now if Silver hadn't stood for me; and doctor, believe this, I can die – and I dare say I deserve it – but what I fear is torture. If they come to torture me – "

"Jim," the doctor interrupted, and his voice was quite changed, "Jim, I can't have this. Whip over, and we'll run for it."

"Doctor," said I, "I passed my word."

"I know, I know," he cried. "We can't help that, Jim, now. I'll take it on my shoulders, holus bolus, blame and shame, my boy; but stay here, I cannot let you. Jump! One jump, and you're out, and we'll run for it like antelopes."

"No," I replied; "you know right well you wouldn't do the thing yourself – neither you nor squire nor captain; and no more will I. Silver trusted me; I passed my word, and back I go. But, doctor, you did not let me finish. If they come to torture me, I might let slip a word of where the ship is, for I got the ship, part by luck and part by risking, and she lies in North Inlet, on the southern beach, and just below high water. At half tide she must be high and dry."

"The ship!" exclaimed the doctor.

Rapidly I described to him my adventures, and he heard me out in silence.

"There is a kind of fate in this," he observed when I had done. "Every step, it's you that saves our lives; and do you suppose by any chance that we are going to let you lose yours? That would be a poor return, my boy. You found out the plot; you found Ben Gunn – the best deed that ever you did, or will do, though you live to ninety. Oh, by Jupiter, and talking of Ben Gunn! Why, this is the mischief in person. Silver!" he cried. "Silver! I'll give you a piece of advice," he continued as the cook drew near again; "don't you be in any great hurry after that treasure."

"Why, sir, I do my possible, which that ain't," said Silver. "I can only, asking your pardon, save my life and the boy's by seeking for that treasure; and you may lay to that."

"Well, Silver," replied the doctor, "if that is so, I'll go one step further: look out for squalls when you find it."

"Sir," said Silver, "as between man and man, that's too much and too little. What you're after, why you left the block house, why you given me that there chart, I don't know, now, do I? And yet I done your bidding with my eyes shut and never a word of hope! But no, this here's too much. If you won't tell me what you mean plain out, just say so and I'll leave the helm."

"No," said the doctor musingly; "I've no right to say more; it's not my secret, you see, Silver, or, I give you my word, I'd tell it you. But I'll go as far with you as I dare go, and a step beyond, for I'll have my wig sorted by the captain or I'm mistaken! And first, I'll give you a bit of hope; Silver, if we both get alive out of this wolf-trap, I'll do my best to save you, short of perjury."

Silver's face was radiant. "You couldn't say more, I'm sure, sir, not if you was my mother," he cried.

"Well, that's my first concession," added the doctor. "My second is a piece of advice: keep the boy close beside you, and when you need help, halloo. I'm off to seek it for you, and that itself will show you if I speak at random. Good-bye, Jim."

And Dr. Livesey shook hands with me through the stockade, nodded to Silver, and set off at a brisk pace into the wood.

THE TREASURE-HUNT

"Jim," said Silver when we were alone, "if I saved your life, you saved mine; and I'll not forget it. I seen the doctor waving you to run for it – with the tail of my eye, I did; and I seen you say no, as plain as hearing. Jim, that's one to you. This is the first glint of hope I had since the attack failed, and I owe it you. And now, Jim, we're to go in for this here treasure-hunting, with sealed orders too, and I don't like it; and you and me must stick close, back to back like, and we'll save our necks in spite o' fate and fortune."

N.C. WYETH

Page 311
I had a line about my waist and followed obediently after the sea-cook, who held the loose end of the rope, now in his free hand, now between his powerful teeth.

"As for hostage," he continued, "that's his last talk, I guess, with them he loves so dear. I've got my piece o' news, and thanky to him for that; but it's over and done. I'll take him in a line when we go treasure-hunting, for we'll keep him like so much gold, in case of accidents, you mark, and in the meantime. Once we got the ship and treasure both and off to sea like jolly companions, why then we'll talk Mr. Hawkins over, we will, and we'll give him his share, to be sure, for all his kindness."

It was no wonder the men were in a good humour now. For my part, I was horribly cast down. Should the scheme he had now sketched prove feasible, Silver, already doubly a traitor, would not hesitate to adopt it. He had still a foot in either camp, and there was no doubt he would prefer wealth and freedom with the pirates to a bare escape from hanging, which was the best he had to hope on our side.

Nay, and even if things so fell out that he was forced to keep his faith with Dr. Livesey, even then what danger lay before us! What a moment that would be when the suspicions of his followers turned to certainty and he and I should have to fight for dear life – he a cripple and I a boy – against five strong and active seamen!

Add to this double apprehension the mystery that still hung over the behaviour of my friends, their unexplained desertion of the stockade, their inexplicable cession of the chart, or harder still to understand, the doctor's last warning to Silver, "Look out for squalls when you find it," and you will readily believe how little taste I found in my breakfast and with how uneasy a heart I set forth behind my captors on the quest for treasure.

We made a curious figure, had anyone been there to see us – all in soiled sailor clothes and all but me armed to the teeth. Silver had two guns slung about him – one before and one behind – besides the great cutlass at his waist and a pistol in each pocket of his square-tailed coat. To complete his strange appearance, Captain Flint sat perched upon his shoulder and gabbling odds and ends of purposeless sea-talk. I had a line about my waist and followed obediently after the sea-cook, who held the loose end of the rope, now in his free hand, now between his powerful teeth. For all the world, I was led like a dancing bear.

The other men were variously burthened, some carrying picks and shovels – for that had been the very first necessary they brought ashore from the *Hispaniola* – others laden with pork, bread, and brandy for the midday meal. All the stores, I observed, came from our stock, and I could see the truth of Silver's words the night before. Had he not struck a bargain with the doctor, he and his mutineers, deserted by the ship, must have been driven to subsist on clear water and the proceeds of their hunting. Water would have been little to their taste; a sailor is not usually a good shot; and besides all that, when they were so short of eatables, it was not likely they would be very flush of powder.

Well, thus equipped, we all set out – even the fellow with the broken head, who should certainly have kept in shadow – and straggled, one after another, to the beach, where the two gigs awaited us. Even these bore trace of the drunken folly of the pirates, one in a broken thwart, and both in their muddy and unbailed condition. Both were to be carried along with us for the sake of safety; and so, with our numbers divided between them, we set forth upon the bosom of the anchorage.

As we pulled over, there was some discussion on the chart. The red cross was, of course, far too large to be a guide; and the terms of the note on the back, as you will hear, admitted of some ambiguity. They ran, the reader may remember, thus:

Tall tree, Spy-glass shoulder, bearing
a point to the N. of N.N.E.
Skeleton Island E.S.E. and by E.
Ten feet.

A tall tree was thus the principal mark. Now, right before us the anchorage was bounded by a plateau from two to three hundred feet high, adjoining on the north the sloping southern shoulder of the Spy-glass and rising again towards the south into the rough, cliffy eminence called the Mizzen-mast Hill. The top of the plateau was dotted thickly with pine-trees of varying height. Every here and there, one of a different species rose forty or fifty feet clear above its neighbours, and which of these was the particular "tall tree" of Captain Flint could only be decided on the spot, and by the readings of the compass.

Yet, although that was the case, every man on board the boats had picked a favourite of his own ere we were half-way over, Long John alone shrugging his shoulders and bidding them wait till they were there.

We pulled easily, by Silver's directions, not to weary the hands prematurely, and after quite a long passage, landed at the mouth of the second river – that which runs down a woody cleft of the Spy-glass. Thence, bending to our left, we began to ascend the slope towards the plateau.

At the first outset, heavy, miry ground and a matted, marish vegetation greatly delayed our progress; but by little and little the hill began to steepen and become stony under foot, and the wood to change its character and to grow in a more open order. It was, indeed, a most pleasant portion of the island that we were now approaching. A heavy-scented broom and many flowering shrubs had almost taken the place of grass. Thickets of green nutmeg-trees were dotted here and there with the red columns and the broad shadow of the pines; and the first mingled their spice with the aroma of the others. The air, besides, was fresh and stirring, and this, under the sheer sunbeams, was a wonderful refreshment to our senses.

The party spread itself abroad, in a fan shape, shouting and leaping to and fro. About the centre, and a good way behind the rest, Silver and I followed – I tethered by my rope, he ploughing, with deep pants, among the sliding gravel. From time to time, indeed, I had to lend him a hand, or he must have missed his footing and fallen backward down the hill.

We had thus proceeded for about half a mile and were approaching the brow of the plateau when the man upon the farthest left began to cry aloud, as if in terror. Shout after shout came from him, and the others began to run in his direction.

SILVER AND I FOLLOWED – I TETHERED BY MY ROPE, HE PLOUGHING, WITH DEEP PANTS, AMONG THE SLIDING GRAVEL.

"He can't 'a found the treasure," said old Morgan, hurrying past us from the right, "for that's clean a-top."

Indeed, as we found when we also reached the spot, it was something very different. At the foot of a pretty big pine and involved in a green creeper, which had

The body pointed straight in the direction of the island, and the compass read duly E.S.E. and by E.

even partly lifted some of the smaller bones, a human skeleton lay, with a few shreds of clothing, on the ground. I believe a chill struck for a moment to every heart.

"He was a seaman," said George Merry, who, bolder than the rest, had gone up close and was examining the rags of clothing. "Leastways, this is good sea-cloth."

"Aye, aye," said Silver; "like enough; you wouldn't look to find a bishop here, I reckon. But what sort of a way is that for bones to lie? 'Tain't in natur'."

Indeed, on a second glance, it seemed impossible to fancy that the body was in a natural position. But for some disarray (the work, perhaps, of the birds that had fed upon him or of the slow-growing creeper that had gradually enveloped his remains) the man lay perfectly straight – his feet pointing in one direction, his hands, raised above his head like a diver's, pointing directly in the opposite.

"I've taken a notion into my old numbskull," observed Silver. "Here's the compass; there's the tip-top p'int o' Skeleton Island, stickin' out like a tooth. Just take a bearing, will you, along the line of them bones."

It was done. The body pointed straight in the direction of the island, and the compass read duly E.S.E. and by E.

"I thought so," cried the cook; "this here is a p'inter. Right up there is our line for the Pole Star and the jolly dollars. But, by thunder! If it don't make me cold inside to think of Flint. This is one of his jokes, and no mistake. Him and these six was alone here; he killed 'em, every man; and this one he hauled here and laid down by compass, shiver my timbers! They're long bones, and the hair's been yellow. Aye, that would be Allardyce. You mind Allardyce, Tom Morgan?"

"Aye, aye," returned Morgan; "I mind him; he owed me money, he did, and took my knife ashore with him."

"Speaking of knives," said another, "why don't we find his'n lying round? Flint warn't the man to pick a seaman's pocket; and the birds, I guess, would leave it be."

"By the powers, and that's true!" cried Silver.

"There ain't a thing left here," said Merry, still feeling round among the bones; "not a copper doit nor a baccy box. It don't look nat'ral to me."

"No, by gum, it don't," agreed Silver; "not nat'ral, nor not nice, says you. Great guns! Messmates, but if Flint was living, this would be a hot spot for you and me. Six they were, and six are we; and bones is what they are now."

"I saw him dead with these here deadlights," said Morgan. "Billy took me in. There he laid, with penny-pieces on his eyes."

"Dead – aye, sure enough he's dead and gone below," said the fellow with the bandage; "but if ever sperrit walked, it would be Flint's. Dear heart, but he died bad, did Flint!"

"Aye, that he did," observed another; "now he raged, and now he hollered for the rum, and now he sang. 'Fifteen Men' were his only song, mates; and I tell you true, I never rightly liked to hear it since. It was main hot, and the windy was open, and I hear that old song comin' out as clear as clear – and the death-haul on the man already."

"Come, come," said Silver; "stow this talk. He's dead, and he don't walk, that I know; leastways, he won't walk by day, and you may lay to that. Care killed a cat. Fetch ahead for the doubloons."

We started, certainly; but in spite of the hot sun and the staring daylight, the pirates no longer ran separate and shouting through the wood, but kept side by side and spoke with bated breath. The terror of the dead buccaneer had fallen on their spirits.

On one of these boards I saw, branded with a hot iron, the name Walrus – *the name of Flint's ship.*

Partly from the damping influence of this alarm, partly to rest Silver and the sick folk, the whole party sat down as soon as they had gained the brow of the ascent.

Silver, as he sat, took certain bearings with his compass.

"There are three 'tall trees'" said he, "about in the right line from Skeleton Island. 'Spy-glass shoulder,' I take it, means that lower p'int there. It's child's play to find the stuff now. I've half a mind to dine first."

"I don't feel sharp," growled Morgan. "Thinkin' o' Flint – I think it were – as done me."

"Ah, well, my son, you praise your stars he's dead," said Silver.

"He were an ugly devil," cried a third pirate with a shudder; "that blue in the face too!"

"That was how the rum took him," added Merry. "Blue! Well, I reckon he was blue. That's a true word."

Ever since they had found the skeleton and got upon this train of thought, they had spoken lower and lower, and they had almost got to whispering by now, so that the sound of their talk hardly interrupted the silence of the wood. All of a sudden, out of the middle of the trees in front of us, a thin, high, trembling voice struck up the well-known air and words:

"Fifteen men on the dead man's chest –
Yo-ho-ho, and a bottle of rum!"

I never have seen men more dreadfully affected than the pirates. The colour went from their six faces like enchantment; some leaped to their feet, some clawed hold of others; Morgan grovelled on the ground.

"It's Flint, by – – !" cried Merry.

The song had stopped as suddenly as it began – broken off, you would have said, in the middle of a note, as though someone had laid his hand upon the singer's mouth. Coming through the clear, sunny atmosphere among the green tree-tops, I thought it had sounded airily and sweetly; and the effect on my companions was the stranger.

"Come," said Silver, struggling with his ashen lips to get the word out; "this won't do. Stand by to go about.

This is a rum start, and I can't name the voice, but it's someone skylarking – someone that's flesh and blood, and you may lay to that."

His courage had come back as he spoke, and some of the colour to his face along with it. Already the others had begun to lend an ear to this encouragement and were coming a little to themselves, when the same voice broke out again – not this time singing, but in a faint distant hail that echoed yet fainter among the clefts of the Spy-glass.

"Darby M'Graw," it wailed – for that is the word that best describes the sound – "Darby M'Graw! Darby M'Graw!" again and again and again; and then rising a little higher, and with an oath that I leave out: "Fetch aft the rum, Darby!"

The buccaneers remained rooted to the ground, their eyes starting from their heads. Long after the voice had died away they still stared in silence, dreadfully, before them.

"That fixes it!" gasped one. "Let's go."

"They was his last words," moaned Morgan, "his last words above board."

Dick had his Bible out and was praying volubly. He had been well brought up, had Dick, before he came to sea and fell among bad companions.

Still Silver was unconquered. I could hear his teeth rattle in his head, but he had not yet surrendered.

Silver hobbled, grunting, on his crutch; his nostrils stood out and quivered; he cursed like a madman when the flies settled on his hot and shiny countenance; he plucked furiously at the line that held me to him and from time to time turned his eyes upon me with a deadly look. Certainly he took no pains to hide his thoughts, and certainly I read them like print. In the immediate nearness of the gold, all else had been forgotten: his promise and the doctor's warning were both things of the past, and I could not doubt that he hoped to seize upon the treasure, find and board the *Hispaniola* under cover of night, cut every honest throat about that island, and sail away as he had at first intended, laden with crimes and riches.

Shaken as I was with these alarms, it was hard for me to keep up with the rapid pace of the treasure-hunters. Now and again I stumbled, and it was then that Silver plucked so roughly at the rope and launched at me his murderous glances.

We were now at the margin of the thicket.

"Huzza, mates, all together!" shouted Merry; and the foremost broke into a run.

And suddenly, not ten yards further, we beheld them stop. A low cry arose. Silver doubled his pace, digging away with the foot of his crutch like one possessed; and next moment he and I had come also to a dead halt.

Before us was a great excavation, not very recent, for the sides had fallen in and grass had sprouted on the bottom. In this were the shaft of a pick broken in two and the boards of several packing-cases strewn around. On one of these boards I saw, branded with a hot iron, the name *Walrus* – the name of Flint's ship.

All was clear to probation. The cache had been found and rifled; the seven hundred thousand pounds were gone!

THE FALL OF A CHIEFTAIN

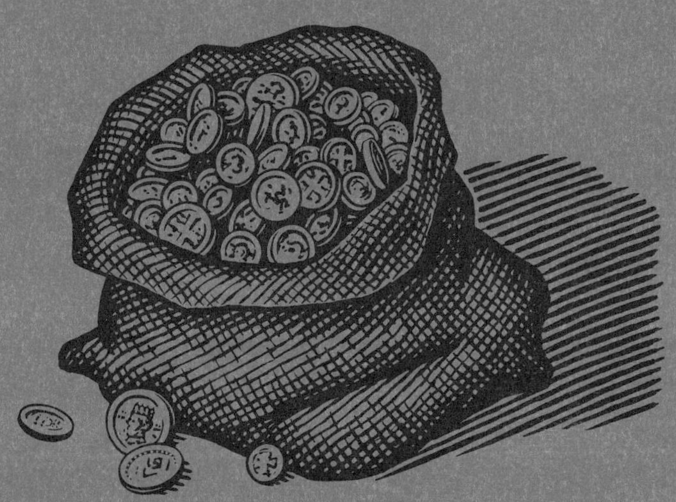

There never was such an overturn in this world. Each of these six men was as though he had been struck. But with Silver the blow passed almost instantly. Every thought of his soul had been set full-stretch, like a racer, on that money; well, he was brought up, in a single second, dead; and he kept his head, found his temper, and changed his plan before the others had had time to realize the disappointment.

THE FALL OF A CHIEFTAIN

"Jim," he whispered, "take that, and stand by for trouble."

And he passed me a double-barrelled pistol.

At the same time, he began quietly moving northward, and in a few steps had put the hollow between us two and the other five. Then he looked at me and nodded, as much as to say, "Here is a narrow corner," as, indeed, I thought it was. His looks were not quite friendly, and I was so revolted at these constant changes that I could not forbear whispering, "So you've changed sides again."

There was no time left for him to answer in. The buccaneers, with oaths and cries, began to leap, one after another, into the pit and to dig with their fingers, throwing the boards aside as they did so. Morgan found a piece of gold. He held it up with a perfect spout of oaths. It was a two-guinea piece, and it went from hand to hand among them for a quarter of a minute.

"Two guineas!" roared Merry, shaking it at Silver. "That's your seven hundred thousand pounds, is it? You're the man for bargains, ain't you? You're him that never bungled nothing, you wooden-headed lubber!"

"Dig away, boys," said Silver with the coolest insolence; "you'll find some pig-nuts and I shouldn't wonder."

"Pig-nuts!" repeated Merry, in a scream. "Mates, do you hear that? I tell you now, that man there knew it all along. Look in the face of him and you'll see it wrote there."

"Ah, Merry," remarked Silver, "standing for cap'n again? You're a pushing lad, to be sure."

But this time everyone was entirely in Merry's favour. They began to scramble out of the excavation, darting furious glances behind them. One thing I observed, which looked well for us: they all got out upon the opposite side from Silver.

Well, there we stood, two on one side, five on the other, the pit between us, and nobody screwed up high enough to offer the first blow. Silver never moved; he watched them, very upright on his crutch, and looked as cool as ever I saw him. He was brave, and no mistake.

At last Merry seemed to think a speech might help matters.

"Mates," says he, "there's two of them alone there; one's the old cripple that brought us all here and blundered us down to this; the other's that cub that I mean to have the heart of. Now, mates – "

He was raising his arm and his voice, and plainly meant to lead a charge. But just then – crack! crack! crack! – three musket-shots flashed out of the thicket. Merry tumbled head foremost into the excavation; the man with the bandage spun round like a teetotum and fell all his length upon his side, where he lay dead, but still twitching; and the other three turned and ran for it with all their might.

Before you could wink, Long John had fired two barrels of a pistol into the struggling Merry, and as the man rolled up his eyes at him in the last agony, "George," said he, "I reckon I settled you."

At the same moment, the doctor, Gray, and Ben Gunn joined us, with smoking muskets, from among the nutmeg-trees.

"Forward!" cried the doctor. "Double quick, my lads. We must head 'em off the boats."

And we set off at a great pace, sometimes plunging through the bushes to the chest.

I tell you, but Silver was anxious to keep up with us. The work that man went through, leaping on his crutch till the muscles of his chest were fit to burst, was work no sound man ever equalled; and so thinks the doctor. As it was, he was already thirty yards behind us and on the verge of strangling when we reached the brow of the slope.

"Doctor," he hailed, "see there! No hurry!"

Sure enough there was no hurry. In a more open part of the plateau, we could see the three survivors still running in the same direction as they had started, right for Mizzen-mast Hill. We were already between them and the boats; and so we four sat down to breathe, while Long John, mopping his face, came slowly up with us.

"Thank ye kindly, doctor," says he. "You came in in about the nick, I guess, for me and Hawkins. And so it's you, Ben Gunn!" he added. "Well, you're a nice one, to be sure."

"I'm Ben Gunn, I am," replied the maroon, wriggling like an eel in his embarrassment. "And," he added, after a long pause, "how do, Mr. Silver? Pretty well, I thank ye, says you."

"BUT THE DEAD MEN, SIR, HANG ABOUT YOUR NECK LIKE MILL-STONES."

"Ben, Ben," murmured Silver, "to think as you've done me!"

The doctor sent back Gray for one of the pick-axes deserted, in their flight, by the mutineers, and then as we proceeded leisurely downhill to where the boats were lying, related in a few words what had taken place. It was a story that profoundly interested Silver; and Ben Gunn, the half-idiot maroon, was the hero from beginning to end.

Ben, in his long, lonely wanderings about the island, had found the skeleton – it was he that had rifled it; he had found the treasure; he had dug it up (it was the haft of his pick-axe that lay broken in the excavation); he had carried it on his back, in many weary journeys, from the foot of the tall pine to a cave he had on the two-pointed hill at the north-east angle of the island, and there it had lain stored in safety since two months before the arrival of the *Hispaniola*. When the doctor had wormed this secret from him on the afternoon of the attack, and when next morning he saw the anchorage deserted, he had gone to Silver, given him the chart, which was now useless – given him the stores, for Ben Gunn's cave was well supplied with goats' meat salted by himself – given anything and everything to get a chance of moving in safety from the stockade to the two-pointed hill, there to be clear of malaria and keep a guard upon the money.

"As for you, Jim," he said, "it went against my heart, but I did what I thought best for those who had stood by their duty; and if you were not one of these, whose fault was it?"

That morning, finding that I was to be involved in the horrid disappointment he had prepared for the mutineers, he had run all the way to the cave, and leaving the squire to guard the captain, had taken Gray and the maroon and started, making the diagonal across the island to be at hand beside the pine. Soon, however, he saw that our party had the start of him; and Ben Gunn, being fleet of foot, had been dispatched in front to do his best alone. Then it had occurred to him to work upon the superstitions of his former shipmates, and he was so far successful that Gray and the doctor had come up and were already ambushed before the arrival of the treasure-hunters.

"Ah," said Silver, "it were fortunate for me that I had Hawkins here. You would have let old John be cut to bits, and never given it a thought, doctor."

"Not a thought," replied Dr. Livesey cheerily.

And by this time we had reached the gigs. The doctor, with the pick-axe, demolished one of them, and then we all got aboard the other and set out to go round by sea for North Inlet.

As we passed the two-pointed hill, we could see the black mouth of Ben Gunn's cave and a figure standing by it, leaning on a musket. It was the squire, and we waved a handkerchief and gave him three cheers.

A gentle slope ran up from the beach to the entrance of the cave. At the top, the squire met us. To me he was cordial and kind, saying nothing of my escapade either in the way of blame or praise. At Silver's polite salute he somewhat flushed.

"John Silver," he said, "you're a prodigious villain and imposter – a monstrous imposter, sir. I am told I am not to prosecute you. Well, then, I will not. But the dead men, sir, hang about your neck like mill-stones."

"Thank you kindly, sir," replied Long John, again saluting.

"I dare you to thank me!" cried the squire. "It is a gross dereliction of my duty. Stand back."

And thereupon we all entered the cave. It was a large, airy place, with a little spring and a pool of clear water, overhung with ferns. The floor was sand. Before a big fire lay Captain Smollett; and in a far corner, only duskily flickered over by the blaze, I beheld great heaps of coin and quadrilaterals built of bars of gold. That was Flint's treasure that we had come so far to seek and that had cost already the lives of seventeen men from the *Hispaniola*. How many it had cost in the amassing, what blood and sorrow, what good ships scuttled on the deep, what brave men walking the plank blindfold, what shot of cannon, what shame and lies and cruelty, perhaps no man alive could tell. Yet there were still three upon that island – Silver, and old Morgan, and Ben Gunn – who had each taken his share in these crimes, as each had hoped in vain to share in the reward.

"Come in, Jim," said the captain. "You're a good boy in your line, Jim, but I don't think you and me'll go to sea again. You're too much of the born favourite for me. Is that you, John Silver? What brings you here, man?"

"Come back to my dooty, sir," returned Silver.

"Ah!" said the captain, and that was all he said. What a supper I had of it that night, with all my friends around me; and what a meal it was, with Ben Gunn's salted goat and some delicacies and a bottle of old wine from the *Hispaniola*. Never, I am sure, were people gayer or happier.

The next morning we fell early to work, for the transportation of this great mass of gold near a mile by land to the beach, and thence three miles by boat to the *Hispaniola*, was a considerable task for so small a number of workmen. The three fellows still abroad upon the island did not greatly trouble us; a single sentry on the shoulder of the hill was sufficient to ensure us against any sudden onslaught, and we thought, besides, they had had more than enough of fighting.

Therefore the work was pushed on briskly. Gray and Ben Gunn came and went with the boat, while the rest during their absences piled treasure on the beach. Two of the bars, slung in a rope's end, made a good load for a grown man – one that he was glad to walk slowly with. For my part, as I was not much use at carrying, I was kept busy all day in the cave packing the minted money into bread-bags.

The transportation of this great mass of gold was a considerable task for so small a number of workmen.

Day after day this work went on; by every evening a fortune had been stowed aboard, but there was another fortune waiting for the morrow; and all this time we heard nothing of the three surviving mutineers.

And at last, one fine morning, we weighed anchor, which was about all that we could manage, and stood out of North Inlet, the same colours flying that the captain had flown and fought under at the palisade.

The three fellows must have been watching us closer than we thought for, as we soon had proved. For coming through the narrows, we had to lie very near the southern point, and there we saw all three of them kneeling together on a spit of sand, with their arms raised in supplication. It went to all our hearts, I think, to leave them in that wretched state; but we could not risk another mutiny; and to take them home for the gibbet would have been a cruel sort of kindness. The doctor hailed them and told them of the stores we had left, and where they were to find them. But they continued to call us by name and appeal to us, for God's sake, to be merciful and not leave them to die in such a place.

At last, seeing the ship still bore on her course and was now swiftly drawing out of earshot, one of them – I know not which it was – leapt to his feet with a hoarse cry, whipped his musket to his shoulder, and sent a shot whistling over Silver's head and through the main-sail.

After that, we kept under cover of the bulwarks, and when next I looked out they had disappeared from the spit, and the spit itself had almost melted out of sight in the growing distance. That was, at least, the end of that; and before noon, to my inexpressible joy, the highest rock of Treasure Island had sunk into the blue round of sea.

We were so short of men that everyone on board had to bear a hand – only the captain lying on a mattress in the stern and giving his orders, for though greatly recovered he was still in want of quiet. We laid her head for the nearest port in Spanish America, for we could not risk the voyage home without fresh hands; and as it was, what with baffling winds and a couple of fresh gales, we were all worn out before we reached it.

It was just at sundown when we cast anchor in a most beautiful land-locked gulf, and were immediately surrounded by shore boats full of Negroes and Mexican Indians and half-bloods selling fruits and vegetables and offering to dive for bits of money. The sight of so many good-humoured faces (especially the blacks), the taste of the tropical fruits, and above all the lights that began to shine in the town made a most charming contrast to our dark and bloody sojourn on the island; and the doctor and the squire, taking me along with them, went ashore to pass the early part of the night. Here they met the captain of an English man-of-war, fell in talk with him, went on board his ship, and, in short, had so agreeable a time that day was breaking when we came alongside the *Hispaniola*.

THE SEA-COOK HAD NOT GONE EMPTY-HANDED.

Ben Gunn was on deck alone, and as soon as we came on board he began, with wonderful contortions, to make us a confession. Silver was gone. The maroon had connived at his escape in a shore boat some hours ago, and he now assured us he had only done so to preserve our lives, which would certainly have been forfeit if "that man with the one leg had stayed aboard."

I was kept busy all day in the cave packing the minted money into bread-bags.

But this was not all. The sea-cook had not gone empty-handed. He had cut through a bulkhead unobserved and had removed one of the sacks of coin, worth perhaps three or four hundred guineas, to help him on his further wanderings. I think we were all pleased to be so cheaply quit of him.

Well, to make a long story short, we got a few hands on board, made a good cruise home, and the *Hispaniola* reached Bristol just as Mr. Blandly was beginning to think of fitting out her consort. Five men only of those who had sailed returned with her. "Drink and the devil had done for the rest," with a vengeance, although, to be sure, we were not quite in so bad a case as that other ship they sang about:

With one man of her crew alive,
What put to sea with seventy-five.

All of us had an ample share of the treasure and used it wisely or foolishly, according to our natures. Captain Smollett is now retired from the sea. Gray not only saved his money, but being suddenly smit with the desire to rise, also studied his profession, and he is now mate and part owner of a fine full-rigged ship, married besides, and the father of a family. As for Ben Gunn, he got a thousand pounds, which he spent or lost in three weeks, or to be more exact, in nineteen days, for he was back begging on the twentieth. Then he was given a lodge to keep, exactly as he had feared upon the island; and he still lives, a great favourite, though something of a butt, with the country boys, and a notable singer in church on Sundays and saints' days.

Of Silver we have heard no more. That formidable seafaring man with one leg has at last gone clean out of my life; but I dare say he met his old Negress, and perhaps still lives in comfort with her and Captain Flint. It is to be hoped so, I suppose, for his chances of comfort in another world are very small.

The bar silver and the arms still lie, for all that I know, where Flint buried them; and certainly they shall lie there for me. Oxen and wain-ropes would not bring me back again to that accursed island; and the worst dreams that ever I have are when I hear the surf booming about its coasts or start upright in bed with the sharp voice of Captain Flint still ringing in my ears: "Pieces of eight! Pieces of eight!"

LOUIS RHEAD

HOWARD PYLE'S BOOK OF PIRATES

Texts and illustrations by Howard Pyle, 1921

An anthology published by Harper & Brothers in 1921, a decade after Pyle's death, *Howard Pyle's Book of Pirates* is described by its sub-title as a blend of "Fiction, Fact & Fancy concerning the Buccaneers & Marooners of the Spanish Main". There is good reason for defining its contents so equivocally. *Pyle's Book of Pirates* provides wonderfully colorful capsule biographies and vignettes of many of the most famous Atlantic World pirates of the 1600s and 1700s, such as Henry Morgan, Blackbeard, and Edward Low, as well as more obscure pirate figures such as the Frenchman Pierre Le Grand. As a whole, the book offers a broad-ranging introduction to Atlantic World piracy and gets a lot right. Pyle acknowledges, for instance, the presence of Black pirates. He also acknowledges longstanding controversies, such as the legitimacy of pirates' privateering commissions. At the same time, he concedes the falsehood of some stereotypes, such as the assertions that Captain Kidd buried treasure all along the U.S. Atlantic coast. Pyle's details are roughly accurate regarding pirate theatres of operations, carnage, and battles at sea. When he tells us that Henry Morgan crossed the Central American isthmus to attack Panama City, we can count on his veracity, and equally, when he identifies Tortuga Island off the coast of Hispaniola as a significant pirate base, he guides us well. Henry Avary (Avery) *did* go to Ireland after he gave up piracy. Blackbeard *did* get a royal pardon for his earlier depredations prior to his last and fatal pirate campaign. Yet Pyle's renditions do also perpetuate and sometimes invent pirate myths, and we should recognize that when he quotes pirate conversation, the source is almost certainly his imagination. We might even wonder about the existence of his unidentified "old historian" who gave him a description of Blackbeard wearing "a sling over his shoulders, with three brace of pistols, hanging in holsters like bandoleers."

PIERRE LE GRAND

Just above the northwestern shore of the old island of Hispaniola – the Santo Domingo of our day – and separated from it only by a narrow channel of some five or six miles in width, lies a queer little hunch of an island, known, because of a distant resemblance to that animal, as the Tortuga de Mar, or sea turtle. It is not more than twenty miles in length by perhaps seven or eight in breadth; it is only a little spot of land, and as you look at it upon the map a pin's head would almost cover it; yet from that spot, as from a center of inflammation, a burning fire of human wickedness and ruthlessness and lust overran the world, and spread terror and death throughout the Spanish West Indies, from St. Augustine to the island of Trinidad, and from Panama to the coasts of Peru.

Page 329
The boat in which the buccaneers sailed might, perhaps, have served for the great ship's longboat.

About the middle of the seventeenth century certain French adventurers set out from the fortified island of St. Christopher in longboats and hoys, directing their course to the westward, there to discover new islands. Sighting Hispaniola "with abundance of joy," they landed, and went into the country, where they found great quantities of wild cattle, horses, and swine.

Now vessels on the return voyage to Europe from the West Indies needed revictualing, and food, especially flesh, was at a premium in the islands of the Spanish Main; wherefore a great profit was to be turned in preserving beef and pork, and selling the flesh to homeward-bound vessels.

The northwestern shore of Hispaniola, lying as it does at the eastern outlet of the old Bahama Channel, running between the island of Cuba and the great Bahama Banks, lay almost in the very main stream of travel. The pioneer Frenchmen were not slow to discover the double advantage to be reaped from the wild cattle that cost them nothing to procure, and a market for the flesh ready found for them. So down upon Hispaniola they came by boatloads and shiploads, gathering like a swarm of mosquitoes, and overrunning the whole western end of the island. There they established themselves, spending the time alternately in hunting the wild cattle and buccanning the meat, and squandering their hardly earned gains in wild debauchery, the opportunities for which were never lacking in the Spanish West Indies.

At first the Spaniards thought nothing of the few travel-worn Frenchmen who dragged their longboats and hoys up on the beach, and shot a wild bullock or two to keep body and soul together; but when the few grew to dozens, and the dozens to scores, and the scores to hundreds, it was a very different matter, and wrathful grumblings and mutterings began to be heard among the original settlers.

But of this the careless buccaneers thought never a whit, the only thing that troubled them being the lack of a more convenient shipping point than the main island afforded them.

This lack was at last filled by a party of hunters who ventured across the narrow channel that separated the main island from Tortuga. Here they found exactly what they needed – a good harbor, just at the junction of the Windward Channel with the old Bahama Channel – a spot where four-fifths of the Spanish-Indian trade would pass by their very wharves.

There were a few Spaniards upon the island, but they were a quiet folk, and well disposed to make friends with the strangers; but when more Frenchmen and still more Frenchmen crossed the narrow channel, until they overran the Tortuga and turned it into one great curing house for the beef which they shot upon the neighboring island, the Spaniards grew restive over the matter, just as they had done upon the larger island.

Accordingly, one fine day there came half a dozen great boatloads of armed Spaniards, who landed upon the Turtle's Back and sent the Frenchmen flying to the woods and fastnesses of rocks as the chaff flies before the thunder gust. That night the Spaniards drank themselves mad and shouted themselves hoarse over their victory, while the beaten Frenchmen sullenly paddled their canoes back to the main island again, and the Sea Turtle was Spanish once more.

But the Spaniards were not contented with such a petty triumph as that of sweeping the island of Tortuga free from the obnoxious strangers; down upon Hispaniola they came, flushed with their easy victory, and determined to root out every Frenchman, until not one single buccaneer remained. For a time they had an easy thing of it, for each French hunter roamed the woods by himself, with no better company than his half-wild dogs, so that when two or three Spaniards would meet such a one, he seldom if ever came out of the woods again, for even his resting place was lost.

But the very success of the Spaniards brought their ruin along with it, for the buccaneers began to combine together for self-protection, and out of that combination arose a strange union of lawless man with lawless man, so near, so close, that it can scarce be compared to any other than that of husband and wife. When two entered upon this comradeship, articles were drawn up and signed by both parties, a common stock was made of all their possessions, and out into the woods they went to seek their fortunes; thenceforth they were as one man; they lived together by day, they slept together by night; what one suffered, the other suffered; what one gained, the other gained. The only separation that came betwixt them was death, and then the survivor inherited all that the other left. And now it was another thing with Spanish buccaneer hunting, for two buccaneers, reckless of life, quick of eye, and true of aim, were worth any half dozen of Spanish islanders.

By and by, as the French became more strongly organized for mutual self-protection, they assumed the offensive. Then down they came upon Tortuga, and now it was the turn of the Spanish to be hunted off the island like vermin, and the turn of the French to shout their victory.

Having firmly established themselves, a governor was sent to the French of Tortuga, one M. le Passeur, from the island of St. Christopher; the Sea Turtle was fortified, and colonists, consisting of men of doubtful character and women of whose character there could be no doubt whatever, began pouring in upon the island, for it was said that the buccaneers thought no more of a doubloon than of a Lima bean, so that this was the place for the brothel and the brandy shop to reap their golden harvest, and the island remained French.

BUT THE VERY SUCCESS OF THE SPANIARDS BROUGHT THEIR RUIN ALONG WITH IT.

Hitherto the Tortugans had been content to gain as much as possible from the homeward-bound vessels through the orderly channels of legitimate trade. It was reserved for Pierre le Grand to introduce piracy as a quicker and more easy road to wealth than the semihonest exchange they had been used to practice.

Gathering together eight-and-twenty other spirits as hardy and reckless as himself, he put boldly out to sea in a boat hardly large enough to hold his crew, and running down the Windward Channel and out into the Caribbean Sea, he lay in wait for such a prize as might be worth the risks of winning.

For a while their luck was steadily against them; their provisions and water began to fail, and they saw nothing before them but starvation or a humiliating return. In this extremity they sighted a Spanish ship belonging to a "flota" which had become separated from her consorts.

The boat in which the buccaneers sailed might, perhaps, have served for the great ship's longboat; the Spaniards outnumbered them three to one, and

PIERRE LE GRAND

Nothing remained for the Spaniard but to yield, for there was no alternative between surrender and death.

Pierre and his men were armed only with pistols and cutlasses; nevertheless this was their one and their only chance, and they determined to take the Spanish ship or to die in the attempt. Down upon the Spaniard they bore through the dusk of the night, and giving orders to the "chirurgeon" to scuttle their craft under them as they were leaving it, they swarmed up the side of the unsuspecting ship and upon its decks in a torrent – pistol in one hand and cutlass in the other. A part of them ran to the gun room and secured the arms and ammunition, pistoling or cutting down all such as stood in their way or offered opposition; the other party burst into the great cabin at the heels of Pierre le Grand, found the captain and a party of his friends at cards, set a pistol to his breast, and demanded him to deliver up the ship. Nothing remained for the Spaniard but to yield, for there was no alternative between surrender and death. And so the great prize was won.

It was not long before the news of this great exploit and of the vast treasure gained reached the ears of the buccaneers of Tortuga and Hispaniola. Then what a hubbub and an uproar and a tumult there was! Hunting wild cattle and buccanning the meat was at a discount, and the one and only thing to do was to go a-pirating; for where one such prize had been won, others were to be had.

CAPTAIN HENRY MORGAN

And now we come to the greatest of all the buccaneers, he who stands pre-eminent among them, and whose name even to this day is a charm to call up his deeds of daring, his dauntless courage, his truculent cruelty, and his insatiate and unappeasable lust for gold – Capt. Henry Morgan, the bold Welshman, who brought buccaneering to the height and flower of its glory.

CAPTAIN HENRY MORGAN

Recruits poured in upon him, until his band was larger and better equipped than ever.

Having sold himself, after the manner of the times, for his passage across the seas, he worked out his time of servitude at the Barbados. As soon as he had regained his liberty he entered upon the trade of piracy, wherein he soon reached a position of considerable prominence. He was associated with Mansvelt at the time of the latter's descent upon Saint Catharine's Isle, the importance of which spot, as a center of operations against the neighboring coasts, Morgan never lost sight of. The first attempt that Capt. Henry Morgan ever made against any town in the Spanish Indies was the bold descent upon the city of Puerto del Principe in the island of Cuba, with a mere handful of men. It was a deed the boldness of which has never been outdone by any of a like nature – not even the famous attack upon Panama itself. Thence they returned to their boats in the very face of the whole island of Cuba, aroused and determined upon their extermination. Not only did they make good their escape, but they brought away with them a vast amount of plunder, computed at three hundred thousand pieces of eight, besides five hundred head of cattle and many prisoners held for ransom.

But when the division of all this wealth came to be made, lo! there were only fifty thousand pieces of eight to be found. What had become of the rest no man could tell but Capt. Henry Morgan himself. Honesty among thieves was never an axiom with him.

Rude, truculent, and dishonest as Captain Morgan was, he seems to have had a wonderful power of persuading the wild buccaneers under him to submit everything to his judgment, and to rely entirely upon his word. In spite of the vast sum of money that he had very evidently made away with, recruits poured in upon him, until his band was larger and better equipped than ever.

And now it was determined that the plunder harvest was ripe at Porto Bello, and that city's doom was sealed. The town was defended by two strong castles thoroughly manned, and officered by as gallant a soldier as ever carried Toledo steel at his side. But strong castles and gallant soldiers weighed not a barleycorn with the buccaneers when their blood was stirred by the lust of gold.

Landing at Puerto Naso, a town some ten leagues westward of Porto Bello, they marched to the latter town, and coming before the castle, boldly demanded its surrender. It was refused, whereupon Morgan threatened that no quarter should be given. Still surrender was refused; and then the castle was attacked, and after a bitter struggle was captured. Morgan was as good as his word: every man in the castle was shut in the guard room, the match was set to the powder magazine, and soldiers, castle, and all were blown into the air, while through all the smoke and the dust the buccaneers poured into the town. Still the governor held out in the other castle, and might have made good his defense, but that he was betrayed by the soldiers under him. Into the castle poured the howling buccaneers. But still the governor fought on, with his wife and daughter clinging to his knees and beseeching him to surrender, and the blood from his wounded forehead trickling down over his white collar, until a merciful bullet put an end to the vain struggle.

Here were enacted the old scenes. Everything plundered that could be taken, and then a ransom set upon the town itself.

This time an honest, or an apparently honest, division was made of the spoils, which amounted to two hundred and fifty thousand pieces of eight, besides merchandise and jewels.

The next towns to suffer were poor Maracaibo and Gibraltar, now just beginning to recover from the desolation wrought by l'Olonoise. Once more both towns were plundered of every bale of merchandise and of every piaster, and once more both were ransomed until everything was squeezed from the wretched inhabitants.

Here affairs were like to have taken a turn, for when Captain Morgan came up from Gibraltar he found three great men-of-war lying in the entrance to the lake awaiting his coming. Seeing that he was hemmed in in the narrow sheet of water, Captain Morgan was inclined to compromise matters, even offering to relinquish all the plunder he had gained if he were allowed to depart in peace. But no; the Spanish admiral would hear nothing of this. Having the pirates, as he thought, securely in his grasp, he would relinquish nothing, but would sweep them from the face of the sea once and forever.

That was an unlucky determination for the Spaniards to reach, for instead of paralyzing the pirates with fear, as he expected it would do, it simply turned their mad courage into as mad desperation.

A great vessel that they had taken with the town of Maracaibo was converted into a fire ship, manned with logs of wood in montera caps and sailor jackets, and

Here were enacted the old scenes. Everything plundered that could be taken, and then a ransom set upon the town itself.

filled with brimstone, pitch, and palm leaves soaked in oil. Then out of the lake the pirates sailed to meet the Spaniards, the fire ship leading the way, and bearing down directly upon the admiral's vessel. At the helm stood volunteers, the most desperate and the bravest of all the pirate gang, and at the ports stood the logs of wood in montera caps. So they came up with the admiral, and grappled with his ship in spite of the thunder of all his great guns, and then the Spaniard saw, all too late, what his opponent really was.

He tried to swing loose, but clouds of smoke and almost instantly a mass of roaring flames enveloped both vessels, and the admiral was lost. The second vessel, not wishing to wait for the coming of the pirates, bore down upon the fort, under the guns of which the cowardly crew sank her, and made the best of their way to the shore. The third vessel, not having an opportunity to escape, was taken by the pirates without the slightest resistance, and the passage from the lake was cleared. So the buccaneers sailed away, leaving Maracaibo and Gibraltar prostrate a second time.

And now Captain Morgan determined to undertake another venture, the like of which had never been equaled in all of the annals of buccaneering. This was nothing less than the descent upon and the capture of Panama, which was, next to Cartagena, perhaps, the most powerful and the most strongly fortified city in the West Indies.

Pyle.

Many who were left were put to the sword, and some few were spared and held as prisoners.

In preparation for this venture he obtained letters of marque from the governor of Jamaica, by virtue of which elastic commission he began immediately to gather around him all material necessary for the undertaking.

When it became known abroad that the great Captain Morgan was about undertaking an adventure that was to eclipse all that was ever done before, great numbers came flocking to his standard, until he had gathered together an army of two thousand or more desperadoes and pirates wherewith to prosecute his adventure, albeit the venture itself was kept a total secret from everyone. Port Couillon, in the island of Hispaniola, over against the Ile de la Vache, was the place of muster, and thither the motley band gathered from all quarters. Provisions had been plundered from the mainland wherever they could be obtained, and by the 24th of October, 1670 (O. S.), everything was in readiness.

The island of Saint Catharine, as it may be remembered, was at one time captured by Mansvelt, Morgan's master in his trade of piracy. It had been retaken by the Spaniards, and was now thoroughly fortified by them. Almost the first attempt that Morgan had made as a master pirate was the retaking of Saint Catharine's Isle. In that undertaking he had failed; but now, as there was an absolute need of some such place as a base of operations, he determined that the place must be taken. And it was taken.

The Spaniards, during the time of their possession, had fortified it most thoroughly and completely, and had the governor thereof been as brave as he who met his death in the castle of Porto Bello, there might have been a different tale to tell. As it was, he surrendered it in a most cowardly fashion, merely stipulating that there should be a sham attack by the buccaneers, whereby his credit might be saved. And so Saint Catharine was won.

The next step to be taken was the capture of the castle of Chagres, which guarded the mouth of the river of that name, up which river the buccaneers would be compelled to transport their troops and provisions for the attack upon the city of Panama. This adventure was undertaken by four hundred picked men under command of Captain Morgan himself.

The castle of Chagres, known as San Lorenzo by the Spaniards, stood upon the top of an abrupt rock at the mouth of the river, and was one of the strongest fortresses for its size in all of the West Indies. This stronghold Morgan must have if he ever hoped to win Panama.

The attack of the castle and the defense of it were equally fierce, bloody, and desperate. Again and again the buccaneers assaulted, and again and again they were beaten back. So the morning came, and it seemed as though the pirates had been baffled this time. But just at this juncture the thatch of palm leaves on the roofs of some of the buildings inside the fortifications took fire, a conflagration followed, which caused the explosion of one of the magazines, and in the paralysis of terror that followed, the pirates forced their way into the fortifications, and the castle was won. Most of the Spaniards flung themselves from the castle walls into the river or upon the rocks beneath, preferring death to capture and possible torture; many who were left were put to the sword, and some few were spared and held as prisoners.

So fell the castle of Chagres, and nothing now lay between the buccaneers and the city of Panama but the intervening and trackless forests.

And now the name of the town whose doom was sealed was no secret. Up the river of Chagres went Capt. Henry Morgan and twelve hundred men, packed closely in their canoes; they never stopped, saving now and then to rest their stiffened legs, until they had come to a place known as Cruz de San Juan Gallego, where they were compelled to leave their boats on account of the shallowness of the water.

Leaving a guard of one hundred and sixty men to protect their boats as a place of refuge in case they should be worsted before Panama, they turned and plunged into the wilderness before them.

There a more powerful foe awaited them than a host of Spaniards with match, powder, and lead – starvation. They met but little or no opposition in their progress; but wherever they turned they found every fiber of meat, every grain of maize, every ounce of bread or meal, swept away or destroyed utterly before them. Even when the buccaneers had successfully overcome an ambuscade or an attack, and had sent the Spaniards flying, the fugitives took the time to strip their dead comrades of every grain of food in their leathern sacks, leaving nothing but the empty bags.

Says the narrator of these events, himself one of the expedition, "They afterward fell to eating those leathern bags, as affording something to the ferment of their stomachs."

Ten days they struggled through this bitter privation, doggedly forcing their way onward, faint with hunger and haggard with weakness and fever. Then, from the high hill and over the tops of the forest trees, they saw the steeples of Panama, and nothing remained between them and their goal but the fighting of four Spaniards to every one of them – a simple thing which they had done over and over again.

Down they poured upon Panama, and out came the Spaniards to meet them; four hundred horse, two thousand five hundred foot, and two thousand wild bulls which had been herded together to be driven over the buccaneers so that their ranks might be disordered and broken. The buccaneers were only eight hundred strong; the others had either fallen in battle or had dropped along the dreary pathway through the wilderness; but in the space of two hours the Spaniards were flying madly over the plain, minus six hundred who lay dead or dying behind them. As for the bulls, as many of them as were shot served as food there and then for the half-famished pirates, for the buccaneers were never more at home than in the slaughter of cattle.

Then they marched toward the city. Three hours' more fighting and they were in the streets, howling, yelling, plundering, gorging, dram-drinking, and giving full vent to all the vile and nameless lusts that burned in their hearts like a hell of fire. And now followed the usual sequence of events – rapine, cruelty, and extortion; only this time there was no town to ransom, for Morgan had given orders that it should be destroyed. The torch was set to it, and Panama, one of the greatest cities in the New World, was swept from the face of the earth. Why the deed was done, no man but Morgan could tell. Perhaps it was that all the secret hiding places for treasure might be brought to light; but whatever the reason was, it lay hidden in the breast of the great buccaneer himself. For three weeks Morgan and his men abode in this dreadful place; and they marched away with *one hundred and seventy-five* beasts of burden loaded with treasures of gold and silver and jewels, besides great quantities of merchandise, and six hundred prisoners held for ransom.

Whatever became of all that vast wealth, and what it amounted to, no man but Morgan ever knew, for when a division was made it was found that there was only *two hundred pieces of eight to each man.*

When this dividend was declared, a howl of execration went up, under which even Capt. Henry

Morgan quailed. At night he and four other commanders slipped their cables and ran out to sea, and it was said that these divided the greater part of the booty among themselves. But the wealth plundered at Panama could hardly have fallen short of a million and a half of dollars. Computing it at this reasonable figure, the various prizes won by Henry Morgan in the West Indies would stand as follows: Panama, \$1,500,000; Porto Bello, \$800,000; Puerto del Principe, \$700,000; Maracaibo and Gibraltar, \$400,000; various piracies, \$250,000 – making a grand total of \$3,650,000 as the vast harvest of plunder. With this fabulous wealth, wrenched from the Spaniards by means of the rack and the cord, and pilfered from his companions by the meanest of thieving, Capt. Henry Morgan retired from business, honored of all, rendered famous by his deeds, knighted by the good King Charles II, and finally appointed governor of the rich island of Jamaica.

Other buccaneers followed him. Campeche was taken and sacked, and even Cartagena itself fell; but with Henry Morgan culminated the glory of the buccaneers, and from that time they declined in power and wealth and wickedness until they were finally swept away.

Once more both towns were plundered of every bale of merchandise and of every piaster.

MAROONING AND CAPTAIN AVARY

The buccaneers became bolder and bolder. In fact, so daring were their crimes that the home governments, stirred at last by these outrageous barbarities, seriously undertook the suppression of the freebooters, lopping and trimming the main trunk until its members were scattered hither and thither, and it was thought that the organization was exterminated. But, so far from being exterminated, the individual members were merely scattered north, south, east, and west, each forming a nucleus around which gathered and clustered the very worst of the offscouring of humanity.

The result was that when the seventeenth century was fairly packed away with its lavender in the store chest of the past, a score or more bands of freebooters were cruising along the Atlantic seaboard in armed vessels, each with a black flag with its skull and crossbones at the fore, and with a nondescript crew made up of the tags and remnants of civilized and semicivilized humanity (white, black, red, and yellow), known generally as marooners, swarming upon the decks below.

Nor did these offshoots from the old buccaneer stem confine their depredations to the American seas alone; the East Indies and the African coast also witnessed their doings, and suffered from them, and even the Bay of Biscay had good cause to remember more than one visit from them.

Worthy sprigs from so worthy a stem improved variously upon the parent methods; for while the buccaneers were content to prey upon the Spaniards alone, the marooners reaped the harvest from the commerce of all nations.

So up and down the Atlantic seaboard they cruised, and for the fifty years that marooning was in the flower of its glory it was a sorrowful time for the coasters of New England, the middle provinces, and the Virginias, sailing to the West Indies with their cargoes of salt fish, grain, and tobacco. Trading became almost as dangerous as privateering, and sea captains were chosen as much for their knowledge of the flintlock and the cutlass as for their seamanship.

As by far the largest part of the trading in American waters was conducted by these Yankee coasters, so by far the heaviest blows, and those most keenly felt, fell upon them. Bulletin after bulletin came to port with its doleful tale of this vessel burned or that vessel scuttled, this one held by the pirates for their own use or that one stripped of its goods and sent into port as empty as an eggshell from which the yolk had been sucked. Boston, New York, Philadelphia, and Charleston suffered alike, and worthy ship owners had to leave off counting their losses upon their fingers and take to the slate to keep the dismal record.

"Maroon – to put ashore on a desert isle, as a sailor, under pretense of having committed some great crime." Thus our good Noah Webster gives us the dry bones, the anatomy, upon which the imagination may construct a specimen to suit itself.

THE PROCESS OF MAROONING WAS AS SIMPLE AS TERRIBLE.

It is thence that the marooners took their name, for marooning was one of their most effective instruments of punishment or revenge. If a pirate broke one of the many rules which governed the particular band to which he belonged, he was marooned; did a captain defend his ship to such a degree as to be unpleasant to the pirates attacking it, he was marooned; even the pirate captain himself, if he displeased his followers by the severity of his rule, was in danger of having the same punishment visited upon him which he had perhaps more than once visited upon another.

The process of marooning was as simple as terrible. A suitable place was chosen (generally some desert isle as far removed as possible from the pathway of commerce), and the condemned man was rowed from the ship to the beach. Out he was bundled upon the sand

"Maroon – to put ashore on a desert isle, as a sailor, under pretense of having committed some great crime."

spit; a gun, a half dozen bullets, a few pinches of powder, and a bottle of water were chucked ashore after him, and away rowed the boat's crew back to the ship, leaving the poor wretch alone to rave away his life in madness, or to sit sunken in his gloomy despair till death mercifully released him from torment. It rarely if ever happened that anything was known of him after having been marooned. A boat's crew from some vessel, sailing by chance that way, might perhaps find a few chalky bones bleaching upon the white sand in the garish glare of the sunlight, but that was all. And such were marooners.

By far the largest number of pirate captains were Englishmen, for, from the days of good Queen Bess, English sea captains seemed to have a natural turn for any species of venture that had a smack of piracy in it, and from the great Admiral Drake of the old, old days, to the truculent Morgan of buccaneering times, the Englishman did the boldest and wickedest deeds, and wrought the most damage.

First of all upon the list of pirates stands the bold Captain Avary, one of the institutors of marooning. Him we see but dimly, half hidden by the glamouring mists of legends and tradition. Others who came afterward outstripped him far enough in their doings, but he stands pre-eminent as the first of marooners of whom actual history has been handed down to us of the present day.

When the English, Dutch, and Spanish entered into an alliance to suppress buccaneering in the West Indies, certain worthies of Bristol, in old England, fitted out two vessels to assist in this laudable project; for doubtless Bristol trade suffered smartly from the Morgans and the l'Olonoises of that old time. One of these vessels was named the *Duke*, of which a certain Captain Gibson was the commander and Avary the mate.

Away they sailed to the West Indies, and there Avary became impressed by the advantages offered by piracy, and by the amount of good things that were to be gained by very little striving.

One night the captain (who was one of those fellows mightily addicted to punch), instead of going ashore to saturate himself with rum at the ordinary, had his drink in his cabin in private. While he lay snoring away the effects of his rum in the cabin, Avary and a few other conspirators heaved the anchor very leisurely, and sailed out of the harbor of Corunna, and through the midst of the allied fleet riding at anchor in the darkness.

By and by, when the morning came, the captain was awakened by the pitching and tossing of the vessel, the rattle and clatter of the tackle overhead, and the noise of footsteps passing and repassing hither and thither across the deck. Perhaps he lay for a while turning the matter over and over in his muddled head, but he presently rang the bell, and Avary and another fellow answered the call.

"What's the matter?" bawls the captain from his berth.

"Nothing," says Avary, coolly.

"Something's the matter with the ship," says the captain. "Does she drive? What weather is it?"

"Oh no," says Avary; "we are at sea."

"At sea?"

"Come, come!" says Avary: "I'll tell you; you must know that I'm the captain of the ship now, and you must be packing from this here cabin. We are bound to Madagascar, to make all of our fortunes, and if you're a mind to ship for the cruise, why, we'll be glad to have you, if you will be sober and mind your own business; if not, there is a boat alongside, and I'll have you set ashore."

The poor half-tipsy captain had no relish to go a-pirating under the command of his backsliding mate, so out of the ship he bundled, and away he rowed with four or five of the crew, who, like him, refused to join with their jolly shipmates.

The rest of them sailed away to the East Indies, to try their fortunes in those waters, for our Captain Avary was of a high spirit, and had no mind to fritter away his time in the West Indies, squeezed dry by buccaneer Morgan and others of lesser note. No, he would make a bold stroke for it at once, and make or lose at a single cast.

AS FOR THE TREASURE ITSELF, THERE WAS NO END TO THE EXTENT TO WHICH IT GREW AS IT PASSED FROM MOUTH TO MOUTH.

On his way he picked up a couple of like kind with himself – two sloops off Madagascar. With these he sailed away to the coast of India, and for a time his name was lost in the obscurity of uncertain history. But only for a time, for suddenly it flamed out in a blaze of glory. It was reported that a vessel belonging to the Great Mogul, laden with treasure and bearing the monarch's own daughter upon a holy pilgrimage to Mecca (they being Mohammedans), had fallen in with the pirates, and after a short resistance had been surrendered, with the damsel, her court, and all the diamonds, pearls, silk, silver, and gold aboard. It was rumored that the Great Mogul, raging at the insult offered to him through his own flesh and blood, had threatened to wipe out of existence the few English settlements scattered along the coast; whereat the honorable East India Company was in a pretty state of fuss and feathers. Rumor, growing with the telling, has it that Avary is going to marry the Indian princess, willy-nilly, and will turn rajah, and eschew piracy as indecent. As for the treasure itself, there was no end to the extent to which it grew as it passed from mouth to mouth.

Cracking the nut of romance and exaggeration, we come to the kernel of the story – that Avary did fall in with an Indian vessel laden with great treasure (and possibly with the Mogul's daughter), which he captured, and thereby gained a vast prize.

Having concluded that he had earned enough money by the trade he had undertaken, he determined to retire and live decently for the rest of his life upon what he already had. As a step toward this object, he set about cheating his Madagascar partners out of their share of what had been gained. He persuaded them to store all the treasure in his vessel, it being the largest of the three; and so, having it safely in hand, he altered the course of his ship one fine night, and when the morning came the Madagascar sloops found themselves floating upon a wide ocean without a farthing of the treasure for which they had fought so hard, and for which they might whistle for all the good it would do them.

At first Avary had a great part of a mind to settle at Boston, in Massachusetts, and had that little town been one whit less bleak and forbidding, it might have had the honor of being the home of this famous man. As it was, he did not like the looks of it, so he sailed away to the eastward, to Ireland, where he settled himself at Biddeford, in hopes of an easy life of it for the rest of his days.

Here he found himself the possessor of a plentiful stock of jewels, such as pearls, diamonds, rubies, etc., but with hardly a score of honest farthings to jingle in his breeches pocket. He consulted with a certain merchant of Bristol concerning the disposal of the stones – a fellow not much more cleanly in his habits of honesty than Avary himself. This worthy undertook to act as Avary's broker. Off he marched with the jewels, and that was the last that the pirate saw of his Indian treasure.

KIDD AND BLACKBEARD

Perhaps the most famous of all the piratical names to American ears are those of Capt. Robert Kidd and Capt. Edward Teach, or "Blackbeard." Nothing will be ventured in regard to Kidd at this time, nor in regard to the pros and cons as to whether he really was or was not a pirate, after all. For many years he was the very hero of heroes of piratical fame; there was hardly a creek or stream or point of land along our coast, hardly a convenient bit of good sandy beach, or hump of rock, or water-washed cave, where fabulous treasures were not said to have been hidden by this worthy marooner. Now we are assured that he never was a pirate, and never did bury any treasure, excepting a certain chest, which he was compelled to hide upon Gardiner's Island – and perhaps even it was mythical.

So poor Kidd must be relegated to the dull ranks of simply respectable people, or semi-respectable people at best.

But with "Blackbeard" it is different, for in him we have a real, ranting, raging, roaring pirate *per se* – one who really did bury treasure, who made more than one captain walk the plank, and who committed more private murders than he could number on the fingers of both hands; one who fills, and will continue to fill, the place to which he has been assigned for generations, and who may be depended upon to hold his place in the confidence of others for generations to come.

Captain Teach was a Bristol man born, and learned his trade on board of sundry privateers in the East Indies during the old French war – that of 1702 – and a better apprenticeship could no man serve. At last, somewhere about the latter part of the year 1716, a privateering captain, one Benjamin Hornigold, raised him from the ranks and put him in command of a sloop – a lately captured prize – and Blackbeard's fortune was made. It was a very slight step, and but the change of a few letters, to convert "privateer" into "pirate," and it was a very short time before Teach made that change. Not only did he make it himself, but he persuaded his old captain to join with him.

And now fairly began that series of bold and lawless depredations which have made his name so justly famous, and which placed him among the very greatest of marooning freebooters.

"Our hero," says the old historian who sings of the arms and bravery of this great man – "our hero assumed the cognomen of Blackbeard from that large quantity of hair which, like a frightful meteor, covered his whole face, and frightened America more than any comet that appeared there in a long time. He was accustomed to twist it with ribbons into small tails, after the manner of our Ramillies wig, and turn them about his ears. In time of action he wore a sling over his shoulders, with three brace of pistols, hanging in holsters like bandoleers; he stuck lighted matches under his hat, which, appearing on each side of his face, and his eyes naturally looking fierce and wild, made him altogether such a figure that imagination cannot form an idea of a Fury from hell to look more frightful."

"NOBODY BUT THE DEVIL AND I KNOWS WHERE IT IS, AND THE LONGEST LIVER SHALL HAVE ALL."

The night before the day of the action in which he was killed he sat up drinking with some congenial company until broad daylight. One of them asked him if his poor young wife knew where his treasure was hidden. "No," says Blackbeard; "nobody but the devil and I knows where it is, and the longest liver shall have all."

As for that poor young wife of his, the life that he and his rum-crazy shipmates led her was too terrible to be told.

For a time Blackbeard worked at his trade down on the Spanish Main, gathering, in the few years he was there, a very neat little fortune in the booty captured from sundry vessels; but by and by he took it into his head to try his luck along the coast of the Carolinas; so off he sailed to the northward, with quite a respectable little fleet, consisting of his own vessel and two captured sloops. From that time he was actively engaged in the making of American history in his small way.

He never did bury any treasure, excepting a certain chest, which he was compelled to hide upon Gardiner's Island.

He first appeared off the bar of Charleston Harbor, to the no small excitement of the worthy town of that ilk, and there he lay for five or six days, blockading the port, and stopping incoming and outgoing vessels at his pleasure, so that, for the time, the commerce of the province was entirely paralyzed. All the vessels so stopped he held as prizes, and all the crews and passengers (among the latter of whom was more than one provincial worthy of the day) he retained as though they were prisoners of war.

And it was a mightily awkward thing for the good folk of Charleston to behold day after day a black flag with its white skull and crossbones fluttering at the fore of the pirate captain's craft, over across the level stretch of green salt marshes; and it was mightily unpleasant, too, to know that this or that prominent citizen was crowded down with the other prisoners under the hatches.

One morning Captain Blackbeard finds that his stock of medicine is low. "Tut!" says he, "we'll turn no hair gray for that." So up he calls the bold Captain Richards, the commander of his consort the *Revenge* sloop, and bids him take Mr. Marks (one of his prisoners), and go up to Charleston and get the medicine. There was no task that suited our Captain Richards better than that. Up to the town he rowed, as bold as brass. "Look ye," says he to the governor, rolling his quid of tobacco from one cheek to another – "look ye, we're after this and that, and if we don't get it, why, I'll tell you plain, we'll burn them bloody crafts of yours that we've took over yonder, and cut the weasand of every clodpoll aboard of 'em."

There was no answering an argument of such force as this, and the worshipful governor and the good folk of Charleston knew very well that Blackbeard and his crew were the men to do as they promised. So Blackbeard got his medicine, and though it cost the colony two thousand dollars, it was worth that much to the town to be quit of him.

They say that while Captain Richards was conducting his negotiations with the governor his boat's crew were stumping around the streets of the town, having a glorious time of it, while the good folk glowered wrathfully at them, but dared venture nothing in speech or act.

Having gained a booty of between seven and eight thousand dollars from the prizes captured, the pirates sailed away from Charleston Harbor to the coast of North Carolina.

And now Blackbeard, following the plan adopted by so many others of his kind, began to cudgel his brains for means to cheat his fellows out of their share of the booty.

At Topsail Inlet he ran his own vessel aground, as though by accident. Hands, the captain of one of the consorts, pretending to come to his assistance, also grounded *his* sloop. Nothing now remained but for those who were able to get away in the other craft, which was all that was now left of the little fleet. This did Blackbeard with some forty of his favorites. The rest of the pirates were left on the sand spit to await the return of their companions – which never happened.

As for Blackbeard and those who were with him, they were that much richer, for there were so many the fewer pockets to fill. But even yet there were too many to share the booty, in Blackbeard's opinion, and so he marooned a parcel more of them – some eighteen or twenty – upon a naked sand bank, from which they were afterward mercifully rescued by another freebooter who chanced that way – a certain Major Stede Bonnet, of whom more will presently be said. About that time a royal proclamation had been issued offering

W.K.
H.P.

And now Blackbeard began to cudgel his brains for means to cheat his fellows out of their share of the booty.

pardon to all pirates in arms who would surrender to the king's authority before a given date. So up goes Master Blackbeard to the Governor of North Carolina and makes his neck safe by surrendering to the proclamation – albeit he kept tight clutch upon what he had already gained.

And now we find our bold Captain Blackbeard established in the good province of North Carolina, where he and His Worship the Governor struck up a vast deal of intimacy, as profitable as it was pleasant. There is something very pretty in the thought of the bold sea rover giving up his adventurous life (excepting now and then an excursion against a trader or two in the neighboring sound, when the need of money was pressing); settling quietly down into the routine of old colonial life, with a young wife of sixteen at his side, who made the fourteenth that he had in various ports here and there in the world.

Becoming tired of an inactive life, Blackbeard afterward resumed his piratical career. He cruised around in the rivers and inlets and sounds of North Carolina for a while, ruling the roost and with never a one to say

him nay, until there was no bearing with such a pest any longer. So they sent a deputation up to the Governor of Virginia asking if he would be pleased to help them in their trouble.

There were two men-of-war lying at Kicquetan, in the James River, at the time. To them the Governor of Virginia applies, and plucky Lieutenant Maynard, of the *Pearl*, was sent to Ocracoke Inlet to fight this pirate who ruled it down there so like the cock of a walk. There he found Blackbeard waiting for him, and as ready for a fight as ever the lieutenant himself could be. Fight they did, and while it lasted it was as pretty a piece of business of its kind as one could wish to see. Blackbeard drained a glass of grog, wishing the lieutenant luck in getting aboard of him, fired a broadside, blew some twenty of the lieutenant's men out of existence, and totally crippled one of his little sloops for the balance of the fight. After that, and under cover of the smoke, the pirate and his men boarded the other sloop, and then followed a fine old-fashioned hand-to-hand conflict betwixt him and the lieutenant. First they fired their pistols, and then they took to it with cutlasses – right, left, up and down, cut and slash – until the lieutenant's cutlass broke short off at the hilt. Then Blackbeard would have finished him off handsomely, only up steps one of the lieutenant's men and fetches him a great slash over the neck, so that the lieutenant came off with no more hurt than a cut across the knuckles.

At the very first discharge of their pistols Blackbeard had been shot through the body, but he was not for giving up for that – not he. As said before, he was of the true roaring, raging breed of pirates, and stood up to it until he received twenty more cutlass cuts and five additional shots, and then fell dead while trying to fire off an empty pistol. After that the lieutenant cut off the pirate's head, and sailed away in triumph, with the bloody trophy nailed to the bow of his battered sloop.

Those of Blackbeard's men who were not killed were carried off to Virginia, and all of them tried and hanged but one or two, their names, no doubt, still standing in a row in the provincial records.

APPENDIX

AUTHOR BIOGRAPHIES

Daniel Defoe
(1660–1731)

Daniel Defoe was born in London, the son of James Foe, a successful businessman, and Annie, both Presbyterian Dissenters who resisted pressure to join the Church of England. His mother died before he was 10 years old, and Daniel was sent to an academy for the education of Dissenters' sons in Newington Green, to the north of London. Its founder was the Reverend Charles Morton (later vice-president of Harvard College in England's colony in Massachusetts Bay), who offered a progressive, forward-thinking curriculum, with lessons taught in English rather than the traditional emphases on Classical languages.

It is possible that Defoe's father hoped he would become a minister, but he instead determined to become a merchant. In 1684 he married Mary Tuffley, the daughter of a wealthy businessman, with whom he had eight children. Their marriage lasted for the rest of his life. Defoe was unsuccessful in business, however, and by 1692 was facing bankruptcy, a misfortune that has sometimes been attributed to the losses he incurred as a result of insuring ships during the Anglo-French naval wars of the 1690s. He was twice briefly imprisoned for unpaid debts.

At the beginning of the 1700s, Defoe emerged as an active political pamphleteer, weighing in on public debates on behalf of the Dissenters. In 1703 he was arrested and sent to prison at Newgate on a charge of seditious libel for his satirical pamphlet from 1702, *The Shortest-Way with the Dissenters*. Upon his release, Defoe resumed his publishing career with the bi-weekly periodical the *Review*, which featured articles on politics, religion, commerce, and morals. It remained in print until 1713, when Defoe turned to writing fiction.

In 1719, *Robinson Crusoe* was published, a novel that went on to be translated and printed in numerous countries. The book's episodic first-person narrative relates the day-to-day adventures of a man stranded on an uninhabited island, while the plot wove together details gleaned from accounts of shipwrecks and travels to the New World alongside the imagined emotional responses of the protagonist. After its publication, Defoe was labeled "the father of the English novel".

Although he lived to write and publish several other novels about rogues, thieves, and rascals, including the infamous *Moll Flanders* (1722), it is without doubt *Robinson Crusoe* for which Defoe is best remembered.

Howard Pyle
(1853–1911)

Born in Wilmington, Delaware, Howard Pyle lived in a place touched deeply by the American Revolution, the U.S. Civil War, and piracy's Golden Age. After art training in Philadelphia under the Dutch immigrant Francis Adolf Van der Wielen and at the Art Students League in New York City, Pyle settled down in the Wilmington area for almost his entire adult life, where he became very active in the local Swedenborgian church, which his mother and then the rest of his immediate family had joined while he was growing up. He sang in the Swedenborg church choir, donated books to the church library, and praised Emanuel Swedenborg's writings, whilst stating that he read the latter's *Arcana Coelestia* continually and even sometimes had it read to him as he painted. Once Pyle had established himself as a magazine illustrator of high adventure stories and an author of adapted tales from England and mainland Europe, he created an art school based upon the philosophy of illustration as text interpretation, hoping that through his classes and disciples he could incubate a distinctive American school of art that broke away from European traditions. Although many of his best-known students, such as Frank Schoonover and Stanley Arthurs, made their greatest mark, like him, in the area of magazine and book illustration, his most admired student, N.C. Wyeth, longed to become a canvas painter of renown, though he was also highly accomplished as an illustrator.

Page 354
George Varian
On arrival in Bristol, Jim Hawkins marvels before "the most wonderful figureheads, that had all been far over the ocean", 1918

Page 356
Frank Schoonover
Pirates Coming through Charleston,
oil on canvas, 1922
Blackbeard's men march into the town he notoriously blockaded in 1718.

Right
Frank Schoonover
Ned Rackham Espied the Derelict Shore,
oil on canvas, 1922
Blackbeard's marooned crew vie for the attention of the passing Ned Rackham.

Pyle and his students advocated thorough research about the history, artifacts, and customs of the eras in which the events they depicted took place, often searching for period costumes to use as guidelines in their establishment of characterization and setting. Pyle's pirate illustrations contained so much drama that at times they seemed like tableaux from the theatre.

Robert Louis Stevenson
(1850–1894)

Robert Louis (originally Lewis) Stevenson was born and raised in Edinburgh, the only child of Thomas Stevenson, a civil engineer, and his wife Margaret Isabella Balfour. Sickly from early childhood, he was put into the special care of a hired nurse by the age of two, a woman to whom decades later he dedicated his poetry collection *A Child's Garden of Verses* (1885). Despite irregular school attendance due to frequent bouts of bronchitis, colds, and pneumonia, he managed to gain admission to the University of Edinburgh in 1867, where his father encouraged him to study engineering. Stevenson was unenthusiastic, being already drawn to writing and was permitted to switch to legal studies. Although he qualified for his license in 1875, he remained committed to writing, and never in fact practised law. His recalcitrance, in addition to his bohemian lifestyle (which included growing his hair long, wearing velvet jackets, and rejecting his father's strict Calvinism), led to an estrangement from his father that was further exacerbated by his romance and marriage to Fanny Van de Grift Osbourne, a married American woman with two children who was more than 10 years older. They had met in France in 1876, and Stevenson traveled to the United States to join her in 1879, although they were not married until May 19, 1880. Cut off from his father's financial assistance, and waiting for Fanny's divorce to be finalized, Stevenson came close to dying as he foundered in financial distress, deprivation, and near starvation.

Stevenson's first publication, a pamphlet about the uprising and suppression of anti-Anglican Scottish Presbyterians in the 1600s, appeared in 1866. During the 1870s, he published works in various genres in *Macmillan's Magazine*, the *Cornhill Magazine*, and other periodicals, as well as travel books based on his trips to continental Europe. In 1878, *An Inland Voyage* was published, about a canoeing trip through Belgium and France, followed a year later by *Travels with a Donkey in the Cévennes*, his often-funny account of mountain trekking in southern France on an excruciatingly slow animal to which he became surprisingly devoted.

After the honeymoon, Stevenson, his wife, and stepson returned to Scotland, where he became reconciled with his father. As his health continued to falter, he resumed his travels and lived for a while in France, seeking a better climate for his respiratory problems. The Stevensons spent the winters of 1880/81 and 1881/82 in Switzerland, and then lived in Hyères on the French Riviera before settling in Bournemouth on the south coast of England, where they lived from 1884 to 1887.

Though none of these residences brought health to Stevenson, he produced his most famous fictional works during this period. *Treasure Island*, passages of which are reprinted in this volume, was serialized in the boys' magazine *Young Folks* in October 1881, and published in book form in 1883, with tens of thousands of copies sold in Stevenson's lifetime. *Kidnapped* followed in 1886, with *Strange Case of Dr Jekyll and Mr Hyde* published in the same year.

In June 1888, the Stevensons sailed from San Francisco to the South Seas, where they explored the Marquesas Islands, Tahiti, and other islands before settling permanently in Samoa. Stevenson continued to write until the end of his life, including *In the South Seas*, which appeared posthumously in 1896 after he died suddenly of a cerebral hemorrhage in December 1894; he was buried on a mountaintop overlooking the ocean. He is remembered as a poet, essayist, book reviewer, and indefatigable letter-writer, as well as for his novels, and although his literary standing is contested, he was indisputably one of the most prominent British writers of the late 19th century.

F.E. Schoonover
'22

F.E. Schoonover

AUTHOR BIOGRAPHIES

Jules Verne
(1828–1905)

Born on February 8, 1828, in the port city of Nantes in France, Jules Verne was the eldest son of Pierre Verne, a bourgeois lawyer, and his wife Sophie Allotte de La Fuÿe. By the age of six, Jules was steeped in stories of shipwrecked sailors told to him by his teacher, a widow whose sea-captain husband had been missing for several years. It was probably her storytelling that influenced Verne's interest in writing, and by his adolescence he was writing poetry and keeping journals. After finishing his childhood education in various local institutions, Verne took up legal studies in Paris in 1847 and earned his license there in 1851. His father had hoped he would return to Nantes, but Verne remained in Paris and pursued a career in the theatre, on which he had already embarked earlier in his life. From around 1848 he had begun writing operetta libretti, and a meeting in 1849 with Alexandre Dumas *père* led to a collaboration the following year with Dumas's son, also Alexandre, on a production of a stage comedy Verne had written entitled *Les Pailles rompues* (*The Broken Straws*). From 1852 to 1854, Verne worked as secretary for the Théâtre Lyrique in Paris, an opera company dedicated to French operettas. Meanwhile, his writing career took off, beginning with a series of witty short stories and scientific pieces for the magazine *Musée des familles*.

In 1857, Verne married Honorine du Fraysne de Viane, a widow with two children, and in 1861 their son Michel was born. Verne's need for a steady income to support his family induced him to become a stockbroker while carrying out research for his fictional works. His authorial ambitions gained traction in 1862 when he met and became associated with the editor and publisher Pierre-Jules Hetzel. Verne's *Five Weeks in a Balloon* was first published in Hetzel's periodical *Le Magasin d'éducation et de récréation* and then issued in book form, a practice the two men would continue to follow in their subsequent collaborations.

Verne's first four novels were collectively labeled "Voyages Extraordinaires", a nod to their common elements which included a highlighting of scientific inventions, travel to isolated locations by technically advanced means, and changing societal norms. Ultimately, this label was extended to the rest of Verne's œuvre of adventure writings as well, over 50 book-length works in all. Aside from the passages from *The Mysterious Island* (1875) retold in this edition, the most popular of this remarkably prolific writer's works include *Around the World in Eighty Days* (1872) as well as the nautical titles *Twenty Thousand Leagues Under the Sea* (1869/70) and *The Floating City* (1871). The episodic character of his stories – often featuring rugged adventurers who overcome physical and psychological trials – seems to have been designed from the start to suit serialization, while their theatrical elements owe much to Verne's familiarity with the stage.

Verne's personal life was marked by frequent travel on ships that he owned, but also family strife and heartache, and when he died on March 24, 1905 he was not a wealthy man. Overcome with diabetes and poor health, he left behind several manuscripts that were later edited and issued by his son Michel. Often called "the father of modern science fiction", Verne is the second most-translated fictional author in the world, surpassed only by the English mystery writer Agatha Christie.

Frank Schoonover
Blackbeard (right) and a mate swarm over a ship's railings in the cover illustration for Blackbeard, Buccaneer, 1922

ARTIST BIOGRAPHIES

Zdeněk Burian

(1905–1981)

Illustrations on pages 27 l., 154, 161, 169, 194, 204, 206, 208, 219, 226, 235, 362, 382

Zdeněk Burian was born in the Moravian town of Kopřivnice, in Austria-Hungary, on February 11, 1905. His talent as a draftsman was recognized and fostered while he was still a young boy, and at 14 he entered the Prague Academy of Fine Arts at fourteen only to leave soon after without taking a diploma to earn a precarious livelihood as a day laborer. During this early period Burian spent a great deal of time working outdoors, which was highly beneficial for the studies of nature he was doing as a self-taught artist. He also taught himself a range of drawing and painting techniques, and in 1921 his first illustrations were published in *Dobrodružství Davida Balfoura* (*Kidnapped: Being Memoirs of the Adventures of David Balfour in the Year 1751*) by Robert Louis Stevenson. Burian was not only an accomplished painter but also worked quickly, a skill that was valued by publishers.

After commissions for various journals and periodicals, by the 1930s Burian was able to support his family – he had married in 1927 – by working as a book illustrator. Numerous adventure and science fiction classics by Rudyard Kipling, Jules Verne, and even Edgar Rice Burroughs were published with illustrations by Burian. It is his illustrations to Verne's *L'Île mystérieuse* for the Czech edition *Tajuplný ostrov*, published in 1939, which are reproduced in this edition.

Burian was not only a distinguished illustrator of books for children and adolescents. He was also known for the reconstruction drawings on which he collaborated with leading paleontologists of his day, continuing to work in this field until he died in 1981. Published in many books and scientific journals, these drawings still play a major role in shaping our perception of prehistoric natural phenomena. *The Lost Worlds of Zdeněk Burian*, edited by Judith Schalansky and published in 2013, provides an excellent overview of the body of work produced by this illustrator whose importance cannot be overstated.

Jules Férat

(1829–1906)

Illustrations on pages 28, 29, 200, 386

Born on November 28, 1829 in the town of Ham to the north-east of Paris, Jules Férat studied with Léon Cogniet at the École des Beaux-Arts in Paris in the early 1850s and regularly exhibited at the annual Salon in the capital between 1857 and 1878. Known for his skill at depicting factory workers and machines, he provided illustrations for many magazines and books and gained his greatest recognition for illustrating Jules Verne's *L'Île mystérieuse*.

While Férat was praised especially for his talent at representing light within dark spaces (as in coal mines) and for the details of clothing (such as their folds), his work has been criticized for portraying his characters' physiques in ways that were excessively muscular. The illustration reproduced on page 200 casts light on a dark space and depicts Tom Ayrton hoisting himself up the side of the pirates' ship. Férat died in Paris on June 6, 1906.

Zdeněk Burian
In an illustration for Jules Verne's L'Île mystérieuse (Tajuplný ostrov), *the settlers' dog Top is frightened by a dugong before being miraculously saved*, 1939

Walter Paget
Title-page to Robinson Crusoe, *depicting the protagonist in a pastoral setting, flanked by two goats and his parrot Poll,* 1897

Frank Godwin

(1889–1959)

Illustrations on pages 20 t., 21, 22, 385

Born in Washington, D.C., Frank Godwin was the son of the city editor of the *Washington Star*, where he began an apprenticeship at the age of 16. Though his art was mostly self taught he attended classes at the Art Students League in New York City, where he shared a studio with James Montgomery Flagg and honed his skills in pen and ink, securing his first illustration assignment in 1908 for the satirical weekly *Judge*.

Continuing into World War I, Godwin's artwork graced many further issues of *Judge*, and his illustrations also appeared in several of the nation's popular magazines, including *The Saturday Evening Post*, *Ladies' Home Journal*, and *Redbook*. Over the course of the war he developed his skills and attention as a cartoonist, and his large cartoon supporting the Red Cross appeared on the first page of Wisconsin's *Watertown News* on May 13, 1917, not long after the United States had entered the conflict.

Between World Wars I and II Godwin made a considerable impact as a book illustrator, and his rich colorings and tones – which have been likened to the work of Maxfield Parrish and Newell Convers Wyeth – turned up in many of the most popular adventure stories of his day, including *King Arthur and His Knights* and the Stevenson works *Kidnapped* and *Treasure Island*. During the same period, Godwin gained perhaps even greater acclaim for his work in comics. He created the syndicated strip "Connie" for the Philadelphia *Public Ledger* (1927–44), and did other strips too, including "Bill Bunting" and "Rusty Riley". While World War II was under way, his cartoons for the oil company Texaco supported the war effort by encouraging people to conserve rubber.

Godwin was a member of the National Cartoonists Society and served as vice-president of the Society of Illustrators. For the last 17 years of his life he lived in Solebury Township, near Hope, Pennsylvania, where he died of a heart attack on August 5, 1959.

Walter Paget

(1862–1935)

Illustrations on pages 65, 70, 76, 80, 82, 89, 92, 93, 106, 111, 113, 117, 120, 122, 133, 137, 144, 365

Walter Stanley Paget (abbreviated to "Wal Paget" in the signature to his pictures), was born in London to a large middle-class family and became, like his two older brothers, prominent in British book and magazine illustration. His style had similarities with that of his brother Sidney (1860–1908), and both illustrated the stories of Sir Arthur Conan Doyle. Certain reports suggest that Sidney in fact used Walter as the model for his illustrations of Sherlock Holmes.

Walter Paget received his professional training at the Royal Academy of Arts in London, where in 1885 he exhibited a decorative design during its annual exhibition. His work included oil portraiture, though he was best known for his black-and-white and halftone illustrations. Paget became an in-house and regular contributor to *The Graphic*, a celebrated periodical that was published in London, and his illustrations were also picked up by various other magazines. Some of his most memorable work dealt with British imperial subjects, as when he served as a war correspondent for the weekly *Illustrated London News* and covered the infamous and ultimately disastrous Gordon Relief Expedition of 1884/85 when British rescue forces were dispatched to Khartoum in Sudan. One of his most famous late-career paintings, meanwhile, the undated *Birth of the Irish Republic*, presents a sympathetic image of the Irish independence movement. Historical subjects also appealed to Paget, as displayed in his *Cleopatra* (*c.* 1901), held by the Victoria and Albert Museum in London.

Paget provided illustrations for both Defoe's *Robinson Crusoe* and Stevenson's *Treasure Island*, and a significant number of his works for the first of those novels appear in this book. He died at his home near Bromsgrove, in the west of England, on January 29, 1935.

H. Pyle

ARTIST BIOGRAPHIES

Howard Pyle
Reproduced in his Book of Pirates, *Pyle's illustration captures a wounded sailor brandishing a belaying pin in the direction of an outstretched hand, firing a flintlock pistol*, 1921

Howard Pyle
(see biography on pp. 357/58)
Illustrations on pages 6, 26, 32 b., 42, 44 l., 50 b., 326, 329, 332/33, 335, 337, 339, 341, 344/45, 351, 352, 366, 375

Louis Rhead
(1857–1926)
Illustrations on pages 51, 261, 299, 300, 307, 325

Louis John Rhead was born in Etruria in Staffordshire, England, in 1857. His father was a well-known ceramic artist, and by the time he was 16 Rhead was already engaged in pottery design and production. Attracted to the graphic-design work of poster illustrators, he developed a style that was similar to that favored by popular artists of the period. In 1883 Rhead left England and moved to the United States to begin work in New York as art director for the publishing firm D. Appleton, where he remained for the next six years.

Rhead's formal artistic training had begun in Paris a decade earlier and continued in London from 1879–81 at the National Art Training School. His preferred techniques followed those developed by the Arts and Crafts artists Walter Crane and William Morris. Rhead's later illustration work included *Bold Robin Hood and His Outlaw Band* (1912), a book that contained his own retellings of the legends with corresponding illustrations, an edition of *The Arabian Nights' Entertainments* (1916), and Stevenson's *Kidnapped* (1921).

Published in 1915, Rhead's copiously illustrated edition of *Treasure Island* also featured an introduction by him that recounted his childhood reading of the story in serialized form and paid tribute to its influence on him as a boy. He remembered that the episodes had contained no illustrations, but in marked contrast his edition contained over 100 illustrations and decorations which Rhead described as flowing from "the scrutiny" of the characters and adventures "who lived with me so closely" throughout the years. There were four full-color illustrations, yet Rhead's masterful use of graphic-design techniques was the book's real jewel. Each chapter featured a dramatic black-and-white frontispiece, while the first letter in the text was boxed and included a visual clue to the action that was to unfold. In his introduction Rhead noted that Stevenson had not wanted the original serialized story to be illustrated; nevertheless, Rhead hoped his own designs and illustrations were noteworthy additions to Stevenson's drama.

George Roux
(1853–1929)
Illustrations on pages 8, 241, 252, 267, 277, 284, 292, 315, 316, 322

Born on April 5, 1853 in Ganges, southern France, George (Alexandre-Georges) Roux began attending the École des Beaux-Arts in Paris in 1878 where he studied under Alexandre Cabanel and Jean-Paul Laurens. Much of his early work was historically themed, although he also made his mark in portrait painting and decorative work, as well as in illustration, where he achieved his most lasting success.

Roux is particularly remembered for illustrations in the works of two of the authors represented in this book, Robert Louis Stevenson and Jules Verne. The publisher Pierre-Jules Hetzel's first illustrated edition of the French translation of Stevenson's *Treasure Island* in 1885 featured 24 plates by Roux, though he did not always get full credit for this work. In some cases his signature and initials became deleted, so that attribution for the illustrations was at times given instead to the engravers, whose names still appeared on the plates. Roux also contributed a large number of illustrations for Verne's *Voyages Extraordinaires*, and was the second-most prolific picture artist for that series after Léon Bennett.

Roux's pictures for *Treasure Island* have long attracted scrutiny because Stevenson himself wrote about them in an unpublished manuscript, which appeared in print after his death. Stevenson approved of the "spirited" quality of Roux's illustrations, but also harbored reservations about the work, particularly regarding Roux's depictions of Long John Silver.

Frank Schoonover
Blackbeard in Smoke and Flame, oil on canvas, 1922
"He stirred his infernal pots and the greasy smoke rolled upward in choking volume." Edward Teach looms menacingly in an illustration for Blackbeard, Buccaneer.

Frank Schoonover

(1877–1972)

Illustrations on pages 18, 38, 40, 43, 356, 359, 360, 369, 378

Frank Earle Schoonover was born in Oxford, New Jersey. Although he briefly considered becoming a Presbyterian minister, by 1896 he was studying art in one of Howard Pyle's early classes in the newly founded "School of Illustration" at the Drexel Institute in Philadelphia. When Pyle opened the Drexel Institute's summer art program at nearby Chadds Ford in 1898, Schoonover was one of the 15 students selected to live and work there together. He remained a disciple of Pyle's throughout his professional career, and contributed illustrations, as Pyle had, for many books and magazines.

Also like Pyle, Schoonover often used black and white line drawings at the beginnings and endings of book chapters, and embellished pages with dramatic illustrations. These scenes, so richly filled with incident, epitomized his training with Pyle. Characters are caught in mid-action and the details reflect the mood of the text, without repeating the story's exact particulars. According to Schoonover, Pyle demanded precision in the details within depicted scenes and encouraged illustrators to use authentic artifacts as guides when they were painting.

Schoonover took this advice seriously, hunting for appropriate period clothing and objects both by visiting the places he illustrated and by carrying out research on details he was uncertain about. His full-page illustrations for the 1922 edition of Ralph Paine's *Blackbeard, Buccaneer* are filled with kinetic verve and atmosphere.

George Varian

(1865–1923)

Illustrations on pages 39, 48, 49, 236, 272, 289, 354

Although George Edmund Varian was born in Liverpool in England, by the time he was four he was living in Brooklyn, New York and it was as an American citizen that he pursued his artistic career. Varian received his formal art education at the Brooklyn Artists Guild and the Art Students League in New York City and became known for his illustration work in magazines such as *McClure's*, *St. Nicholas*, and *Youth's Companion*. He was also deeply engaged in book illustration, which was a common profession for artists who trained at the Art Students League. By 1900 Varian was the sole illustrator of Alice Balch Abbot's *A Frigate's Namesake* (published by Century in 1901), with 15 illustrations. The book's plot centered on a young girl's seafaring adventures and contained settings that Varian would draw again and again, namely ships and scenes involving open water.

Varian's artistic reputation had already been established when on May 2, 1902 Mount Pelée, an inactive volcano on the French island of Martinique, began to erupt. Another eruption followed on May 8, and most of the inhabitants of the island's town of St. Pierre were killed. As U.S. interest in this disaster in the Caribbean heightened, the American journalist and explorer George Kennan traveled to the area near the volcano, accompanied by Varian. On May 26, the pair were told to flee as further volcanic activity was expected, but Varian went back into the house where they were staying and retrieved his sketchbooks. Kennan subsequently wrote that as he did so the volcano was "ablaze with lightning" from the volcanic fire and smoke, but Varian calmly declared he was fine. His artwork was featured in Kennan's account of their adventures, *The Tragedy of Pelée: a narrative of personal experience and observation in Martinique* (Outlook, 1902), and his reputation as an illustrator of themes of adventure was duly consolidated.

Varian's illustrations in Robert Louis Stevenson's *Treasure Island* represent his typical standard for this form of

Alice Bolingbroke Woodward
Untitled, watercolor on board, 1907
Captain Hook escapes the clutches of the crocodile, in an illustration for J.M. Barrie's Peter and Wendy.

artwork: the 20 illustrations included a series of black-and-white portrait images for the main characters and various action scenes, interspersed between full-color representations. It seems likely that Varian was only expecting to be able to sell some of the color pictures as artwork after the book was completed, since the only ones he signed with his last name were the ones that look like fully developed paintings. It is also noteworthy that his obituaries throughout the United States only mentioned his work in *The Tragedy of Pelée* and as an illustrator for children's books.

Edward Henry Wehnert

(1813–1868)

Illustrations on pages 58, 62, 66, 73, 84, 87, 121, 127, 130, 147

Edward Henry (E.H.) Wehnert was born the son of German immigrants in London, and when he was only 14 his father, a tailor, sent him to Germany to be educated at the University of Göttingen. While he was there, Wehnert often drew pictures for his friends and took their responses as encouragement for him to study art. His art training and first professional work began following his return to England when he made drawings and studied from the different collections in the galleries of the British Museum, and painted a large work in oil for an exhibition. He further honed his skills during a stint in Paris where he took advantage of the Louvre's resources and was given formal instruction in the studio of the painter Paul Delaroche. Following several years' residence in Paris he moved to Jersey in the Channel Islands, where he stayed for two or three years and then, in 1837, returned to London where he joined the Society of Water-colour Painters. Although he had several pictures chosen for the society's exhibitions, he was not a commercially popular painter.

However, since he was not able to earn enough from his fine art on its own, Wehnert turned instead toward illustration as a more promising outlet for his talents, though he still continued to paint oils and watercolors and several of his works were shown at the Royal Academy. In his later years he also made a trip to Italy, where he sketched a number of scenes that he hoped to develop into major oil paintings. At the same time Wehnert had become adept as a woodblock illustrator and secured graphic-design work for several important literary publications, including a translation of the Grimm brothers' *Household Stories* (C.S. Francis, 1853) and Defoe's *The Life and Adventures of Robinson Crusoe* (Bell and Daldy, 1862). Wehnert's full- and quarter-page depictions of Crusoe's island adventures are mostly character sketches, with Crusoe himself placed in the center of the action. Although these illustrations may now seem stylistically dated, they nevertheless anticipated the representations that appeared in later illustrated versions of Defoe's classic. At the time of the 1862 edition, the printing of color illustrations had yet to be perfected and Wehnert's scenes were all in black and white. Future editions would occasionally add color to them.

Alice Bolingbroke Woodward

(1862–1951)

Illustrations on pages 46, 47 b., 370, 381

Alice Bolingbroke Woodward was the daughter of the respected geologist and paleontologist Henry Woodward, who was Keeper of Geology at the Natural History Museum in London while she was young. Born in Chelsea, she and her siblings were educated at home, and they were all encouraged to draw. Alice enjoyed doing scientific illustrations, and drew several examples for her father's lectures. Her formal art training began at Westminster School of Art, and while studying there she met the famous American illustrator Joseph Pennell. He trained her as an artist to work in commercial publishing, and by 1898 she had become an established book illustrator. When her illustrations were published in *The Peter Pan Picture Book* in 1907, the reviewer in the December 1907 issue of *The Publishers' Circular and Booksellers' Record,* issued in London, called her work "remarkably accurate". Woodward's illustrations depict a nursery tale full of very young children, who might be enacting the famous tale of piracy that had been adapted and edited into a children's book by Frederick Orville Perkins, with J.M. Barrie's blessing. These fanciful illustrations are still considered her strongest work in the field of children's literature.

Newell Convers Wyeth

(1882–1945)

Illustrations on pages 2, 4, 20 b., 24, 25, 27 r., 55, 56/57, 79, 90, 95, 99, 100, 103, 109, 115, 116, 141, 150, 157, 163, 164, 171, 174, 179, 183, 187, 189, 190, 193, 203, 211, 225, 231, 242, 247, 255, 262, 271, 274, 279, 283, 295, 303, 311, 373, 376/77, 389

Newell Convers Wyeth was born in Needham, Massachusetts on October 22, 1882. His mother encouraged his interest in art, and he attended two art institutions in Massachusetts prior to joining Howard Pyle's School of Art when he was 20. In February 1903, Pyle advised Wyeth, who was in the process of beginning a career in commercial magazine illustration when he joined Pyle's school, to "drop all outside work for publishers" while he was enrolled there. This was a primary requirement expected of students in Pyle's course of study at his studios in Wilmington, Delaware. They were expected to follow his judgement on when they had reached a point when they were ready to take on paid work, and then to depend on his contacts with publishers in order to secure such assignments. Wyeth soon emerged as one of Pyle's star students, in the process collecting a large costume wardrobe and thoroughly researching the scenes he illustrated. In fact, Wyeth showed so much artistic talent that by 1905 Pyle was encouraging him to turn his interest from illustration to canvas painting, a highly unusual piece of advice from a master of illustration who taught students to follow his example.

After marrying and establishing himself in Chadds Ford, Pennsylvania, Wyeth enjoyed a remarkably successful career in illustration, which included his work for Robert Louis Stevenson's *Treasure Island.* The large-scale paintings he produced set high standards. Like Pyle, Wyeth depicted larger-than-life scenes darkly situated in a representative countryside and complemented by strong characterization, although his pictures often went further than the texts they accompanied. *Treasure Island* is an interesting early example of his sense of realism. By the time he illustrated Jules Verne's *The Mysterious Island* for Scribner's 1918 edition, Wyeth had perfected a storytelling formula that would fully engage his audience. The chapter endings featured carefully drawn black-and-white portrayals of characters in motion, adding a sense of drama and personality to the full-page color scenes and the panoramic vision they confer on Verne's engaging novel.

Newell Convers Wyeth
Title-page illustration to
Treasure Island, 1911

1911

THE ILLUSTRATOR

Michael Custode
(* 1963)

The Canadian artist Michael Custode is known for his evocative, black-and-white illustrations which imitate the technique of woodcut engraving.

Custode was born in St. Catharines, Ontario, though since his father worked in the steel industry the family moved on several occasions when he was young. He lived in Montreal, Newmarket, and Fonthill before settling in his current home of Toronto. In 1986, he graduated from the Communications and Design department at the Ontario College of Art (now OCAD University). He worked for three years as a graphic designer before moving into freelance illustration, a field in which he has since been active for over 35 years.

His illustrations have been reproduced in a range of printed media, including the newspapers *The Globe and Mail*, *The Toronto Star*, and *The Washington Post*, as well as the magazines *This Old House*, *Outside*, and *Sports Illustrated*. In addition to his work for periodicals, Custode has illustrated the covers of several books, including Woody Tasch's *Inquiries into the Nature of Slow Money* (2010). The clarity of his artistic style lends his illustrations a versatility which has seen them applied to various media, from packaging and stationery to website design. For his illustration and graphic design the illustrator has won awards from the Art Directors Club of Toronto (1992) and the Advertising and Design Association of Ottawa (2000).

The scene-setting vignettes composed by Michael Custode for this book, shown at the beginning of each chapter, are derived faithfully from the texts of the pirate tales reprinted. In their refined, precise linework, they offer a clear counterpoint to the vivid drama and exuberance of the book illustrations by the Brandywine School artists that are also featured in this volume. Furthermore, the icons created by Custode for this book – such as the treasure chest (p. 3), Jolly Roger (p. 7), and glossary symbols (pp. 379–387) – demonstrate his experience in graphic design, effortlessly distilling the world of piracy into a clear and striking visual language.

Right
Howard Pyle
The Flying Dutchman, oil on canvas, 1900
Pyle's painting of a foundering ship doomed to sail for eternity and its captain, both named "The Flying Dutchman", was reproduced in the magazine Collier's Weekly *in December 1900.*

Pages 376/77
Newell Convers Wyeth
Absconding with the Treasure, oil on canvas, c. 1929
Two pirates carry a chest by the sea's edge in the Caribbean, followed by another holding a pistol, in a scene inspired by Wyeth's series of paintings from 1911 for Treasure Island.

GLOSSARY

After-deck
A part of a ship's deck located toward the vessel's rear, or *stern*.

Age of Sail
The period ranging from roughly the late 1500s, when sailing vessels dominated the high seas and naval warfare, to the mid-19th century, when steam power replaced wind power as the primary means of naval propulsion.

Anchorage
The locale where a vessel drops its anchor in the expectation of remaining in place.

Articles of War
A term used at various times in British and U.S. history to describe the regulations governing either a part or the whole of their military establishments.

Barbary Pirates
Pirates operating along the North African Mediterranean (or "Barbary") coastline of the Muslim states and semi-dependencies of the Ottoman Empire of Algiers, Morocco, Tripoli, and Tunis, as well as from Morocco's Atlantic coast.

Black Spot
Fictional device deriving from Robert Louis Stevenson's novel *Treasure Island*, connoting a pirate's curse against or warning to another pirate, delivered in the form of a round piece of paper blackened on one side.

Bow
The forward part of a ship. In the *Age of Sail*, firing a single shot across another ship's bow was a means of averting battle by indicating hostile intent and inducing the targeted ship to submit to a search or surrender without resistance.

Bowsprit
A spar projecting forward from the *bow* of a sailing vessel, to which forestays (ropes supporting foremasts) are attached.

Brig
A ship with two square-rigged masts, smaller and with fewer cannon than the *Age of Sail*'s large warships, which were known as frigates. Generally, brigs had a crew of about 150 men.

Broadside
When all the guns along one side of a vessel are fired simultaneously or near-simultaneously.

Buccaneer
A synonym for pirate or *privateer* most commonly applied to marauders sailing the *Spanish Main* during the *Golden Age of Piracy*.

Bulwark
Wood planking running along a vessel's sides above the level of the deck. The term evolved from a late medieval word for protective defensive works on land such as ramparts, which were sometimes called bulwarks.

Capstan
A mechanism on sailing ships consisting of ropes wrapped around a barrel or cylinder; the device uses the pulley system, as it extends and retracts rope, to supply the necessary tension to raise sails and hold them in place.

Page 378
Frank Schoonover
The Press Gang, oil on canvas, 1923
In a painting reproduced in Ralph Paine's novel Privateers of '76*, the citizens of Plymouth flee an onrushing press gang, clad in Royal Navy uniforms.*

Right
Alice Bolingbroke Woodward
Untitled, watercolor on board, 1907
Kicked overboard by Peter Pan, Captain Hook falls into the outstretched jaws of the awaiting crocodile.

Corsair
Synonym for pirate or *privateer* applied most commonly to *Barbary pirates*; some authorities consider the Barbary State naval raiders to be *privateers* rather than pirates because they held quasi-legitimacy as agents of the Ottoman Empire.

Coxswain
The helmsman of a ship's boat. In Stevenson's *Treasure Island*, coxswain Israel Hands is a "wily, old, experienced seaman, who could be trusted at a pinch with almost anything."

Cutlass
A sword, commonly associated with pirates and especially *Barbary pirates*, with a wide, slightly curved blade and a single cutting edge.

Dead Man's Chest
Term deriving from Stevenson's *Treasure Island* alluding to a pirate's trunk or treasure chest. Famously, in the opening scene of that book an old seaman sings the refrain, "Fifteen men on the dead man's chest."

"Dead men don't bite"
A phrase that appears several times in *Treasure Island* suggesting that, in certain instances, pirates found executing captives and disaffected crewmen preferable to offering them some form of lenity, such as *marooning* them on an island. Anything less than capital punishment left open the possibility that a captive might find an opportunity in the future to avenge his ill treatment.

Doubloon
A Spanish gold coin used as currency in New Spain during the Spanish occupation of territories in North and South America, and also in the Philippines and nearby islands. Today the word is commonly used to refer to the money or plunder sought by pirates.

Filibuster
A term deriving originally from the Dutch word *vrijbuiter* that was often used as a synonym for pirates or *freebooters* during the *Age of Sail*, especially throughout the *Spanish Main*. In the mid-19th century the word was applied to U.S. adventurers who invaded Latin America on private military expeditions.

Freebooter
A word nearly synonymous with pirate, but highlighting the plundering intentions of marauders. The term has typically been applied to the career of the Englishman Sir Francis Drake, who during the *Age of Sail* plundered Spanish colonies in Latin America.

Gentleman of Fortune
Phrasing employed several times in Stevenson's *Treasure Island* as an ironic euphemism for pirates, who in fact rarely came from such privileged backgrounds.

Golden Age of Piracy
Period from the late 1600s to the 1720s when piracy was particularly rampant and many of the most famous pirates of legend roamed the high seas.

Grog
An alcoholic drink served regularly aboard pirate and English naval vessels during the *Golden Age of Piracy*; at the

GLOSSARY

Zdeněk Burian
"Gideon Spilett remained motionless... his gun to his shoulder, without moving a muscle." A tiger on Lincoln Island is hunted by the settlers, from Verne's
L'Île mystérieuse (Tajuplný ostrov), 1939

time, it generally consisted of rum and water, but for some while during the 19th century and prior to its abolition of grog rations, the U.S. Navy replaced the rum component with whiskey.

Hawsehole
A hole in a vessel's *bow* that allows a thick anchor cable or *hawser* to pass through it.

Hawser
Large heavy rope constructed from three filaments braided together that was used to moor a ship. The heaviness of the rope and the repeated twisting produced a strong cable that resisted water absorption.

Hull
The body of a vessel. During the *Age of Sail*, ship frames were made of wood and hulls were vulnerable, especially in tropical waters, to damage from shipworms and deterioration from sea matter such as barnacles. This meant careful caulking when portside with tar, pitch, and oakum was necessary while ships were in port.

Jack Tar
A common/non-officer seaman or sailor on a merchant or naval vessel. The term derives from the importance of tar as a caulking agent to prevent leaking in the *Age of Sail*'s wood-planked vessels. Ships' officers assigned such labor to common seamen.

Jolly Boat
Light, small boat carried aboard sailing vessels, used when lowered into the sea for tasks such as conveying persons to another ship or point on land.

Jolly Roger
The inimitable black flag with white skull and crossbones emblazoned on the sinister background, which has become emblematic of pirate ships and their marauding crews. According to legend, flags with this symbolism were routinely employed by notorious pirates such as Blackbeard.

Letter of Marque and Reprisal
Formal, often written permission from a government allowing private citizens to commit actions at sea against the persons and property of a hostile power; during the *Age of Sail*, such authorizations provided legal cover for *privateering* as compared to piracy, which was illegal under international law and custom.

Loot
The treasure that pirates seized at sea and along coasts from the persons and places they attacked and pillaged.

Lugger
A type of small, square-rigged ship used for trading and fishing or for *privateering*, which subsequently became a favorite with pirates because it traveled quickly and could hold a crew of up to 100. This two- or three-masted ship was the idealized vessel often depicted in illustrations of early pirate legends

Maroon (verb)
To force a person ashore from a vessel and strand them on a deserted island or stretch of coast; pirates sometimes also marooned captives or rivals aboard ship as an alternative to executing them.

Frank Godwin
"I fixed my umbrella also in the step at the stern." Crusoe fashions a makeshift mast for his boat as he makes his way around the island, 1925

Messmate
A ship's crew member who regularly sits in the galley at mealtimes and eats with the same companions. In Defoe's *Robinson Crusoe*, the protanist takes a liking to a ship's captain who wants him to sign on for a voyage and indicates they will be messmates together if he does so.

Mutineer
Derived from the French word *mutinier* to denote a rebellious crew member who opposes the ship's authority. While one person aboard ship can begin a protest over a personal dispute, the mutineer rarely acts alone and instead intends to incite a spirit of insurrection amongst his comrades.

Pieces of Eight
Silver coins produced in Spain's American colonies during the *Age of Sail* that circulated as currency there and elsewhere.

Privateer
During the *Age of Sail* and the early steam era, privateers were privately owned vessels given license by the authorities of a given country (see *letter of marque and reprisal*) or by informal understandings to attack the seaborne commerce of a country at war with the authorities of that country.

Prize Courts
During the *Age of Sail* these tribunals judged the legitimacy and value, under *letters of marque*, of vessels and cargoes captured by *privateers* in wartime; such courts also ruled on the disposition of the vessels and cargoes, in particular how the proceeds should be distributed.

Rig (verb)
To ready a vessel for sea travel, most specifically its sails, cables, and other materials constituting its rigging.

Schooner
Vessel developed in the 1600s fitted with two or more masts, notable for its lightness and speed; pirates often sailed in schooners.

Scuttle
A hole in a ship's deck used for communication, lighting, ventilation, or other purposes; alternately, *to scuttle* was to make one or more holes in the *hull* of a vessel with the intention of sinking it.

Sea Chest
Historically, this was a large trunk used to contain a crew member's belongings, but it has since become part of the language to describe the hidden plunder that any pirate obtained during his voyages. By the late 19th century, periodical publications were running tales such as Stevenson's *Treasure Island* that hinged on a pirate's personal sea chest and its contents.

Sea-dog
Sometimes a synonym for pirate, the term more generally signals a weathered, oldish sailor. When the author R. A. J. Walling needed the appropriate term to title her book about the 16th-century English naval commander, slave trader, and nemesis of Spanish shipping, John Hawkins, she called him *A Sea-dog of Devon*.

Left
Jules Férat
"In the rapid flash of the lantern, he had recognized his former accomplice." Ayrton is confronted by Bob Harvey on board the Speedy, *in an engraving for* L'Île mystérieuse, *1875*

Page 389
Newell Convers Wyeth
Robinson Crusoe marks the passing of time on his improvised calendar on the beach, 1920

Seaboard
Although the term can be simply defined as the coastline alongside the sea, pirate legend has changed its depiction into a long beach, often on the eastern seacoast of the United States, where pirates landed, left their hidden treasures, and raided landowners in the vicinity.

Sloop
One-masted sailing vessel of light draught appreciated by pirates for its maneuverability in coastal waters and inlets; as naval sloops-of-war during the *Age of Sail*, these vessels usually mounted around 20 guns, far fewer than the large warships of the day.

Spanish Main
A term used widely in the 1700s and 1800s for Spanish-controlled parts of the Caribbean Basin following the European conquest and control of the Americas. It was variously applied either to the continental coastline running from southern North America through Central America and along South America's northern shores, or to the entire area embraced by Spanish colonization, including the territories in Caribbean waters and islands such as Cuba.

Spy-glass
Old-fashioned word for a handheld telescope, an item that increased rapidly in stature because of its importance to early sailing vessels. Such telescopes – a popular device in pirate tales – enabled seafaring captains to view ships in the distance, survey nearby coastal areas for possible landing problems, or watch for storms.

Stern
The rear portion of a ship where any guns would be mounted in case the ship needed to make a rapid escape from another vessel. It is also the section where the rudder is installed, used to maneuver the ship, and often the captain's quarters would be located at the stern.

Thole Pin
A pin attached to the upper edge of a boat's side to function as an oar's fulcrum.

Tiller
A beam or horizontal bar connected to a vessel's rudder whose movement determines a ship's steering. In Stevenson's *Treasure Island*, the narrator Jim Hawkins knows he is catching up with another ship when he can view "the brass glisten on the [other ship's] tiller."

Yellow Jack
Colloquial term for yellow fever, a viral, often-fatal tropical disease spread by mosquitoes and so called because of the jaundice it induces in some of its victims.

SELECTED BIBLIOGRAPHY

The Tales

Defoe, Daniel, *The Life and Strange Surprizing Adventures of Robinson Crusoe of York, Mariner*, London, W. Taylor, 1719.

Pyle, Howard, *Howard Pyle's Book of Pirates: Compiled by Merle Johnson*, New York, London, Harper & Brothers, 1921.

Stevenson, Robert Louis, *Treasure Island*, London, Cassell, 1883.

Verne, Jules, *The Mysterious Island*, trans. William Henry Giles Kingston, London, Low, Marston, Searle & Rivington, 1875.

Further Reading

Birkin, Andrew, *J. M. Barrie and the Lost Boys: The Real Story Behind Peter Pan*, New Haven, Yale University Press, 2003.

Bonner, William Hallam, *Pirate-Laureate: The Life and Legend of Captain Kidd*, New Brunswick, New Jersey, Rutgers University Press, 1947.

Chet, Guy, *The Ocean is a Wilderness: Atlantic Piracy and the Limits of State Authority, 1688–1856*, Amherst, University of Massachusetts Press, 2014.

Cordingly, David, *Under the Black Flag: The Romance and the Reality of Life among the Pirates*, New York, Random House, 1996.

Dolin, Eric Jay, *Black Flags, Blue Waters: The Epic History of America's Most Notorious Pirates*, New York, Liverlight Publishing, 2018.

Exquemelin, Alexandre Olivier, *De Americaensche Zee-Roovers*, Amsterdam, Jan ten Hoorn, 1678.

Gerassi-Navarro, Nina, *Pirate Novels: Fictions of Nation Building in Spanish America*, Durham, North Carolina, Duke University Press, 1999.

Hanna, Mark G., *Pirate Nests and the Rise of the British Empire, 1570–1740*, Chapel Hill, University of North Carolina Press, 2015.

Johnson, Steven, *Enemy of All Mankind: A True Story of Piracy, Power, and History's First Global Manhunt*, New York, Riverhead Books, 2020.

Konstam, Angus, *Pirates: The Complete History from 1300 BC to the Present Day*, Guilford, Connecticut, Lyons Press, 2008.

Lane, Kris E., *Piracy in the Americas: 1500–1750*, New York, Routledge, 1998.

Lapouge, Gilles, *Les Pirates: Forbans, flibustiers, boucaniers et autres gueux de mer*, Paris, Phébus, 1987.

Latimer, Jon, *Buccaneers of the Caribbean: How Piracy Forged an Empire*, Cambridge, Massachusetts, Harvard University Press, 2009.

Leeson, Peter T., *The Invisible Hook: The Hidden Economics of Pirates*, Princeton, Princeton University Press, 2009.

Lincoln, Margarette, *British Pirates and Society, 1680–1730*, Farnham, Ashgate, 2014.

Little, Benerson, *The Buccaneer's Realm: Pirate Life on the Spanish Main, 1674–1688*, Washington, D.C., Potomac Books, 2007.

Meier, Dirk, *Seafarers, Merchants and Pirates in the Middle Ages*, Woodbridge, Boydell and Brewer, 2009.

Owens, W. R., "Defoe, Robinson Crusoe, and the Barbary Pirates", in *English*, vol. 62, March 2013, pp. 51–66.

Puhle, Matthias, *Die Vitalienbrüder: Klaus Störtebeker und die Seeräuber der Hansezeit*, Frankfurt, Campus Verlag, 2012.

Rediker, Marcus, *Villains of All Nations: Atlantic Pirates in the Golden Age*, Boston, Beacon Press, 2004.

Ritchie, Robert C., *Captain Kidd and the War against the Pirates*, Cambridge, Harvard University Press, 1986.

Thompson, Janice, *Mercenaries, Pirates, and Sovereigns: State-building and Extraterritorial Violence in Early Modern Europe*, Princeton, Princeton University Press, 1994.

Turley, Hans, *Rum, Sodomy, and the Lash: Piracy, Sexuality, and Masculine Identity*, New York, New York University Press, 1999.

Weaver-Hightower, Rebecca, *Empire Islands: Castaways, Cannibals, and Fantasies of Conquest*, Minneapolis, University of Minnesota Press, 2007.

Woodard, Colin, "The Last Days of Blackbeard", in *Smithsonian Magazine*, vol. 44, February 2014.

Yolen, Jane, *Sea Queens: Women Pirates Around the World*, Watertown, Massachusetts, Charlesbridge, 2008.

Zachs, Richard, *The Pirate Hunter: The True Story of Captain Kidd*, New York, Hyperion, 2002.

ON SHORE HERE
OF SEPTEMBER

NOTES

Truth or Vision? Piracy of the Past

1 John Esquemeling, *The Buccaneers of America*, 1678, London: Swan Sonnenschein, 1893, 15.
2 Howard Pyle, *The Story of Jack Ballister's Fortunes*, 1895; New York: Century, 1922, 73.
3 Robert Louis Stevenson, *Treasure Island*, New York, Charles Scribner's, 1905, preface by Mrs. Fanny Stevenson, viii.
4 *Literary World*, 26, (Dec. 1895), 473.
5 Robert Louis Stevenson, *Treasure Island*, London, Cassell, 1883, 115.
6 Howard Pyle picture *Kidd at Gardiner's Island*, for Thomas A. Janvier, "The Sea Robbers of New York", *Harper's New Monthly Magazine* 89 (Nov. 1894), 813–27 (image on p. 825).
7 W.S. Gilbert and Arthur Sullivan, *The Pirates of Penzance or The Slave of Duty*, 1879; New York: Hitchcock Publishing Company, 38.
8 Quoted in Ann Wilson, "Anxiety, Gender and Technology in Peter Pan", in *Modern Drama: Defining the Field*, ed. Ric Knowles, Joanne Tompkins, and W.B. Worthen, Toronto: University of Toronto Press, 2003, 140.
9 *New England Courant*, July 22, 1723, quoted in George Francis Dow, *The Pirates of the New England Coast, 1630–1730*, Boston: Jordan & More, 1923, 308.
10 "Rare Jolly Roger Goes on Display at Portsmouth's Navy Museum", *BBC News*, Dec. 14, 2011 (https://www.bbc.com/news/uk-england-hampshire-16164191).

EDITORIAL NOTE

The tales reprinted in this book are extracts from the literary works *Robinson Crusoe*, *The Mysterious Island*, *Treasure Island*, and *Howard Pyle's Book of Pirates*.

A number of expressions used in these texts reflect the attitudes and prejudices of the times in which they were written, and should be viewed in historical context.

THE AUTHORS

Robert E. and **Jill P. May** were career-long professors at Purdue University, Indiana, prior to their retirements. Robert May is an internationally recognized scholar of the "filibusters," 19th-century adventurers who invaded foreign territory in private and illegal military expeditions, and the author of *Manifest Destiny's Underworld* (2002). Jill May, whose research, writing, and teaching have illuminated multiculturalism in children's literature, is the co-editor of *Exploring Culturally Diverse Literature for Children and Adolescents* (2005). They are the co-authors of *Howard Pyle: Imagining an American School of Art* (2011), a study of America's most famous illustrator of pirates, and a leading writer of pirate tales.

ACKNOWLEDGMENTS

We would like to thank the museums, libraries, private collectors, and all other persons and institutions listed in the photo credits for their helpful and forthcoming support of this publication.

For their illuminating texts, and for their significant expertise and steadfast support of this publication, we would like to extend our sincere thanks to the authors Robert E. and Jill P. May.

Finally, we would like to express our gratitude to Michael Custode for lending new perspectives to these timeless tales with the illustrations featured in this volume.

PHOTO CREDITS

We thank the following museums, libraries, and other institutions named below for kindly permitting the illustrations and photographs used in this publication to be reproduced.

When not otherwise specified, the remaining illustrations have been reproduced from works held by private collections.

© Michael Custode: cover, back cover, endpapers, pp. 3, 5, 7, all chapter openers, vignettes, and glossary symbols.

Illustrations by Alice B. Woodward. © HarperCollins Publishers Ltd. Taken from the book *The Peter Pan Picture Book*, published 1907 by George Bell & Sons. Licensed by HarperCollins: pp. 46, 47 b., 370, 381.
Baldwin Library of Historic Children's Literature, Special and Area Studies Collections, George A. Smathers Libraries, University of Florida, Gainesville, FL.: pp. 58, 62, 66, 73, 84, 87, 121, 127, 130, 147.
Bibliothèque nationale de France, Paris: pp. 8, 28, 29, 32 l., 50 l., 200, 241, 252, 267, 277, 284, 292, 315, 316, 322, 386; fonds patrimonial Heure joyeuse, médiathèque Françoise Sagan, Paris, sur gallica.bnf.fr: pp. 28, 29, 200, 386.
The Box, Plymouth, United Kingdom: p. 15 t.
© Brandywine River Museum of Art: Anonymous gift, 1989: p. 211 (89.23); Bequest of Ann Wyeth McCoy, 2006: p. 247 (2001.12); Bequest of Gertrude Haskell Britton, 1992: pp. 242 (92.16.1), 311 (92.16.2); Gift of Mr. and Mrs. S. Hallock du Pont, Jr., 1992: p. 27 b. (92.8.1); Purchased through the generosity of Mr. and Mrs. Bayard Sharp, 1995: pp. 279 (95.11.2), 283 (95.11.1); The Andrew and Betsy Wyeth Collection: pp. 255 (NCW 13), 262 (NCW 18), 271 (NCW 20), 274 (NCW 15), 303 (NCW 327).
Bridgeman Images: © Archives Charmet / Bridgeman Images: p. 34; © British Library Board. All Rights Reserved / Bridgeman Images: p. 23; © Look and Learn / Bridgeman Images: pp. 15 b., 44 t., 45, 52, 53, 54. Photo © Christie's Images / Bridgeman Images: pp. 4, 25, 56/57, 79, 95, 103, 141.
© Clifford Harper: p. 1.
The Collection of Joel and Suzanne Sugg: pp. 193, 231.
The Collection of Joseph and Louise Huber: pp. 99, 109, 115.
The Collection of Maurice and Marcia Neville: p. 203.
David & Annabelle Stone Gilbert & Sullivan Collection, Special Collections & Archives, George Mason University Libraries: pp. 30–31.
Delaware Art Museum: Gayle and Alene Hoskins Endowment Fund, 1990: p. 41; Museum Purchase, 1912: pp. 6, 42, 326, 329, 338, 344/45, 375.
Delaware, Biggs Museum of American Art: pp. 40 (1993.28), 43 (1992.28).
© Eldred's Auctions, East Dennis, MA / *The Bonadventure* by N.C. Wyeth from the Collection of Elizabeth E. Meyer: p. 190.
Courtesy of Frank E. Schoonover Fund, Inc.: pp. 18, 38, 40, 43, 356, 359, 360, 369, 378.
Image Courtesy of Freeman's: p. 100.
Harvard Library, Harvard University: p. 51.
Used with permission by The Kelly Collection of American Illustration: pp. 50 b., 164.
Library of Congress, Rare Book and Special Collections Division: p. 19 l.
© John Carter Brown Library, Brown University, Providence, RI: pp. 12–14; Box 1894, B. 02912: pp. 19 r., 35.
Courtesy of the Museum of Texas Tech University: Photography by Carolina Arellanos: pp. 171, 189.
New Britain Museum of American Art, Harriet Russell Stanley Fund (1953.18): p. 295.
New York Public Library: pp. 10, 16/17, 33, 36/37.
Philadelphia Museum of Art: Gift of Franklyn L. Rodgers, 2018, 2018-117-1: p. 157.
Private Collection, Boston, Massachusetts: p. 24.
Private Collection, Connecticut: p. 90.
Photograph Courtesy of Sotheby's, Inc. © Private collection: p. 2.
St. Paul's School, Concord, New Hampshire: p. 163.
University of Michigan: p. 55.
Vallejo Maritime Gallery, California: pp. 376/77.
© VG Bild-Kunst, Bonn 2024: pp. 27 l., 154, 161, 169, 194, 204, 206, 208, 219, 226, 235, 362, 382.

IMPRINT

Cover, back cover, and endpapers:
Michael Custode

Page 1: Clifford Harper
The Female Pirate Anne Bonny, 2020

Page 2: Newell Convers Wyeth
Stand and Deliver!, oil on canvas, *c.* 1921

Page 4: Newell Convers Wyeth
For a Mile, or Thereabouts, My Raft Went Very Well, oil on canvas, *c.* 1920

Page 58: Edward Henry Wehnert
Crusoe stumbles across the print of a man's foot, from Daniel Defoe's Robinson Crusoe, 1862

Page 150: Newell Convers Wyeth
Endpaper illustration, from Jules Verne's The Mysterious Island, 1921

Page 236: George Varian
Jim Hawkins packs away his spoils in the cave, from Robert Louis Stevenson's Treasure Island, 1918

Page 326: Howard Pyle
Kidd on the Deck of the "Adventure Galley", crayon and watercolor on illustration board, 1902 (detail)

Hohenzollernring 53, D–50672 Köln
www.taschen.com

Project management: Mahros Allamezade, Tom Pitt-Brooke, Cologne
Art direction: Andy Disl, Los Angeles, Claudia Frey, Cologne
Production: Daniela Asmuth, Cologne

ISBN 978-3-8365-8476-0
Printed in Italy

64°42'
64°40'
20
20
12
18°26'
6
4
6
4
Safe anchor
3
3
Swamp
Josiah buried
2
18°24'
12
8
8
4
6
Cliffs
6
6
Safe anchor
12
12
8
18°22'
64°42'
64°40'